4 WEEKS

P9-DMU-856

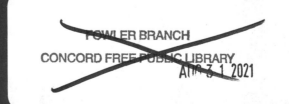

FORESTBORN

FORESTBORN

ELAYNE AUDREY BECKER

A TOM DOHERTY ASSOCIATES BOOK
NEW YORK

FORESTBORN

Copyright © 2021 by Elayne Audrey Becker

Map by Rhys Davies

A Tor Teen Book
Published by Tom Doherty Associates
120 Broadway
New York, NY 10271

www.tor-forge.com

Tor® is a registered trademark of Macmillan Publishing Group, LLC.

Library of Congress Cataloging-in-Publication Data

Names: Becker, Elayne Audrey, author.
Title: Forestborn / Elayne Audrey Becker.
Description: First edition. | New York : Tor Teen/Tom Doherty Associates,
  2021.
Identifiers: LCCN 2021010726 (print) | LCCN 2021010727 (ebook) |
  ISBN 978-1-250-75216-1 (hardcover) | ISBN 978-1-250-75226-0 (ebook)
Subjects: CYAC: Magic—Fiction. | Shapeshifting—Fiction. | Fantasy.
Classification: LCC PZ7.1.B434746 Fo 2021 (print) | LCC PZ7.1.B434746
  (ebook) | DDC [Fic]—dc23
LC record available at https://lccn.loc.gov/2021010726
LC ebook record available at https://lccn.loc.gov/2021010727

Our books may be purchased in bulk for promotional, educational, or business use. Please contact your local bookseller or the Macmillan Corporate and Premium Sales Department at 1-800-221-7945, extension 5442, or by email at MacmillanSpecialMarkets@macmillan.com.

First Edition: August 2021

Printed in the United States of America

0 9 8 7 6 5 4 3 2 1

For my mom and dad,
who never doubted.

Map of ALEMARA

The Decani Mountains

Elrin Sea

Caela Ridge

WESTERN VALE

Land of Giants

Oraes

ERADAIN

Niav

GLENWEIL

The Purple Mountains

Grovewood

The Old Forest

Roanin

Briarwend

TELYAN

Fendolyn's Keep

Elrin Sea

Poldat

FORESTBORN

ONE

I find her deep in the Old Forest, facedown in the dirt.

Sharp pain needles my palms where I've balled my fists so tight, the nails have carved half-moon marks into the skin. Snaking across the twig-strewn ground, gnarled roots press against my boots like a warning as I roll the young woman onto her back. Best to be sure.

No, she is certainly dead. Cold, stiff, and hungry like the rest; even with forest debris masking much of her shirt, the threadbare cotton dips in unmistakable rivulets across her bony frame. I swallow my disappointment and push her eyelids shut, wanting to spare her kin the sight of those empty, pointless eyes.

"Sorry," I murmur, sitting back on my heels. "I'm guessing you didn't deserve this."

Around us, the trees lean inward and down with ominous uniformity, leaves and branches straining against their holds, drawn to the dead woman as if tethered by ropes. The sway, the humans call it. I ignore the prickling in my belly. They'll straighten out soon enough when the magic leaves her body.

With a final nod, I push to my feet and wend my way back to the forest's edge. It's a close wood, with broad oaks in summer bloom crowding the grassy floor, their leafy canopy admitting shafts of sunlight that glitter like crystal chandeliers. All in all, too peaceful a setting for someone driven to madness to die alone. I breathe it in deep to savor the scent while I can, grateful that, for whatever reason, these trees never seem drawn to the magic in my own blood. I've had enough of vengeful wilderness to last a lifetime.

"Well?" Seraline asks, her knuckles nearly white where they clutch the hem of her shirt.

I shake my head. "Dead."

Her shoulders sink. Though Seraline is sturdy as iron when she's in her aunt's tannery shaping leather into draft horses' yokes, standing a determined two paces behind the tree line now, she seems shakeable as snow.

"Come on," I say, looking to the stony town just across the open fields. "You're going to be late." I don't ask if she plans to examine the body for herself. Seraline may have insisted on coming as a show of support, but our friendship has many limits, her discomfort with the dead and dying the least of them.

After a brief hesitation, Seraline falls into step at my side, sweeping her seeing stick across the ground in broad strokes. "Poor thing."

I mumble my assent, my jaw clenched tight.

This time of year, the late summer air hangs heavy even in the early morning, enough that the back of my neck is already slick with sweat. The barley fields remain mercifully empty as we pick our way through the dusty rows, but still I plow forward with my head down and shoulders bent, half from habit and half spurred by the hour. Seraline isn't the only one who's running behind.

"Will you not come with us?" she asks, her head tipping to the side as we near the town. "Aren't you due back in Roanin, anyway?"

"I can't," I reply, making it sound like an apology. I'm not really sure why we still play this game when we both know it's futile. "I have a few things to take care of first."

"Today of all days," she snorts.

"You know how it is." In truth, I'd give my right arm to stay away from the capital today. But there's no help for it.

"Her husband deserves to know," Seraline adds after a while. "The two of them were inseparable."

"He will know. The trail wasn't hard to follow."

Seraline is always trying to persuade me to talk to the deceased's families. She believes I have a softer manner than many in uniform, and once she even called me heartless for refusing. That time hurt the most. But it isn't my job to report any deaths I uncover to next of kin. Only to the king. And it's not like she's stepping up to volunteer, anyway.

Briarwend is a humble farming town that stretches all of three streets, a collection of squared-off stone shops that deal in necessity rather than charm. Its weather-worn residents are the same. When I began seeking intel here four years ago, long days tending the surrounding fields made the people lazy and open over a couple of pints. Lately, they're just hungry, poor soil and rising taxes leaving gaping holes that only tempers seem to fill.

Each night under dwindling oil lamplight and over stained, sticky tables, the pub dwellers deal out anger and judgment like tossing seeds across the earth. The battered forest walker I helped home last night is not the only magical person I've found bleeding on cobbled streets. The humans' ire is growing fists.

Seraline's family is fixing their horse's harness to an old wooden cart when we reach their cottage home. Most locals have long since departed.

"Where have you been?" her mother demands, tightening the leather straps. The roan mare stamps a hoof, ears flicking nervously in my presence. "We should have left hours ago!"

"Lela needed my help. And you're not ready, anyway." Seraline shrugs.

"Nor are you. Breakfast is gone, so you'll just have to wait. Go get changed." She studiously avoids my eye, as if I'm not even there.

Seraline bids me farewell with a light touch on the shoulder, which causes her little sister to quickly interlace two pairs of twisted fingers and pull them apart. The sign to ward off bad fortune.

"You shouldn't indulge my sister," the dreadful Arden says once she's gone, sauntering over and swiping a greasy hand across his forehead. By far the weakest sibling in this family of four. "Seraline is delicate. She can't be tramping about the kingdom with the likes of you."

Which is ironic, really, since he was eager enough to sidle close last year, when he thought empty flattery might earn him a kiss. That was before a too-often empty belly soured his tongue, before he learned who and what I am. And though I truly could not care less what this boy thinks, I'm dismayed to find my stomach still burns with anger and something close to shame. My gaze drops to his pant leg, which bears splotches of dried blood from the night before.

"Problem?" Arden sneers, white skin burned red from long days in the sun.

A slow tingling feeling bubbles up from my core, threads of numbness that tiptoe across my arms and legs. I force myself to breathe deeply, to beat the threads back. "I know it was you," I mutter.

He traces his chapped lips with two fingers, beady eyes darting to his mother before he leans forward, his smile stiffening. "You know nothing," he hisses.

"You forget I have certain resources at my disposal." I raise a hand in front of his flaking face, where my nails have sharpened into claws. "And that I know where you live."

I stare until a satisfying trace of fear tinges Arden's expression before heading toward the town's single inn, which is little more than a guesthouse with four creaking rooms. If my brother, Helos, were here, he would tell me to not take the bait, that I'm better than that. What he never seems to understand is that I'm not better than anything at all.

Annoyingly, the innkeeper is absent as I climb the stairs and unlock my room, shifting as soon as I've closed the door behind me. Coolness rushes through my tingling limbs like liquid as I release my hold on the borrowed matter, shedding my Briarwend disguise.

In place of Lela's face and features, my own natural ones take shape—taller height and stronger calves, olive skin a shade darker than Lela's pale white complexion, narrow eyes and dense, nut-brown hair in waves that fall just below perpetually tense shoulders. A face Seraline's family would never know as my own. Then I open the single window, considering.

I prefer to pay the innkeeper directly for his discretion, and I'm not keen on the thought that someone below might see me fly away from here. But I suppose most homes are empty by now, and anyway, I really can't afford to wait. Placing a silver coin on the corner table, I strip off my clothes and focus on a place deep within my core, using it to pull from the air around me. Intuitive as breathing, my body numbs as the bones shrink and settle into those of a goshawk, my gray and creamy white feathers ruffling with pleasure. The knot between my ribs loosens slightly as my wings carry me through the window and out into the morning light.

It's about an hour's flight from Briarwend to Telyan's capital city, Roanin. In this form, my tail is straight as an arrow shaft, my hooked beak sharp as Telyan steel. Tendrils of cool breeze skim my feathers, and my heart sings at the freedom of it all. But only briefly.

Far below, a single wide road cuts north across the farm plots and deciduous woods. Already it's packed with travelers on foot and horseback. Many, particularly those from farther south, will have set out during the night. It's the one day each year the Danofers open Castle Roanin's gates to the public, and many people derive huge pride from actually making it through and securing a place within the grounds.

Even the relief flight brings is not enough to offset my hatred of this day.

Ahead, at last, my destination comes into view: an open expanse of granite buildings gleaming gray in the rising sun, the occasional gabled roofs and spires fracturing the skyline. Encased within the shadow of the Purple Mountains to the north and bordered by dense woods stretching east and west, Roanin is an insular city, its residents increasingly wary of outsiders. With natural barriers on three sides, there is only one way to enter, and even then, strangers would find it difficult to navigate. The layout is a dizzying array of twisting, narrow streets and stone buildings, wild and winding as the Old Forest surrounding it. Lofty and angular, Castle Roanin stands sentinel at the back.

Upon entering King Gerar's service four years ago, I had been foolish enough to trust in that castle. To hope that, after years of struggling to survive in the wilderness with only my brother beside me, I might have found a home at last. Turns out, solitude is lonely, but being surrounded by people who want nothing to do with you hurts even worse.

I sweep over the castle complex and alight on the roof of my house, a small, single room situated behind the smelly stables and close to the outer wall; the work I do for King Gerar permits me to live on the royal estate, but barely. A city clock tower taunts me with the hour as I throw on a soft blue dress and flats, frown at the dark circles ringing my eyes, and hasten toward the castle's eastern entrance. Though the oak-lined lawn separating the castle from the complex's front gates must stretch four hundred paces deep at least, even this far back, the gathering crowd's gentle roar hums loud as the distant shore.

Through the wooden door, the east kitchens are a flurry of motion. Apprentices chopping, pots boiling, cooks scurrying, all preparing already for midday. Poorer girls like Seraline may have to skip meals now and again, but here in the castle there are always three, served on tablecloths and gold-rimmed platters polished to a shine. I cut through the tempting scents of rosemary and thyme, around the young men pouring carrots and turnips over thinly sliced venison, with my head held high as if the workers' sidelong glances mean nothing to me. Rude gestures and hardened faces no more than raindrops pattering glass.

By the time I reach the exit, my chest feels tight as a pinprick.

Beyond the empty corridor, the castle's central atrium is equally chaotic. Tension drags at my shoulder blades as I weave through the men and women rushing about, each step echoing painfully off the polished marble floor. Spanning three stories and lined with lead-paned windows twice my height, this foyer seems designed to make occupants feel small. Wrought-iron banisters guard a covered gallery two floors up, a walkway which traces the room's perimeter and culminates at a set of glass double doors gleaming in the castle's southern façade. Within the hour, the Danofers will

pass through those doors and out onto the narrow balcony beyond
to read the Prediction everyone is gathering to see.

I take the steps on the atrium's grand staircase two at a time.

It somehow feels easier to breathe on the second floor, where
thick green carpets wrap the paneled corridor in a protective cloak
of quiet. My heart sinks when I round the corner and see who's on
duty outside the parlor's double doors.

"You're late," observes Dom, one of King Gerar's most senior
guards, in a tone of quiet delight. At his side, Carolette sniffs and
looks down her nose.

"Just open the door," I say.

Carolette clicks her tongue, pushing her long brown plait over
her shoulder. "Manners, shifter. You're in the company of royals
now."

At my side, my fingernails stretch into claws. "Open the door,
or I'll open you."

The members of the esteemed Royal Guard look far from impressed by this threat, but Dom turns the knob and steps inside
nevertheless.

"You reek of death," Carolette hisses as I pass, her breath hot
in my ear. And though I clutch my anger close like a second skin,
I can't stop the old fear from sweeping its clammy hand down my
spine.

"The shifter to see you, Your Majesty," Dom announces, his
purple-accented gray uniform appearing washed out amidst the
upholstered furniture.

At the far end of the gauzy pearl parlor, three members of the
royal family are milling about by the curtained windows. King
Gerar with his emerald-encrusted crown, the one reserved for formal ceremonies only, along with the crown princess, Violet, and
Weslyn, the elder and far less endearing of the two princes. All
three wear the customary funereal black.

The day of the Prediction. The anniversary of Queen Raenen's
death. By a perverse turn of events, this black-hearted day marks
them both.

"Rora, good," King Gerar greets. His tired smile falls flat against the grief shadowing his face. Behind him, Violet spears me with a glance before continuing to pace in her floor-length gown, her dark hair cropped short above bare, rigid shoulders. Back and forth, she taps a long, red-and-gold feather quill lightly against her palm. The one her father gifted to her to cement her place as his successor.

I'd yank that quill from her grasp and snap it in two, if I didn't think that would crack the kingdom as well.

"Your Majesty. Forgive me, I was following a lead." I dip into a hasty bow once the door clicks shut behind me.

"Go on."

"Five more cases in Briarwend," I tell him. "One of them dead. Two that have reached the sway and the silence." Five added to nearly two hundred other cases scattered throughout the kingdom. Eighty-seven afflicted already dead, and those only the ones I've found. This magic-induced illness with no set duration—it could kill its victims in days or months, adults and children alike. No name beyond the Fallow Throes. No cure that healers have yet discovered. It's spreading.

"Any links between the afflicted?" King Gerar asks, folding a hand into his suit pocket. His features are a collage of his children's— the crown princess's stern brow, the younger prince's crystal eyes, the elder prince's trim beard and thick, dark curls, though the flecks of gray peppering his own have become more prevalent in recent months. While he has the tanned white skin of his two eldest children, to my eyes, in this moment, the emotion in his expression is all his youngest son, Finley.

"None that I could tell, sir. Except the usual."

The usual. That no shifters, whisperers, or forest walkers are falling ill and dying. Only humans. I twist my hands behind my back, watching King Gerar process this information in silence. "There's something else," I add, more hesitant now.

Violet's head swings in my direction, but King Gerar's brow only furrows. "Speak freely."

"I found a forest walker who had been beaten badly, not far

from the town center." Safely hidden from sight, my hands constrict into fists. "I think I know one of the persons responsible."

"Do you have proof of guilt?"

My mouth thins. "Not exactly."

King Gerar runs a hand along his beard, looking troubled. "Without proof, I can do nothing. But I will send word to the magistrate. Such behavior is unacceptable."

Violet begins to pace again, her head now bent in thought.

My focus strays to Weslyn a few paces behind, who hasn't looked away from the window since I arrived. He keeps his back to me now, apparently indifferent to the news that another magical person was mugged in the streets. But then, he's never shown a shred of concern for anything I have to say. Not since the day we met, four years ago today.

The annual Prediction and Queen Raenen's death day. Also the anniversary of Helos's and my arrival at Castle Roanin. A coincidence his flint-edged apathy never lets me forget.

"Thank you, Rora," says King Gerar, and the threads of numbness dissipate just as quickly as they surfaced. "You may go." He diverts his gaze to a painting of his late wife mounted above the unlit hearth.

"Sir, shall I do another sweep?" I ask hopefully. "I can leave right away."

"No." He waves an idle hand in my direction, and my shoulders droop. "No, I may have something new for you. In the meantime, take the rest of the day off."

I open my mouth to ask what he means when Dom reenters the parlor.

"Your Majesty, it's nearly eleven. They're ready to open the gates unless you say otherwise."

"Fine, fine." King Gerar gives another wave of his hand. Then he asks, seemingly to no one in particular, "Where is Finley?"

"I can fetch him, sir," I say at once, just as Weslyn finally swivels round. His cold eyes narrow, and I feel a vague sense of victory.

In contrast, King Gerar has brightened a little. The signs are nearly imperceptible, scarcely more than a smoother brow and a slackening in his jaw, but I've learned to look for them whenever Finley's presence is promised. "Very well."

I'm gone before his eldest son can protest.

In the time it takes me to reach the lofty, brown-stoned northern wing and climb the stairs, the noise from the assembling crowd has grown close enough to permeate the castle's thick walls. Hundreds, if not thousands, of people ready to flatten the carefully tended lawn with eager footsteps. Anxiety tightens its familiar grip around my chest.

I round a corner and nearly collide with Finley headlong.

"Rora!" he exclaims, a broad grin overtaking his slender face. "Not looking for me, I trust?"

Finley is the total opposite of his two siblings, and wonderfully so, all tangling limbs and frenetic energy. Wispy blond waves of hair fall across a kind face dotted with freckles, the mark of a childhood spent under the sun. Already, I can feel my mask dropping for the first time in two days.

"Your father sent me to find you." I run a critical gaze over his wrinkled suit and the half-made tie hanging loose around his neck. "Lowering your standards, I see."

"A low blow," he says, shoving my shoulder before falling into step beside me and fixing the tie. "But possibly deserved."

"You promised to at least try," I remind him.

"I know."

"Today seems a good day to start," I add, finding the relaxed set of his shoulders far too free from guilt.

"I had something to attend to," he says. "Royal duties, you know."

I raise an eyebrow. "Don't lie to me."

"Fine. I overslept. Headache—a bit too much to drink last night, I suppose. You know how it is."

"Actually, I don't."

"A fact I'm determined to change one day." Finley trips over a bump in the bloodred runner underfoot, catching himself on the stone wall.

"Are you . . . nervous?" I ask, biting back a smile.

He glares at me sidelong. "Now you're just being rude."

Being with Fin is easy, so much so that I permit my guard to drop more than I should. So by the time we're nearing the parlor doors, the old dread settles over me all the stronger for its temporary absence. The figures sewn into tapestries along the walls take on new meaning, mocking expressions that seem to warn of the trouble to come. I imagine them reaching for me with greedy hands, wanting to pull and flatten my body until I'm like them— still, silent, and unable to cause any more harm.

"I've just remembered," Finley exclaims, so suddenly I flinch. "I'm supposed to bring flowers today."

I appraise him skeptically. King Gerar didn't mention any flowers.

"Come on, or Father will have my head." And without waiting for an answer, he turns on his heel.

I glance at the parlor doors, just at the other end of the hall. But I have no intention of returning there without him, so I resign myself to following.

"Why flowers?" I ask, as he leads me down a winding staircase and past baffled, bowing servants.

"For Mother, you know. To represent her."

"The gardener couldn't fetch them for you?"

"It's more personal this way."

To avoid any possible sightings by the crowd now gathering on the grounds' front lawn, Finley sneaks us out a rear door hidden in the castle's northern façade, nodding to the curious younger recruits on guard. Hot air dampens my skin in what feels like mere moments as I follow him through the hedgerow garden and groves of red maples, past the groundskeepers' shed and an old, rarely used carriage house, all the way to a secret door hidden in the outer wall. Creeping ivy and moss-strewn cracks hide the iron key ring from view.

"Finley," I warn, the back of my neck prickling.

"Fine, I lied." Pulling a heavy key from behind a loose stone, he heaves the door open and gestures for me to step through first. "But you have to admit, the fact that you didn't catch on sooner proves I was right to do so."

"What are you talking about?"

"We both know you were suffocating in there." Finley closes the latch, then uncrosses my arms with a grin.

"Have you lost your mind?" I ask with no small measure of sincerity.

He shrugs and marches straight into the Old Forest.

"You can't miss the ceremony," I persist, even as I fall into step beside him. "It's the most important day of the year!"

"No," he says, his expression sobering. "It's a day for silly tradition and baseless speculation. You don't need to suffer through the aftermath this time. You do enough."

I bite my lip. "You think it will be the same today?"

Finley runs a hand through his hair. "It's been six years. I don't see why not."

"Please tell me you're not subverting an eight-hundred-year-old tradition on my account."

"Come on, Rora. I'm nice, but I'm not *that* nice."

But he is. He's done so before, deftly extricating me from tense situations under the pretense of needing my assistance, only for me to discover through a later series of gripes and eye rolls that he was meant to be somewhere else.

As we climb, the crowd's distant chatter ebbs into the forest's gentle melody—wind-ruffled leaves over creaking branches, chattering robins and cardinals, screeching insects, and small animals scuffling through briars and dens. At first, I think he's leading us to his mother's grave, an ornate headstone erected here in accordance with her will. Today of all days would make particular sense, though he and his family visit often anyway. Well, except his brother; if there's any truth to kitchen gossip, Weslyn hasn't set foot in these woods since the day Queen Raenen fell.

Soon, however, our idle course tracks south, the wrong direction for a grave visit. The ground underfoot grows rougher, wilder, grass giving way to coarse vegetation and dirt-encrusted rocks. Oak trees, beech trees, hickory, elm—a forest ancient and unyielding, giants from a time long lost. Despite my concern for how King Gerar will receive Finley's absence, I can't deny the snags in my stomach are unraveling with every breath of wood-scented air.

The annual tradition of publicly reading the year's Prediction is almost as old as life on Alemara itself. Nearly eight hundred years ago, after a whisperer named Fendolyn united magical and non-magical people under a single banner for the first time since magic surfaced on the continent, divisions regarding the line of succession fractured her followers into warring camps.

Some thought her daughter, Telyan, was the natural heir with her added gift of magic. Others thought it unfair that her son, Era-dain, be cast aside simply because no magic ran in his veins. Then Willa Glenweil, one of Fendolyn's closest advisers challenged both children for the right to rule, for why should the crown be inherited rather than earned?

To spare the mobs from mutual slaughter, Fendolyn proposed a compromise—Eradain could take the north, Glenweil the middle ground, and Telyan would remain in the south, the land from which her mother ruled. But the giants, fearing the seeds of resentment taking root in humans and wanting no part in future trouble, asked that the continent instead be split into four, that the wilderness west of the river remain neutral territory no one could claim. All agreed.

Before departing, as a sign of good will, the giants gifted each of the three new rulers with the continent's rarest type of bird: a loropin. A bird coveted by most, because a quill made from its feathers will write the truth about the future, but only for the one gifted a feather, and only on each anniversary of the day it was given. Having witnessed the rivalry wrought by jealousy, fear, and anger, the giants urged their gift to be symbolic: a reminder to let truth and logic dictate their reigns, rather than bleak emotion.

Every year since then, as a show of unity throughout the three realms, each ruler uses their quills to write a message—one which always seems to write itself—and reads it publicly. Always vague words of comfort or warning, rarely comprising more than a sentence, to guide their people in the year to come and to solidify their role as the wielder of truth. And relative peace did hold—until seven years ago today, when for the first time in seven hundred and forty-one years, all three quills yielded the same words for all three rulers: *two shifters death*.

Two years later, the day Queen Raenen, her hunting party, and her two eldest children stumbled upon Helos and me squatting in the Old Forest was the day of the Prediction. The third of what would become six consecutive annual readings all producing the same three words. Seven, if today's reading yields the same. It was the day the first earthquake in nearly eight hundred years shook the land, striking terror into Telyan hearts that the Day of Rupturing which once broke the world might happen again. The day the queen, an expert rider by all accounts, fell from her horse, broke her neck, and died.

An omen, King Gerar's advisers saw it. A tragedy portending the end of the Danofer line, the royal bloodline that stretches all the way back to Fendolyn, though the magic in it has faded without a magical marriage in almost two centuries. A sign that an explosion of magic could once again crack the continent apart. And trapped at the center of it all, in their eyes, were my brother and me.

"Rora," Finley says, calling my attention back to the present. "As I said, my gesture was not entirely selfless. I thought—now we're here—you could help me with something."

"Oh?"

"Yes, and I think—I'm going to need your help sooner than I realized."

I turn in time to see him trip on a root like he did the runner. Only this time, when he straightens, his face looks alarmingly pale.

"What's wrong?" I demand as he leans against an oak, breathing heavily. "What do you mean, help?"

But Finley's eyes are glazing over, far too fast, the pupils dilating as if he's concussed. He shakes his head, holds out a hand, clutches mine when I step close to steady him. "I think—"

"Finley!" I cry, catching him when his knees suddenly give way. I'm dismayed at how easy it is to support his weight, considering he's only one year younger than I am. Or two, or three. It's all a guess, really. "Fin, talk to me," I say, my heart flinging itself wildly against my rib cage as I watch his eyes lose focus once more. His hand loosens its grip on mine, and both of us sink to the forest floor.

"Let him go," I beg, bending over the body gone rigid, the heaving chest, the quivering, waxen skin. Alarm bells are screaming through my head, loud as the clock tower tolling the hour, and with them, the tingling in my core returns. Threads of numbness engulf my limbs. Fur along my back, then feathers all over—my body torn between the urge to hide or to flee, far away from this scene I never saw coming. "Please. Not him, too."

I ignore the gathering sounds of creaking, groaning wood overhead with a vengeance. Tears are welling in my eyes, but I blink them away and shake my head, refusing to let them fall. Refusing because this day of truth has always been tainted by lies, so what's one more to add to the tally? In the darkening wood, I set each one before me, all of the lies I reach for when the nightmares, the dirty looks, the hidden scars and endless self-loathing begin to drag me under—that my mother loved me before she left me, that my brother and I are not a curse, that I can be good and selfless and worthy of love in spite of the things I've done. I assemble them all, then set one more on the shelf: that my best friend, my only true friend aside from Helos, isn't dying.

But the trees around me, leaves and branches straining against their holds, limbs pointing to Finley like a circle of swords—the trees all tell a different story.

TWO

It takes several tortured, endless minutes for Finley to come to.

"Rora?" he croaks, blinking slowly.

My stomach drops onto the forest floor. "I'm here."

Placing one of his arms around my shoulder, I help him into a sitting position. Finley remains quite still for some time, his hands pressed into the leafy ground as the haze gradually recedes from his eyes. His face remains composed as he takes in the ring of trees bending toward him.

"I see," is all he says.

It's old, the warning that thrums through my blood then. Familiar, how the edges brush my skin. *Out,* they whisper. *Away.* "Are you feeling well enough to walk? We should get you home."

"Rora." Finley resists the tug of my hands, his forehead creasing. "Listen."

Though I'd give anything not to, I divert my attention to the forest around us, which has long since grown unnaturally quiet. No birds chirping, no leaves hissing in the wind. All of the sound has dropped away.

"I had to be certain," Finley murmurs, and my heart hammers at the pitch of his voice, far too loud in the smothering silence. He does not sound surprised.

"You suspected?"

"Don't tell me you did not. You of all people."

I press my lips together in a thin line. For four years, I have worked as a spy for King Gerar, traveling throughout Telyan and observing the mood of the populace. Listening for any issues or points of discontent to report back to the crown, and each time wearing a different face—my animal forms may be limited to three, but I can change my human features to match any person I've seen before.

This duty changed a few months ago, when people started falling sick, and it became my job to identify new cases. The illness presents like countless others at the onset: roaming pains, reduced appetite, nausea, fatigue. General enough in its early stages that it's impossible to detect the magic taking root inside—at least, impossible in human form. My mouse nose can detect the earthy, ash-bitten scent with ease.

Only, I'm never around Finley in an animal form.

My fingers curl into fists at my side. As the Fallow Throes progresses, the affliction becomes easy to identify. Aside from a few strange cases in which those who smell of magic develop no symptoms at all, victims fall prone to episodes of delirium, and then there's the way that nature responds to them. The sway and the silence. The turning point from ordinary symptoms to not, and the sign that patients won't last the year. After a time, their voices shift higher or lower, cruel distortions of their former selves. Worse, their senses heighten many times over—sharper vision, acute hearing, an awareness of vibration and movement as far as several rooms away. Patients say it's like a hurricane, far more than any human is built to experience, with a never-ending headache hammering their skulls. The overstimulation drives most to madness even before the final stage: when they lose the power of language, and only nonsense falls from their tongues.

"Rora," Finley says with a smile, lifting an eyebrow when I don't respond. As if I'm the one who deserves to be pitied and not him.

Finley is surely the least royal-acting royal in all the realms.

"Come on." I brush a twig from my dress with shaking hands. "Let's get out of these woods. You can lean on me for support."

"Always one for practicality."

This time, I can hear the sadness coloring his voice, and it feels like a needle puncturing my lungs.

Accepting my outstretched hands without fuss, Finley wobbles to his feet and hovers in place a moment, pressing the heel of his palm to his temple. With him newly conscious and unsteady on his legs, we can't manage anything faster than a walk. The pace soon sets my teeth on edge. If Helos were here, he could carry Finley to healers and help much more quickly. But sweet Helos hasn't been permitted on the castle grounds—or near our friend—in just over a month. Not since Finley lost some of the usual spring in his step, come to think of it.

Rage boils deep in my belly, turning quickly to fear when I think of how King Gerar and the rest of his court will react to learning his youngest son is—is—

Even in the far corners of my mind, I can't bring myself to say it. But other sinister threads worm their way into focus with ease. The terror of being punished, cast out, of my actions forcing Helos and me to move yet again, when the lives we've built here in Telyan are as close as we've ever come to a stable home and shreds of community. As if I would ever do *anything* to deliberately hurt Finley. Finley, who studies maps and charts out plans for escape, the architect of infinite, imagined voyages free from constraint. Who chafes at the bindings restricting his lot in life, same as I. The only one aside from Helos who's dared to love me and not leave.

The woods ripple around us as we retrace our steps. Chestnuts, oaks, and hickories lean in, then straighten once we've moved three or four paces away. It's a sight better fitted to the Vale of my childhood, that dreaded wilderness west of the river, where magic still thrives in an ever-changing landscape. Not here in a kingdom that's mostly reduced to human subjects, many magical people having left, and the magic embedded in the land only a shade of its former self.

Finley loses his footing with a grunt.

"You're shaking," I realize, cursing myself for giving way to distraction. The pocket of silence envelops us still, as if nature is holding its breath.

He folds his arms across his narrow chest, cradling his elbows in his hands. "I'm all right."

"Don't be absurd. You need medicine." I chew the inside of my cheek, having hoped we would have more time before the delirium's aftereffects began. "The grounds will still be packed with people for another hour at least. There's no way to sneak you in unseen."

"We can just wait until they leave." Finley shrugs, then sways on the spot.

"Or—" I reach out a hand to steady him. Deliberate further, then decide. "Or we stop at Bren and Tomas's shop. It's much closer, and that neighborhood will be empty by now."

"Bren and Tomas will be at the castle like everyone else," says Finley, his tone light with feigned ignorance.

I shift my weight to the other leg. "Their apprentice won't."

Finley shakes his head at once.

"You must have seen how this works," I press. "The more you let your temperature rise, the more likely it is you'll lapse into another episode."

"I'll be fine until the crowds disperse."

"And if you're not?"

Finley scrapes the toe of his boot through the grass.

"You know Helos can help, and we can be there in a quarter of the time. Please, Finley." Visiting my brother will mean disobeying King Gerar's orders. Neither option is good, but I'm afraid chancing another episode would be worse.

I can only hope King Gerar feels the same.

Finley unfolds his arms at last, and some of the tension lifts from my back.

"Thank you."

It doesn't take long to descend the remaining stretch of woods. Mercifully, sound rushes in and sweeps the eerie silence away as soon as we pass the tree line and cross the grassy strip hugging Roanin's outer edge. Finley says nothing when I alter my appearance; though I'm required to maintain my natural form on castle grounds in order to be identifiable, and thus held accountable, outside the castle I can look as I wish. The shift is a simple matter of envisioning the person I want to become—not their body as a whole, but the pieces of it. Hair curled and lengthened to my waist; narrow, dark eyes exchanged for doe-like, chestnut ones; my typically tall frame shrunk half a head shorter. I pull matter from the air and direct it to the skin, the eyes, the bones, which each become numb until their transformation is complete.

Though nothing about my natural form marks me as anything other than human, changing my face when I can has become a matter of course—always safer to have a disguise, should anything go wrong. For most of Alemara's history, magical and nonmagical people lived together in peace. Forest walkers encouraged timber woods to flourish, and whisperers kept wild animals away from livestock through their powers of persuasion. Humans delighted in watching shifters change form and wished they could do the same.

But ever since the cursed Prediction deviated from its usual course, tension between magical and nonmagical people has heated to a steady boil. Telyan may not have gone so far as to emulate its neighbor to the far north, where the king of Eradain forges fear into law, but the atmosphere here grew unpleasant enough that most magical people left anyway. Unwilling to live hidden, and tired of the street fights and hurled insults, of new suspicion and centuries-old human jealousy mingling into something nastier, dangerous.

Most moved across the river, into the Western Vale.

Helos and I dare not return.

Stepping into the unwalled city, my nose wrinkles at the sudden onslaught of late summer urban air, staler than the forest breeze and smelling faintly of the horses that walk the wider sections after dawn. It's a relief to find the stretch of merchant homes and local craft shops are indeed unusually quiet. Finley trails with hunched shoulders and restless hands stuffed into pockets as I lead him through a series of side streets often so narrow that the sapphire sky thins to a ribbon overhead. Around us, russet and gray buildings crouch in silent wait, tight and close-quartered in their impervious brick and granite shells. I force us to move at a fast clip in case any onlookers remain at their windows.

Around another corner, and the apothecary shop comes into

FORESTBORN   21

view at last, half-hidden behind the bend in the road. Its wooden door is closed, but I try the handle anyway. Locked.

"Helos," I whisper, looking up at the second-story window; he lives in the cramped apartment above the shop, Bren and Tomas's former residence before they married and moved somewhere nicer. No head pops out. *"Helos."*

At my side, Finley shuffles his feet a little, stealing glances over his shoulder, then at a tear in his dusty black suit, then down at the stones beneath his feet. Anywhere but the door.

We don't have time for this. I pound my fist against the wood.

There's a noise behind the wall. The door swings open and Helos appears, the dark hair that falls midway between his jaw and shoulders thoroughly mussed.

"Can I help you?" he asks, fingers fumbling with the top button on what was once a crisp white shirt. I frown at the sight of the worn fabric; his salary is far less than mine, but he refuses to accept money from me no matter how many times I offer it.

Before I can reply, he catches Finley's eye and freezes.

"Hello," Finley says, sounding a lot more composed than his shuffling feet suggest.

Helos takes in the face of the friend he hasn't seen in more than a month, then switches his attention to the stranger by his side. I mutter my name to confirm it's me, and the floorboards creak as the three of us step into the lamp-lit shop.

A counter bisects the room toward the back, guarding the entrance to a narrow hallway with rows of cubbies to either side of it. My brother latches the door while I shift back to my natural form, regaining the brown waves, olive skin, and height that we both share. Finley crosses to the counter and lifts a weekly leaflet from the surface.

"A bit of light reading?" he guesses with a wry grin, holding up the creased parchment.

His face stares out from the leaflet, along with his siblings' and his father's, in a family portrait reproduced near the centerfold.

"What are you doing here?" Helos says, jostling the question aside. "Is something wrong? Why aren't you at the ceremony?"

"We went for a walk in the Forest," I reply, and Finley purses his lips like I've betrayed him. "He had an episode, and now he's feverish." I pause. "I saw it, Helos. The sway and the silence."

My brother stares at Finley.

Fallow Throes. Incurable. Fatal. The unspoken prognosis hangs over the room like a veil.

"Stay here," he instructs before disappearing down the narrow hallway. Finley scratches the back of his head, sidling idly around the clean-swept perimeter. Moments later, Helos reemerges with a tightly cinched cloth bag in hand. "Sit."

Finley sinks onto a wicker bench set against the wall as Helos withdraws a gnarled stem from the bag, tears off two mottled green-and-purple leaves, and places them in a mortar on the counter. I lean against the painted wall opposite Finley.

"What other symptoms? Fatigue?" Helos asks, grabbing a pestle from one of the cubbies.

Finley watches him work. "Does it matter?"

"What symptoms?" he repeats, keeping his eyes on the leaves he's grinding. "Any pain?"

The sound of stone scraping stone fills the lavender-scented room.

"My legs," Finley admits at last. "And my feet."

Now it's my turn to look betrayed. He never told me he was in pain. My skin tingles when I think of the pace I set to get here.

I didn't even ask.

But then, Helos has always been the better of us. When King Gerar granted an audience a week after his wife's death, his spineless advisers recounted the ominous circumstances of our arrival and urged execution or exile. King Gerar chose mercy over fear, refusing to inflict punishment in the absence of demonstrable crime. *These are frightened children,* I remember him saying, running a weary hand along his face. *What harm do you imagine them capable of?* To the throne room's barely suppressed outrage, he then offered us a job—only one, since our joint presence in court was controversial enough to endanger us. One job that meant food and coin and all the other benefits that come with being in the king's favor.

Helos told me to take it. Just like that. That's the kind of person
he is.

So I took it.

That's the kind of person I am.

When Helos has reduced the leaves to a fine powder, he nudges
the substance into a glass with water and walks it over to Finley,
who has been staring. "Drink this," he says, crouching in front of
the wicker bench.

Finley accepts the glass with two hands, gaze flitting away from
Helos now that my brother is near. His discomfort chafes the cracks
in my core. I rub my arms and start to pace.

"Your father won't be happy you came here for help," Helos
says quietly.

I glance at Finley, suddenly reluctant for him to admit that this
detour was my idea.

"He'll forgive me this once, I think," Fin says, his gaze softening.

"Not enough to lift the ban, I suppose."

Silence descends with smothering tension, so sharp I can practically taste it. Finley may be able to feign ignorance with ease, but
my brother has always been a landscape of earnestness.

"I'm sorry, Helos." Finley's shoulders droop. "My hands are tied."

"Don't apologize. It's not your fault."

Helos takes the empty glass and tidies up behind the counter,
while Finley studies the lines of his palms. Though I've ached for
things to return to the way they once were, when conversations
were effortless between us, I suddenly find myself longing to be
anywhere else. It's not that King Gerar seems to have given into
the court's suspicions at last, though the notion that my brother
and his healer hands could ever cause someone harm is absurd. It's
the stifling awareness that Finley, a person so willing to flout the
rules he would skip a Prediction reading, has made no attempt to
break this one.

"You should go home," Helos says at last. "The city's always a
madhouse after the reading. Everyone floods the taverns and streets
for ale and gossip. It isn't safe for you."

"That sounds more fun," Finley drawls, resting his head against the wall and closing his eyes. "And the people love us. I bet they'd welcome the sight."

Helos and I exchange a look. The Danofers may still retain the majority of their people's favor, but King Gerar's military tax has hit farmers and even the merchant class pretty hard in recent months. Magic's recession east of the river may have made the land here quieter and more predictable, but the soil has undeniably suffered as a result. Telyan is largely farming country, and fields just aren't as fertile as they used to be. And while the army does have a reputation for giving its soldiers a good life, it can be difficult to sell those who haven't enlisted on devoting already limited income to weaponry and supplies instead of clothing and food.

Not for the first time, I wish that Finley's joy in learning extended more to the present, not just the future.

"My point still stands," Helos argues. "It would take you hours to get through a mob. What if you have another episode?"

Finley doesn't respond.

"We'll go back through the Forest and wait it out," I say. "Now that you've treated the fever."

"Spoil sports," Finley grumbles. But he doesn't object.

Likely he, too, knows my brother's concern is well-founded. Despite the crown's efforts to stem panic among its people, the spread of a mysterious illness has everyone on edge. Seeing a prince with the symptoms would only stoke the flames.

"I'm coming back with you," Helos says abruptly, looking to me, then back at Finley.

Finley's eyes snap open, and my heart sinks. "Helos."

"The royal healers are idiots. I should be the one tending you." He takes one step forward, then stops. "Come on, Fin. They don't know what they're doing."

No one knows what they're doing, because no one knows how to fix this. "You're still just an apprentice," I remind him gently. I'm resorting to the arguments I know the healers in the castle will make, even if King Gerar decides to lift the ban. "You don't have enough experience."

"I managed to keep us alive, didn't I?" There's no bitterness or accusation in the statement. Just truth.

"That was different," I mumble.

He waves a hand. "Let me see if I can help."

"Look, you know his stance on this. The Prediction—"

"The river take the Prediction," he says. "It means nothing. You've said so yourself." He glances to Finley for backup, but Finley's looking away.

When I don't respond, Helos crosses to the window and slumps against the ledge, helpless.

"It doesn't matter what we think," Finley says at last, running a hand over his neck. The feverish flush is clearing from his cheeks. "The court fears the Prediction, and my father is not immune to the pressure they exert on him."

Helos's knuckles are turning white where he grips the ledge. "At least let me walk you back. Just to the door, and then I'll leave. I promise." Finley's bent with his arms resting on his legs. He's watching Helos intently. "Please."

Though I'm still shaking my head, Finley seems to fracture under the strength of my brother's plea. He drops his chin.

"I could lose my job for this," I remind him. "I'll be in enough trouble for not delivering you like I said I would. Helos can't come." I know my brother. He doesn't hide behind borrowed forms like I do.

"I'll tell my father this was all my idea," Finley says, pushing to his feet. "He will just have to blame me instead." He smiles, but there's a trace of pain behind it. "Let's go."

After the miserable morning we've had, the walk back through the woods feels almost like a gift. The tension in Bren and Tomas's shop, so heavy with the weight of unspoken things, softens a little in the fresh forest air. Helos offers an arm when Finley proves shaky on his feet, and the added support seems to steady Fin in more ways than one. The gloom recedes from his expression, familiar warmth blossoming in its wake. Soon enough, he has lapsed into a smug recounting of some horse he raced to victory the other day, and the coin he won off the Royal Guard who failed to beat him, because Finley has always been good at finding the light.

As always, it draws in Helos and me like moths to a flame. Whether he's in denial or simply desperate for distraction, Helos finds a smile and points out the questionable ethics of a wealthy royal making bets with his hapless, overworked Guard. Fin insists he was simply proving the strength of his word by honoring their agreement and elbows me in the side, waiting for me to back him up. I don't, because Helos is probably right, but the weight pressing against my chest eases all the same. Soothed by the tug of friendship, the old rhythm between us temporarily restored. These precious moments of dappled sunlight and bird-song on the breeze in which we can pretend that nothing has changed.

For many seasons following our arrival in Roanin, Finley would call for my brother and me. Almost all disapproved, particularly given the Prediction, but no one would challenge a prince. So the three of us spent countless afternoons wandering the wilder parts of the gardens and grounds—the groves of red maple and sycamore trees, and dogwoods laden with blue jays. Around the stream that cuts through the carefully tailored grass, partially shrouded in the shadow of the mountains beyond. Finley is keen with charcoal and parchment, and some days he would ask me to alter my features so he could replicate them on paper. Helos, he never asked to change.

Those days ended with a few simple strokes of King Gerar's pen.

The midday sun has curled around the mountains north of the city by the time the grounds empty and we reach the castle wall's secret door. Fin pulls the heavy key from his pocket and gestures for Helos to step through first—newly reluctant, judging by his frequent glances, to part ways once more. At the sight of the door, however, my mood has sobered, falling back to grim reality. I watch my brother go, nerves blazing.

Ahead, Castle Roanin's northern face is kindling in the light.

The building is a complex collection of sloping walls and narrow turrets topped with spires. Wings stretch east and west, encasing a vast interior that took me weeks to learn to navigate. Mounted high on a post along the roof's crenellation, Telyan's standard catches the wind—a gray cut of cloth, and at the center a green oak encased within a broad purple mountain.

As the rear entrance comes into view, so does a handful of men and women gathered before it, all but one wearing the purple-accented gray uniforms marking them members of the Royal Guard. My stomach curdles when I see the figure heading the pack.

At sixteen, Fin is still very much a boy, but with only four years on him, Weslyn seems to have stamped out the remnants of youth with a vengeance. He studies our hesitant approach now with a broad stance and crossed arms, forever Finley's opposite in so many ways: sturdier, steadier, stronger. He is also harder—to read, to talk with, closed off to the point of absurdity, considering the world seems to fall at his feet. In fishing harbors and community halls, the people of Telyan whisper that one look from his red-brown eyes will give strength in the darkest of times. But I know that is a lie.

I have seen the way he looks at me.

"Where have you been?" he demands of Finley, having shed his suit jacket since I saw him last, but none of his gloomy mood. He walks toward us, away from the guards, his enormous, wiry gray deerhound named Astra close on his heels. "You do know what today is, I assume?"

"I know, and I'm sorry." Finley hovers a couple of paces before him, hands in his pockets. Our brief attempt at levity at an end. "There was something I needed to take care of."

"Today?" Weslyn's eyebrows arch in disbelief as Astra wags her tail at us, tongue lolling.

Standing side by side, the two brothers could not look less alike. While Finley is fair-haired, pale-skinned, and blue-eyed, his brother is everything darker. Loose brown curls crown a tan face lined with stubble. If Finley is a sail, then Weslyn is the ship. Finley is an ever-flowing river; Weslyn is an oak, rooted to the ground.

"I'm afraid so," Finley replies. "Couldn't be helped. They're not to blame," he adds, when his brother's gaze falls to Helos and me just behind.

"And I suppose you needed them both for this very pressing matter."

I dig my fingernails into my palms and focus on releasing the tension in my shoulders. Control is the key to ensuring I never risk an ill-timed shift from emotions getting the better of me. Interactions with Weslyn make it all too tempting to give in to the lynx's aggression.

Helos opens his mouth—to say what, I don't know—but Fin quickly speaks up. "As a matter of fact, I did."

"What exactly were you doing, then?"

Finley pauses, then shrugs a little.

"This is low, even for you, Fin." Weslyn shakes his head. "Rules don't exist to be broken."

Even to my ears, the chastisement sounds rather halfhearted, as if he recognizes the futility of the words even as they leave his lips.

Finley must hear it, too, because he straightens, suddenly encouraged. And just like that, the tension between them slips away.

"Is Father furious?" Finley asks, a smile working his jaw. I just stand there, trying to look unbothered by the guards' meaningful stares. I have no doubt what message today's reading must have yielded.

To my astonishment, the corner of Weslyn's mouth twitches, as if he might actually smile back. "Furious might be an understatement," he replies. "But only if you mean Violet. Father is more . . . resigned."

Finley is the only one who seems to escape his brother's usual judgment and severity. A courtesy Weslyn no longer extends to me.

"Come on, then. Let's get this over with." Weslyn uncrosses his arms. "*You* should not be here," he adds pointedly to Helos. Then he turns to me. "And you should know better."

"Fi—His Royal Highness needed my help!" I say, wanting to rip the condescension right out of his mouth.

"Well, he——"

Weslyn breaks off when Finley starts to sway. Both he and I reach out reflexively, but it's Helos who gets there first, catching Finley around the shoulders.

"He needs rest," my brother says, looking thoroughly unimpressed by the entire tense exchange. "And an infusion of willow bark. I gave him tarryleaf already."

Finley straightens again with obvious effort. "Helos——"

"I'm sorry, Fin, but he needs to know. It's the Throes," he tells Weslyn in an undertone, his expression painfully somber.

Hearing it said aloud is like watching Finley collapse in the Forest all over again. Instant and eternal all at once. Without looking back, Weslyn raises a hand to stop the tide of guards who started forward when Helos caught Finley. He doesn't criticize my brother's lack of formality. He doesn't tell him to let go. He just stands there, unmoving, staring at Finley.

"Are you sure?" he asks after an endless silence, addressing Finley directly.

My heart aches as Finley says nothing, just drops his gaze to the ground.

This, at last, seems to spur his brother into motion. Weslyn starts barking out orders abruptly, shifting Finley away from Helos's support. Fin begins to object, a torn expression coloring his features, then stops and yields to a throng of guards who surround him before we can even say goodbye. Helos's arms drop. I make to follow, but an elbow hits me between the ribs, hard.

"Back," snarls Simeon, one of the most respected members of the Royal Guard, like I'm no better than a dog caught underfoot. Like I haven't just rescued his sovereign's third-born.

I lurch forward again, my nails blades against my palms.

"Shifter."

The word roots me to the spot, motionless, fuming. I meet Weslyn's stony stare, fire licking my veins. *Rora,* I want to say. *My name is Rora.* It's one of the only things I know to be true, a certainty I cling to in a life shaped by unpredictability.

"My brother no longer requires your assistance. Do not leave the grounds. My father will send for you tomorrow, once the emissaries have departed."

He knows. Somehow, King Gerar knows I let Helos near his son, and soon he'll know his son is dying. The two of us together, just like the Prediction warned.

Normally I can brush aside that look in Weslyn's eyes, the one that says I'm a poison he's determined to draw out. But right now my feet ache, and my thoughts are growing murky from the morning's exhausting string of events, and I have no idea if the punishment for defying King Gerar's orders might be dismissal from his service. For once, Weslyn's expression does what he intends. It wounds me.

He turns to my brother, not a single sign of gratitude or concern for our fate coloring his expression. Unable—or unwilling—to see anything more in Helos or me than our shifter blood. "My father's orders were clear. Go. Now."

Helos remains fixed in place. Staring at me, willing me to protest.

Pressure is building in the back of my skull. Exhaustion and memories. Trauma and time. Go, that quiet, lingering word, the cast that molds my bones. I was five and Helos six the night the humans came and burned our village to the ground. The night our mother abandoned us to die. Go! Helos had shouted after she'd fled and saved herself, when the men discovered our hiding spot. But my ankle was twisted and I could not run, so he shifted to elk and carried me on his back, and to safety.

It was the first time he had shifted to an animal. His first of the three animal forms all shifters gain throughout our lifetimes, in addition to the ability to change our human features. The latter, we have all our lives, but our animal forms are born only from a moment of greatest need, recognized as such by instinct.

Helos's second animal—the fox—came later, when I was half-starved, feverish, and clinging to life. Though his third has not yet come, his two moments of greatest need thus far have been moments spent helping me.

As I meet my brother's eyes and see the hurt brimming to the surface, I long to set concern for my job aside and defend his right to be here. To assure him that Finley will recover, and that things will return to the way they once were. This period will pass.

But we cannot revive the past any more than we can escape it. And my brother and I are beyond empty promises.

"I'm sorry," I whisper, before turning to head for home.

How I wish I were that selfless.

THREE

It's difficult not to feel like a prisoner as I trail Captain Torres of the Royal Guard through the windowless corridor the following morning. Mounted oil lamps flicker along the granite walls, the space beneath them swathed in shadow, while the quarry-like chamber flings the sound of our boots about as if in mockery of my nerves. When the low ceilings begin to feel too confining, I run a hand along the walls and refocus my attention on the stone beneath my fingertips. It's cold.

King Gerar has requested my presence plenty of times, but not after a direct violation of his policy, or after learning his child has fallen ill. Torres's grim expression—and the fact that the revered captain of the Royal Guard herself has been sent to collect me—suggests I should start begging fortune for good news instead of bad. But right now I'm finding it difficult to focus on much of anything. Last night brought little sleep, and the thoughts in my head are a jumbled, spiraling blur.

We pass through a wide hall of silk drapes and candles mounted on crystal chandeliers, then into the adjoining antechamber, where an attendant is dusting the portraits of old kings and queens hung along the wood-paneled wall. Despite the hour, the curtains are still drawn across the long windows; it's as if the castle has curled in on itself, gradually growing as quiet as the city beyond its walls. The boy startles when he sees us and actually drops his feather duster, so dramatic it's almost comical, before abruptly leaving the room.

Captain Torres hesitates before plowing ahead, broad-shouldered beneath her uniform's silver epaulets, her dark hair pinned above copper skin reminiscent of polished amber. I only roll my eyes. Nerves among the staff always run especially high in the days following the Prediction. After King Gerar hired me and helped Helos find work in Bren and Tomas's shop, he ordered castle staffers to keep our identities a secret; no one outside the complex was to know the circumstances of our arrival. While that mandate has enabled us to lead relatively normal lives out in Roanin—any mistrust leveraged toward us born from broader tension rather than pointed hatred—our story spread among the castle staffers like wildfire. I glance at the cracking portraits, the red rug muffling our footsteps, and feel grateful that at least the painted monarchs can't flee like the attendant.

"Hold on."

Captain Torres flings an arm out just as she reaches the door, head cocked to listen. The quiet intensity in her bearing always reminds me of a great bird of prey; a horned owl, perhaps, or a golden eagle. Able to detect the slightest disturbances from far greater a distance than seems possible. Sure enough, beyond the antechamber, the sounds of an argument grow louder, and I hesitate to imagine what sort of disagreement would spur such a breach in decorum.

"Is the—"

"Shh," she waves. "It's the Eradain emissary. Wait here."

I swallow the retort on my tongue with some effort. Apparently it's not enough that the emissary would not recognize me by my appearance; the Danofers refuse to risk an accidental shift in a foreigner's presence. Not with the Prediction stoking fear of shifters like me. Emissaries from Glenweil and Eradain come to Telyan each year for the public reading, and every time, I'm not even allowed in the same hall.

Ignoring Captain Torres's protest, I peek around the corner just enough to see a man pound past, his red-and-blue uniform traced with lines of gold. My stomach churns at the sight.

Expulsion. Executions. Families vanishing in the night. Legislation restricting magical people and creatures, and rumors of worse, relayed in hurried whispers amid the wilderness I grew up in. All stories told of the kingdom to the north, a realm founded on the fear that humans might become second-class to those with magic in their blood. It's the kind of place I worry Telyan might become, should the tension between humans and magical people continue to rise.

Safe from my vantage point, I watch the emissary storm through the far door the moment a flustered valet pulls it open. I guess the talks did not end well.

The thought offers some comfort as an annoyed Captain Torres delivers me to the study two floors up. I'm in no hurry for King Gerar to make peace with a kingdom that would see my kind destroyed.

The minutes tick by as I stand alone in the dark-stained, wood-paneled study, waiting for King Gerar to arrive. The more time that passes, the shallower my breathing becomes. He's probably considering which words he'll use to dismiss me, and the thought nudges me closer to panic.

I massage the sides of my head with my fingers and attempt to cobble together some semblance of a plan. Perhaps I could try another job in Roanin or even elsewhere in Telyan, where no one recognizes our natural forms, and none suspect us to be the two shifters tied to the Prediction. But this job is the closest I've come to experiencing a stable home and real friendship. It's a chance to repay the man who showed mercy and the boy who showed kindness, long enough to show them they didn't make a mistake, that I'm worth keeping around, that I can be good. It's atonement for the way I failed Helos that day by the river, and distraction from what my mother did to me.

Each time I adopt a disguise, I can sink into the role and cast aside the sight of those relentless, haunting eyes—my mother's eyes as they flickered between the attackers, the open woods, and me. The moment when she looked between her children and freedom, and chose freedom. On my best days, I can even pretend there's not a snag caught deep inside me, nothing to do with cryptic words or the magic in my blood and everything to do with the person I've become. This anger and inexplicable sorrow that hang around my neck like a willful child, stubborn and insistent even when I've no cause to feel them at all.

I scan the book spines lining the far wall in an attempt to steady my nerves, then switch my attention to the enormous map spanning a table at the room's center.

It's a map of this continent, Alemara, the narrow landmass stretching north and south, longer than it is wide. An enormous river bisects the continent vertically, the dreadful water that separates the Vale from the three realms east of it—the two kingdoms, Eradain and Telyan, with the republic of Glenweil between them. The first persecutes our kind, while the last exiled Helos and me from its borders, going so far as to distribute leaflets bearing our faces sketched in ink. Beneath the illustrations ran a warning to report any sightings of us. I blot it out on the map with my palm.

My gaze drifts left, across the Purple Mountains curving upward along Telyan's northern border, then west of the river, to the land labeled WESTERN VALE. Terrain with a will of its own—moving, trapping, breaking, alive. Where most magical beings now make their home, and perhaps habitable enough if you have a people, protection. But not for a pair of children endeavoring to survive on their own. Even now, the mere memory of it sends my heart into a gallop.

Clutching the edge of the table, I allow myself just one glance at the dot labeled CAELA RIDGE, a circle of land once made stable thanks to a gift from the giants, where my family had made its home. A single tap of ink to remind others that someone *was* there, that we lived before raiders destroyed our village and every person in it aside from Helos and myself. By now, that part of my life is little more than a collection of shapes and shadows in my mind. The memories taunt me with their nearness, always just out of reach until, on occasion, I manage to snatch one from the fold. The collection of small wooden structures built around and up in the trees. The bridges suspended between age-broadened trunks where Helos and I used to sprint right to the edges, swiveling back only at the last possible moment. Trying to trick our bodies into thinking we would fall and force a bird form to take shape. (My bird would come later, of course—the result of a different kind of running.) The thuds of our feet hitting wooden planks. A fire to shut out the winter wind. Father's bloodied back.

I push off from the table and pace the length of the room, forcing myself to breathe deeply. I have never been able to figure out who those men were or why they came, and the uncertainty is maddening.

"Good, you've come," says King Gerar as soon as he enters the study. He's wearing the dark jacket lined with Telyan purple and green that he always wears for the emissaries' visits. Unease strengthens its grip on my chest when I see the group tailing him: Captain Torres returned, her oval face impassive, along with Weslyn and Violet. No Finley in sight. Though Violet looks immaculate as always, Weslyn's navy button-down is uncharacteristically rumpled, the collar askew, and I wonder if he, too, spent the night awake.

King Gerar glances at the two guards flanking the doorway, awaiting orders. "Leave us," he says.

Just before they shut the door, Astra streaks in and plops down by Weslyn's side. Then I'm left facing King Gerar, the most powerful man in the southern end of the continent.

"Sit. Please," he offers, gesturing to a straight-backed, beige lounge chair. "You look as though you've had a long night."

I do as he asks, perching on the edge. Violet remains by her father's side while Weslyn positions himself in a far corner. Torres stands at the door, and it's then I realize none of them are going to sit as well.

I feel my future here slip further from my grasp.

"I want to thank you for aiding my son," King Gerar continues. "Finley told me what you did for him in the Forest."

"Of course, Your Majesty."

"And Helos. He aided you?" Violet asks.

I will myself not to wilt under the force of her gaze. Unlike Finley, Violet exudes royalty. It's there in the way she carries herself, posture regal in a plum, silk shirt tucked into wide-legged trousers. It's there in the calm and calculating expression with which she appraises me now. It's even in the way she always towers over most people in the room, the cut of hair above her shoulders as straight and severe as her bearing. A born leader, and I admire her for it.

I've overheard the conversations between her and King Gerar, her demands that he send me away.

"Well?"

"His Royal Highness was feverish, ma'am." I clutch my hands before me. "He needed medicine, and there was no way to get him back into the castle unseen. Helos treated him."

"All the way to the door, I hear."

Violet's eyes could cut through bone, but I keep my expression neutral. "He's a healer, ma'am. His Royal Highness asked him to come."

She lets us stand in silence for another few moments. One of her questioning tactics. By now I'm familiar with it, but still it takes all of my concentration to remain motionless under her stare, to ignore my prickling skin. Though Violet will not inherit the throne for many years yet, the influence she maintains in court is growing stronger by the week. Once she turns twenty-five this winter and begins her first solo tour of the kingdom, that influence is sure to extend to the people as well.

She frowns slightly.

"Rora," King Gerar says at last. "There is a matter we need to discuss."

My stomach hits the floor. "Please, sir. Don't dismiss me. It won't happen again."

King Gerar gives me a searching look, as if he can read my emotions in spite of the effort I make to dampen them. "Dismiss you? No, child. I have an assignment for you."

Relief. Breathtaking solace, trickling through my bones like a stream over stones. I have never known him to lie. "I'll do what you need me to do, sir," I tell him earnestly.

His smile is no more than a flicker, there and gone in an instant.

"Almost every week now, my people are dying from this malady."
He pauses, as if to see if I'll contradict him. I don't. "I had hoped
our healers would have found an antidote by now. But nothing
they have tried has worked, and now you say my son is dying, too."

Violet folds her arms, her expression clear but grim. Weslyn
stares at the ground.

"As of this morning, the situation has become graver than I anticipated. It seems Eradain's young king has issued an ultimatum."
King Gerar leans over the table and glances down at the map. "We
have two months to agree to his terms or refuse, and it is clear that
the penalty for resistance will be war. Meanwhile—"

"Agree to what?" *Expulsion, executions*—the question is out before I can stop it.

"That is not your concern," King Gerar replies, in a tone that
curtails further questioning. Torres shoots me a warning glance.
"Meanwhile, the Fallow Throes is spreading, and the healers are no
closer to curing it, nor to understanding why there are some who
don't appear symptomatic at all." He presses his lips tightly together,
perhaps wishing he could deny the words they've let through. "I
will not be cowed into submission by this boy-king, yet we cannot
hope to face the threat beyond our borders if we're being weakened
from within. If this illness is rooted in magic, perhaps therein lies its
antidote. There is still one remedy we have not tried, and that is our
course now. Your course. Stardust."

I just stare. Rendered speechless in the face of his words.
Stardust?

If Helos had spoken thus, I would have laughed in his face. As
it is, I can't keep my mask from slipping, and the royals clearly notice. I've overstepped my boundaries, I can see that, but I can't do
what they're asking. Not this.

"Your Majesty—"

"I am not asking for your opinion," he says, holding up a hand.
"The records speak of its healing powers clearly enough. What I
need—what my people need—is action, and you must be quick.
No one outside of this room is to know; if Eradain learns we are

seeking stardust, they will take that as a refusal before the deadline even comes. You will leave tomorrow."

Tomorrow. A single sunrise until I'm to leave for the place I never wish to see again.

I notice he doesn't frame it as a question.

Even in my worst nightmares, I never would have predicted this. The healing power of stardust is a story as old as Alemara's creation itself—and feels as distant.

Long ago, magic was woven into the earth's core. Magic that grew over the centuries, expanding and pressing against all sides beneath the surface, creating a series of increasingly violent earthquakes. People believed the rumbling earth to be a great, slumbering beast stirring underground, but they soon learned they were mistaken. When the energy became too immense to be contained, the magic shattered in an explosion so great it cracked the land into several smaller continents—the Day of Rupturing, nearly eight hundred years ago, when cities and homes and families were ripped apart. And as the land splintered, so did the magic; hundreds of thousands of fragments, bursting forth and taking root in whatever they could find.

Some remained in the earth—the soil, the flowers, the mountains, the trees. Others embedded themselves in the bodies of some of the land's inhabitants. Over time, those with magic in their blood evolved to have abilities as unpredictable as the magic. Humans learned to hear the hearts of trees and nurture floral growth, to influence the land, to speak with animals, to shift—magical communities of forest walkers, giants, whisperers, and shifters. Animals grew stranger, bolder—mountain lions with hypnotic eyes, foxes with wings, bighorn sheep that fed on bone. Bats with toxic venom and wolves with the power of camouflage. The land changed as well; terrain shifted with no notice, hills sprang up, caves collapsed within moments. Trees grew taller and wider, ensnaring creatures in their branches, cradling others in beds of leaves. And the most powerful strands of magic stretched all the way to the sky—to the stars.

Yes, stardust has the power to heal anyone or anything, even on the brink of death. King Gerar knows the lore as well as I do—it's common knowledge among the educated circles, and I have passed many lonely hours studying scholars' texts in the Queen's Library. But the hoard is closely guarded, hidden deep within the Vale— the wilderness to the west. And there is no way to get to it without bartering with—

"The giants. You would have me negotiate with them?" My voice quivers on the words. The ancient, magical people who gifted loropins to the three realms before isolating themselves at the continent's edge. Human, once, with magic that gave them a slight measure of influence over the land, just enough to send small patches into slumber or alter it according to their will, before that magic made them huge, and frightening, and different in many people's eyes.

To my dismay, King Gerar nods. "They have occupied the Western Vale for longer than any of us have been alive, and you are the only one here who knows how to navigate that terrain. My guards can barely navigate the Old Forest." He pauses. "You have already shown me that you can be discreet, and the road seems clear enough. They won't be hard to find."

The idea of any road marking the Vale is laughable. Because the terrain often changes without warning, many of the landmarks Helos and I may have used have likely altered or vanished by now. Surviving there on our own for so many years nearly cost us our lives. With no elders left to guide us, we had no one to teach us which plants carried poison. No strength in numbers against predators we were never trained to avoid. It was years of trial and error, injuries and sickness. A place of dark memories and abandonment. Hunger and hunters and death.

"My brother and I always avoided the circle of land bordering the giants' domain," I respond carefully, my mind searching desperately for a way out. "It's the most volatile part of the Vale."

"Volatile—how?"

I turn to Weslyn, surprised. He's always studiously avoided the paths I tread, and I'm not sure why that should change now. In fact, I'm not sure why he's here at all.

"The land there, it's—it's where the magic is strongest," I explain, struggling to find the words under four pairs of watchful eyes. Weslyn's expression darkens.

"But it is possible to cut across it," King Gerar persists. "Is it not?"

Deadly rockslides. Poisonous vines. The images flood my mind.

"I—"

Finley's body buried deep in the ground.

"I imagine it's possible," I concede at last. "But I told you—that stretch of land is the most dangerous in Alemara. What if bringing stardust here causes a similar effect? How would Eradain react then, or your own people?" My voice chokes on the last words, and I draw a steadying breath. Old injuries are ghosting my limbs. "Awakened land is unpredictable. The Old Forest may flourish with new life, or it may just as easily turn lethal. Meadows may stretch into hills, or a crack could split the ground beneath a house in two. Plants could become so poisonous as to kill you with their odor alone." I look him in the eye, willing him to understand. "That kind of uncertainty, a life of never knowing what new reality you might wake up to . . . you don't know what that's like."

"You forget that there are benefits to reviving magic in the land," says King Gerar. "The soil would grow more fertile, food more plentiful. We might discover new plants that remedy illnesses we cannot normally treat." He raises an eyebrow, and my face heats. "In any case, we may find out what it's like soon enough, with or without the stardust. Magic seems to be driving the Fallow Throes; it is only a matter of time before it makes its presence known elsewhere." He turns his gaze about the room. "Why is magic awakening east of the river now, when it has lain dormant for so long? What else might it be reviving each night, while we lie here, unaware, asleep in our beds? Magic has not appeared in ordinary humans for centuries, so there must be a reason why it's doing so now. It does not simply materialize out of nothing; these strands must have a source."

Violet makes a noise of distaste.

"That's another reason why I need you to go, Rora. If the heart of magic is rooted in the Vale, perhaps traveling there is the only way to find the cause of this resurgence. If something else is going on, we need to be prepared."

"But for all we know, bringing stardust here could make Telyan as erratic as the land outside the giants' domain!" I exclaim, shooting to my feet. King Gerar's reminder of the benefits is still ringing in my ears, but all I can see is the terrain of my past, which I made certain to leave behind for good. "Wouldn't that simply hasten Telyan's fall, to be forced to contend with an ever-changing landscape in addition to everything else?"

The tension crackling through the room is a near-tangible thing. Torres visibly shifts her weight closer to where I'm standing, lips pursed as if my continued resistance is making her job more difficult. No doubt I have spoken out of turn, but they must understand. They must.

"Without an antidote, the Throes will spread," King Gerar says, almost distantly. "Who knows how many lives it will claim? How far it will reach?" He runs a hand along the map. "We do not know for certain if the stardust's presence alone would be enough to awaken the land—that is purely speculation, nothing more. What we *do* know is that it is the only chance my people have at survival. What does predictable land matter if my people are not here to experience it?" Suddenly he straightens, his gaze hardening. "I will not see my kingdom fall to it without a fight, and in any case, we have no choice. In the wake of Eradain's pronouncement, Telyan must strengthen itself in the weeks to come. That includes eradicating this illness before it runs rampant. The hazard you speak of is a risk we'll have to take."

I still can't help but feel he might only be trading one threat for another, if my theory about the stardust proves correct. But he's right: if war truly is to come to Telyan, the kingdom can't hope to face it with its soldiers being picked off one by one.

"I have full confidence in your abilities, Rora," he continues, watching me carefully. "And we will make it well worth your while. Four hundred gold pieces."

Images of the Vale are scalding my insides, but his words are nearly enough to douse the flames. Four hundred gold pieces.

It's eighty times what I make on a regular job. That kind of coin would buy Helos a new home, a proper one. It would feed us for a year. Or it would enable us to set up somewhere new without squatting, if we do ever decide to leave Roanin. That kind of money would make us rich—if war or reawakened magic don't wreck the land first.

Four hundred gold pieces.

"What will you offer the giants in exchange for the stardust?" I ask, unable to deny that payment would have its advantages.

"Seeds from the eldest strand of trees in the Old Forest. Weslyn will secure them for you."

Weslyn? "Your Majesty?"

"My son will be accompanying you on your journey."

No. Not him.

My gaze cuts to Weslyn. He hasn't spoken since our brief exchange, but for once, I can guess his feelings easily enough; he hasn't yet mastered his sister's art of keeping her eyes fully devoid of sentiment. He faces me now, arms crossed, chin raised. Daring me to object. Astra has lain her head across his shoes, like she knows.

Please, I nearly beg. *Anyone but him.*

"I can manage better on my own," I protest. And it's true. Weslyn's of a different cut—military bound, an officer-in-training meant to leave for Fendolyn's Keep, the garrison in the south of Telyan, in less than a year. A city-born prince who won't even enter the woods bordering his home. Surely he knows nothing of traversing wilderness.

But King Gerar is shaking his head. "Minister Mereth controls the only river crossing there is, and she has kept it inoperable for many years now. She will not reopen it for the sake of a civilian." He rubs his bearded chin. "Weslyn is trained to handle this type of negotiation. He'll persuade her to give you both passage."

Minister Mereth. I'm familiar with the name, and her city on the river—it's where Helos and I first crossed into human territory, though we had not been able to secure passage on any ferry. Boats departed from the eastern shore, not the west. Glenweil is all that stands between Eradain and Telyan, the middle ground that stops the stain of Eradain from seeping into King Gerar's domain. But I have no love lost for that land, or wish to return. She already sent us away when she thought we might have anything to do with the Prediction; for all I know, she may have grown more fond of her northern neighbor's policies in recent years.

And if I give us away again?

"I could—"

"This is not open to discussion. Weslyn will go."

—*shift to look like him,* I finish my objection in my head. The minister would never know the difference. Though I suppose I would not be able to match the knowledge inside his head, however well I could his features.

It's clear it wouldn't matter, even if I could impersonate a royal in both body and mind. The rigid stances permit no argument. They're determined that he should come.

I fight back the only way I dare.

"My brother will come, too," I say. Weslyn opens his mouth, but I shake my head. "You won't be able to keep him away. You know this, sir," I add, addressing King Gerar directly.

It's true; Helos needs some way to help Finley, even if it means leaving his job. But it's bold, maybe too bold. King Gerar holds my gaze, no doubt considering three hastily scribbled words.

"Two of them?" Weslyn practically spits. "No."

"You believe that nonsense?"

Violet's measured challenge surprises me.

"Of course not." His eyes gleam a little too defiantly for that to be the truth. "But one is enough."

No one contradicts him this time, and my heart begins to pound. My control is slipping. I need leverage.

One is enough. I will never be more than "the shifter" to him. To any of them, except Finley and perhaps King Gerar, or friends like Seraline who don't even know my real name. And maybe that's the way it ought to be. Maybe that's all I am—a cobbled-together collection of features. The eyes, the nose, the fingers, the skin—all of it changeable. None of it enough to earn their loyalty any more than it earned my mother's love.

No.

"You need me." He scoffs at my words, but I know they're true, and that fuels my anger further. Besides, at the thought of my brother, a new idea has occurred to me. "You're asking me to risk my life traveling to the edge of the continent, to barter with giants and find out why magic is resurfacing. You may insist on coming, but you cannot do it alone." Torres fists the hilt of her sword, but for once I don't care if I've gone too far. They need me, they *need* me, and the knowledge has set me free.

"That's—"

"I'll do it. I'll go." I'm speaking only to King Gerar now. "But this is my condition. Helos comes."

He'll come, and how proud he'll be to see me. A journey back into the wild. Setting aside my own safety, facing my nightmares for the chance to save others.

He'll see how selfless I can be. Violet will see how useful. And if we can retrieve the stardust and save the afflicted, really save them, maybe the court will see how wrong they are about the two of us. Maybe things can change.

The Vale flashes before my eyes, and hope is tainted by fear.

"Agreed," says King Gerar, before his son can object, or I can change my mind. "Thank you, Rora. We will meet by the north entrance at dawn."

I dip my head and look again to my travel companion. His glare is fire.

The road will be long, and it won't be the miles that make it so.

FOUR

As soon as I tell Helos the news, he marches straight into the Old Forest and shifts to elk to sharpen his antlers against an enormous elm. A way to prepare, he tells me, but there must be more to it. Dogging his steps, I sink into a patch of grass nearby, falling quickly into a much-needed nap. By the time I wake, the sun already perches high in the sky, and Helos has sharpened each tip of horn into a deadly point.

It's wrong. So wrong. Helos is the good one. Helos is hope. And here he is, transforming himself into a weapon.

I can't stand it.

"Pass me that boot, won't you?" he asks, after shifting back to human and dressing.

He swerves to avoid the boot soaring toward him.

"Rora." Spoken like an offering.

"Helos." Spoken like an accusation.

He brushes a few strands of hair from his face and grabs the shoe, his movements bafflingly relaxed compared to an hour ago. "It's a good idea. Stardust can save him. All of them."

"But we'd be bringing it *here*," I counter, pushing to my feet and crossing my arms. Just because I agreed doesn't mean I have to like it. "This is the safest place we've ever lived. What if it becomes no better than the one we escaped? Because of *us*?" The mere suggestion of replicating the Vale east of the river sends forbidden tears to the corners of my eyes. I blink them away rapidly.

He has to see my fears are well-founded. There's only so much magic a living creature can host, but a star? Its capacity is greater than any being's on the earth, a burning expanse filled with the most staggering power there is. It's old magic, strong magic, more potent than any fragments found in nature or animals. We've seen what the Vale is like where stardust is present, and that was only on the outskirts.

Helos bends to tie his laces. "We either take that risk, or let Finley die. Which are you willing to endure?"

I don't have to ask what his answer would be. He would endanger his life for the sake of Finley's without question. Placing others above himself, as always.

Selflessness requires sacrifice. The meaning is clear, and I do my best to absorb the words and prioritize them above my mounting concerns. *No more selfish decisions.*

Once I accepted the assignment this morning, King Gerar had beckoned me over to the map, where Violet walked me through the route we're meant to take. First, to Grovewood, a town two days' walk from Roanin, to collect the Old Forest seeds that Weslyn will attempt to exchange for stardust; if the records are to be believed, anyone bartering with the giants must offer an item emblematic of the traveler's home, one they can use and do not already have. From there, we'll follow the roads northeast, cross Telyan's border, and trek west through Glenweil until we reach Niav, the city on the shore. Weslyn will secure passage for us on Minister Mereth's ferry across the river, and then we'll enter the Vale.

The plan sounded straightforward coming from her mouth. Simple, even, and King Gerar nodded his approval as Captain Torres offered a few recommendations. I just continued staring at the map. The circle of woods marked LAND OF GIANTS jutting out from the Vale's western shore. My heart plummeted at the thought of crossing that hateful river to get there. Twice, if counting the return journey.

"Will you be armed?" Weslyn asked, so abruptly that I had glanced at him in surprise.

"I don't own any weapons, sir."

He appraised me critically, brows rising at my tone. "Yes, well, I doubt you would need one, anyway."

My blood boiled over. My fiercest animal form is a lynx. That doesn't make me invincible.

"Tell your brother what we have discussed. Tomorrow morning, we'll—"

He broke off, staring at my hands where they gripped the table. I followed his gaze and saw how my fingers had grown longer, the nails sharper. Quickly, I dropped my hands to my thighs. There were half-moon marks in the wood.

Captain Torres took a casual step closer. Astra whined, sensing the change in mood, and for a moment the Danofers seemed to ponder the wisdom of sending their second heir to the throne into the wild with a girl who can shift to a lynx.

Torres added a handful of Royal Guards to our traveling party after that.

"I know you want to help him," Helos continues in the present. "We both do, and this is our best chance."

"Even if it means traversing the Vale?"

Helos shrugs, his features devoid of concern.

I don't understand it. I may have trouble leaving the past, but his solution is to pretend it never happened at all.

"What if he dies and we're not here to say goodbye?" My final fear laid bare.

"He's not going to die," Helos says, quite calmly now.

I tug at the hem of my shirt. "Your expression yesterday said otherwise."

"Yesterday, this plan didn't exist. Today it does."

I don't reply. I just turn away, my jaded heart struggling to share his optimism, yet wishing to, desperately. In the silence that follows, the charged air gradually deflates.

"Rora."

I don't look at him.

"Listen to me," Helos says. "This can work."

I shrug a little.

"It's okay to be scared."

"I'm not scared," I reply, too quickly.

"I'll be there, too."

Guilt washes over me. City life has always suited Helos far better than it has me. He loves it here—the work, the people, the noise. Cheerful nights at the pub with casual friends and flings who know him only as Helos, not as one in a pair of shifters. The afternoons off with Finley and me, until recently. I'm sure if it were up to him, we would never leave. "I roped you in without asking. You shouldn't have to come. And your job—you love it. You can't lose it. What if—"

"Don't be stupid. Bren and Tomas can't argue with a royal summons, and I'm too good an apprentice for them to not rehire me when we're back. Anyway, I'm not leaving you. You don't have to do it alone."

Alone.

Images from the last time Helos and I lived on the road swarm my thoughts, the old fear still fresh enough to sting. The constantly pinched nerves and tingling skin. The gnawing emptiness in our stomachs. The ache, ache, ache in feet abused by terrain and time. And always, the weight of having so much love to give, if only someone would let us love them.

I drag my attention back to the present.

Control.

"I should go," I say, brushing dirt from my pants. "Finley asked to speak with me before we leave."

Helos frowns, his lack of invitation tainting the air between us. "It's not right," he mutters.

"I know."

"By the river, I'm going to get Finley's *antidote*. The king should let me say goodbye."

I place a hand on his shoulder. "I know."

Helos glowers at the ground a few heartbeats longer. Then he leads us from the woods without another word.

Finley's quarters are situated in the northern wing of Castle Roanin, the one built closest to the mountains. His request—Fin has always admired what cannot be tamed, always chased the indomitable.

A couple of chambermaids toting linens shuffle by as I cross the airy, brown-stoned corridor. They avert their gaze until they're past me, then swap assessments under their breath when they think I cannot hear—or don't care if I can. One claims it's a shame my parents didn't drown me and then each other back when they had the chance, and I suppose I should be grateful. I've heard worse.

The entrance to Finley's rooms appears around the corner. I drag my feet when I see Weslyn's personal guard, Naethan, manning the door alongside the ever-quiet Ansley. Both are roughly Weslyn's age and have been his friends since childhood, or so the story goes. The way I see it, any friend of his is no friend of mine, but before I can change course and come back later, Ansley exchanges a glance with Naethan and slips inside to announce my arrival.

I hover awkwardly a short distance away, avoiding Naethan's gaze. From the pieces I've gleaned, his visits to Castle Roanin began at a young age; his father was good friends with Queen Raenen and, as an antiquarian, became actively involved in filling out the Queen's Library. Ansley, on the other hand, has always kept tight-lipped about her past, but I've caught her sending portions of her pay to Poldat, a coastal village on Telyan's southern tip. Nothing incriminating about either one, but then, neither has ever seemed too pleased by my presence.

Weslyn emerges from Finley's sitting parlor shortly after.

Judging by the long sword belted at his waist, and the slight trails of dust lining his face and loose shirt, I assume he came here straight from a final session with the arms-master. Training to become an officer before he even leaves the keep. We both pause for a bit, each considering the other, until Astra appears and lopes to my side, licking my fingers and wagging her tail—far friendlier to me than her master ever is. The interference seems to chip at some of the tension between us.

After a glance at the open door, Weslyn gestures for me to follow him a few paces down the corridor. Naethan feigns disinterest as I move to his side.

"You're fond of Finley?" he asks, speaking quietly.

I narrow my eyes, trying to make out the intent behind the question, since the answer should be obvious. "Yes, sir." *Very much.*

He nods once, watching me warily and, perhaps, a bit sorrowfully. "He will try to persuade you not to go. Don't let him."

I lift my chin a little higher, off-guard.

"Rora!" Finley calls through the open door.

At that, Weslyn walks away, whistling for Astra to heel. I follow the voice inside.

At the far end of the blue-paneled, high-ceilinged parlor, the double-doors to Finley's sleeping chamber are shut. Along the walls, half a dozen framed maps gleam with colored illustrations of ships and serpents, mountains and stars. Finley is standing beside the unlit fireplace, staring at one of those maps, back straight and unconsciously regal despite the casual shirt coming untucked in the front.

"Thank you, Ansley. That's all," he says, without turning around.

Dust swirls through the sunlight beaming onto the patterned rug. As soon as the door clicks shut behind me, I step to Finley's side, my hands in my pockets. Together, we study the old drawing in silence.

"I always said I would leave one day, duties or no." Finley's voice is uncharacteristically soft. A half-made tie hangs loose around his neck, as if once again, he got distracted halfway through. "I guess my father will have his way after all."

"Don't say that," I exclaim. "Your father would never want this."

"Then I suppose, for once, he and I are in agreement."

"Finley." For all his repeated insistence that King Gerar is disappointed in him, I have never seen his father treat him with anything less than adoration. "Your father loves you."

"Oh, I know." He still isn't looking at me. "He gives me everything he thinks I could want. Gardens, horses, tutors who speak to me like a person instead of a prince." Finley pauses to consider, grimacing. "Intel on all the boys he believes will one day make good husbands."

I laugh a little at his imitation of King Gerar's measured voice, a middle-aged father trying to matchmake for his son. Then it occurs to me that, as with all of the afflicted, Finley's own voice is going to change. Sooner or later, it will rise or fall into one that will take him further from himself. A stranger's voice.

The base of my throat tightens abruptly.

"But what I want isn't in his power to give, and he knows it."
Finley looks over at last, his forehead creased. And despite the
words, I'm suddenly just grateful that he at least still sounds like
him. "So you see, Rora, I am a constant reminder that all of his
efforts aren't enough."

Finley musters a small smile when he sees the look on my face,
then shrugs off the words and heads for the tray of tea and biscuits
set on an end table by the fireplace. As if to say, *hey, don't worry about
me. I'm only joking.*

I don't buy the nonchalance, any more than I have to ask what
it is he wants. The proof is in the maps along his walls, the wooden
ship upon the mantel, the stacks of drawings, and the curiosity that
burns inside him like candlelight, a flame of restless energy spur-
ring his hands and feet into constant motion.

"This one will be enough," I vow, stepping away from the wall.
Standing here, safe within Finley's parlor, it's easier to let Helos's
confidence strengthen my own. He said this plan could work, and
there's no one I trust more. "We're going to find the stardust."

And then, I add silently, *I will persuade your father to lift the ban,
whatever it takes.* I saw Finley start to object out in the courtyard,
before the guards shunted him away. He doesn't like this separation
any more than Helos or I do.

Fin shakes his head. "You shouldn't have to be the ones that go.
They could find somebody else, or simply send the Guard without
you. I would go myself if only everyone would stop treating me
like an invalid."

"They would fail. None of the Royal Guard knows the Vale
like we do."

"But you could instruct them first. Tell them where to go, what
to look out for." He waves a hand in my direction, desperate for
me to understand. "You and Helos have spent enough of your lives
in danger."

I grant a thin smile, though Helos and I have always shielded
him from the worst parts of our orphaned upbringing. "We're the
best fit for the job. We'll be okay."

"And Wes—"

"He'll be fine, too." Truly I don't know, since humans have not traversed the Vale in years. But I don't know what else I'm supposed to tell him. Certainly not that it will be difficult to give his brother guidance when even the sight of me incites such animosity. "Although," I can't stop myself from adding, "it would be a lot easier if he just stayed behind."

Finley scratches the back of his head. "I know you've never really gotten along, but—"

"A bit of an understatement, don't you think?"

"But that's because you don't know him," Finley plows ahead, as if I haven't spoken. "He has his reasons for being the way he is, but you can trust him. I promise."

"I know enough to know that he could stand to take a few lessons from you in civility."

Finley leans over the back of a chair, his attention shifting to one of the dusty sunbeams. He's silent awhile before shaking his head. "My brother is a better person than either of us," he murmurs, unusually somber as he studies the light. "Trust me, Rora. I should be more like him."

I fold my arms and start to pace, but don't manage a reply. It's true I thought I saw a flicker of goodness in Weslyn once, the day we met. But that was only one day, scarcely more than an hour. Not nearly enough to offset the years of tension that followed.

That afternoon is burned forever into my brain—the thundering earth shooting ripples up my legs, baying hounds whose howls rang like death in my ears, the sting of a troubled past come back to bite. Not an earthquake, but hoofbeats, fast approaching the campsite where Helos and I were squatting homeless in the Old Forest. Perhaps another child would have screamed, but by then, I had long since learned to fear in silence. So no sound came out as terror closed its ghostly fist around my lungs, its grip nearly as tight as my own around a bit of sharpened rock.

Run, Helos had urged me. *Go on ahead. I'll follow.*

And I had actually considered it, traitor that I am, but already, Queen Raenen and the rest of the Royal Fox Hunt party were circling us on their snorting, skittering mounts. My gut sank like a stone when I realized the futility of feigning human; already, the horses' nerves had betrayed our shifter nature.

I remember with perfect clarity the queen's confident posture and long, plaited, yellow hair. I remember her calm, thoughtful expression as she watched the feathers shoot through my skin before Helos's hand on my shoulder comforted me enough to stop them. I remember her concern when she asked where our parents were, then told us, *You need not be afraid*. And though by then, I knew how futile it was to find comfort in a stranger's glance, I remember the ghostly fist loosened its grip on my chest just a bit.

Then the fox they chased had erupted from its hiding place, flushed out by the mad hounds' desperate, prying paws. The startled horses nearly unseated their riders, and when the ensuing panic settled once more, their prized fox—a symbol of the monarchy—lay trampled and broken on the ground.

I watched the change break upon the riders' faces like waves against the shore—calmness into anger, curiosity into naked fear, all apparently stunned into silence as they stared at the dead fox. And then, to my horror, the ones in uniform slowly turned to Helos and me and reached for belted swords.

Queen Raenen had stayed their hands and ordered us to Castle Roanin, to be bathed and fed before an audience with King Gerar, while they finished their hunt. When even the guards proved reluctant to heed her request, clearly unsettled by our presence, it was Weslyn who nudged his horse forward and volunteered to accompany us to the castle. Weslyn who quietly asked me my name and ushered us into the kitchen without judgment, who stood whispering and laughing with Naethan against the wall while Helos and I wrung our hands before King Gerar's empty throne. And when the teary-eyed steward burst into the grand hall scarcely a minute after King Gerar, it was Weslyn's smile that had faded the slowest.

Whatever kindness I thought I'd glimpsed in him that day vanished the moment the steward announced Queen Raenen had fallen from her horse and broken her neck. From then on, his sudden frown became a permanent fixture, one he wields like a weapon. If the boy I met four years ago is still in there, he's buried deep.

"It seems." Finley runs a hand through his wispy hair, then drops it. "It seems I cannot talk you out of it, either."

I step suddenly to his side, wanting to reassure him. "We're going to find it, Finley, I promise. We'll find it and come back. All of us."

"I wanted to tell you," he cuts in, taking my hands in his. "I wanted to say, if I'm not here when you return—"

"Finley—"

"If I'm not here," he repeats, brushing the objection aside, "I want you to know how much your friendship has meant to me. You tell Helos for me, okay? I want you both to learn to be happy without me."

This time I can't stifle a breath of disbelief. Yet his expression is clear as he looks at me. Full of purpose. Determined. For a moment, I see the leader he could be, if he weren't the youngest of three and utterly indifferent to the crown.

"You will be here," I say firmly, unwilling to engage in deathbed talk. "But why didn't you call for Helos as well? He deserves to hear this from you himself, and surely your father would allow one more visit between you. Ask him to lift the ban."

Finley steps away and sinks into a chair, pressing a weary palm against his temple. "My father enacted the ban at my request." It comes out almost a whisper.

I just stand there, staring at my friend, completely blindsided. Of all the answers he could have given, I never would have expected this.

Before I can summon a response, the door swings open, and Ansley walks in with a blue-robed woman at her side. "The healer Mahree here to see you, sir."

My eyes bore into Finley's, demanding an explanation, but he keeps his fixed on the people in his doorway. A muscle works in his jaw. There's a sadness here I can't seem to breach, one I see reflected in my brother's face but cannot understand, because Helos and Finley have always been two sides of the same leaf.

When Ansley steps to my side, her meaning clear, that's when Finley returns my gaze at last. He's blinking rapidly, and the sight imprints on my heart as one I know I'll never stop seeing behind closed lids, one I want to scream at him to take back, because it feels far too much like an ending.

"Take care of yourself, Rora," he pleads, the hitch in his voice driving a dagger through my ribs. His hair has fallen across his forehead. "And tell Helos . . . tell Helos the answer is no."

I blink at him in surprise. The answer is no. But what was the question? I don't even know when he would have asked it— certainly not during our visit to the apothecary shop, and that was the first time Helos and Finley had spoken in more than a month.

"Finley—"

Ansley steps in front of him, blocking my view, and I have no choice. Without another word, I leave to pack my things and wait for dawn.

The world is still dark when I awaken with a start, breathing heavily.

My skin is drenched in sweat, and I cast the sheet to the foot of the bed, lingering a few moments in the cool, early morning air. It was a night of fitful sleep and nightmares that have already begun to lose their shape. The blackness and the quiet are a balm to my wasted nerves; perhaps I can get more sleep in before the journey.

The journey.

Breathe in. Breathe out.

The first trill of birdsong serrates the silence, and I resign myself to the day.

Despite my house's small size, the room is decently furnished; there's a chair, a wooden table big enough for two, and a small set of drawers topped with shelves that hold plates, pots, utensils, and a few well-worn books. In the corner opposite the bed, there's the tub and tiny washroom that I've hidden with a standing screen I intercepted on its way to the garbage. A small stove stands against the left-hand wall. By royalty standards, it isn't much. But it's more than I've ever had.

I wonder if I'll ever see it again.

I pour water heated from the fire into the bath, waiting until it's only half-filled before scrubbing my skin and my hair enough to wash the night away. A backpack the color of pine rests against the wall nearby; I found it by my door when I returned home. A hooded, woolen cloak was inside, the dark gray cloth of much higher quality than the one I already owned, along with a collection of travel food: nuts, cheese, some sort of way-bread, and dried fruits and meats. I'm trying not to look at it.

My stomach constricts as the first fingers of light seep into the room. I'd like nothing more than to walk to the window, shift to goshawk, and fly. To take comfort in the steadiness of my powerful wings as creatures flee the shadow sweeping across the treetops below. To know, for a few moments, that I am the fiercest predator in the sky. Unbeatable. The lynx is a joy, the deer mouse an unwanted reminder, but the goshawk—that is by far my favorite of my three animal forms.

I don't want to start this mission by arriving late, though, so I pull on dark pants and an olive shirt, lace my boots, grab my pack, and lock the door behind me.

When I arrive at the rear door in Castle's Roanin's northern façade, Helos is already waiting beneath an ancient hickory in the courtyard. He's dressed all in black with a new pack slung across his shoulders—someone must have sent him one, too. The sky has brightened to a pale, milky color, as if it hasn't yet decided whether to be gray or blue.

"How was Finley?" he asks without preamble. "Yesterday, when you went to see him."

Panic flares, but I'm spared the burden of shaping a response when the door opens and Captain Torres steps out, nodding somberly in our direction, followed by King Gerar, then Violet and Weslyn, then four members of the Royal Guard. No Astra, which is rare. No Finley, either. I try to swallow my disappointment.

Weslyn has dressed for traveling: long pants, fitted shirt with the sleeves rolled up to his elbows, boots that rise just past his ankles. Of finer make than my own similar garb, and likely to be ruined by journey's end. A particularly foul expression shadows his face. I wonder if it's because of the farewell he's no doubt had to endure, the task before him, or simply the early hour.

His mouth curls when he spots me, and I match his scathing countenance with a frown of my own. He should know better than to come along; his presence will only slow us down. The arrogance of royals.

"Do you have everything you need?" asks King Gerar, intercepting the silent battle.

I drop my hands to my sides and dip my head.

"As discussed, Naethan, Ansley, Carolette, and Dom will accompany you three to Niav to ensure you arrive safely. Once you cross the river, stealth will become your greatest defense. You will be on your own."

I slide a glance toward the four guards who stand at attention near Weslyn: Naethan, prudent and quietly ambitious, one of Captain Torres's prodigies, with his toned figure and handsome dark brown skin; Ansley, soft-spoken and uncommonly skilled at the sword, with her long tangle of red curls and freckled white skin; wide-framed Carolette, the former spy turned guard who has resented me ever since I made her old job obsolete; towering Dom, a pillar of formality, with deep-set eyes, raven hair, and a sour mouth. None of them are allies, but except for Carolette, I suppose it could have been worse.

Only Ansley nods back at me.

"Remember, Eradain's emissary will be taking the same route to the northern border as you," says Violet, folding her arms across her chest. Her riding breeches and jacket are already dirty—she must have woken with the dawn, same as I. "His coach left yesterday morning, so by now, he should have progressed far ahead."

Since no coach will bear my brother or me, we'll be trekking on foot, and as humans, in order to shoulder the packs with all our supplies.

"But be careful," she continues, drumming her fingers above the crease in her arm. "Word can travel fast on the road, and it's vital he does not catch wind of your mission."

I nod shortly. Considering their concern over the emissary, I don't think one day's head start seems an awfully long one, and Violet's thin-pressed lips suggest she agrees. But King Gerar has insisted it's all we can afford to give.

"Helos." King Gerar looks at my brother and opens his mouth to speak, then shuts it.

Helos seems to understand. "We'll find it, Your Majesty." His tone is tinged with resentment, and discomfort nips at my core.

King Gerar nods once, a flicker of emotion returning to his deadened eyes. Then he turns to his son and braces his hands on either shoulder. Weslyn rests his hands on his father's arms. It seems too intimate a moment for me to be witnessing, so I glance at the castle above us, wondering if Finley might be watching from one of the windows. *I'll come back for you,* I resolve silently. That night outside Caela Ridge threatens to break through my mental shields, arcing flames and screams and a pair of frightened eyes, but I force it back. *I'll save you.*

It's a promise. My mother didn't make one, but I can.

"Take care of him until I return," Weslyn says quietly, looking first to his father, then his sister. Violet stands rigid and regal as always, her eyes locked on to the pair. But she doesn't approach.

"Go safely, Son." King Gerar's voice doesn't break on the words; he's dignified even in sorrow. Still, seeing the way he looks at Weslyn, I think that maybe he's a father before a king. Another trait that has earned my loyalty. He puts a hand on the back of Weslyn's head and draws him into an embrace, and it tugs at me then, that feeling I sometimes get watching King Gerar with his children. That nagging curiosity for what it would be like to have a parent who cared. Who protected.

Weslyn breaks free and hugs his sister. Then he walks away from the castle, leaving Helos, me, and the guards to follow.

I dip into a bow, but I make it only a few steps in his wake before I'm called back.

"Rora."

I swivel round, and Violet quirks her head to the side. "A moment. Please."

Nine pairs of eyes bore into me as I return to the group, stomach contorting with unease. Violet places her palm on my shoulder and guides us aside. I flinch at her touch, at the unfamiliarity of it, and can feel myself hunch a little in response. She stops us a short distance away from the others and drops her arm.

"I want you to know that I have set aside your gold. The full amount will be kept safe for your return."

A small ripple of disgust rolls through my bones. As if I'm no more than a mercenary, and money is the only incentive here. I force a look of surprise and dip my head. "Thank you, ma'am."

"My brother is very stubborn, but he'll need your help," she continues, and my surprise becomes genuine. "Please. Watch over him. Losing one brother would be difficult enough. I cannot bear the thought of losing two."

I marvel at her honesty nearly as much as the fact that she's asking me for help. She has never done so before.

Then she hugs me.

At once, my body freezes to ice and stone. I glance at Helos in astonishment, noting my own shock reflected on his face. This cannot be real, though the quiet strength of her arms around mine and her hands on my back feel real enough.

Slowly, as if they've forgotten how this works, my arms curl around her slender figure.

She gives a quick squeeze, and then it's over. My eyes are itching, but I refuse to let her see me cry. To cry for something as stupid as being touched. Anyway, it means nothing. She can't know how long it's been since anyone other than Helos has hugged me.

But I study her face and realize she suspects exactly how long it's been. And suddenly I know.

Finley is a river, and Weslyn's an oak. Violet is the mountain.

"We'll come back," I say, the promise little louder than a whisper. Violet doesn't smile, not really, but she nods before gliding back to her father. It's an effort to lift my feet from where they're rooted to the spot, but I force myself to walk, step by step, back to the group. Weslyn and Helos. My two charges.

Weslyn's expression brims with mistrust, but he says nothing. With a final glance at his home, he leads us out of the castle complex.

FIVE

We follow the stone road due north for the rest of the morning, trekking parallel to the Old Forest until we hook east around its edge. The track is just wide enough for a cart to pass by in either direction, and far more open than I would like. Given how often Weslyn's portrait is reproduced in the weekly leaflets distributed throughout the kingdom, odds are a passerby would recognize the prince in our company, not to mention the presence of four uniformed Royal Guards. We want to avoid detection to the extent that we're able, particularly while the emissary may still be within earshot of any witnesses with loose tongues—a prince on a quest for magic, accompanied by two shifters, trailing the representative of a king who loathes magic and is waiting for an excuse to strike. Best not to let word of our party precede us.

We stick to the road in silence, only entering the forest to hide when someone appears on the horizon ahead or behind. Though I anticipated that Weslyn and his entourage would remain in the lead all afternoon, I suppose I'd expected *some* hesitation in the moments we have to step off the road, considering his rumored aversion to these woods. I was wrong. Weslyn only plows ahead like one with a vendetta to settle, snapping away twigs, sidestepping blackberry thickets, bullishly striding through bracken and moss.

Several times, I want to suggest that my brother or I go first instead. The footing in these instances is laborious, and we're the ones who actually know what we're doing, after all. But every time I try to swerve in front, Weslyn throws himself forward rather than giving way, and one of the guards—usually Carolette—blocks my path with a hand on her hilt. The frustration in my core bubbles closer to the surface.

There's a small tap on my back.

I swivel round and half smile at Helos, but I don't make the guess. It's a game we used to play growing up in the Vale, to keep us entertained when words were slow to come. One person tosses an object from their surroundings at the other, who then has to guess what hit them. When Helos first came up with it, he reasoned it would help familiarize us with the natural world. I figured it was just an excuse to pelt objects at his little sister.

Another tap. Chestnut. Obviously. But I'm reluctant to break the quiet, lest I lose my temper—and my remaining control—so I simply mouth the answer and shake my head. Helos grins.

By the time night falls, I'm longing for a bit of solitude. Which won't do, I tell myself. This is only day one. Weslyn calls a halt when we've cut a decent enough course through the tangled wood to set up camp, and though the clearing is barely more than a stretch of relatively unobstructed ground, I grudgingly admit to myself that it will do.

Carolette, Ansley, and Naethan set about gathering tinder and kindling for a fire, while Dom orders Weslyn to stay put and slips away to scout the perimeter. The shadowed woods have darkened this far in, and what little we can see of the sky has settled into twilight. As Helos tosses a few sticks and rocks through the gaps between trees, I'm baffled by his apparent indifference to Carolette's sidelong glances or the times Naethan shuffles a few steps farther away. I bend to help him clear the forest floor, my stomach churning.

It's obvious all of us are feeling the strain of the deadlines hanging around our necks. The answer King Gerar owes King Jol in two months. The Throes reaching its vile hand farther across Telyan, killing innocents every week. And, of course, the unknown duration of Finley's own ticking clock.

Weighted silence hangs heavy among the group. When Helos and I have finished, we find seats on the leafy floor while Weslyn tramps over to the uniformed trio for the second time. Again, they reject his offer of assistance with exaggerated courtesy and insist he rest instead. As if we haven't all walked the same distance today. Pulling a pouch of almonds from my pack, I watch Weslyn run a hand along his face, then eye the surrounding woods, before seating himself on a decaying fallen trunk.

I debate for a few moments before speaking up. "You don't want to sit there."

Weslyn glares at me while continuing to rummage through his pack, oblivious to the centipede slinking across the log.

"Your Royal Highness," I amend.

He waves a hand in my general direction. "Drop the title. We have a long road ahead of us."

Well. That's something. But he still hasn't acknowledged my advice. Behind him, his dutiful guards raise scandalized brows.

"You should move," I try again, and my pulse races when I'm met with silence once more. Fine. Let him rot with the bugs.

But he looks at me again once he's pulled bread and cheese from his bag. "Why."

I nod my head toward his throne. "There are probably things living in there. Little things. Bugs."

Weslyn shoots to his feet.

The trio snaps up from their seemingly endless work and reaches for swords, as if they've been expecting him to drop dead in our presence at any moment. I have to suppress the urge to smirk as he searches for alternate seating.

"Talented, aren't they?" Helos says in an undertone, bumping my shoulder and nodding to the fire pit only now taking shape.

Helos is right. We could have built it in half the time.

When Dom has returned with a new scratch on his face and everyone has eaten, the group sets their bedrolls in a rough circle around the fire. Carolette catches my eye and forms the sign to ward off bad fortune, always eager to make her harbored bitterness known, while Weslyn pulls a black book from his pack to read by the flames' soft glow. Ansley's watching Naethan, and Naethan's watching Weslyn, and suddenly I can't bear the thought of lying this close to strangers.

"I'll take first watch," I announce, frowning as everyone looks to Weslyn for approval.

Weslyn studies me briefly, as if weighing the odds I'll murder him in his sleep, then nods and returns to his book. Before anyone can protest, I grab a wedge of bread, push to my feet, and take up my post against a tree at the periphery, considering the journey ahead.

I knew Weslyn was of a different cut, but after watching his movements tonight, I have no trouble believing he hasn't set foot here in years. It doesn't bode well for our chances in the Vale, which is far more difficult to navigate than this. My heart begins to race as the images edge nearer: strands of ivy that curl around a victim's neck, squeezing playfully—until they crush; a bed of piping flowers, red-and-purple streaked, luring animals with their sickly scent and sending them into endless sleep. *For Finley,* I remind my ever-tightening throat. *We're doing this for Finley.*

Helos appears at my side, and the memories reluctantly retreat.

"Here," he says, stepping close and holding out an apple. We have the same amount of food in our packs, and still he offers me his.

I smile and brandish the bread at him. "I've got my own, remember?"

After a beat, he nods and bites into the fruit. We fall silent, looking out at the trees, their shapes slowly becoming indistinguishable from the darkness surrounding them. For most folk in Roanin, this forest is where bedtime tales are born. They fear the shadows deeper than night. But we're used to wilder corners of the world, and for me, this darkness is the familiar sort. The kind that's soft and warm. There's a rustle a few steps behind us as our companions settle in for the night.

"You never answered my question," Helos murmurs after a while. "About Finley."

I wish I could withhold the truth from him longer, but I know the guilt will only continue to gnaw at me if I do. "There's something I have to tell you."

He leans his back against the nearest trunk. Waiting.

"Finley told me your expulsion from the grounds was his doing. Not King Gerar's."

Just enough light remains for me to see Helos's mouth drop open. "What?"

"He's the reason his family won't allow you in anymore." My voice is scarcely more than a whisper, lest Weslyn be listening. "He also—he said to tell you the answer is no. And that you should understand why."

"He told you that?"

I've rarely heard him sound so angry, and I find it doesn't fit any better than the blade-sharp antlers he'd carved before we left. My courage wavers. "Why is he keeping you away, Helos?"

He hurls the apple core into the dour woods and paces to the side, throwing his hands behind his head.

"Did you have a fight or something?" I'm not sure when that even could have happened, given Helos's expulsion from the castle and the fact that he and Finley never argued before it. I would know—he never visited the grounds without me present. But one piece at a time.

Silence yawns between us, so long I'm preparing to ask his forgiveness—though for what, I can't say—until at last, he sighs. "You could say that."

I want to press him further. To hear an explanation that denies my growing suspicion, because surely he's too smart to have fallen for royalty. Yet his voice sounds so sad that although I don't have all the answers I need, I drop the issue.

"You should get some sleep," I say at last, knocking his arm a little.

He doesn't object, though I'm not sure how much rest he'll find in his current state. "Wake me in a few hours. I'll take over."

I stand there staring into space my human senses can no longer interpret until the breathing behind me finally deepens into sleep.

The storm clouds break the following dawn. Once we leave the cover of the forest, the beating rain makes for a miserable slog through the mud patches peppering the road like constellations. Resigned, I mark the progress of the muck slowly soaking through my travel-worn boots and wrap my new cloak around me and my pack. The wool is nearly suffocating in the humid summer heat, but at least it repels the water for a while.

We reach Grovewood midmorning, passing under the broad archway with a nod to the gatekeeper, who gapes a little at the sight of the royal party. As we've only come to collect the seeds for bartering before moving on, I can't imagine we'll be here long enough to wait out the thunderstorm. Already, my wet feet ache in protest at the thought, but grim recollection of Finley's condition tempers the discomfort. *Selfless,* I tell myself, my new mantra.

Sandwiched between the Old Forest and the base of the Purple Mountains, Grovewood is Telyan's northernmost town, and one of the more pleasant to work in. Instead of Briarwend's cracked, aching stones, here tree-lined streets of packed earth weave among a smattering of dark-grained, wooden buildings to create an atmosphere like an extension of the forest. Tailors, leather-workers, booksellers, and smithies—a town of craftspeople and quiet specialists, close enough to do business in Roanin without having to spare the city rent.

Fortunately, though someone has kindled the tall oil lamps lining the roads, the gloomy weather allows us to pass through the main streets without amassing spectators. Well, except for one: midway through, I notice a seated tabby cat, seemingly indifferent to the rain, marking our progress with eerie intensity—too much, surely, for an ordinary house cat. I nod in greeting, but the shifter, who doubtless can smell the magic in me, turns tail and flees.

Sadness pricks my heart. I wonder how long they've been here, hiding in their animal form.

The shop with the seeds we need sits at the end of a street at the edge of town, a stretch I've rarely had any reason to visit. Towering pines peek out from behind it; when we're done here, our road lies just east of them. Around three blocks from our destination, Weslyn halts without warning outside an antiquarian shop, its thinly curtained windows glowing from oil lamplight within.

"Go on inside," he tells Naethan, raising his voice against the downfall. "He'll want to see you, and we can manage alone."

I peer again at the painted sign jutting out from the overhang, then it clicks. Naethan's father, once Queen Raenen's close friend.

"You too," Weslyn adds to Ansley, who's studying Naethan and biting her lip.

"If you're sure." Naethan smiles and claps Weslyn on the back, unbothered by Dom's disapproving scowl.

He and Ansley are already stepping into the shop, Weslyn and the other guards walking away, when Helos says close to my ear, "I'm going to have a look inside."

I turn in surprise.

Shielded by his cloak's large, gray hood, my brother's eyes have taken on a slightly misty quality, no doubt lured by the promise of worn bindings and old words. But still—

"What about the seeds?" I ask.

"Weslyn will get them," Helos says. "There's something I want to look for here first. I won't be long."

Since I suppose there's no real reason not to separate, I nod and hasten after Weslyn's party, irked by their indifference to our whereabouts. A pair of lawkeepers, civilians who maintain the peace and report crimes or indiscretions, study my passing approach with idle interest. My face starts tingling, only a little, but enough to prompt my anxiety about giving way to ill-timed shifts. Today, I don't have the luxury of hiding behind a borrowed face.

I find Weslyn just outside the wooden shop with the seeds, speaking to Dom and Carolette in a voice too low to make out. The two of them nod and set off on their own, not looking particularly pleased with whatever he's ordered them to do.

I catch up to Weslyn right as he's opening the door.

"I don't require assistance, or a spy," he says pointedly, when I reach his side.

Clearly, as he's managed to dispose of all four guards already, though I can't imagine why. But unlike them, I'm as much a part of this mission as he, and not in the mood for taking orders, so I ignore the callous remark and follow him over the threshold. Weslyn balls his hands into fists but doesn't object again.

Stepping inside the shop is like walking into a forest itself. The space is dimly lit, and there are plants everywhere, crowding the wood-planked ground, creeping up walls, and hanging from the ceiling. Some are so tall or meandering that I can't find the pots that house their roots. It's beautiful.

Weslyn brushes a vine from his shoulder and calls out for the owner.

"With you in a moment!" cries a deep voice from afar.

I cradle a leaf between two fingers while Weslyn fiddles with his sleeve.

"Your Royal Highness," says a different voice, softer and just to our right. "Anything I can assist you with?"

Weslyn smiles at the older woman who emerged through a side door. "Thank you, Nelle, but this request requires Geonen's particular expertise."

Nelle's lips press into a thin line. Dismay hits the pit of my stomach when I'm close enough to see the slight curve in the older woman's back, the sweat beading along her warm brown skin, the flecks of gray peppering her dark, plaited hair. I included her in my last report on the afflicted population in Grovewood, which means the sway and the silence can't be too far off. "Might I have a word first, sir? Please. It's important."

Weslyn gestures for her to lead the way, and she takes us through the side door, into a brighter space lined with windows adjoining a garden just outside. A blond, yellow-clad girl with white skin is organizing herbs at the far side, but her hands grow still when she sees Nelle's company.

Not wanting to get told off for hovering, I feign interest in one of the cabinets near the door. Rows of jars crowd the shelves, their labels sounding medicinal in nature.

"—third year in a row," Nelle is saying in an undertone. "I've tried planting elsewhere, but it's no use. Waste of time."

"No," Weslyn counters. "You were wise to try. Have you applied for a loan?"

"It wouldn't matter. My business depends on the earth, and you can't negotiate with dirt."

"My brother would disagree with you there." I peer over my

shoulder and see Weslyn smiling a little, though his sunken posture doesn't mirror the lightness of the words. Nelle's apprentice is making a good show of attending to her work, but I don't miss the look she gives Weslyn, unabashedly scanning him up and down when his back is turned. Something I've never been bold enough to do with anyone; at least, not in this form. Not when half-hearted kisses in stolen bodies are easier. Safer. "What of the supplies you have?"

"Growing fewer with every passing day. Lots of children here, sir. Children get sick."

"Not just children," he says gravely. Then he bends closer, just a little. "Any illness in particular giving you trouble?" I'm certain his thoughts have taken the same grim turn as mine: she looks worn out, her eyelids drooping a little.

Nelle shifts her weight onto the other leg. "It's that magical one. The Fallow Throes." Her words take on a decidedly disapproving tone. "I can't do anything for them, other than offer herbs that treat the symptoms. Once the extra senses hit, it's . . . it's bad, sir. The pain."

Weslyn places a hand on her shoulder. "We'll discover the remedy soon enough, Nelle. I know you're doing all you can."

"With respect, do you—" Nelle hesitates a moment, then drops her voice even lower. "None of the patients I've tended to have magical blood. Does the crown not think it odd?"

Dread pools in my veins as I glance behind me again, bracing for Weslyn's reply. I can tell by the way Nelle speaks that this is the matter she wished to discuss all along.

"Odd?" Weslyn echoes, his tone noncommittal.

"I'm not the only one who's concerned, sir. It's beginning to feel, well, targeted, if you take my meaning."

She lets that hang for a long moment.

"I appreciate your honesty," Weslyn says at last. "But I'm sure you understand we cannot base policy on conjecture." I straighten in surprise. "I would encourage you to dispel these rumors going forward. For now, there is no need to worry." His focus drops to the woman's feet, where she's shifting her weight from one to the other. "Are you in pain, Nelle?"

She waves a crinkled hand, visibly disappointed. "Don't worry about me, sir. What of His Majesty? Your family, are they well?"

"Quite well," Weslyn replies, the lie slipping from his tongue as easily as any of mine ever have. As easily, I suspect, as hers. "I'll consider what you said about the soil. In the meantime, I'm afraid my companion and I have business to attend to."

At a quick glance from Weslyn, I follow him back into the first room, determinedly avoiding Nelle's gaze. I can hear the blond girl whispering rapidly behind us.

"Your Royal Highness!" greets the store owner as soon as we're back among the hanging plants. "Forgive me, I didn't want to interrupt."

My back tenses.

It's not the green, needlelike hair that makes me stare, nor the furrowed, gray-brown skin that must mirror the bark on his home tree. It's that he's here, a forest walker in Grovewood, greeting us like nothing at all is wrong.

Slandered by his own colleague, moments ago.

"How are you, Geonen?" Weslyn asks, smiling graciously. Another person he knows by name, and a magical one, no less. Perhaps it shouldn't surprise me, but it does.

Geonen wipes his knobby hands on his apron and nods a greeting my way. "Fine, fine. Business is as usual." I raise my eyebrows, but he sounds genuine enough. "How is His Majesty? Is it the grounds again?"

Weslyn shakes his head. "No. I'm here for another reason. I need seeds from the Old Forest, for trees that don't grow anywhere else in Alemara."

Geonen scratches an eyebrow, which looks like plated scales of pine bark. "From the Old Forest, eh? I should have some in the back. Come with me."

Following him is easier said than done. The shop extends farther back than I'd realized on prior visits, and broad leaves crowd thick around us. I'm passing through a doorway into a back room when I collide with someone small.

"Apologies, miss," Geonen says on the girl's behalf. "My daughter."

She's young, likely no more than eight or nine, with hair as green and needling as her father's. She stares up at me with wide, clear eyes.

I offer her a smile, now doubly angry with Nelle's gossiping tongue. "That's all right."

"Sorrell, come with me."

The girl steps quietly to her father's side, and the two of them lead us into the back room.

This area is cooler, and much neater; the sea of plants has been replaced by several bags and boxes lining shelves built into the walls. Darkness hangs even heavier here than in the front rooms, and I sink into its embrace with relief.

By the time my eyes have adjusted to the dimness, Geonen has evaluated several cloth bags, weighing them briefly in his palm before shaking his head and placing them back on the shelves. The bag he finally hands to Weslyn is rather small, about the size of my fist.

"These should do well," he says, looking between me and Weslyn, while Sorrell clutches his leg. "Just make sure to keep them dry, and in the dark. Here, since you'll want to leave the bag closed until you're ready to use them, I'll show you now so you know what you're getting."

With a bit of work, Geonen unfastens the tightly knotted string that seals the top. Then he holds the bag out to Weslyn, who carefully sticks his hand inside and captures a few seeds in his palm. After a quick examination, he holds them out for me. I can't think why he should suddenly want my opinion or approval—maybe it's just for show—but I nod all the same.

"Perhaps," says Weslyn, "given the weather we've had, it would be best to seal them further, just in case."

Geonen considers this. "Well, they should be all right, since Roanin isn't far. But—" He breaks off and pulls a small box from the shelf, setting its previous contents aside. "Take this just in case."

Trading Weslyn the box for the seeds, Geonen reseals the bag and places it in the open container.

Weslyn pulls a few coins from his pocket. "Thank you, Geonen."

The man's eyes widen slightly, and he runs a hand along his face. "That's too much, sir."

Weslyn keeps his palm outstretched. "Then take what I owe you."

The man takes three of the five pieces offered and bows a little. Weslyn hands the other two to the girl, who holds them delicately in her tiny palms. "For your help," he says, and a ghost of a smile crosses her lips.

I nod to Geonen and follow Weslyn out of the shop, torn between budding confusion and resentment. Outside, the rain has tapered to a misty drizzle.

It's strange to watch him interact with his people, the lightness in his bearing so unlike the rigid way he storms around Castle Roanin. His care for them is obvious, and perhaps I ought to respect him for it, or at least be grateful for the respite. But every time he greets another one by name, all I can think about is the fact that he's never called me by mine since the day he asked what it was. And somehow, that hurts worse than if he didn't know it at all.

"We shouldn't linger," he says when we're outside, keeping his voice low. "We'll leave this afternoon. There's something I have to take care of first."

"I can—"

"Alone," he adds, rather rudely.

I fold my arms. "Your father gave me this assignment, too, you know."

"And?"

"*And,* that means I'm here to help. You can't do everything alone."

"He asked for your help in the Vale," Weslyn clarifies. "And we're not there yet, in case you hadn't noticed."

I might have to kill him, promise to Finley and Violet or no.

"Just find something else to do for an hour or two, if you think you can manage that. Here," he says, drawing a few coins from his pocket and dropping them in my palm. "Consider this an advance on your payment. Buy yourself some new shoes. Yours are wrecked."

Before I can reply, he simply walks away, indifferent. His back to me, like always.

I study his retreat with temper rising. "What could be so urgent that you have to do it now? What's more important than saving Finley?"

Weslyn is back in a few short strides, and the fire in his gaze is enough to frighten me. "Nothing is more important. Nothing. I can't believe you'd even suggest it."

I've rarely heard him sound so angry. Still—

"If you really felt that way, you would leave now instead of touring the town."

Weslyn releases a tight breath, clearly striving for control. "Good to know you think so little of me," he says at last, quiet. "But there is work to be done here before we leave, and it does not concern you."

"It does when we travel together," I insist. "I'm sick of being treated like I'm worthless. Either that or some sort of curse. Ignore me all you like when we return, but things are different out here, and I won't stand for it any longer. As you said, the road is long."

His eyes narrow. "Are you threatening a prince?"

I place my hands behind my back. "You told me to drop the title."

Weslyn says nothing for a while, just stands there, staring at me. I wring my hands, grateful that my back hides them from view. They're shaking.

"We will leave this afternoon," he says, drawing the words out slowly. "In the meantime—"

"Your Royal Highness," says a raspy voice to our left. "I hope I'm not interrupting."

We turn as one to the wavy-haired, middle-aged man hovering a few paces away, flushed white skin creased with laughter lines. He's smiling in a manner reminiscent of a hound cornering a fox. Though he's not dressed in the telling red-and-navy uniform, I recognize his face from that morning at Castle Roanin nonetheless.

The Eradain emissary.

SIX

He won't recognize me. He can't. So long as I keep my emotions under control, nothing about my appearance screams *shifter*. Logically, I know this.

But being so close to a man from that land, a place where death and disappearances are rumored to stalk the streets, makes my insides shrivel with fear. Who knows how many families have suffered at his hand—or, at the very least, the hand of the king he works for. I have no idea how he could stomach it, if the whispers are true.

Weslyn stiffens beside me. "Ambassador Kelner," he says with a nod. "Well met." And to his credit, he almost sounds as if he means it.

"It's lucky I've run into you, really." Kelner's gaze remains fixed on Weslyn alone, predator to prey, and it's clear to me this meeting is not the work of chance at all. I shift backward a step, wishing only to melt into the shadows. "I wonder if I might have a word."

"Do you," Weslyn says, voice flat.

"If I may. See, you seem to—"

Kelner breaks off when his attention flicks to me at last. His eyes widen at the sight.

For a long moment, we both stare at each other. Forehead wrinkled, Kelner appears just as startled as I feel. No messenger here to intercept me, no wall to hide behind. I focus on beating back the tingling in my shoulders, the forbidden strands of coolness teasing my skin. My body sensing fear and offering ill-timed escape in the form of a mouse. *Expulsions, executions—*

I fasten my mask back into place and mold my expression into one of polite confusion.

"Apologies, miss," he says, recovering himself. "For a moment, I thought you were someone else."

"Your message, Ambassador?" Weslyn presses when I open my mouth to respond.

Kelner inclines his head and gestures to a pub nearby. "Perhaps we can speak somewhere more private?" *Perhaps* and *private* come out more like *praps* and *privt* in his deep, gravelly voice; his northern accent clips the words short. There's something vaguely familiar about that accent, but the recognition is too fleeting to grab hold of.

"Perhaps another time," Weslyn says. "I have business I must see to."

"On a gloomy day like this? No trouble, I trust."

I twist in time to see Weslyn's expression calcify. "I would have thought our position quite plain, Ambassador."

Kelner summons a saccharine smile. "I regret the manner in which His Majesty and I parted ways, it's true. But you seem to me the type who listens to reason."

"As opposed to the king, you mean."

His smile falters a bit. "I would never suggest—"

"You already have, so let me be clear. If you have come seeking a traitor in my father's court, you will not find one here." Kelner looks somewhat startled by this direct approach, but Weslyn only crosses his arms. "I trust your stay has been comfortable? I would hate for you to have to travel this evening with aching joints."

Kelner frowns at the obvious dismissal, but there's nothing he can do about it. He's a representative; Weslyn's royal. A prince out-ranks him without question. "Indeed," he replies grudgingly. "It is always a relief to escape the confines of a city for such a . . . quaint town."

Weslyn ignores the slight and shakes his hand. "By your leave, then." He catches my eye meaningfully before striding away.

Kelner seems to wilt a little, his expression sour, as I follow briskly in Weslyn's wake, wondering how this changes things. Violet had said, *It's vital he does not catch wind of your mission.* From here, only one road leads north to Telyan's border—the road, it seems, our party and Kelner will now have to share. By this point, he was meant to be far ahead.

I wait until we've turned the corner before speaking up. "What did he—"

"Not here," Weslyn says, and he doesn't say another word, doesn't even look at me, until we've entered the antiquarian shop.

Inside, warm scents of leather and parchment fill the cozy room, a low-ceilinged maze of crowded stacks and narrow halls that appear, fortunately, empty.

Weslyn verifies there's no one in sight before shutting the door and rounding on me. "Do you think he recognized what you are?" he asks in an undertone, an edge of desperation to his voice.

Not who, but *what*. I fold my arms and attempt to brush past the insult. "I don't see how he could have. I wasn't going to shift for no reason. I'm not stupid."

"Then why did he look at you like that?"

My stomach prickles with unease. "How should I know?"

Weslyn pinches the bridge of his nose with thumb and forefinger before exhaling softly. "Come on, then."

We wind through the stacks, the polished wooden floorboards slick underfoot, to a wider, brighter area in back. Helos is chatting amicably with a man who's wrapping a small parcel in paper behind the counter. Naethan hovers nearby, frowning slightly until Ansley taps his arm and whispers in his ear, while his father—a tall, lean man with dark brown skin smartly dressed in a tie and delicate, gold-rimmed glasses—laughs robustly at something Helos said. Not for the first time, I marvel at my brother's ability to connect with strangers.

Naethan snaps to attention at our approach. "What happened?"

Helos looks up, his smile fading when he sees us.

"Feryn," Weslyn says to the man instead. "It's good to see you."

"You look tired, my boy," Feryn says, placing a broad hand on the side of Weslyn's face. "Always tired. You work too hard."

"You worry too much." Weslyn smiles. "I'm perfectly well."

"Mm." The corners of Feryn's mouth curl up. "You hear that?" he says, glancing back at his son. "He's perfectly well."

Naethan raises a brow. "He's an idiot. And he hasn't answered my question."

Ansley leans against one of the stacks, peering closely at Weslyn. Helos and I just stand there, unsure how to navigate this dynamic.

"I'll leave you kids to talk," Feryn says when the silence stretches long, smiling at me. He lifts the brown parcel. "And I'll get this where it needs to be," he tells Helos with half a wink. Then he's gone.

Weslyn's composure seems to fracture in Feryn's absence. He leans against the counter and runs a hand over his face. "Eradain's ambassador is here. He intercepted us."

"He's here?" Naethan exclaims. Ansley glances at me for confirmation, her face grim.

Familiar frown returning, Weslyn begins to pace the room, waving his hands as he recounts the exchange. Helos, Ansley, and Naethan take turns studying me while he talks.

Trying to ignore the feeling of being trapped, I glance longingly toward the front of the shop, wishing I could fly out and face the afternoon from the skies. Maybe I'd fly back to the castle to check on Finley, say a new goodbye that scrubs those rapidly blinking eyes from my mind. Or maybe I'd fly farther south, beyond the rolling hills and hazel thickets encasing the heart of Telyan, the hidden lakes and deciduous woods stretching far toward the horizon. All the way to Beraila, the closest continent south of ours. A tropical landscape of towering rainforests and misty mountains, jaguars and monkeys, grassy steppes holding far more human realms than Alemara's three—I've studied Finley's maps.

I would leave this dreaded continent's Predictions behind, and never mind the fact that I don't know whether magic still exists in life overseas, or whether it's long since gone to ground. Trade relations and alliances among the thirty continents may have flourished once, but Alemara's three realms have confined their ships to silent harbors for more than fifty years now. Rumblings of power struggles abroad they wanted no part in, alliances shattered between monarchies too afraid to see one another's cracks reflected in their own façades.

"This emissary—he and my father did not part on friendly terms," Weslyn is saying when I come back to myself. "I wouldn't put it past him to put a tail on us."

"That will make our road more difficult," Naethan says, folding his arms. "Do you know how many others he's traveling with?"

Weslyn shakes his head.

"We could delay long enough to let him get ahead." Naethan pauses, considering. "Or leave right now and double the pace."

"You're forgetting one important thing," I say at last, frustrated. Though they're continuing to shield the terms of this ultimatum from me, I'm desperate to learn what exactly King Gerar is so reluctant to agree to, and whether it involves further restricting people like me. "Kelner didn't seem all that shocked to find you here. Somebody must have told him." I'm tempted to accuse Carolette, but then, I suppose I'm biased.

There's a beat of silence.

"Will this escalate things with Eradain?" Helos asks, since no one seems eager to offer up any names.

"I don't know." Weslyn shakes his head again, apparently too distressed to remember to be mean. "Kelner's report may heighten Jol's suspicions that Telyan has begun to mobilize."

"Not necessarily, Wes."

Ansley's quiet voice surprises us all.

"If Kelner had spotted us farther along our road—closer to the border, for instance—he would have had more of a reason to suspect something is going on. But right now, he has no real evidence to support that claim. He doesn't know where you're going or why, or even that you're going anywhere beyond Grovewood at all." She rubs a palm along her forearm. "He certainly doesn't know that Helos and Rora are shifters."

I blink at her, taken aback. She used my name.

Weslyn grips the edge of the counter, facing the room. "I hope you're right. In any case, I made it clear he was to depart tonight. Perhaps we should stay until later tomorrow, like Naethan said. Give him a chance to get ahead."

"There's no need to wait that long," I say, making up my mind. "Every day wasted is a day closer to the deadline his king set for Telyan, and in any case, dragging our feet is not going to help Finley. If Kelner's taking the road, we'll simply have to avoid it entirely. We'll trek to the border through the backcountry, and we'll leave today."

"But that rou—"

"Helos and I have walked it before. It won't be a problem." My confidence is rising in the face of his doubt.

Naethan studies me a heartbeat longer, then nods slowly. "No tail of Kelner's will be able to follow us out there."

Bears, maybe. Coyotes and wolves. But not like the magical ones in the Vale, at least. These are far safer.

It feels a little strange to be the one making the plan, but the others only look to Weslyn for their cue, and Weslyn doesn't balk at my instruction. Instead, he appraises me another moment, then nods stiffly and grabs a piece of parchment from Feryn's workspace. "I'll send a letter to Roanin by raven, to tell my father what happened."

After ensuring that Kelner has already departed, we leave Grovewood behind beneath the early evening's golden haze, winding through the pines behind Geonen's shop and following the remnants of a trail that likely used to guide townsfolk on a safe loop through the woods. Now it leads to nothing, so overgrown it's nearly indistinguishable from the surrounding weeds. Helos and I have used it before, though, so it serves as our departure point into the wild.

It's a four days' journey through the backcountry to the border with Glenweil.

We spend the days mostly in silence, traversing the slopes at the foot of the Purple Mountains. To our right, meadows stretch as far as the eye can see, and beautiful flowers blanket the curving land: echinacea, coreopsis, butterfly weed, and bluets, a dawn-colored canvas of brilliant pinks, yellows, oranges, and purples. To our left, the mountains serve as constant sentinels. The spruce-fir forest lining their jagged peaks gleams blue-gray in the sunlight, while the lower faces are a patchwork of mixed oak. The footing becomes rougher and rockier the closer we come to the base of the range, and I hear Carolette and Dom grumbling more than once. But we're to trail in the range's shadow until it ends abruptly, farther to the northeast. Where the mountains end, so does Telyan.

We could track farther east, where the land flattens out closer to the kingdom's coast. Such a route would likely turn four days into three. But east is where the road lies, and here there are no settlements under the open sky, only windswept grass and wildflowers. Stealth is well worth the slower pace.

Fortunately, by the end of the second day, my new boots have started to break in. I had a time that first night, massaging the soles of my feet and wishing that replacing my blistered pads with healthier skin would not require the heavy maintenance that all healing attempts do.

On our third day trekking in ankle-sore quiet, the temperature becomes nearly unbearable. The air sits thick and humid, so heavy I can almost taste its salted tang, and my pants stick to my calves like gloves. At least that's all it is: heat. Summer sun. Not sinking sand, or clouds of dust that notch one's skin. The thought nudges my heart rate higher.

"We should stop," Helos announces from his position near the rear, when we reach a rare pair of drooping willows. "Make camp for the night."

"No, we still have a good hour or two before the sun sets," Weslyn says. "We should keep going."

"His Royal Highness is right," Dom huffs, his corded forearms shiny with sweat. "There's no need to waste the day."

I shake my head a little. I don't know whether they're stoic or just stupid, but with the amount of time we have spent hiking in this heat, unshaded, it's not a good idea to push it even further.

Helos places his hands on his sides, breathing heavily. "Would you prefer a stroke, or sun poisoning?"

Dom's scowl promises danger to come, but Naethan backtracks from Ansley's side, where he's become a semipermanent fixture—quietly philosophizing about some text or other, brightening when he teases out a laugh. "I agree we should stop, sir," he nods to Weslyn, shading his forehead. "Carry on, and we would be asking for trouble."

"I wouldn't say no to a little rest," Carolette puts in.

"You always want to rest," Dom growls, shifting his weight.

"Except when I'm in the sparring ring, beating your ass to the ground."

Ansley smiles a little from the front of the line.

"Enough," Weslyn says, wiping the sweat from his neck. "We'll stop here."

Snorting as if he would have stopped regardless, Helos drops his pack and sits, using a trowel to clear a fire hole in the ground for later. After a brief hesitation, Naethan bends to help him. I start gathering twigs, Carolette and Ansley refuse Weslyn's offer of help once more, and Dom looms over us all, a muscle working in his jaw.

We reach Telyan's border with Glenweil the next day.

A prickle of apprehension pinches my spine. Forest has given way to a river of grass, and there's not much here to mark the divide between kingdom and republic. Just a strip of shorn field and two small watchtowers positioned a couple of arrow-lengths apart on either side. Set back a short distance to our right, there's a squat home with two long-legged horses paddocked nearby—ready to run should any message require sending.

Weslyn looks fully at ease as he takes the lead, which is good because even Helos is hesitating a little. No doubt he, too, is remembering the time we crossed here, years ago.

There had been a brief line of questioning on the Glenweil side of the border. Names? State your business. You're young to be traveling alone. Where are your parents?

Dead and gone, I had almost replied.

"They sent us on ahead," Helos answered, sounding admirably sure of himself. Noticeably lacking the Telyan people's lilting accent.

The border guard, whose tone had betrayed concern up until that point, had suddenly eyed us with open suspicion—two half-starved kids, a tangle of dust and fatigue and matted hair. "For what purpose?"

Helos didn't have an answer to that, malnourishment and too many sleepless nights having addled our brains. After a minor hesitation, he opened his mouth to speak, but the damage had been done.

"All right," the guard said. "It's all right, lad. We'll wait for them, eh? How about a cup of tea?"

My grip on Helos's arm had tightened. I couldn't have told which weighed stronger—fear or longing.

My brother sensed my mood and smiled rather weakly. "Thank you," he told the guard. "Maybe later. We'll head back and see if we can find them."

The guard started to object, but Helos took my hand and led us back in the direction we'd come from, so we could hide out of sight. When night had fallen, we shifted to fox and mouse—me clinging to the fur on his back—and stole across the border.

In the present, the Telyan guard hails a greeting, which Weslyn returns with confidence. The gray-haired woman gapes a little when she sees whom she's stopped, placing a fist across her brown leather breastplate and bending into a crooked bow while her younger counterpart emerges from the house. Weslyn exchanges a few words with them about our need for subtlety, and then we're over the border and making for the pair of Glenweil guards waiting on the other side.

Neither of those two recognize Weslyn for who he is, and Weslyn makes no move to inform them, simply stating in a rather quiet

voice that we're heading for Niav. The pair seems satisfied enough
with his story and lets us pass without further interrogation. I
suppose Telyan's border is not the border that concerns them.

We make for the open hills.

It takes us several days to traverse the sprawling countryside,
an isolating expanse of horse pastures, sheep enclosures, and cattle
farms. Naethan has softened toward Helos, as most usually do after
a few days in his amiable presence. Ansley, whose pale complexion
has suffered more than anyone else's under the summer sun, even
thanks me when I help her cross a stream, and I find myself returning her friendly smile. If we were closer, I might reassure her that
her interest in Naethan is obviously mutual, at least to me, and ask
what's holding her back. But that kind of close friendship is still
relatively uncharted territory, and I don't want to risk offending
her and losing her newfound warmth.

Unlike the younger guards, Dom remains unmoved by my lack
of incriminating activity. He continues to appraise Helos and me
with unmasked skepticism, his presence an impenetrable thundercloud over the group. Carolette's attitude is hardly better, her
well-worn bitterness manifesting as a constant string of challenges
to every suggestion I make. But at least, for the most part, Weslyn
simply ignores us.

Four years have gone since I last traversed this land, and I
cannot say I've missed it. Before leaving Glenweil's borders for
Telyan, we'd spent a week crossing its level grasslands and winding
riverbeds to the north, then south among the rolling blue-green
meadows, hugging the shadow of the Purple Mountains. The grasslands weren't forgiving—violent winds burned our skin and lack
of coverage made food sparse—but at least they weren't predisposed
to fear us.

In the present, I steal a glance at my brother, wondering if he's
reliving the same memories.

His bearing is no different than usual, his expression no less
relaxed. Of course. He's built that wall in his mind. I wonder how
hard he's had to work to make it solid as stone.

When at last we reach Glenweil's capital city, it's nothing like

Roanin. Nestled primarily between rolling hills and river, Niav has a rather sprawling look to it. Unconfined by dense forest, the roads and buildings spill across the open land in an almost haphazard way. A palace of dark, weathered stone crowns the slope overlooking the city. That palace is our destination, the final leg of our journey before we cross the river into wilderness. Into magic.

The thought triggers the usual buzz of nerves and flash of trauma. Instead of seizing up, I try breathing into it. Through it. I survived it once. I could do it again. Perhaps my memory has even exaggerated its potency.

The effort only partially works.

When we can't put it off any longer, Helos and I tell the others that we have to alter our forms for the duration of our stay. The entire group responds with stony silence. Resentment nips at my core as I watch the distrust return to their faces, as if the mere mention of shifting has slotted us back into the Prediction's narrow box.

"Isn't that risky?" Weslyn asks at last, looking between us.

Helos shakes his head. "We can hold it for a couple of days. Longer if we can sleep and make up for some of the time, but we'll only be here the one night, right?" He doesn't hesitate in his explanation, even when Weslyn's brow creases. Not afraid to speak openly of his abilities. In contrast, I'm only listening, and still my back tenses reflexively.

"And you refuse to explain why."

Dom goes so far as to fist his sword hilt. I almost wish he'd pull it, just to make something happen at last.

"Bad blood," Helos says with a small shrug. I clasp my hands behind my back. "You're just going to have to trust us."

He omits the fact that Minister Mereth has seen our natural forms before. Seen, and expelled, with the promise of harsher consequences if we should return and jeopardize her people's safety. I don't know much about politics, but I've enough sense to suspect we can't afford to lose her as an ally, should things end poorly with Eradain.

My brother adopts the form of one of his casual, pub-going friends, matching Weslyn's weather-worn complexion, shortening his hair and darkening it to black, trading brown eyes for green, and shrinking until he's bonier, more spindly. Since we're doing this for Finley, I decide to mirror Evaline, one of his usual guards—shorter and stouter, widemouthed in a heart-shaped face, with thick brows and frizzy hair brushing the tops of my shoulders. A few other small adjustments and I'm unrecognizable from my natural form.

Carolette makes the sign with her hands to ward off bad fortune, a sight with which I've now grown thoroughly bored. I do feel a prickle of regret, though, when Ansley's pained expression reminds me that I've just duplicated her former partner, who's now happily engaged—to a different girl. So much for our tentative friendship.

Weslyn stares for a moment after I change, his expression difficult to interpret for once. Then he plows ahead without speaking, leading us down into the city.

SEVEN

After the relative solitude of our journey thus far, Niav is an explosion of sounds and sights and smells.

Residents tug on cattle leads and sweep the streets with wiry wooden brooms, their motions light and buoyant, voices unexpectedly cheery as they call out. The women wear blouses tucked into crinkled skirts that reach their ankles, and the men wear shirts that fall past their hips, most of the fabrics garishly patterned in vibrant shades like tulip yellow, sunset orange, fern green, and clay red. All together, the composite's a jarring contrast to the grays, browns, and greens our party wears in the more muted palette characteristic of Telyan fashion.

Unlike Roanin's twisty, cobbled roads, Niav's streets of packed earth stretch wide across, even broader than the crowds, with the buildings to either side set a few paces apart. A layout no doubt meant to give the city an open feel, but I only feel on edge. Once we reach the bottom of the hill, the road swells alarmingly with vendor stands marketing patterned cloth and racks of sizzling beef. I find myself shrinking away from those hawking the city's renowned metalwork—items of adornment, tools, and weaponry—my mind on the street fights and beatings back in Telyan, and the fact that Glenweil's Prediction has produced the same words the last six years.

Weslyn glances back once or twice, like he can feel the tension emanating from my body. His guards are too preoccupied with cutting a path to care one way or another, but Helos smiles and squeezes my shoulder, and the connection relaxes me a little. The city's clamor and closeness may overwhelm me more often than not, but my brother feeds off the energy like drawing water from a well, and I can't help but feel safer in his shadow.

Descending into Niav, it was impossible not to notice the river coursing just beyond it. The one the humans swear by, the one we have to cross. From that distance, it looked almost peaceful, grayishwhite and gleaming innocently beneath the unbroken sun. No sign of the raging current, icy spray, or slick, muddy shore.

Though I had tried not to look at it, my eyes would not obey my brain.

Across that river lurks the vast wilderness, a realm of changeling wolves and nightwings. Caegars, marrow sheep, and, once, my home. A land impassive and unforgiving, one that sheltered my brother and me for years while slowly, simultaneously, guiding us to the brink of starvation and death. From my raised vantage point on the opposite shore, I could see the colossal peaks of the Decani Mountains, the slate-gray stone capped with snow even in late summer, set back deep in the Vale and stretching northwest all the way to the continent's tip. The conifer woods blanketing the lower mountainsides spilled over the hills and around the hidden lakes crowded along the base of the range. Save for a few alpine meadows and a bare patch faintly visible from here, the tree coverage continued all the way south, where the region flattened out—and where a thick, gray veil of mist peeked out, creeping toward the river.

Helos and I always steered clear of the mist, but this time we'll have to delve straight in. Somewhere beneath it lives the band of giants we're seeking. As for whatever might be driving strands of magic across the river and into nonmagical bodies—I have no idea what disruption could be so forceful, or where we might find it, but we can't just search the entire Vale for it. Not when Finley's life hangs in the balance. We'll simply have to procure the stardust first and go from there.

Chin up, Fin would say if he were here. *Fear is just a story waiting to be told. Learn the story and remember every part of it so you can tell me.*

You've always been the better storyteller between us, I argue in my head. *You're the one who gives them happy endings.*

We pass a hulking bookshop with its merchandise spilling out onto the street, and Helos breaks away to check the metal stands. He catches up with us shortly after, waving a local leaflet from inside.

"Look at this," he tells the group, handing it to me.

TROUBLE FROM THE NORTH

The headline screams from the top of the page in big, bold letters. Weslyn backtracks and grabs a corner of the parchment.

"They had the same Prediction again." Helos's mouth curls in distaste. "'Two shifters death' for the seventh year in a row. It seems the author felt that was important to mention alongside the rest. The article hints at a series of King Jol's demands, though it doesn't go into detail." He pauses expectantly.

Weslyn's fingers tighten around the leaflet as he scans its contents. "I'm guessing he has given Glenweil the same ultimatum as Telyan. Glenweil's emissary suggested as much after Kelner stormed out."

Trepidation claws its way up my throat. That would escalate the conflict beyond contention between two kingdoms. King Jol's demands could result in a continent-wide war.

Of the eight weeks he gave King Gerar to accept or reject Eradain's terms, one and a half have already passed.

"But what exactly—"

"Not here," he interrupts, unbothered by the way Helos glowers. "Let's move. I must speak with Minister Mereth."

Seeking a quicker route to the palace, we round the corner onto an emptier street. A couple of officers pass us by, their straight-backed postures more rigid than the ones we saw in Grovewood. My hands close into fists. I've spent so many months fearing the rot of Eradain might bleed into Telyan, I've not thought enough about whether it has rankled here in Glenweil already.

Stupid. It's your job to discover these things.

I track the patrol out of the corner of my eye, even though I know we have done nothing wrong. Old habits are hard to kill.

Beneath a bronze monument of some long-dead general on horseback, a man donned in an orange tunic is shepherding a line of sheep between the buildings. Streaks of silver and gold hair fall from the crown of his head, and his irises are a bright, metallic gray, like molten silver. He's a whisperer—animal speaker—the first magical person I've seen since we arrived. He must be compelling the sheep with his mind.

Carolette huffs with impatience as we press against a wall, waiting for the herd to pass. Movement from above snares my attention, and my eyes dart to the flower boxes strewn beneath the windows.

My stomach drops.

The pink and purple blossoms are bending on their stems, angling down toward the sheep in the street like bees drawn to nectar.

One by one, the sounds of the city drop away.

Into an undertone, then a whisper.

And finally, into silence.

The rest of the group notices all at once, eyeing one another apprehensively. One of the sheep must have the Fallow Throes—which is new. In Telyan, I've identified only humans.

"It's here," Naethan whispers, disconcertingly loud in the muted quiet.

Dom watches Helos and me with open mistrust.

Though it's not a huge surprise to find the Throes have spread beyond Telyan's borders, it's another thing entirely to see it for oneself. It may be my job to root out new cases, but probably, few in our group have experienced the sway and the silence in person.

Roanin. Grovewood. Niav. I cannot make sense of it, how an ordinary animal could harbor even a sliver of magic, considering magical beings are born, not made. It's almost as if this sickness is following us wherever we go, except that makes no sense. Three hastily scribbled words taunt the back of my mind, but I dismiss the fear at once.

I won't let myself believe the Prediction is about us. If it were, surely the messages would have stopped the year we arrived, when Queen Raenen broke her neck.

The herd moves on, and sound sweeps back in like the tide: jumbled conversation, a door snapping shut, the metallic jangling of the harnesses attached to horse-drawn carts. The whistle of wind tunneling through the alleys and the river's distant roar.

Apprehension needles my spine. "Let's keep—"

"OUT! Get *out!*" someone howls, the voice so close that gray feathers burst from my skin before I even draw breath.

Pain ignites along my collarbone, sudden and huge, as Dom slams into me with what feels like the force of a bear. My teeth rattle as he pushes me onto a side street half-swathed in shadows.

"Get off of me!" I say through gritted teeth, my heels scraping the ground as he forces me back. The feathers retreat beneath my skin as my fingers stretch into claws, long and curved and brutally sharp. Saved, I dig the points into his upper arms until I feel them pierce the skin.

Dom hisses and steps away, the manic glint in his eyes fringing on madness. With no warning, he looses his sword and swings it at me.

There's no time to scream. Flinching backward, I only just manage to clear the blade, and now it's a concentrated effort not to yield to my wildcat instinct. Every bit of it is screaming to defend, attack.

"What are you doing?" Weslyn demands, thundering down the alley toward us, his footsteps practically turning the packed earth to ash. "What are you planning to do, kill her?"

Just behind him, I see Naethan grab Helos's arm when my brother lurches toward me.

"She could have given us away." Dom snorts, spits, and swipes a hand beneath his nose, still pointing the sword at me. He's mad if he thinks I'm going to die by his blade. "I'm sorry, sir. I can't do it anymore. She puts you at risk. They both do."

"Dom, lower your sword," Weslyn says in a quiet voice, as I curl my clawed hands in warning. Just a moment, one single breath, is all it would take to give into the spreading numbness and shift to lynx. "Now."

Dom wavers. It's plain he wants to defy Weslyn, but he seems reluctant to disobey a royal command, no matter how quietly it's uttered. He doesn't put away his blade, though.

Losing patience, I look him straight in the eye and say, "You will lose."

"We have a job to do, Dom," Weslyn continues, as if I haven't spoken. Back with the rest of the guards, Helos has stopped struggling, as if afraid any sudden moves might shatter Dom's remaining control.

"But it's not right, sir, working with *them*." Dom's features contort. "I took an oath to protect your family. If you cross that river with them, you will not return, I promise you that. It'll be Her Majesty's fall all over again. Look at her hands. She's a monster."

I flinch, then hate myself for it. The claws disappear.

Weslyn's face has paled, but the severe set of his mouth doesn't change as he watches me, unblinking, before focusing back on the guard. "You will lower your sword, Dom. Now."

At last, Dom's compulsion to obey wins out. He drops his sword and spits in my direction. "The river take you," he mutters, murder in his eyes. Then he slams the blade back into its sheath and swivels back to Weslyn. "Apologies, sir. I meant no offense."

"Wait with the others."

After a long moment, Dom marches away.

In the silence that follows, Weslyn studies me with a furrowed brow. I can't tell if he's expecting me to thank him for stepping in, or weighing the senior guard's warning in his mind. Sudden panic flares—that he might listen to Dom, might send me away after all. Instead, he asks a single question: "Why would you risk it?"

Relief mingles with dismay. I don't know how to explain that it isn't a choice, that this is just how the Vale raised me. How, while he was engaging with high-end tutors in matters of diplomacy, history, and geography, the wilderness was grinding different lessons into my bones—the amount of time fresh kills remain edible, the tells in animals' postures that signify peace or aggression, the methods for maneuvering through ivy tunnels and muddy banks, the importance of responding immediately to the first sign of trouble.

"That voice," I say quietly, realizing it must have come from a window above us. "I thought that she was shouting at us. It startled me."

"Do not let it happen again."

The force of his judgment is burning through me, searing my skin. *Fight back,* that rapidly fading part of me urges, implores. *It's not your fault. Fight back.*

But the spark won't catch, and my flicker of fire vanishes in a wisp of smoke, leaving me hollow and cold. A memory whispers victoriously in my ear. Another pair of eyes appraising my worth, judging me *not enough.* Seeing the darkness inside me and turning away while she still could. Close behind, another memory stirs—a head sinking beneath the torrential current, gasping for air.

Monster.

"I'm sorry," I whisper, but he's already turned away.

Nobody speaks as we climb the hill that leads to the minister's palace. There are no businesses lining this road, only elaborate homes whose doors have been thrown open to admit the river breeze. People stare openly, though not antagonistically, as we pass.

Still stung by Dom's remarks, I stick to the rear and concentrate all my energy on keeping my emotions in check. *Do not be a distraction.* To our left, the river glitters in the sunlight like diamonds under flame, and I quickly divert my attention to the ground in front of us.

When we crest the hill, the road stretches straight toward Willahelm Palace, which is set back a good distance on the wind-tussled plateau. The iron gate cutting across our path is tall and wiry, with decorative spindles crowning slender rods twice my height. Two guards stand behind the bars, marking our approach with rather indifferent expressions. They're dressed in the same fitted, green-accented brown uniforms, hands resting casually on the hilts of the long swords belted at their sides.

Speaking in an undertone, Weslyn tells the guards who he is and requests an audience with the minister. "My travel companions," he supplies, when the guards' attention switches to Helos and me. I curl a lock of hair behind my ear and clutch the hem of my shirt, taking comfort in my borrowed form and Helos's quiet surety.

Weslyn clears his throat, and the guards snap to attention. Seeming alarmed by the fact that they've held up a royal, they throw open the gate, eyes wide.

"If you please, Your Royal Highness." The shorter one gestures for him to step through and leads the seven of us toward the entrance. I study her back in confusion.

For an instant, she had appeared . . . blurry around the edges, like a half-finished painting with the figure not quite filled in. The sight tugs at something in my brain, some memory that sets my heart scampering through my chest, but in the next moment, she's already walking away and looking completely ordinary. It must have been a trick of the sun.

While Castle Roanin stands tall and elegant, limbs winding and wild as the forest surrounding it, the heart of Glenweil's republic is heavy and grounded, its palace walls stacked with enormous stones easily the length of a leg each. The estate borders on barren, trim grass dotted with only a few young trees and low-cut hedges, all clearly planted rather than naturally grown.

Wind buffets our backs as the road gives way to a broader, paved courtyard, and a chill passes through me despite the season. Ahead, Glenweil's standards snap a violent dance on matching posts just outside the double doors—deep green cloth boasting two black arrows pointed in opposite directions, with a gold-stitched rendering of the river winding between them. When Helos and I were here before, we never made it past those flag posts. Minister Mereth appraised us just beyond them.

It was about two weeks before we first came to Roanin, after seven or eight years of living in the Vale alone. Helos and I had finally decided that we couldn't do it any longer. We needed support, *community,* and hadn't found another home in the Vale since the massacre that destroyed Caela Ridge also disrupted the giants' influence that had kept the land there stable.

The one time we dared to return after the attack, we found little more than smoldering wood and overgrown vegetation—the trees had begun to reclaim what was theirs. Our house had collapsed inward like parchment crushed in one's fist. Some of the elevated bridges we'd raced upon still stood, while others had broken or burned to the ground. That ground—a horrid mess of arrows and gore, bodies and ash, half the bones lost to marrow sheep within hours. Maybe I had friends there, or tutors, or toys. But I can't remember their names. I can't remember a single face clearly, aside from Father's. Facedown in the grass with an arrow in his back, exactly as we'd left him the night before.

No shifters we met in years to come would take us under their wing. All seemed afraid to congregate in groups, lest the humans who killed our family come after theirs, as well. So we had grappled with the river at last and entered Niav, completely overwhelmed by the buildings and the faces, the wheeled carts and the cadence of conversation—and the relief at being able to understand the words.

Once we had gotten over our initial shock and worked up the courage to remain within the city borders for more than a few hours, we began seeking employment. Many people turned us down when they took in our grimy faces and tattered clothing, the garments salvaged from the wreckage of Caela Ridge by then riddled with little tears and holes. Others were swayed by the sight, and a few offered jobs and lodging.

But I'd ruined it for us. We had heard the rumors of Eradain but were ignorant of the other realms, unaware of the unprecedented event the year before, the second time all three Predictions yielded the same three words. I revealed our shifter nature within a couple of weeks, after a man had scared me badly enough that mouse instincts wrenched my core. Whiskers burst from my cheeks, and officers dragged Helos and me in front of their newly elected minister.

Minister Mereth. The leader who won that year's election in a landslide, a visionary with publicized plans to improve access to education and reduce the damaging impact of overgrazing livestock. A pragmatist who opted for logic over sentiment and exiled a couple of starving kids with nothing more than small sacks of food, out of an abundance of caution for her people. *You will find no work here,* she said, before summoning an artist to copy down our natural forms, to prevent us finding work. She gave us one week to leave the realm.

The guard bangs twice on the doors now—enormous, gilded, bronze creations standing nearly as tall as the flags. I dig my nails into my palms, suddenly eager for distraction. A sculptor has carved tiny pictures into the bronze, but I barely have time to examine them before the doors heave inward, metal hinges groaning with the effort.

The entrance hall is far more welcoming than I expected from the looming exterior. Candelabras affixed to the walls cast the high-ceilinged foyer in a muted but surprisingly warm light. Thick rugs woven with reds and golds blanket the floor and keep the stone's chill at bay, while a grand staircase, twice as wide as I am tall, doubles back a dozen or so steps up so that we can't see where it leads.

Our guard speaks to a nearby manservant, who disappears around a corner in the back.

"If you'll just wait here a moment," says the guard.

There are no chairs in the hall, so we hover in silence while Weslyn straightens the cuffs of his sleeves. I wonder if it's an intentional move on Minister Mereth's part, forcing visitors to stand. Helos nods to me, and I return the gesture stiffly.

When Minister Mereth breezes around the corner, she's just as I remember her. With one exception: the expression on her face is decidedly kinder. Her tall, curvy form is draped in a blouse and rippling skirt of deep scarlet, while smooth, deep brown skin peeks out from beneath a lacy, cream-colored shawl. Her gaze sweeps over all of us, but to my relief she glides straight to Weslyn.

"Prince Weslyn," she greets with a smile, though her eyes remain wary. He takes her proffered hand and shakes it once. "To what do I owe the pleasure?" Her cadence is measured, softer than the lilting accent with which Weslyn speaks.

"Minister," Weslyn replies. "I seek an audience with you."

"On behalf of King Gerar, I presume?"

"Of course."

Minister Mereth's eyes narrow shrewdly, and I have the distinct impression there's some game going on here I don't understand. "And your companions?"

Weslyn gestures to Helos and me. "These two would sit in, if you grant it."

I fight hard to keep my astonishment from showing.

Minister Mereth shifts her focus to us, and though I make sure to keep my face devoid of recognition, I can feel my limbs freeze a little on instinct. Her gaze, though penetrating, isn't omniscient, but it lingers on Helos longer than it had on me. "I grant it. First, though, you must be tired. Go and freshen up after your journey. Are my hands attending to your horses?"

It seems for all the world like she's directing the question at Helos, and I can sense his confusion as clearly as my own.

"We came on foot," Weslyn replies, wresting her gaze from my brother at last.

She doesn't bother trying to conceal her surprise. "Indeed."

There's a moment's silence, during which a look passes between them that I can't interpret. Then she smiles. "We'll dine together tonight. For now, Elias will show you to your quarters."

A slight fellow with long lashes, pronounced cheeks, and copper skin steps forward and inclines his head. "If you'll follow me," he says to the seven of us, gesturing to the grand staircase.

Minister Mereth sweeps from the room before we have a chance to turn our backs to her.

EIGHT

Elias leads us to the second level, where the staircase opens up to a broad stone gallery lined with vertical, rounded windows. The view looks out onto a tailored courtyard below, a tame, square plot cut into the palace's center that's altogether too artificial for my taste. Down the hall, a handful of finely dressed people toting pens and parchment look us over, their faces bloated with a self-importance that screams "state officials." I try and fail to read the documents as we pass.

Since working for King Gerar, I've gleaned no tales of discontent with Minister Mereth's term, of which two years remain. Only latent apprehension among Castle Roanin's court, lest their neighbor's continued success inspire democratic sentiment among grumbling Telyan royalists. In a rare stroke of political interest, even Finley has worked to prevent that happening.

"This is clever," Helos remarked one afternoon, his voice echoing in the castle grounds' old carriage house. We had thrown open the shutters to create a musty, private studio for Finley's latest project—a wooden ship he was constructing based on intricate diagrams.

Finley's face had popped over the wall of an unused tacking stall. "You mean me?"

"I mean this," Helos replied, smacking the top of Finley's head with a leaflet.

Finley snatched the creased parchment and scanned it, then grinned. "So you do mean me."

"'*Princess Violet fights the flames*,'" *Helos recited from the caption. I grabbed the leaflet's edge, the air crisp with autumn's chill. It was a drawing of Violet with a bucket, dousing a fire licking the edge of a nest of chicks. In the air, the water droplets formed beaded words. Foresight. Courage. Justice.* "*No mention of any Prince Finley.*"

"*Whose idea do you think it was to put the story in the papers?*"

"*Your sister's,*" *I said at once.*

"*Well, yes. But as an image?*"

I studied the sketch more closely. "You drew this?"

He winked. "Pictures hold more power than words, sometimes."

"*And deflection,*" *Helos added, with a decidedly arched brow. Violet's first public initiative, a proposal to replace old wood with stone to reduce the spread of fire, had been met with widespread approval. So much so that the press had ceased reporting the fire that spurred it in the first place.*

"*There's a reason the people have not tried to overthrow us yet.*" *Finley shoved the leaflet into Helos's chest. "We do more than keep systems running. We promise to do good and then follow through."*

"*Sounds like royal arrogance to me.*" *But Helos had been smiling.*

At the end of the hall, we round the corner and halt almost immediately.

"Your Royal Highness," Elias says, opening the door to the first chamber. Weslyn nods and steps inside.

The next two rooms are for my brother and me. Mine is bright and spacious, with an enormous four-poster bed set against the left wall, a mirrored dressing table and impressively carved wardrobe, and an array of upholstered couches and chairs arranged before the windows. Blues and yellows adorn the room, down to the thick rug lying underfoot.

While Elias leads the group on, I shed my pack and dash to the towering windows, leaning against the sill. Our quarters are at the back of the palace, right at the edge of the hilltop. After our view from afar, I know how sheer the drop is just below.

There's a knock on my open door, and Helos pokes his head through a moment later. "She's making a statement, I think," he says, stepping inside.

"What do you mean?"

Familiar despite his borrowed form, Helos sits on the arm of a couch and nods at the view. "Only one way out of here, and it isn't through the window."

He was quicker on the uptake than I was, but he's right. Where they've placed us, our movements can be tracked.

"She doesn't trust us," I observe.

"No, she doesn't."

I turn again, not having heard Weslyn arrive.

"But it's not surprising," he adds, closing the door and coming to my side. "It's highly unusual for a visitor from another court to show up unannounced. Even more unusual for them to travel with such a small party, and on foot. A dead giveaway that we traveled in secret, and all this on top of the pressure she's already feeling from Eradain." He shrugs. "I wouldn't trust us, either."

I make no move to fill the silence that follows. This is the first time he's chosen to be alone with us, and I don't know what to make of it, any more than I do his civil tone. As if nothing could be more normal.

"I want to apologize for Dom's actions today." Weslyn leans against the windowsill, collared shirt crinkling. "He's my responsibility. It will not happen again."

Helos and I exchange a look. Where was this sentiment when Carolette was hurling insults, or he himself treated us like a curse?

"Do you believe him?" I ask, feeling the need to test his apology. "That if you go with us tomorrow, you won't return."

He appears to consider the question carefully. "If I don't return, it won't be because of any prophecy."

That surprises me. "And dinner tonight? You asked if we could attend."

"You two have a part in this mission that the others do not. You have a right to hear what Mereth has to say." Briefly, he studies his hands on the sill. "In any case, since we're about to travel together, just the three of us, I thought we ought to . . ." He trails off, drumming his fingers along the wood.

"Bond?" Helos supplies in a dry voice.

Weslyn's face flushes. "Something like that," he mutters, twisting back to the window. If I didn't know better, I'd call his reticence discomfort.

Following his gaze, I locate Glenweil's northern border not far beyond the palace hill. The plains on the other side are barren and flat, shaded with burnt umber, the coarse, yellowed stalks covering them withered and listless. Divots and cracks are flecked with fading hawkweed and silvered sagebrush, and to the east, jagged buttes of stone and clay sever the horizon. The sight conjures other images—murky bogs, stagnant pools, birds crouching mutely in their roosts. Plants that burn when you graze their sides. I imagine the land weeping through its roots.

Everything about it speaks of silence.

"Eradain," I remark in a small voice.

Weslyn nods. "That's it."

And since he's clearly trying, and he's right we're about to travel alone, I decide it's only fair to return the effort. "Have you ever been?"

"Once." He frowns a little. "Long ago."

I chew the inside of my lip.

It feels strange to stand on the doorstep of the place Helos and I never ventured in all the years of living on our own. When the time had come at last to trade the wild for city life, we spent a long time searching for a place to cross the river. It had taken two treks along the shore, top to bottom and back again, before we conceded there were no natural crossings. The river barely even narrowed at any point, aside from a steep gorge to the south. No, the only place a swim seemed feasible at all was over to Niav, where we could see the city and tiny dock lining the opposite shore.

Helos decided to go first, of course, intending to signal back to me if he deemed the water safe enough. We'd waited for early evening, when the sun was just beginning to set. Then he'd waded into the river and—

"What exactly has Eradain demanded of Telyan?" I ask abruptly, to stem the tide.

Weslyn's jaw tightens, and seeing this, my brother folds his arms.

I recall the way I learned more of Eradain from refugees in the Vale than from my employer's own mouth. How King Gerar never granted me more than closed doors any time that kingdom came up. Shoved aside when my presence was no longer useful, and never trusted enough to share the truth. A small fire kindles within.

The brand of shame.

"Never mind," I say crossly.

Weslyn glances at me, eyebrows arched. "It's complicated."

"And I suppose I'm too dull-witted to understand?"

Helos kicks my foot, but I ignore the warning.

Weslyn fists his hands on the windowsill. "All I said was it's complicated."

"If it's private information, you can trust me to keep it to myself."

He says nothing.

"Never mind. The solution is always to keep me in the dark, isn't it?"

Weslyn fixes me with a level stare. "What am I missing here?"

"You tell me Eradain, whose laws are notoriously prejudiced against anyone with magic in their veins, like me, issued terms for your father to agree to, but you won't tell me what they are." My temper is rising fast and hot. "Telyan may go to war in a matter of *weeks,* a time frame you were quick enough to hang over my head when it meant securing the stardust faster, but I'm not permitted to know why. Instead, you keep the truth to yourself and expect me to do your bidding half-blind. Have I not done enough to earn your trust? Are you all so ashamed of your association with me that you dismiss me the moment it stops benefiting you?"

He crosses his arms, regaining his usual condescension. The stubborn ass. "You have no idea what you're talking about. It's a king's place to keep things from his subjects."

But I spy for him, gather intel for him. I'm on a quest to save his people and his *son.* I am more than an ordinary subject. Or maybe . . . maybe I only hoped I was.

Foolish hope.

I turn back to the window.

"He does trust you," Weslyn insists.

I note the use of *he,* not *we,* and keep my eyes on the horizon.

"Listen. Relations between Telyan and Eradain are . . . strained. King Jol is young and ambitious, only twenty-five and two years into his reign, yet already working to distinguish himself from his father. He's become vocal in his belief that the world would be better off without magic."

Yes, I've heard loose renditions of the climate there, snippets repeated on southern tongues spitting envy rather than disgust. As if Telyan, too, should persecute magic within its borders. I laugh without humor. "Haven't Eradain's people always felt that way?"

"No, they rebelled against the idea of a magical monarch. This is different." He presses a palm to his forehead, suddenly weary. "Since assuming the throne, Jol has sent several envoys to my father, all bearing the same message: reclaim the continent. Join him in a mission to conquer the Western Vale, to rid the land of magical beings once and for all."

"What?" Helos exclaims, voicing my outrage. "The Vale has always been neutral territory! Is it not enough to target people within his own kingdom?"

"It may have been, once. But it seems the Prediction has changed that." Weslyn's gaze darts to me, inscrutable, before returning to my brother. "The first year the Predictions aligned, my father met with Mereth and Jol's father, Daymon. My father and Mereth both advised prudence without mobilization, but Daymon disagreed. He ordered his staff to assemble a list of every shifter in Eradain, so that he might keep tabs on them." He pauses. "Then the earthquakes began."

I feel a tremor of nerves despite myself. "There's no proof it will happen again. The Rupturing."

"No, but we know an explosion of magic caused it, and a series of earthquakes preceded it. It is not unreasonable to fear that new earthquakes means it's starting again, especially with them happening in all three realms."

"But to tie that to the Prediction," Helos says. "As if two shifters could cause the continent to break apart. The idea is absurd."

"It isn't to Jol," Weslyn counters. "And it wasn't to Daymon. Not with earthquakes suggesting a buildup of magic and Predictions repeatedly warning of death. Daymon originally saw two shifters as the heart of the issue, but when the Predictions began to repeat, he expanded his identification system to include all magical civilians." His forehead creases. "I'm sure you heard what followed. Shops and homes vandalized, jobs lost, marriages broken. It wasn't unusual for people to vanish and not reappear until several days later, in considerably worse shape than before."

My stomach twists.

"Daymon's death left the kingdom in a state of unrest. Jol smoothed the chaos. He enacted a new code of law that exiled magical people and punished those who fought to stay. Some moved south, but I believe more went west, across the river."

As have many from Telyan. The Vale must be a much more crowded place than it was when Helos and I lived there. "That's sick," I say. "I don't know how his people could have allowed it."

"It's what they wanted. The humans, anyway. Remember, Eradain's resentment of magic stretches all the way back to its foundation. It's ingrained into the fabric of their culture." Weslyn runs a hand along his beard. "Jol didn't create that tension, he only acted on it. To most of his people, he's a hero."

"He sounds like an asshole," Helos retorts.

"Maybe, but he holds his people's favor." Weslyn frowns. "They pitied him as a child. He and Daymon had a famously tense relationship throughout his upbringing. Public ridicule, constant belittlement, rumors of beatings. To outsider eyes, Jol was a model son, but Daymon always acted like he hated him, and no one knew why. Then, of course, there's the fact that his own mother tried to kill him."

"What?" I can't help but feel a shred of sympathy.

Weslyn's face brims with skepticism. "My father never believed it. The official story is that Mariella went mad and tried to murder Jol when he was four. She failed, fled the castle in Oraes, and went into hiding. Later, Daymon caught her and ordered her execution, then had her head mounted outside the castle for many months." He stares out the window at the desolate land to the north. "Barbaric, really. My father met Mariella several times and liked her, even attended their wedding. He's always said there was nothing mad about her." After a moment, he shakes his head and leans back against the glass. "But this is what the people see when they look at Jol—a boy who emerged from a difficult childhood triumphant, grown into a man perfectly poised to lead them. Daymon was unstable, his manner harsh and his moods erratic. Jol is more . . . controlled. Strict, maybe, and certainly not to be crossed, but intelligent, confident, more commanding of respect. They adore him." He shrugs, his mouth twisting in distaste. "Personally, I don't like him. He smiles too easily for someone who rules the way he does."

"You've met him?" I ask, surprised, though I don't know why.

"A few times. Most recently, when he visited Roanin just over a year ago."

"But I don't—"

"You wouldn't remember," he interrupts. "You were not summoned to the castle at any point during his visit. There were people in place to steer you away if needed."

It takes a moment for the words to register. When they do, vexation quickly overpowers my confusion.

"You were watching me?" I demand, offended, and angry it isn't altogether surprising.

Weslyn does not look apologetic. "If he had seen you and recognized you for what you are, the consequences would have been beyond your own neck. Listen," he adds, holding up a hand when I open my mouth to argue. "My father has maintained peace with Eradain, albeit a tenuous one, by disassociating himself with magical people, at least when one of Eradain's representatives is around. He doesn't hide his distaste for Jol's methods, but nor has he ever tried to interfere. If he had, Jol likely would have launched his armies into Telyan long ago." He inclines his head toward me. "Now imagine if Jol found a *shifter,* of all people, in my father's court. Think of the Prediction."

Instead, I think back to that day in Grovewood, when Kelner stared at me so openly. But no, he couldn't have known.

"But that's wrong," Helos says. "To do nothing and allow those people to be treated so horribly, for fear of upsetting the northern king."

Weslyn casts a withering look in his direction, and I wonder if it's considered treasonous, even out here, to speak ill of one's king and the choices he makes. "My father's duty is to protect his kingdom to the best of his ability. He and Mereth both walk a fine line. They do not ban magic from their borders like Jol does, but nor do they actively push back against his government. Right or wrong, that is the decision they both made."

Helos runs his boot back and forth across the carpet, his eyes downcast and mouth pinched tight. I agree. I understand why King Gerar chose the course he did, but it was the wrong one.

"It no longer matters," Weslyn continues, "because Jol has grown tired of the stalemate. You asked what ultimatum he gave." His face flushes red with anger, and it occurs to me that this is the longest he and I have ever spoken without one of us storming away. At least he's finally answering my questions, for a change. "He demands that Telyan adopt his laws that exile magical people. He also demands we join his campaign to rid the Vale of magical beings. Which, given the laws, would amount to eliminating them from the continent entirely." He crosses his arms. "Eliminate them, and we stand the best chance of preventing another Rupturing, he reasons. And if the land grows quieter as a result, all the better. To resist will mean open war."

The truth is a breathtaking punch to the gut. All this time Helos and I have spent building a life in Roanin, and now we might have to leave Alemara entirely? Never see Finley or do the jobs we love again? My heart climbs into my throat. *Useless. Unwanted.* "And how does your father plan to respond?"

"He hasn't decided. But my sister has long advocated standing up to the north. She believes there's something going on there that the envoys aren't telling us." He glances at me, a glint in his eyes I can't interpret. "She wants your help with that, actually. She has argued to send you north for a long time now, to spy for us. But my father has always refused, he won't even consider it. He is convinced it would be too risky for us and you."

I can't tell which amazes me more—the idea that Violet would trust me enough to send me on such a mission, the idea that King Gerar would refuse on account of a risk to me, or the idea of being discussed when I'm not there. Discussed as an asset. As someone firmly of use. And suddenly it clicks into place—the times I heard Violet demand that her father send me away. She didn't want to be rid of me. She wanted to *use* me.

A twinge of excitement blossoms in my core.

"And Glenweil?" Helos asks. "What kind of dinner conversation are we walking into tonight? Has Mereth received similar demands?"

Weslyn studies Helos's face for a moment before answering. "It's my job to determine that, and to gauge her relationship with Jol. If conflict does turn to combat, my father needs to know whether or not we'll have an ally in her." He scrapes a foot across the ground. "For now, as I said, Glenweil remains neutral. As does Telyan."

My heart sinks at these words. I can see the effort it takes for Helos to keep his thoughts to himself, and since he's already risked treason, I suppose it's my turn to voice it.

"What you're both doing is not neutral," I murmur, so quietly my words are almost lost. But when Weslyn pushes off from the glass, his body is etched with tension, and I know he heard me.

"Speaking of dinner, I'll do the talking tonight," he says, not acknowledging my remark. "You have a right to sit in on the conversation, but try to avoid speaking as much as possible. This is going to be tricky enough as it is."

I roll my eyes.

"Look, she won't expect you to speak in any case. I'm sorry, but it's true. There's an order to these things. I'm trained to navigate conversations like these—"

I laugh derisively. "Four years in your father's service, and you think it's any different for me? Any different for either of us, for that matter?" I know he has to be the one to negotiate, of course, but still I chafe at yet another reminder that he and I are not equals. "We're sh—"

My voice falters, then drops to a whisper, wary of eavesdroppers. "We're who we are, living in a world *your people*," I thrust a finger in his direction, "have decided is not for us, on account of three stupid words. We have spent our lives learning to do the same as you, and if you think it's any different, you're a fool."

There's a terrible silence, and I'm sure I've spoken out of turn—calling a royal a fool! But the words have been building inside me, and I won't try to take them back.

This is usually the point when Helos would caution me with a warning touch on my arm or a knock of the foot, but he's made no move to interfere. I wrest my gaze from Weslyn's and am dismayed by the sight of him.

Ire is etched into Helos's furrowed brow and taut arms, an awful combination of sorrow and fury. Almost as if this conversation has wakened a stroke of vengefulness within, an impulse that doesn't belong to him. Not to someone as good as my brother.

I lurch away from the window.

This room of luxury and comfort, of soft things and stone walls and shelter from the outside world.

Those rolling hills and ancient woods and open stretches of sky. The moonlight on my skin and the wind in my wings.

All of it is rotten, the world a hunter that rivals the best of them—a ruinous beauty that ensnares my heart and sets me aflame before reminding me, over and again, that none of it is meant for someone like me.

The door opens and closes, and I stare at the wood. I didn't even see him leave.

A hand falls on my shoulder, and though the touch is gentle, I still flinch instinctively. I know my brother wants to help, but he doesn't ask me if I'm okay. He doesn't bother, because how could I be? How could he be?

For a single moment, just one, I wish that we were children again and he could keep us safe. All I'd have to do is hold on. But my heart won't accept the thought. I don't want to be protected any longer. I want to protect *him* for a change. And we haven't been children for a long time.

"I'll see you at dinner," is all Helos says before crossing to the door and shutting it behind him.

Biting back a scream, I grab my pack and hurl it hard as I can at the wall, wanting to shatter the world as it's shattering me.

The afternoon passes in a blend of frustration and exhaustion. I pace the room. I try to nap but abandon the attempt after a period of restless nothing. I fill a bath and scrub every layer of dirt from my skin, comb my knotted hair, and pull on the only dress I brought. Then I sit by the window, marking the sun's descent with a dim sense of dread.

Almost time.

My hands trace idle lines across the skirt of my dress. The lavender fabric is a little worse for the wear, wrinkled and slightly musty from the days spent in my pack, but I like the feel of it, anyway—like brushstrokes against my skin. I pad over to the dressing table, barefoot, and stare at my borrowed reflection in the oval mirror, the dress nearly hitting my ankles in this form, though it usually ends midway down my calves. With a pinch of disappointment, I realize I only have the boots, which are dirty and heavy and ruin the whole look. Well, that can't be helped.

There's a knock on my door, and I find Helos waiting in the hall with a young woman dressed in Glenweil green. I fall into step beside him while she leads the way to Weslyn's quarters.

"Nice shoes," he mutters, looking scarcely better rested than I. He's cleaned up rather well though, his dark hair shining and combed smoothly back.

"Nice shirt," I reply, noting the grass stains discoloring the dark red fabric.

He grins.

The woman knocks on Weslyn's door, then opens it hesitantly when he calls for her to enter. Bathed in reds and browns, his room is much darker than mine, though adorned with similar furniture.

Weslyn is lounging in a chair by the unlit fireplace, holding a pen and a brown, leather-bound book he's been writing in for several nights now. I've never caught a glimpse of what's inside; he always keeps it well hidden from intruding eyes.

At our appearance in the doorway, he sets the book aside and says nothing to either Helos or me, only closes his door and trails the woman down the hall, his expression unreadable.

Our guide leads us a different way than we came, and our shoes clatter uncomfortably against the polished wooden floors, the sound knifing high into the arched ceiling. Every corner we turn is sharply angled, every door fastened shut. Though I'm trying to memorize the route, I keep getting distracted. Weslyn's shirt is a blinding shade of white, the collar and cuffs crisp and bright, like a beacon in the darkening corridors.

I'm trying not to look at it.

By the time we reach the dining room, I'm thoroughly disoriented. There are no windows in here, just dank stone walls and the flickering light of candelabras. The feeling of entrapment intensifies.

Atop a rug shaded black onyx and jade, a rectangular table has been set with four places. Minister Mereth looms in the high-backed chair at the far end, her posture immaculate, black curls drawn into an elegant knot. Her earlier smile is gone.

She gestures for us to sit, beckoning Weslyn to the place at her right. Helos offers me the place to her left, and though I have no wish to be so close, I don't dare protest in front of her. Feigning gratitude, I sit and count the items before me: two stacked, cream-colored ceramic plates etched with pink detailing around the edges; two glasses with bands of gold around the lips, one filled with water and the other with wine; two forks; two knives; one spoon; one cloth napkin; all set atop a mat the color of Helos's shirt, with threads as fine as spider's silk, woven in a dizzying, lacy pattern. It's a familiar game, one I've used often to soothe my nerves, but the sense I'm being watched forces my eyes up after only a few moments. Minister Mereth is surveying me with unmasked curiosity.

Trying to swallow my apprehension, I clasp my hands in my lap and return her gaze. She switches her attention to Weslyn.

"Your rooms are comfortable, I trust?"

That seems to be a signal, because four servers instantly appear with wide, shallow bowls in hand. Mine holds a creamy bisque, and I cast a surreptitious glance at Weslyn, who picks up his spoon without hesitation. I do the same. This is by far the nicest meal I've ever attended, and I have no idea what the rules of etiquette might be. Glumly, I imagine how the Minister Mereth might react if she knew she'd invited two shifters to her table, let alone the two she'd specifically ordered to leave Glenweil.

"Very comfortable. Thank you," Weslyn replies, when the servers are out of sight.

"And your family? How is your father?"

"He's well."

Minister Mereth nods. "Yet he doesn't know you're here."

By the river, she's direct.

Weslyn continues to sip at his soup, seemingly unperturbed. "On the contrary, he's one of the few who does."

Minister Mereth sits back and appraises him. "If you bring trouble with you, I won't have it in my borders."

"We bring none." Weslyn's response is immediate, his voice clear and calm, no trace of defensiveness or alarm. The fact that he fits so naturally into the polished surroundings—his tailored clothing, the beard he's trimmed to shadow, the silver ring on his middle finger—only makes me feel further out of place. "Though according to your local distribution, trouble is already here."

She sits forward a little, fingering the stem of her wineglass. Though she appears a few years younger than King Gerar, her force of presence is just as strong. I imagine her and Violet facing off, and the lightning storm that would surely follow. "Jol has been a thorn in my side since before he was crowned. He is a child playing king, and this, simply his latest tantrum."

Weslyn sets down his spoon and folds his hands before him. "Then you don't think him serious?"

"Serious," she echoes faintly, sipping her wine. "His policies have never been against the likes of us."

My fingers curl into fists.

"He considers everyone who stands against him a threat," Weslyn contradicts. "He's like his father in that regard."

Minister Mereth fixes him with a piercing look. "He's nothing like his father. Daymon was unhinged. Jol knows exactly what he's doing, foolish as his decisions may be. Is the soup not to your liking?"

Her head whips toward me, quick as a blink, startling me into a frozen sort of silence. My eyes flicker to the spoon clutched tight in my hand. I haven't eaten a single bite.

I dip my head and start eating, unsure whether she expects an apology. Her attention drifts to Helos.

"Your face is vaguely familiar. Have we met?"

My body ices over. Helos has never learned to hide behind masks the way I do; his feelings are usually easy to read upon his face. But to his credit, he only leans back a fraction, clearly surprised to be addressed. "No, Minister."

She continues to appraise him, tapping the side of her glass lightly. "Hm."

"We were speaking of the north," Weslyn reminds her in the pause that follows.

"First I would like to know who sits at my table." Minister Mereth trades her wineglass for a spoon and dips it into her soup. "Your name?" she asks me.

I straighten a little, resisting the urge to smirk at Weslyn. She won't expect us to talk, indeed. "Evaline, ma'am."

"Evaline," she echoes slowly, testing the syllables on her tongue. "That's a pretty name. And what do you do, Evaline?"

"I'm in the Royal Guard, ma'am." If she ever solicits information on King Gerar's court, she'll find that there is indeed a short, frizzy-haired member of the Royal Guard named Evaline. I'm leaving no trail to the secret shifter in their midst.

"And you?" she asks Helos, a calculating gleam in her expression.

I don't like it. My brother has always turned heads, and the form he chose today probably doesn't help, but now is not the time to be attracting extra attention.

"What's your name?"

"Helos," he replies, opting for the truth. "I'm a healer."

"A healer and a fighter," she muses, appraising Weslyn with open interest. "Why do you speak of Eradain?"

Weslyn appears slightly relieved to be back on topic. A point on which we can agree. "He's given Telyan the same deadline to adopt his legislation. He also requested we join his campaign to take the Western Vale."

The article we read didn't mention the campaign, and Weslyn pauses to gauge Mereth's reaction. Though I've already heard this news, the reminder still unsettles me.

Her silence is telling, and Weslyn picks up on it immediately. "You received the same request."

She nods, setting her spoon down. "He'll be disappointed with my lack of enthusiasm, I imagine. That land has remained untouched for centuries, and for good reason. I have told his messengers as much."

"Then you plan to say no?"

"I haven't decided yet on my response, and if I had, I would not share it here. But I have no wish to expand Glenweil's borders, nor to risk my people's lives in such a foolish and needless endeavor."

"Nor the lives of those living in the Vale?" Weslyn adds. In my peripheries, Helos straightens in surprise.

Minister Mereth holds Weslyn's gaze long enough to be disconcerting. Whether she's impressed or offended, it's difficult to say. At last, her lips curve in a slight smile. "Why are you here, Prince Weslyn?"

He sips from his own wineglass. "We'd like to cross the river."

Minister Mereth coughs a little on her soup. "Is that so?" This time, when he doesn't bend beneath her gaze, her expression clouds over. "You have no business crossing the river, any more than Jol does."

"No law prohibits us from crossing, so long as we do so in peace and with no intention to settle. So that's not for you to decide. My actions are guided by my father, and my own conscience."

A server enters the room with a pitcher but hastily retreats when he sees his minister's face.

"Is that a threat?" she asks, in a voice carved from ice.

"On the contrary," Weslyn replies, "it's an invitation. In exchange for passage on one of your boats, we will happily share our findings with you."

"And what exactly is it you hope to find?"

"With any luck, nothing." Weslyn drains the last of his wine. "Our intention is to see whether Jol has begun his campaign before the deadline is up. To judge the state of the Vale, and whether it yet bears the mark of Eradain, with or without our help."

No mention of the stardust, then, or the other riddle we're aiming to solve: why magic is reviving in pieces east of the river. Nor do either of them acknowledge the Fallow Throes in their midst. The leaflet Helos picked up didn't mention it, and Minister Mereth isn't raising the topic any more than Weslyn has.

It's all a show of strength between them.

"You wish to spy." Mereth's eyebrows shoot up, and she sits back again.

Weslyn nods, gesturing to Helos and me. "You understand our need for stealth."

She grants him nothing, though her eyes blaze with curiosity. "And your companions are what, your bodyguards?"

He smiles without humor. "Of a sort."

Minister Mereth's gaze whisks over Helos and me once more before returning to Weslyn. "If you do find his people there, what then?"

"We'll report our findings and call a summit. If he's begun, we must intervene now before open war becomes unavoidable."

"And you really think Jol would violate a centuries-old neutrality agreement on his own?"

Weslyn stares at her. "Do you not?"

Minister Mereth is silent for a time, so long that the servers come to clear away our bowls and replace them with another steaming plate of food. Weslyn, too, remains still, staring down the ruler by his side.

At last, she looks around the table, first at me, then Helos, then Weslyn. "You must return here first to share what you find. If you wish to use my crossing, those are my terms."

Weslyn nods. "Agreed."

Minister Mereth smiles then, a small, victorious smile that reminds us the people of Glenweil elected her for a reason. "The boat will sail at dawn."

NINE

The walk to the water is quiet, save for the hissing of the wind and the distant rush of rapids. Dirt muffles our footsteps as we cling to hooded cloaks and wind our way through a city shrouded in predawn shadows. Helos, Weslyn, and I have moved in silence this morning, and none of us seems keen to break it.

We bade farewell to Ansley, Naethan, Carolette, and Dom at the base of the palace hill; Weslyn asked them to remain in Niav for three days, to gather intel on the city they could take back to King Gerar. It was a relief for me to leave them behind, but I noticed the tightness in Weslyn's frame, despite the confidence in his parting words. Naethan had embraced him, once again ignoring Dom's insistence on formality, while Carolette shot me a glance that promised death should anything happen to him. Ansley had murmured "good luck" and actually squeezed my shoulder before doing the same to Weslyn.

Now my stomach sits in knots, my joints feel cramped and achy, and I know it's the strain of maintaining the shift as much as anxious tension. Resuming my natural form while I slept negated some of the hours I spent holding the borrowed one all of yesterday, but I didn't sleep enough to cancel it out, and today, adopting Evaline's form requires more of an effort.

I suppose we'll be across the river shortly enough. With every miserable step, my apprehension deepens.

I tell myself the fear is irrational. That the land on the opposite shore is just that: land. But I can't stop the adrenaline coursing through my limbs, the tingling spine and tightening chest, the way my skin quivers as if overrun with insects. My heartbeat is thrumming in my ears, so loudly I'm sure somebody else must hear it, and by the time the city ends and the river comes into full view, my heart's roar nearly rivals that of the churning water.

If we succeed in fetching the stardust, we could awaken the land east of the river once more. These could be our last steps on nonmagical ground.

Helos is a few paces ahead of me, and suddenly I'm filled with a desperate need to close the distance between us. Clutching my cloak, I scramble forward until I'm walking so close I actually knock him sideways a couple of steps.

"Okay?" he asks in a low voice. His posture radiates calmness, but there's a stiffness to his gait, and his eyes are wary. Haunted. I can tell his façade is an effort.

I don't answer.

Without speaking, he slips an arm around my shoulders. Together, we follow Weslyn to the port.

It's a small thing, little more than a sturdy-looking dock. A single-tiered boat, much longer than it is wide, tugs at its tether at the end, looking pitifully fragile against the powerful current despite the several pairs of rowers on deck. As we approach, the sight dredges up unwelcome images, along with those ever-present whispers of *not enough, not enough.* I try to drown them out with thoughts of Finley instead. Of golden hair and crystal eyes.

"Turn your face to the left. No, not that far—there. Hold it." Finley *adjusted his grip on the parchment pad and studied my face with renewed intensity. It was a warm, clear spring day, a couple of years back, when Finley's body had not yet started attacking itself.*

"You're not looking at me," he chided with a trace of laughter.

He was right. I was looking at the trees.

"Perhaps I'll just have to draw Helos instead."

I reined in my thoughts enough to feign offense, but it was an empty threat. He had drawn Helos only once and had made no move to do it again.

My brother grinned lazily, stretched out on his back with an arm strewn across his eyes. "Rora's the better subject," he objected. I scoffed at the notion of being better in any sense.

Finley smiled, open and honest, and it won me over. I held his gaze and allowed him to sketch my eyes.

"There," he said after a time, handing me the pad with charcoal-smudged fingers. "That wasn't so bad, was it?"

It was, but I flashed him a small smile. The drawing was good, a little too good. When I handed it back, he tore it from the pad and offered it to me. "Your payment for sitting."

"Miss?"

I turn my attention to the captain before me, a short, androgynous person with warm beige skin and close-cropped ebony hair. They gesture for me to step onto the boat Weslyn is already boarding, and I place one foot onto the wooden slat connecting the ferry to the dock.

Then stop.

The seconds pass. The captain makes a few reassurances about the current and the size of the crew, but half the sounds are lost to wind and water. The current is indeed slower this close to the shore, gentle even. But I don't want to cross. The land on the other side almost cost Helos and me our lives. It left us scarred and hungry and so deeply, frightfully alone. And I do not want to go. I can't go.

I take a step back.

"Please."

I wrest my gaze from the distant shore to find Weslyn watching me carefully, one foot on the boat, the other still on the board.

"Please do this. For Finley." Strangely, the request doesn't sound like an order. It sounds more like the river close to shore. He looks at the wood, then back at me. And then, very slowly, he offers a hand.

The gesture awakens a flicker of shame. I should be able to do this myself. I shake my head and board the boat, wringing my hands before me.

When I next look behind, Helos is halfway down the slat. His body is rigid, no longer an illusion of calmness. I try to catch his eye, but he's not looking at me. He's looking at nothing.

At last, he's across, and together we follow the captain down the center. The boat is larger than I thought but still creaks disconcertingly underfoot. Weslyn chooses a seat at the front, but Helos and I plant ourselves on a bench firmly in the middle, as far from the edges as possible.

The man to my left has the same muscular build as the captain on the dock. When I sit, he points south to a spot on the western bank, farther down the river. It's close to the place where Helos and I first crossed. We'll be following the current for a short distance rather than rowing directly across, he explains. I nod and straighten my spine, pretending not to hear the curiosity in his voice.

Indeed, all the rowers look curious, but they keep their mouths shut. I suspect they've been ordered to do so.

As soon as we're settled, they release the boat. The captain barks a command, and we push off from the dock.

Fortune save us.

The rowers do their work in silence, with far greater efficiency than I anticipated; we're into the center of the river in no time at all. In an attempt to distract myself from our destination and the way the boat rocks back and forth, I focus on my breathing. In. Out. In. Out. Why is Weslyn staring?

I force a challenge into my gaze, and he flicks his attention to Helos before turning forward once more. I'm the picture of stillness, but next to me, my brother can't stop fidgeting. He bounces a leg, he twists his hands, he brushes the hair off his forehead. Giving himself away with each movement, and the experience is strange to me. He's always had this restless energy when he gets nervous, but this—I haven't seen Helos so on edge in a long time.

I can't help but wonder if he's remembering the rapids closing over his head. The heaviness of the river as it fought to drag him under. I wonder if he's remembering the way I didn't save him.

Or perhaps the sight of the opposite shore—inescapable now—has suddenly made this whole journey far too real. Forced him to confront the trauma of his past in a way he's managed to avoid for years.

Tiny points of pressure prick my skin from beneath. Alarmed, I refocus on my breathing, determined to steady my racing heart.

The pricks are feathers, threatening to break through to the surface.

Not this time, I think resolutely. I won't fly. I will not flee.

Hold it, said Finley.

"Easy, crew," the captain calls as we make our way past the half-way point. The woods are growing steadily larger. I press my shoulder to Helos's, attempting to offer some reassurance. His leg stops twitching, but his hands are still clasped in a death grip; upon closer inspection, I notice a tightly folded piece of paper clutched firmly between them. He's running his fingertips over the creases.

A letter, perhaps? Or a map? The only bits I can see are blank. I resist the urge to reach for it, fixating instead on the long line of trees coming closer.

Weslyn hasn't looked back in a while.

By the time the rowers guide the boat into the shallows, resolve strengthens me. I know what I have to do. I have to be strong for my friend. I have to be strong for my brother. And this time, I will not fail.

The pinpricks disappear.

Three people leap into the water and grab the front of the boat. Three more take it from behind, and slowly, they push and pull it onto the pebbly bank.

Weslyn is the first to exit the boat. The captain promises to set a daily lookout at Niav's port, so we can catch our ride back by flagging them with smoke signals. Weslyn nods his thanks before stepping down onto the rocks, hands fisting the straps of his pack. Keeping my eyes trained on the tree line, I shuffle forward until I'm right at the edge. The captain offers me a hand, but I shake my head. I have no need of it.

For Finley, I think resolutely. And I step onto the shore.

TEN

Every step is an effort.

The sky has settled into a dull gray color, which I suppose matches the mood. It was difficult to stand and watch our only means of escaping this shore surge into the river and away to the opposite bank. We exchanged glances after that, Helos and I having released our borrowed forms to great relief—and to no comment from Weslyn—but no one was quite willing to splinter the silence, or take the lead. So the three of us just walk side by side up the rocky shore, boots grating against the tricolored stones, toward a mass of scaly juniper shrubs tangled along the forest's edge. Helos halts us right at the tree line.

"Now that we're out of the open," he says, in a constrained sort of voice, "we need to establish our plan."

Weslyn gazes farther down the river. "The giants live near the southwestern tip, don't they? So we track south."

"It's not as simple as that," I say, pausing my examination of my brother. Weslyn's forehead creases. "We don't want to walk the shore; it's too exposed, and we'll have to move farther inland anyway to reach the giants."

"Too exposed—to what?"

He doesn't sound as nervous as he should, and I can't tell if he's acting, arrogant, or vastly unintuitive.

"Marrow sheep," I reply, sheathing my own apprehension in annoyance. "They come down from the mountain ledges hunting bones to grind between their teeth and strengthen their rutting horns. Widow bats that spin toxic webs of saliva. Changeling wolves whose fur camouflages to match their surroundings. Caegar wildcats that hypnotize you with their eyes, paralyzing your legs and lulling you into a false sense of security before killing you. Not to mention timber bears, even more dangerous than grizzlies, which are so strong, they can fell trees with the slightest push."

"You make it sound as if this whole place is a death trap."

"It's not a death trap," I retort. "It's just the wilderness. The terrain here is unplotted. The trees are centuries old; the woods won't be as easy to navigate as the Old Forest. There are boulders that could twist loose and pits of dirt hiding two-headed snakes and biting insects. Water sources don't just appear when you need them. And all while we're making our way across the Vale, we're invading other creatures' territories, and we're walking a land where magic is steeped into the plants and the animals and the earth itself. That means unpredictability. A landmark could be there one day and gone the next. Leaves might produce a mist that puts us to sleep for a hundred days. And if we get hurt, there is no one to call for help. No one. *We are alone.*"

I've moved slowly forward throughout this speech, to the point where I'm now somewhat close to Weslyn. I resist the urge to step back. He needs to understand.

For a while, he doesn't reply. Just studies me as if working out a puzzle.

"And this is where you grew up," is all he says.

I'm not sure I can bear the pity tingeing his voice, so I shake my head and gesture dismissively. "This isn't about our past," I tell him, not sure how true that is. "This is about saving Finley, and every other afflicted person before they end up underground. Not to mention finding the source of this resurging magic. And to do that, we have to stay alive. That means staying alert, traveling as stealthily as possible, and listening to my brother and me. Got it?"

I half expect Weslyn to respond in anger, but he only holds my gaze a few moments more, then nods.

"Got it," he echoes, rather quietly.

Just as quickly as it flared, my impatience ebbs away. "All right then," I say, satisfied and strangely flustered. "Helos?"

My brother flinches a little as our gazes connect, as if jolted from a bleak trail of thought, then quirks his head toward the trees. "I say we head west through the forest. We can make camp at the central lake, then track south to the giants from there."

The base of my throat tightens. It's been four years since we've been here, and already our familiarity with the landscape is returning to us.

As if we could ever be free of it.

I nod my assent, and he moves to take the lead. But I quickly stride past him; he's been eyeing the woods apprehensively, and this, at least, is something I can do for him.

The forest is alive with the sounds of bugs, breeze, and the occasional yelping cry of a golden eagle. Given the summer season, the trees are in full bloom, ponderosa pines and silverleaf oaks whose canopy crowds thick above us. Needles shiver on their perches, the branches swaying and creaking intermittently. We climb steadily through a maze of roots, twigs, stones, and dirt, gaining enough elevation to accrue minor headaches, our sides nudged by mountain sagebrush and white-flowered stalks of bear grass. Every once in a while, I catch glimpses of a squirrel or a similar creature reveling in the disarray.

As I predicted, the going is slow. It's a dark wood—the tree-tops catch most of the light before it can filter through—and we're making an unfortunate amount of noise. Though the air at this height is colder than that of the lower slopes back east, I shed my cloak and stuff it into my pack when my face grows flushed with exertion. The others have long since abandoned theirs.

For all my brave talk about listening to Helos and me, I can't help but feel I'm setting a poor example. I flinch at every snapped twig. I can't go more than a handful of steps without looking over my shoulder. I'm not even positive I'm heading in the right direction; the cloud cover is making it difficult to track the sun's position in the sky.

It doesn't matter how long I've been away. Each step forward feels like stepping into the past, back into that state of prolonged uncertainty and dread, teasing out the threads of fear woven into my core. I try to remind myself that this is a different time. I'm older now, stronger, and nightmares are not destined to repeat, not necessarily. It's no use. Memories cling to me like cobwebs, and it's impossible to shake them loose.

My own mother left me. The knowledge is certainly nothing new, but being here makes the wounds I have worked so hard to suppress gnaw at my insides with renewed intensity. Father is dead, and our mother abandoned us. She was supposed to protect me. Supposed to love me.

Wasn't she? Isn't that what mothers do?

Another crack to my right, and this time I swivel so quickly that my feet tangle in the undergrowth. Helos catches me before I can fall.

It's only a ginger-furred holly hare, his enormous eyes four times larger than an ordinary rabbit's. The pupils constrict rapidly, and he bears two rows of serrated teeth before dashing back into the brush.

Weslyn gapes at the sight.

"Let's rest," Helos suggests, letting go of my arms when I've regained my balance.

I shake my head, blood heating my face. "I'm fine."

"You're not, and neither am I." My brother and his honesty. "A few minutes won't hurt."

But they will. Every minute we waste is another minute trapped in this cursed place. And if we stop, I won't even have the distraction of hiking to help me.

My brother is already pulling food from his pack, though, so I sink to the ground and draw my knees up in front of me. Minister Mereth gifted us plenty of provisions for the journey, but the thought of food turns my stomach heavy as stone, so I only sip a little from my waterskin. Weslyn watches the quivering bushes awhile longer before sinking slowly to my other side.

"How long did you live here?" he asks, when I'm halfway lost to memories. It's a difficult question to answer, considering we didn't have much of a method for measuring time.

I look to Helos, but he appears preoccupied with monitoring our surroundings, slightly wide-eyed. I'm still watching him when I answer. "Don't know. Twelve, thirteen years in total, maybe."

A pause. Then, "What made you leave?"

I glance at Weslyn sharply. When Helos and I met with King Gerar a week following Queen Raenen's death, we had shared only the slimmest details of our situation. He had asked us where we'd lived before—Caela Ridge—and for our parents' names, which we couldn't remember beyond Father and Mother. But despite his thoughtful gaze, he never pressed us to uncover the full truth of our past. No one had, except for Finley.

"It became difficult to survive on our own," I reply, stifling the urge to ask him why he wants to know.

His brow furrows. "And how long were you on your own for?"

The food in Helos's hand remains untouched. He's just . . . sitting there. Leg bouncing. Fiddling with his sleeve.

I stand abruptly, brushing the debris from my backside. Being here is difficult enough without rehashing the details of our tragic past out loud. "Let's keep moving. I want to reach the lake by nightfall."

Weslyn looks like he might object, then appears to think better of it and pushes to his feet.

"I'll lead for a while," Helos offers automatically as he shoulders his pack.

I shake my head. "No, I'll—"

Weslyn sucks in a breath, and my fingers stretch into claws before I've even assessed the danger. He's tugging his leg upward, hands clasped just above the knee.

"I can't get free," he says with thinly veiled panic as I survey the rippling ground caressing his feet.

"Just stay calm," Helos directs, back in protector mode. "That's—"

"Sinking sand," I finish for him, sheathing the claws and scouring our surroundings for fallen branches. Well aware of the fact that the sand wasn't there when we sat down.

"What makes you think I'm not calm?" Weslyn says, the objection falling flat against the pitch of his voice.

"Helos!" I exclaim, and an instant later he joins the search. I'm kicking leaves and twigs aside, hurling rocks, moving farther from the boys as my search grows more desperate.

"It's getting higher," Weslyn calls, and I slam backward a handful of steps—but it's only at his ankles. Relief quickly overpowers my confusion, and I find what I was searching for shortly after.

Rough bark digs into my palms as I hoist the branch back to Weslyn and plunge an end into the vile sand, moving it in a way that mimics a creature's footsteps. The sand gathers around the branch, sucking at it like poisonous kisses, and the distraction is enough. Weslyn takes Helos's outstretched hand and hauls his feet onto stable ground.

I drop the branch to its fate while Weslyn regains his bearings. My brother's attention continues to flit behind us—the initial cry would have alerted any creatures in the area.

"Thanks," Weslyn breathes, lifting one foot after the other, as if he no longer trusts the ground beneath them.

"You're lucky," I tell him, and his eyebrows arch. "It usually moves much faster."

To my surprise, the corner of his mouth twitches. A moment, a blink in time—then gone. "That's comforting to know."

Helos hands Weslyn his pack before pulling mine from the forest floor. "Let's keep moving," he suggests, and neither of us objects.

I take the lead as promised, both boys falling into step behind me. Weslyn doesn't ask any more questions for the rest of the day.

By the time twilight falls, my nerves are so frayed, my body so exhausted, that I'd likely be useless if anything else did attack us. Luckily, the land has lain quiet, and the handful of creatures we've come across have been no larger than my foot. Which seems odd, but I don't voice my misgivings out loud. It's only been one day. Plenty of time for danger to materialize.

The lake is even larger than I remember, a vast expanse of open, empty space that looks forbidding in the dusky light. Long shadows skim the rippling, blue-gray surface, racing the surrounding conifers for a prominent spot in the gathering dark. Tomorrow, we'll follow its shore south for a good while, continuing toward the low-lying mist that I spied from Niav. I still have no idea what that mist might do to us when we reach it.

Weslyn suggests we spend the night directly on the shore, but Helos insists we set our camp fifty paces away. I scour the forest floor for pieces of kindling, sparking memories from another quest for firewood.

It was close to winter, perhaps a year or so after our village burned. I had crept through the gathering dusk, wandering farther from Helos than was wise, yet determined to be of use. My small hands reached for a leafy stick on the ground—and closed around a tail.

I had heard stories of the changeling wolves that can alter their fur to camouflage with their surroundings better than any chameleon. Father admired them, believed their presence a sign of prosperity in the Vale. "If you ever see one, take heart," he'd say. "That means the world is at balance." Though the rest of his words are mostly lost, I still recall the low hum of his voice spinning tales for Helos and me, a fire's warm glow dancing playful silhouettes across the log walls. A woolen blanket and a pair of slender hands—my mother's, I guess, for all the good they'd do me later. But he never taught me how to evade one, and here was a pair of eyes gleaming in the shadows, a lip curled back in warning, a coat returning from nut brown to gold-streaked gray.

The wolf was small, not yet a yearling as later comparison would reveal. I must have come close to the pack's den. Those were the only conclusions I reached before heat surged through my limbs and numbness engulfed me, and my body bent and lengthened into a lynx for the first time—fluffy, gray winter coat flecked with white, tufts of thicker fur encircling my face, eyes a brighter yellow than the amber ones before me.

The transformation startled the wolf, whose cry alerted the family. I barely had time to test my new paws before bolting away as fast as they could carry me, unwilling to wait and see if the pack would attack.

In the present, I gasp and lose my grip on the dry twigs I've bent over to collect. When the landscape before me solidifies once more, I straighten and place a hand over my thundering heart. There's no way to know whether any changeling wolves might be lurking in these trees. And if there are?

A sign of prosperity; that's how Father would see it. But I never learned how to find the beauty in them. Only the danger.

When I return with the kindling, Weslyn asks to take first watch. Again, Helos contradicts him. Maintaining a smokeless fire requires diligence and care, and knowledge that he doesn't have. My brother will take first watch.

The glower on Weslyn's face, visible in the dim light of the small fire when it's made, suggests that he, too, has felt the power balance shift. There's nothing for it, though. Helos and I have spent years honing the craft of survival. The wild is our domain.

Without another word, Weslyn busies himself with the small black book he's been reading—a war history, according to the fading spine—though he glances around nervously when scrabbling noises penetrate the dark. The flames crackle and pop, and the soothing scent of burning wood lingers in the air. I collapse onto my bedroll as soon as I've finished eating, swatting at a few idle gnats and banishing further rumination on wolves. Nerves spent, I stare up at the night sky.

In the sliver visible beneath the treetops, the stars are vast and brilliant, flickering in the expanse. A band of white sweeps across the blackness like brushstrokes over canvas. Gradually, I let them lull me into what I hope will be a dreamless slumber.

It never is.

At first, I'm not sure what snaps me awake.

Blinking a few times to combat my swollen eyelids, I push myself onto my elbows and survey the camp. Helos and Weslyn are both asleep, Helos snoring softly, Weslyn with an arm bent beneath his head. Fading shadows drape the surrounding wood like gray gossamer curtains, mingling with patches of early morning fog. I tip my head to the sky, which is heavy with storm clouds, robbed of the dawn. With the sun obscured, it's difficult to judge the hour.

Twisting around, I force myself to focus on each individual noise, cataloging them in my head: leaves chattering in the breeze, ptarmigans rustling the vegetation, twigs snapping, insects buzzing and chirping.

My heart rate picks up. I lean forward a little, straining to hear it again.

Several moments pass. Nothing.

"Is something wrong?"

Weslyn has sat up and is rubbing the sleep from his face, his navy shirt crinkled around the sleeves.

"I thought I heard footsteps." I keep my voice low.

Weslyn scans the perimeter, unblinking. "And now?"

"My senses are too limited like this," I say, pushing to my feet. Weslyn quickly mirrors me. "I'm going to shift and scout around."

"What do—"

"Wake Helos and tell him where I've gone. I won't be long." I reach to pull my shirt over my head.

With a strangled protest, Weslyn turns his back to me, though not before I catch his look of intense alarm. "Fortune's sake," he says, "I would have given you privacy. You don't have to just . . . strip."

I have to suppress a laugh as I stuff my clothing into my pack. Sometimes I forget how bashful humans are about nudity. For shifters, it's just another body, same as any of our animal forms.

Coolness rushes through my tingling limbs as they shrink and settle into lynx, my fur silver brown in the summer season. Already, my fluffy coat has blocked out the morning chill as my tufted ears sift through the minute sounds of clicking, chirping, biting. Much better. I flex my claws, then lope away from the campsite.

The mingled scent of magic—soil and ash—drapes the wilderness like a second skin. I venture far from the boys and our things, appreciating the solitude and the dappled sunlight on my back, the earth packed beneath my massive paws. About forty paces away, a tiny body's urgent scurrying cuts abruptly into a cry of anguish. Someone is hunting, and my tufted ears pick up the sounds as if the scene were laid out before me. *Prey,* demands that inner voice, the bit of animal instinct that accompanies each shift. But my human impulses are always stronger, and I have other priorities right now.

The weight of the footsteps I heard had called a bear to mind, but so far, there is no bear in sight. When the undergrowth makes it difficult to navigate on foot, I retrace my steps to clearer ground, and suddenly I'm running. Running and then rising, body shrinking and wings bursting forth—through the trunks, above the canopy, into the open sky.

Where I'd see only blurs of green and teal as a human at this distance, my hawk eyes can make out leaves, branches, and the negative space between. Shafts of cooler breeze skim my feathers as I circle the woods, riding pockets of air. Once. Twice. I can't help myself; the feeling of freedom is intoxicating.

On the third circle round, I take stock of my surroundings. The Decani Mountains loom far to the north, their jagged peaks dusted with snow and patches of conifers. Just west of them lies the sapphire Elrin Sea. I turn my attention to the trees below and sweep lower, searching for movement. What I find makes my heart drop.

There is indeed a bear lumbering toward the lake. It's heading right for Weslyn, and Helos isn't with him.

My wings beat the air furiously as I shoot toward him. Weslyn must have heard the footsteps, because he has his sword out. It's difficult to judge what type of bear it is from here, but if it's a timber bear . . .

Please, Violet had said—pleaded—and I don't intend to fail her.

I twist and swerve through the narrow gaps between branches, dropping low as I go. This body is built for maneuvering through forests. Launching straight over the bear's head—just a black bear, thank fortune—I burst into the clearing and shift, my bare feet slamming into the ground with more force than intended.

Weslyn nearly jumps out of his skin and pivots toward me faster than seems possible. The tip of his outstretched blade grazes my stomach.

There's a moment in which we both freeze, struck by the knowledge that he was a finger-length from killing me. His wide gaze drops to the thin line of red now trailing across my olive flesh. Then he lowers his blade and swings round, tossing my pack behind him without looking back.

Keeping an eye on the trees around us, I dress as quickly as I can, my shaking hands fumbling with the fabric.

"Are you all right?" he asks, his back still to me.

I nod, then remember he can't see that. "I'm fine."

"Why did you—"

But he doesn't finish, because the bear has moved closer. He's raven black and gorgeous, his waggling nose sniffing the air, beady eyes watching us.

"He's probably just curious," I say quietly.

Weslyn makes a soft noise of disbelief. "Bit close for curiosity."

I'm just grateful those powerful paws don't possess any magical abilities. I glance at Weslyn, then at his hand, which is maintaining a vise-like grip on his sword. If he spooks, he'll use it, and there's no need for that. No one here is going to die on my watch.

"GET!" I yell without warning, clapping my hands together.

Weslyn starts. "What—"

"Scaring him off." I shout again, once, twice, clapping my hands and throwing them in the air. Weslyn does the same, swinging his sword a bit.

It works. The bear decides we're not worth his trouble and turns tail to retreat.

Weslyn rounds on me as soon as he's out of sight. "You didn't see it while scouting?"

"I did. That's why I'm here," I retort, realizing with a pang of guilt that I probably could have spotted it sooner if I hadn't given in to distraction. "Where's Helos?"

"He left to look for you."

"He left you *alone*?"

Weslyn shrugs a bit, then blanches at the sight of my stomach. "You're hurt."

He's right; blood is seeping through the front of my shirt, the stain expanding at a disconcerting rate. I almost wish he hadn't pointed it out, because now that he has and the shock has worn off, the pain is starting to register.

Quick as a flash, Weslyn drops his blade and kneels by his pack.

"I've got bandages in here somewhere," he mumbles, rummaging through the contents.

I should reply and tell him that it's fine. And I will. As soon as I can open my mouth without the risk of crying out.

"Okay, I—hey," he says, scrambling over to where I've sunk to the ground. I note the small drop of panic in his voice with grim satisfaction.

"It's nothing," I insist, a little breathless because of what feels like dozens of needles now sticking my skin.

"Don't be ridiculous," he snaps, but his hands are hesitant as they reach for the bottom of my shirt. I flinch away, and a small gasp escapes my lips at the movement. The needles cut deeper.

Weslyn holds my gaze. "I need to take a look." Slowly, he lifts my shirt enough to reveal the wound just below my navel.

The cut is shallow, but it's long. There are no needles lining it. Just blood.

"Okay, hold on," he says, like I'm going anywhere. He produces a vial of sharply scented liquid and dabs a bit onto a small square of cloth, then presses the cloth to the cut with both hands. Tears prick my eyes when it touches my skin.

"I can do it," I grumble, but he ignores me and presses firmly on the wound for a full minute. I don't know what to do, so I stare at the ground.

"I'm sorry," he says in a quiet voice, after a while. "I didn't mean to cut you." I risk a quick glance at his face, where a few strands of hair have fallen across his brow, reminding me sharply of his brother. Expression grim, he's staring fixedly at his hands, which have been careful not to touch anything but cloth. "You startled me."

I look back at the ground. "It's all right."

Using one hand to hold the cloth in place, Weslyn grabs his roll of bandage tape and pulls at the end with his teeth, ripping it once his piece is sufficiently long. Delicately, he lifts a bit of the cloth, then replaces it with a new one when the blood keeps flowing.

"Thanks for coming back," he mutters, catching my skin while bandaging the wound tight.

I risk another glance, and this time our eyes connect. His are a dark shade of honey, edged with a hickory-brown ring. They're watching me cautiously.

"It's all right," I say again, since I don't know what else to.

My brother races into the clearing in fox form, bushy tail brushed out, a rabbit clutched between his narrow jaws.

Weslyn pulls away.

"I'm fine," I say hastily, since Helos's panic is evident. Barely any time later, he's fully dressed and has thrown himself down in front of me.

"What happened? How bad is it?"

"Not bad," I assure him. "You went hunting?"

"The rabbit practically begged to be caught. I went looking for you." He sits back on his heels.

"Why? You should have stayed with Weslyn."

"You shouldn't be out there on your own. What happened?"

My guilt over precipitating Helos's concern subtly morphs into annoyance. I can look after myself. "Weslyn—"

I don't have time to explain further, because Helos's wandering eyes have landed on the sword lying a few steps away, a tiny splotch of blood coloring the tip.

In a flash, my brother's on his feet with Weslyn's shirt grasped tight in his hands, slamming him against a tree.

"Helos!"

He ignores me and continues to glare at Weslyn, the muscles in his arms straining at the edge of his white sleeves. Bewilderment thrums through me at the sight of that relentless grip, gentle healer hands suddenly tightened into weapons. The entire picture is completely unlike him—my brother is no fighter.

"I'm fine," I insist for the third time, forcing myself to march over to them despite the vicious pain that causes. Weslyn isn't saying anything, nor is he making any attempt to free himself, even though he can probably match Helos in strength. Somehow, that only makes it worse. "It was an accident. There was a bear."

Helos still won't acknowledge me, that frightening, slightly wild-eyed intensity overshadowing his face. A stranger's face. My heart hammers in alarm.

"Helos," I say, more urgent this time. "Come back."

Something in my voice must have broken through, because at last, my brother blinks and loosens his hold a little. "A bear?"

I release the breath I've been holding. "Just a black bear. We scared him off. We should move, though, if we don't want to run into him again." I look pointedly at the fists pinning Weslyn in place.

Helos hesitates a beat longer, then fixes Weslyn with a look that would rival Violet's best. It's a look that reminds me of antlers sharpened to a point. It promises death.

"You don't touch her again," he commands in a low voice. "You don't touch her. Understand?"

I marvel at how not even two weeks have passed since we were standing outside the castle, yielding to Weslyn's authority. Now we're here, with Helos clutching his shirt in a death grip.

Weslyn says nothing, and Helos appears to take that for assent. He releases him.

ELEVEN

As soon we've broken down our meager campsite, Helos takes us back to the lakeshore. The Vale has a penchant for casually leading its inhabitants astray, and growing up, we could lose hours in a day trying to amend a broken course. But for whatever reason, this lake has always stayed in place, unchanging, so we'll follow its shoreline south until we reach the end.

Helos remains in the lead throughout the morning. Weslyn trails behind me, mostly studying his feet to avoid tripping. Grim silence has tainted our group since the altercation. Though it hurts to stand up straight and hurts even worse to walk, I do my best to match their pace. I won't provide any unnecessary distractions, and at least I'd managed to bury my scarlet-soaked shirt in the ground before leaving the campsite. No need to lure predators with the scent of dried blood.

The patchy forest near the water's edge is a good diversion from the pain, lush and alight with an ongoing symphony—the woodpecker's rapid knocks, quivering bushes, the shrill whistles of deer mice and voles. The knot that's been building inside me for days unwinds a little at the sound. As we walk, we cross paths with squirrels and grouse, rabbits, and even a couple of ravens. None are their magical counterparts, and I study their retreats in confusion.

At one point, Helos catches my furrowed brow and reaches back to knock my arm. Then he scoops an object up from the ground and tosses it at me.

"Really?" I scoff.

He shrugs.

"I could see what it was before you threw it."

"Sounds like you're avoiding guessing."

"I don't have to guess," I say with feigned disgust, drawing out every syllable. "It was a lump of dirt."

His mouth curves into a small smile. "Dirt, was it?"

Immediately, I stop and stare at the small mark on my lilac shirt. Then I scan the ground.

"Helos."

He doesn't break stride.

"Helos, I swear to—"

"What's wrong?" Weslyn asks from behind, sounding weary.

I bite my tongue, unwilling to admit that Helos may have thrown scat at me.

My brother grins wickedly, aware of my dilemma.

"Nothing," I mutter, continuing ahead. Anyway, it was dirt.

The next time Helos looks back, the corners of his mouth fall. "Hold on. You're limping."

"I'm fine," I say, though really, the ache that each step aggravates runs deeper than the small stretch of torn skin; pain lances through my abdomen and toward my back, radiating throughout my midsection.

I've been determined to say nothing; every hour that passes carries Finley and the rest of the afflicted closer to death, and every moment not spent helping them is a moment wasted. Selflessness requires sacrifice. I know this, and can push through the pain for my friend's sake, if no one else's. It's what Helos would do. What *I* will do.

But my brother grabs my arm and forces me to stop before we've gone nearly far enough.

"Let me see," he instructs.

"I said I'm *fine*."

"You're not, and I should have noticed sooner. Let me look at it."

Weslyn steps up behind me. "Do we need to stop?"

"No," I reply, at the same moment that Helos says, "Yes."

Weslyn looks between the two of us, then back the way we came. My brother reaches for my shirt, and I slap his hand away.

"Rora." Helos speaks as someone schooling an unruly child. I bristle at his tone. "You're only going to slow us down the worse it gets," he reasons, anticipating my argument.

Resentment spears through me. A burden if I stop, a burden if I keep going. Why must he confine me to the role I'm determined to escape?

Weslyn takes a step closer, and finally I relent, if only to prevent him from getting too near. I keep my back turned to him and lift my shirt to my navel, revealing the bandaged sword wound.

Helos peels away the wrapping as delicately as he can, but I still have to grit my teeth while he works. "It looks clean," he announces, examining the cut. "Just healing."

"Great. So we can keep moving."

He shakes his head. "We should stop for the night. You're in pain."

"No need," I reply. "I can handle it."

"Be reasonable."

"I *am* being reasonable. You're the one letting emotion cloud your judgment. As usual."

"By the river, Rora—"

"One night," Weslyn says, stepping between us with a compromise. "We'll stop early one night. What about over there?" He points to a cave mouth just visible to the west.

As dark clouds have been rolling in overhead, finding shelter is likely not a bad idea. "It could be all right," I concede with as much dignity as I can muster.

"Unless someone else is living there," Helos mutters.

Weak, my brain whispers. *Weak. Weak.*

I clutch the hem of my shirt, tired of that voice.

Weslyn scratches the back of his head. "Maybe we should check it out, then."

"*You* stay here." Helos sheds his pack roughly. "*You* check nothing. Rora, keep an eye on the horizon."

With that, he breezes toward the cave, presumably to search the darkness with his fox eyes, ears, and nose.

Weslyn and I stand without speaking, studiously avoiding each other's gaze. I monitor the perimeter, then glance back at Weslyn, who's crossing his arms, then swatting at bugs, then dragging a foot along the ground. It seems he doesn't like feeling useless any more than I do.

I bite my lip, then decide. "You can't let your attention linger on one spot for too long. When you're scouting," I add, noting his puzzled expression. "Keep your eyes moving and your ears open. Help me look. Please."

He waits, appraising me silently, as if trying to determine whether the request is genuine.

"I can't look everywhere at once, and I don't really fancy being eaten today. Join me or don't." I turn away.

Weslyn doesn't reply, but in my peripheries I catch the new alertness in his posture, the way his wordlessness changes to a different kind of silence.

I work my mouth back into a straight line.

When Helos returns with the all clear, we pick our way over to the cave. The round, uneven monolith juts out from a grassy ridge, its stone walls red-toned and ribboned with white and pale pink sedimentary bands. Moss hugs the walls to either side of the entrance, while delicate ferns grow in swaying lines below.

Inside, the stone's color skews more tan than pink. With strands of sunlight kindling half the main cavern in watery light, I circle the various rock shelves protruding from the sides, then the shallow basin of water set into the smooth floor. A thick, clear liquid creeps down the walls farther back. I examine it more closely. Pine sap.

"It's a good find," I tell Weslyn, the words blunted, slightly muffled by the stone. Though the cave narrows to a recess farther back, the space beyond it is too dark to make out.

Helos picks a spot to skin and gut the rabbit he caught, while I collect sticks for a fire outside. Seated a short distance away, Weslyn divides his time between watching us work and doing something with his hands that I can't see—he's blocked the view with his pack. Reading, maybe. The rabbit is restorative when cooked, but no sooner have we all finished eating than Helos pushes to his feet and grabs his pack.

"I'm going to look for a plant that will help with the pain while we have the light."

I watch him shoulder his bag and smooth his hair back, crackling with unspent energy.

"You don't have to rush off," I protest. "You shouldn't—"

"Stay here," he says.

Then he's gone.

The air in the cave hangs close and cold, and carries a faint sound of dripping water. Without looking at Weslyn, I shuffle to the side to rest my back against one of the entrance walls. The movement is difficult to endure, but the relief the added support brings is already immense.

Weak—

Stop it, I say, silencing the voice. It feels good to rest.

Helos shrinks as he recedes farther into the distance, then disappears from view entirely. I study the spot where he vanished.

"I'm sorry," Weslyn says, claiming my attention. He's bent over what I have now determined to be the leather-bound book. The one he writes in. Hair curling loosely over his forehead, he gestures to my stomach with his pen. "I should have been more careful."

"I'm really okay," I reply, massaging my temples with my palms.

He snorts. "You sound like my brother."

Dropping my hands, I glance at him sharply, taking in the neutral set of his features. For a moment, I thought the stoic soldier prince had actually smiled.

"Can you not heal yourself?" he asks, shifting the conversation away from his family.

I resume my massage and shut my eyes. "No."

A sliver of wind whistles through the cave's opening, lifting my hair from my shoulders. The air carries the scent of rain to come.

"Why?"

Though I raise my eyebrows pointedly, he appears unfazed by my annoyance. Typical royal.

"Shifting requires a certain amount of give-and-take," I say. "In order to change my features, I have to change my body's composition. And if part of that becomes damaged or goes missing, I can't just create a permanent replacement out of nothing. So I can't heal myself."

"I don't understand."

The note in his voice relaxes me a little. As if his questions are truly just that: questions. Not accusations, like I've grown accustomed to whenever my shifter nature comes up. I start again in a calmer voice.

"As long as I've seen a person at least once, I can shift to assume their form. To do this, I can change the shape of my eyes, or my nose, or my mouth. I can grow taller or make myself shorter. I can lengthen my hair or my waist. I can change my bones if I want to." I brace myself for a flinch, a grimace—some sign of apprehension to color his face. Nothing comes. "All of those parts are made of matter, so making them bigger means taking on more, and making them smaller means getting rid of some. Since I can't create matter from nothing, I have to either borrow from the world around me or shed some of my own for a while."

"You borrow it."

Now he does look a little skeptical. Irked, I wave my hand for him to scoot closer. After a minor hesitation, he sets down the pen and sits opposite me.

As it had this morning, his sudden nearness feels strange, the calm energy unfamiliar. Like we're friends having a normal conversation, not two people with one mutual friend and a history of avoiding each other. But he's here, so I point to a spot on the cave floor and tell him to watch it carefully. "Look there, not at me," I repeat, when his eyes wander back to my face. Frowning, he stares at the ground as instructed.

Warmth rushes through my body, and I feel my waist shrink and my feet lengthen, curly hair hitting midway down my spine.

There's a hole in the stone Weslyn is studying.

He jerks backward and stares at me, eyes widening as he takes in Ansley's face, then the rest of her duplicated body. "What did you do?"

"I borrowed from the rock." I hold my long tresses out for him to see. "Usually I'd pull from multiple spots, not just the one, so you wouldn't even know anything's missing. Or the air; that one is unnoticeable."

"Deceptive," he says, but his voice is traced with light. Almost like respect, but that makes no sense. Weslyn holds little regard for my shifting abilities. He's made that clear enough.

I nod at the hole. "Now watch it again."

This time, I don't have to remind him to keep his gaze in place.

The dip in the stone becomes smooth once more as my body returns to its natural form. A shiver passes through me.

"You gave it back," Weslyn observes, leaning on his hands and watching me curiously.

"Matter always returns to its original source sooner or later. It pulls back of its own accord. The longest I've ever held on to borrowed matter was two days, and it was exhausting." I mirror his posture, resuming my position against the wall. "I can't heal myself, because to replace damaged or missing parts, I would have to borrow matter. And nothing borrowed can remain a part of me forever. To heal myself that way would be to enter an eternal, draining cycle of pulling and releasing. There'd be no point to it."

Neither of us speaks again for a short while. I take a few swigs of water when Weslyn returns to his pen and book, then pull some dried raspberries from my pack, relishing the tartness that lingers on my tongue. A raven alights on a branch outside, and my thoughts turn to its magical counterpart, a black-tipped caw with feathers thin and sharp as rapiers. That's the one that should be out there.

"Does it hurt?" Weslyn asks, as if we've been talking this whole time. It's clear he isn't referring to the wound.

I place the fruit down slowly. "No one has ever asked me that. Except Finley."

"He asked?"

"Yes. The day we met."

Weslyn's definitely smiling now, though only a little, as his attention shifts to the horizon. "That sounds like Fin."

"He was always kind to me," I continue, while I still have the nerve. The implication behind the words hangs clear enough. *Unlike you.*

Weslyn holds my gaze for a long moment before replying. "He thinks a lot of you and your brother. Always has."

It's a jolt to the system to hear him admit that, a confession I didn't expect—and don't entirely understand, given Helos's recent expulsion. The ban—has Finley told his brother the reason behind it? I search Weslyn's face for a clue, but none comes. "You haven't."

The river take me, those were not the words I meant to say. But they're out now, can't take them back. Nerves buzzing, I watch the brief light fade from his face, hard edges regaining their hold.

Weslyn looks down at his book. "It's complicated."

"How?" I press. *It's complicated*—the same excuse he used for keeping us politically in the dark. But this time, my prodding doesn't work. Weslyn cloaks himself in silence, unpersuaded, immovable as stone.

You don't know him, Finley had said, and he was right. But I was right when I said that everything about him is harder. A few tentative steps toward breaking the wall between us, and already, it's rebuilding. I cast about for something else to say, reluctant to leave it there now that we've begun, and when there's still so much road ahead. "I think a lot of Finley," I settle on, since he seems the safer topic, "but I get the sense he doesn't care what people think one way or another."

It works—Weslyn nods, back on stable ground. "He has always known how to ignore the voices around him. A fault, perhaps. Or a talent." His breath huffs out, an amused sound, as his fingers toy with the sticks reserved for feeding a fire. "It drives Violet a bit mad, but I think my father pities him. Training for a life of diplomatic functions, standing in at ceremonies, perhaps marrying for political advantage."

I bite the inside of my cheek.

"My sister was born to rule. Fin couldn't care less." He says it with a touch of humor, which hints at his own feelings on the matter, I think. Then he drops the sticks. Regretting his openness, perhaps, or remembering his brother's future looks different now.

Finley's easy laughter rings in my ears. The way his distractable gaze gleams like topaz in the sunshine, always moving, always searching. The times he hid with the horses or shadowed the gardeners, stablehands, and kennelmasters working the grounds, determined to be out of doors and out of sight of the court. "He told me he wants to go to university."

Weslyn's chin tilts upward, as if he's surprised his brother would entrust me with this scrap of information. "He does."

And something about the way he says it, the way he's at his books every night, makes me ask, "Do you?"

He drops his eyes and looks away, out to where the trembling leaves catch the light of the sun. "I did."

It seems we have fallen back into personal territory, the kind that shuts him down. But as he's just interrogated me, I feel it's only fair. "That's why you read so much."

He shrugs and turns his head away. Only a little, but still I catch it, and now I'm the one who's left surprised. He rarely acts uncomfortable in front of me.

"Why didn't you?"

Weslyn doesn't answer straightaway, just continues to stare into the distance. Certain I've blown it again, I wait a few moments before searching for the object of his scrutiny.

"In light of the mounting tension with Eradain, my father has spent the last three years strengthening our army." His voice has dropped quieter. Softer. "Increased recruiting efforts, more tax and treasury funds delegated to weaponry, food supplies, training. Alemara's three realms have never warred internally since their foundation, you know. But to me, war seems inevitable now."

Unfortunately, I'm inclined to agree. It's like a flower blooming in reverse, the way the realms are folding in on themselves. The petals curl inward and down.

"One of us had to serve," he continues, "and it wasn't going to be Violet. Not as the crown heir."

I say nothing when our eyes connect again, but I don't bother hiding my surprise.

His mouth twists into a half smile. "I gave my father plenty of reasons why I should accompany you. Presented a case he wouldn't be able to ignore, and I figured it could be useful, anyway—there's only so much you can learn in a castle. But I would have come regardless." The smile vanishes. "I would do anything for Fin."

I'm staring at him long after he's looked away again.

From the way Finley admires him, and the times I've watched Weslyn soften toward Fin, I suppose I knew the two of them were close. But I've never understood it. They're too different—the light and the dark, showy and solemn, playful and reserved. Fin is a wandering soul, the spinning needle on a compass, while Weslyn is the fixed point north—grounded, unyielding. But the pieces before me now are hinting at a different picture, one that doesn't match up with the arrogant, entitled person I have always thought him to be. "Why are you telling me all this?"

His brow furrows a little. "I don't know." And there it is again, that strange quirk of the mouth, almost like a genuine smile. Again. "You didn't answer my question."

I blink a couple of times before tracing a tiny tear in my pants. The black dye is fading, the fabric wearing thin on the knees and thighs. Some ridiculous part of me feels like I owe him more than an answer in light of his honesty. Like an assertion that I would do anything for my brother, too. Like a confession that I once left him to die instead. I can't bring myself to admit either.

"It doesn't hurt," I murmur at last. "No."

By the time Helos returns—with the herbs, two freshly caught rabbits, *and* another bundle of sticks, fortune's sake—the sky is growing dark. He smiles a little when he reaches me, but there's a shadow lurking beneath the gesture. He's tired.

"Cat's tongue," he says by way of explanation, waving the stalks of small, rounded pink leaves in his hand. "It doesn't grow east of the river. Chew a small amount into a pulp and apply that to the wound. It will help with the pain."

I take the proffered herbs and thank him as he walks away and drops the rabbits near Weslyn, who's reading the black book once more. Weslyn starts a little when the bodies hit the ground beside him.

"Let me do that," I say, pushing to my feet, as my brother starts rebuilding the fire. He shakes his head. "Come on. You've been out walking and hunting while we've sat and done nothing. I want to do it."

"I'm fine," he insists, a bit too sharply to be believable.

"Helos—"

"Make your salve, Rora."

Frustrated, I sink down opposite him and place a couple of leaves in my mouth, probably chewing with more force than necessary. Helos grabs a few bits of tinder and pulls the trowel, flint, and knife from his pack. I track his weary movements relentlessly, pausing only to press the mushy leaves onto the cut.

I'm tempted to ask if he, too, has thought of Finley. During the long, silent treks, I've reflected often on our exchange in the Old Forest, his confession to a fight but nothing more. My mind has cycled through recent memories searching for clues—a prolonged glance between them here, a touch on the shoulder there, whispered words, and the kind of laughter that emerges only when the other is around. Finley's guilt, Helos's quiet sadness. *The answer is no.*

The picture they come together to suggest does not surprise me. Helos and Finley, two sides of the same leaf. Always. It's my own stupidity that's exasperating, my inability to see what was right there before my eyes.

It's that Finley said no.

But even though I have watched my brother for any signs of heartbreak or conflict within, up until crossing the river, his step was as lively as ever. It's maddening. I can probably count the number of things my brother has ever hidden from me on one hand, yet this is one truth he refuses to entrust to me.

No, if he does suffer any uncertainty or sorrow, if he, too, is having a resurgence of nightmares—nightmares that haven't surfaced for quite some time—he seems determined to bury them.

Helos lays out bark and leaves, but he has barely started assembling when Weslyn walks over and squats in front of us. Despite the delicate peace we seem to have struck, I eye him warily.

"Show me," he says. "Please."

Helos looks at him, then at the tinder, then back at him. "What, how to make a fire?"

Weslyn nods.

My brother studies him a moment longer, then hands him the trowel. "We start by digging."

Weslyn drops his knees to the dirt and digs until Helos tells him to stop.

The cat's tongue goes to work quickly. The sharp stabbing pains recede to a dull ache, and my mind begins to dim when remnants of the drug hit my bloodstream. I spread my wool cloak across the cold stone shelf beneath me, which helps reduce the chill seeping into my legs, even if it doesn't much soften the seating. We've each claimed a spot in the cave, me on a low-hanging rock shelf, Helos and Weslyn on opposite ends of the floor. A small fire crackles near the water basin—more practice for Weslyn.

Though afternoon light still filters into the cave, the cat's tongue and the smell of the fire are lulling me toward sleep. When something cracks outside, my ears only snatch at the tendrils of sound with fading resolve. I drift in and out of consciousness, chin drooping, limbs sinking into heaviness.

The cavern begins to tremble.

I snap awake. My gaze connects with Weslyn's, then falls to Helos.

"Out!" my brother says, right as the wood supporting the fire collapses. We snatch our things and hasten toward the entrance, but the ground outside has begun to rise.

"Wait!" I cry, grabbing their shirts from behind as sharp-peaked stones tear through the dirt just beyond the cave mouth. The boulders soar upward faster than the raven flies, scraping against the cave's outer shell, cutting off our escape.

The jagged pillars crest the cave mouth, and the cavern plunges into darkness.

TWELVE

The rumbling subsides.

Our haggard breathing severs the quiet.

"We need to make a torch," I manage, gesturing to the smoldering twigs scattered across the floor. The sparks won't catch on stone, but the flames will soon go out.

At once, Helos stops pushing on the boulders and hurries to the stack of spare wood. Weslyn is still staring at the blocked entrance. Of course. This kind of thing is still new to him.

"Come on," I tell him, wresting his gaze away from the stones. "We'll have to find another way out."

Not waiting for his reply, I reach up to scrape moss from the entrance walls. He watches me work a moment, then rummages through his pack and offers me a stretch of cloth.

"Use this."

"Tear it into strips," I instruct, relieved to see he isn't panicking. "We'll need fuel. And something to bind it with."

"I don't suppose you have wire in that bottomless pack of yours," Helos grumbles.

Weslyn crouches at Helos's side shortly after. He has wire.

"The sap," I say, remembering abruptly. "There's sap on the walls farther back."

"In a cave?" Weslyn's skeptical.

"Don't ask me to explain it." I head for the back, then have to catch myself against a rock shelf when my vision teeters. The cursed drug is pulling at my consciousness. I slap the sides of my face.

"Drink some water," Helos says, breezing past me to soak the cotton in sap. "It should dilute the effects." He dips the torch in the dying embers, and the top flares to life.

With impatient hands, I find my waterskin and down several gulps, then kneel to examine the pool of clear liquid collected in the basin. It gives off a sharp scent. "Nobody drink this," I warn, stomach sinking. "I don't think it's actually water."

Weslyn's forehead creases in the wavering light. "How much do you both have in your waterskins?"

He reports three-quarters full, while Helos's nearly reaches the top. Mine is half empty.

A danger that has nothing to do with threats or injuries.

"Well, that dripping is coming from somewhere," I reason, forcing myself to stay calm. "There might be water farther back."

"What did you find when you searched there?" Weslyn asks.

Helos hesitates. "No water that I remember."

"Then what exactly is making that sound?"

The rhythm plagues the heavy silence that follows. *Drip. Drip. Drip. Drip.*

"Come on." Helos quirks his head toward the cave's narrowing. "I didn't scout the whole place, just checked for other inhabitants. There might be a back door." Torch in hand, he leads the way without waiting for a response.

Weslyn only gestures for me to follow, then falls into step behind.

There's no easy path through the funnel-shaped passageway. Rock formations jut out of the ground like pointed teeth, their undulating sides reminiscent of hardened candle wax. We navigate around them, endeavoring to ignore the mirror image above our heads—dozens of triangles at varying lengths, most little wider than icicles.

"Step quietly," I whisper. "While we pass. Just in case." Since the fire's glow stretches only a short way ahead, we can't tell when the tunnel will end.

Please let the ground remain still.

Above and below, torchlight bounces off the rocky icicles, creating the impression that some of the points are twitching. The illusion disorients my already muddled mind. My eyelids keep drooping of their own accord, and my feet feel clumsy, weighted down. Knowing the danger of dulled reflexes, I take a few more sips of my precious water supply.

Fortunately, the tunnel has been widening around us. Soon the ceiling drops away, and the space broadens into an expansive cavern. My nose wrinkles against a metallic tang in the air, but Helos only leads us forward, bootsteps echoing. The dripping noise has faded away.

Near the center, upright stones the size of timber bears have collected in a loose ring. For reasons I can't explain, the hair rises along the back of my neck as we step inside the strange circle, scouring for an exit. The massive obsidian blocks flicker eerily in the dancing torchlight—or maybe that's just the drug.

"Up there." I point to a gap near the cavern's domed ceiling, trying to shake the dizziness away. *Focus.* "There's a hole in the wall. It might be large enough to pass through."

"We would have to get up there first," Helos replies, circling the walls for another exit. The opening I spotted is a good two stories above our heads.

Acute awareness of my winged form teases my thoughts, but I push the selfish notion away. We need a route that works for all of us.

"We could climb," Weslyn suggests quietly.

I follow his gaze to the rock shelves stepped along the sloping walls. My back tenses. Though there appear to be enough footholds to get us from here to the hole up top, many of them slant downward, and some are less substantial than others. One stretch scarcely juts out from the wall at all.

"It might work," Helos concedes, sounding more confident about the hand-sized footholds than they merit. He glances at me sidelong. "How's your head?"

"Getting better." I sip on the water again. The drowsiness is finally starting to fade, thank fortune. But as clarity grows, so does the pain.

"We'll wait a little longer. Don't want you falling and cracking your skull." He pauses, watching me carefully. "Or you could fly."

"I'll climb," I say firmly. "But what about the light? It doesn't stretch very far."

Helos tugs at the short sleeves of his dark shirt, the coverage scant in the cave's crisp air. Weslyn has already freed his from their usual roll above the forearm. "We'll just have to go slowly," my brother responds at last, sounding doubtful.

I rub the tender stretch of my stomach.

"Rora, fly up there," he says, more insistent now. "It makes the most sense."

"No." I drop my hand, furious he noticed.

"There's no point in all of us risking the climb if the opening is a dead end. You can tell us what you see."

"I'm not leaving you down here!"

"The fire will light two sets of feet more easily than three." Helos pushes his hair behind his ears. "Please, Rora. For me."

In the shadow of the obsidian blocks, Weslyn watches us spar without comment.

Having an audience only makes the shame hit harder. I know my brother is right, and that my resistance must sound juvenile to an outsider like Weslyn. But he doesn't understand how the situation feels too similar to that horrible day I swore never to repeat—the day I gained my goshawk form. The waves and the distant head sputtering for air, memories that set my body aching even now.

Common sense, I decide at last, shedding my bag and ignoring the tightness at the base of my throat. *Not selfishness. There's a difference between them.*

Once I've stripped and repacked my clothes in the privacy of a stone, it takes little more than a moment to fly up and into the opening. Fluttering my wings for stability, I perch on the edge and peer inside.

"What do you see?" Helos calls.

After hopping farther in, I pull from the cramped air and shift to lynx to study the hole. My whiskers brush the sloping walls, but it should be wide enough. I shift back to human. "There's a passageway," I call down, the tear in my stomach stinging fiercely. The stone sets a sharp chill into my bare skin. "It's very narrow, but I think we can use it. I saw a bit of light near the other end."

"We're coming up then," Helos says. "Stay there."

The boys begin to climb.

Helos maintains the lead, torch in hand, his worn boots sliding across the stone more than once. Each time they slip hits like a dagger through the heart. If he falls, smashing into one of those obsidian blocks could break his neck.

Since Helos carries the light, Weslyn has slung my pack across his own shoulder. The closeness makes me a bit uncomfortable, but all I can do is follow their progress from shelf to shelf, their bootsteps scraping in the quiet.

When they're maybe three-quarters up the wall, they both pause.

It's the tricky bit I spotted from below, not far now beneath my shadowed opening. I poke my head out farther, lips pressed tight. The ledge they have to cross is only five or six paces long, but it's scarcely wider than two hands put together. The drop is a long way down.

"Hug the wall," I suggest, hoping I successfully masked the tremor in my voice.

"We'll be—"

But whatever Helos was starting to say cuts off as a shudder runs through the walls.

The vibration buzzes against my back.

"Hurry up!" I say. "You're almost here!"

But it's as if the very walls are echoing my uncertainty. Earthquake or just a trick of the Vale, the stony chamber quivers with affected nerves, loosing a few jagged rocks from the ceiling. They crumble and clatter against the floor, smacking the ground like pellets of hail. The torchlight flinches when one of the pieces strikes Helos's arm.

"Come on!" Weslyn shouts against the din. Though his expression remains determined, nervous sweat is shining along his brow. "I'll hold the torch. My shoes have better traction."

Helos hands it over with a glance up at my face. His is morphing into a landscape of fear.

Feeling utterly helpless, *useless,* I can only watch as Weslyn shuffles in front of Helos, then sweeps his free hand across the trembling wall. Clearly, he's searching for a handhold to latch on to, but the rock face is maliciously slick. He abandons the search and just presses his palm against the wall, keeping the torch in the hand closest to Helos. With my teeth rattling between clenched jaws, mouse fur threatens to poke through my skin as Weslyn steps out onto the ledge.

"Almost there," I call, as the two of them sidestep along the shelf.

As soon as Weslyn reaches the other, wider side, he sheds my pack and tosses it up into the hole with his free hand. Then he finds a notch in the wall, grabs it, and leans back over to light Helos's path.

My brother takes another step, but his boot doesn't stick. It slips.

"Helos!" I scream as his body teeters away from the wall. His arms spiral, foot hitting nothing but air, all of it happening too fast, *too fast.* Weslyn makes a grab for him, and the abandoned torch splinters on the ground below, the impact echoing through the cavern.

The walls stop shaking as the light goes out.

"Helos?" I breathe into the newfound silence, hopeful and terrified all at once. The space is overwhelmingly black, the fire remnants dwindling to the barest glow.

"We're okay."

It's Weslyn voice, sounding tight with exertion.

It's a miracle, and I bite back a sob, throwing on clothing as quickly as I can. Then I pop my head back out to listen while they feel their way along the wall.

"Grab my hands," I say, still regaining my panicked breath, ignoring my stomach and extending my arms as far as they'll go. "I'll pull you up toward the hole. Can you feel them?"

Labored breathing cuts through the dark. The sound of rubber soles scraping stone. Then—pressure on my palm, the hand wide and calloused, unfamiliar. Sticky with blood where it clutched the wall.

Involuntarily, my muscles lock up.

You don't touch her again, Helos commanded. *Understand?* But there's Weslyn's palm against mine, trapping my fingers firmly between his own, and Helos is doing nothing.

I find his other hand and haul him up.

Weslyn squeezes in next to me, swearing when his head bumps the wall.

"Careful," I mutter, releasing my grip. The muscles in my abdomen are screaming. "You can scoot a little way down. It isn't very steep."

I reach back out for Helos while Weslyn moves farther into the opening, his shoulder grazing my arm in the narrow space. Familiar hands find mine, and then my brother is there beside me. His palms are shaking.

"Nice try," I say at last with false cheer. "But no one here is dying today."

I can hear his ragged smile in the blackness.

"What now?" Weslyn asks, the space around us painfully close. "You said there's a passageway?"

"It's narrow, I couldn't actually see the end. But it must let out somewhere—you can see a faint light."

Though now that I'm looking with human eyes, there really doesn't seem to be any light at all.

Weslyn says nothing.

"I'll go first," I decide, sliding forward on my rear. My foot connects with some part of him, and I yank my leg back, startled, clenching my teeth at the pain in my stomach.

"Be careful," Helos warns, his voice rather faint. "Weslyn, you go next. I'll bring up the rear."

Curse it. I pull from the air and heal my stomach, stitching it shut with new skin. Just until we're out, I reason. The aching fades at once.

Slowly, using my hands and feet to craft a picture in my mind, I move my pack to my front side and slide forward once more. The stone scrapes roughly against my arms, the air cool and slightly stale on my tongue. Wordlessly, Weslyn shuffles behind me.

As we progress through the tunnel, the undulating sides narrow and widen at irregular intervals, the resultant gap so small at times that I have to lay back to fit through. In an effort to ease some of the crackling tension, I do my best to narrate the path as I go, warning the boys when the tunnel bends or constricts. The muffled words hang close.

It would be easier to navigate this as a mouse, of course. But I never consider making the shift. Weslyn's silence is speaking volumes to me.

"You know," Helos mutters through gritted teeth. "I have a strange feeling Finley would enjoy this."

I almost smile in spite of the circumstances. He would.

Gradually, the space brightens enough to see the outlines of my hands. When at last, the tunnel lets out onto an open ledge, I slide onto the flat rock face and wait for them to emerge. It's lighter out here, though still indisputably dim, and I note the vastness of the space and the rush of running water somewhere below. Water—we must be close to an exit. Relief rushes through me.

Weslyn slips out next. He switches his pack onto his back and scoots straight to the opposite end of the ledge, as far from me as possible. I don't take it personally. His movements seem very tight.

"Is your hand okay?" I ask, realizing I should probably just ask if *he's* okay. I promised Finley he would be. I want to thank him for saving Helos, for carrying my pack, but even in the comforting mask of darkness, I still don't really know how to talk to him.

"It's fine," Weslyn replies shortly. He's looking away.

Helos emerges last, blinking at the newfound glow. Probably because he's the tallest, his arms look a little more scraped up than ours, but otherwise he seems all right. Better than all right, really. *Alive.*

"Look at this," he breathes, moving right to the edge.

The cavern before us is at least three times the size of the one with the obsidian stones. While that had held only bare rock and metallic air, this has the look of an enclosed forest—a tangled heap of trees down below, taller and broader-topped than the Vale's native conifers, with vegetation crowding the bases and sprawling

ivy clinging to the surrounding walls like spiderwebs. A broad
stream winds through the forest and out, then disappears into a
dark tunnel set into the wall opposite our ledge. Around us, spo-
radic birdsong spirals through the air, and in a far corner—

Cursed fortune.

"Do you see that dark mass over there?" I lean forward to look
at Weslyn. "Up against the ceiling?"

After a moment, Weslyn peers up to where I'm pointing. "Bats?"

"Widow bats," I correct him. "They have—"

"Toxic saliva."

I blink in surprise.

"That's what you said yesterday, right?"

"I—that's right," I reply, addled, and he nods. "We'll have to be
careful not to disturb them."

The three of us pick our way down the rocky slope connecting
our ledge with the ground. Once down, we hesitate on the outskirts
of the forest, unspoken wariness threading between us.

"I don't see how this could grow here," Weslyn says quietly.
"There's no sun."

"And where is this murky light coming from?" Helos adds.

Sweat is already beading along my face in the hot, humid air. I
shake my head. "Come on. I think I see a way out."

Sticking close to the outer wall rather than cutting through the
trees, I circle around to the stretch of black water that flows through
a ravine and into a tunnel. The stream only spans five or so paces
across, and the current doesn't look strong. "It has to lead somewhere, right? Otherwise it would be stagnant."

Helos dips a hand in. "Cool, but not too cold."

"The lake?"

He nods. "I reckon so."

"Our packs would get wet," I muse. "We'd have to lay them out
to dry."

"Overnight should do it. We could light a fire to help them along."

Realizing the third member of our party hasn't spoken in a
while, I twist toward Weslyn to gauge his thoughts.

His face is ashen.

"What do you think?" I ask, feeling an unexpected twinge of pity.

He stares at the water, then the tunnel it flows into—maybe ten paces high—the details inside too dark to make out. After a while, his attention falls to me.

"You want to ride the stream," he says flatly.

I nod. "We think it lets out at the lake."

"You think."

"Yes."

"But you're not certain."

Helos scrapes a foot along the ground, watching the bats.

"Can you swim?" I ask.

Weslyn folds his arms, his shoulders taut. "Yes, but I'm not sure if—"

He breaks off when the trees begin to sway.

One heartbeat. Two. Three. Four. That's how long they bend in one direction before swerving back the other way. The trunks creak and snap under the canopy's shifting weight, wood groaning in a ghostly drawl, broad leaves hissing as they scrape against one another. With a flurry of high-pitched cheeping, yellow-bellied tanagers erupt from the wood on frantic wings. Back and forth, the forest sways.

Helos throws his arms behind his head and says, "Shit."

The word has hardly left his mouth when the colony of widow bats shudders awake. Suspended from the ceiling in a far corner, the dark mass ripples like a perverse mirror of the stream. It's impossible to judge how many there are. Two hundred at least, likely more.

"We have to move!" I say at once, jumping back to the water's edge. My hair sweeps across my face in the wind churning forth from the shaking wood.

Helos squats beside the stream, ready to lower himself in. But despite the commotion, Weslyn still hesitates.

A few of the bats drop out of the close-knit colony, shrieking at the swaying trees.

"Get in!" Helos shouts.

"What if it dead-ends?" Weslyn counters.

"This entire cavern is about to be covered in *giant toxic webs*. You want to die here?"

"You have no idea where this leads!"

"I know what will happen here if we stay!"

After the trees' next rotation, the colony decides it's had enough. Hundreds of bats peel away from the ceiling in a dark, flapping, shrieking mass.

"Remember what I told you," I shout at Weslyn. "Staying alive means listening to Helos and me!" Then I shove him into the water.

Strands of white saliva beam across the swaying woods, laying a patchwork of solid lines that weave together like rope. The treetops begin to smolder, but that's all I see before the stream sweeps us into the tunnel.

In the sudden blackness, keeping my eyes open or closed makes no difference. Only the cool air sweeping my face and the babbling rhythm of the water, magnified in the stone chamber, tells me we're moving forward. My sodden boots hang heavy and uncomfortable as my legs churn the dark stream to counter the weight of my pack. To my relief, by the time I've counted to fifty, the space around us has brightened considerably. Light floods in when the ceiling drops away, and before I have time to assess what's ahead, we plunge down a tiny waterfall.

Trapped.

For an endless moment, I have been buried alive, dragged under by the force of the drop and the stream cascading overhead. Fighting panic, I struggle to the surface and gulp in air, circling my arms against the downward pull of the pack. Helos and Weslyn emerge heartbeats later, spitting water and scraping wetness from their eyes.

We're back in the lake.

Though we must have spent hours inside the cave, twilight blue still hangs in the air. Crickets chirp a relentless tune, a welcome to usher us back to the outside world. Clinging to the noise like a lifeline, I swim the short distance to shore, my boots scraping stones from the soft, sandy bottom when it becomes shallow enough to walk. Helos and I pull ourselves onto the bank in synchronized motion, followed, soon after, by Weslyn.

"Not even a hill," Helos grumbles, shaking his hair dry and nodding over to where the stream spat us out. A few damp strands have stuck to his face.

He's right; that last cavern was huge, practically the height of Castle Roanin's central atrium, but the land around the lake barely rises higher than ant hills. I roll my eyes, wringing the water from my shirt.

"Are you okay?" he asks Weslyn, who hasn't risen from the ground.

Weslyn doesn't meet his gaze. "Fine," he mutters.

"I'll build the fire, then." Helos makes for the tree line.

I watch my brother go, the spring already returning to his step—remarkable. But I don't follow. Weslyn's expression by the water's edge, before we rode the stream, remains fresh in my mind. Shivering a little in my waterlogged clothes, I pace over to where he's still sitting back on his heels.

He's breathing rather heavily, drenched clothes clinging like a second skin. Winding his fingers through the weed stalks, he stares into the forest with unfocused eyes and doesn't seem to notice me standing there. He's tossed his pack aside as if it bites.

"Only so much you can learn in a castle, right?" I say at last. And then, remembering the river crossing, I shake aside the strangeness of it and offer a hand to help him up.

Weslyn keeps his eyes on the sodden ground. But he takes it.

THIRTEEN

Things are different the next day. We still exchange few words as we walk, but it's a slightly easier sort of silence. At least there are no walls to hold us here.

Dawn has scarcely broken when we leave the lapping shore to our right and continue our trek through the patchy forest. Black bugs nip and flit around us, sensing a meal, their wings catching the light of the sun. Helos made me another salve after I released the matter holding my wound together, but this time I've applied it sparingly, wishing to remain as alert as possible.

As we walk, I begin pointing things out to Weslyn—an upturned root, the brand of moss that burns rubber soles, sugar-laced pine-cones, and a razor-winged, black-tipped caw on a branch. Taking the fire request as a cue, I'm teaching our third to observe his surroundings.

Weslyn rarely comments, just listens quietly. Prior to this journey, I'd only ever seen him in the bustling castle or among a retinue of staffers or guards. Away from all that, though, I'm finding he's an introspective sort, less vocal when not required to lead. After a while Helos joins in, too, though judging by his indifferent tone, it's more for the sake of complementing my efforts than any genuine interest in Weslyn's outdoor education.

"Look here," I say midafternoon, pacing over to a thick, tall shrub covered in yellow-white blossoms and teardrop leaves.

Weslyn steps to my side and cradles a tubelike flower between two fingers. "Honeysuckle." He nods with a faint smile. "We have these back home."

"You have a variation on them," I clarify. "The nectar in southern honeysuckle is sweet to drink, but not much more. These contain an added benefit." With a gentle touch, I choose a flower and peel back the petals, revealing the tiny white bead inside. "Honeysuckle pearls. They melt like powder on your tongue and will cure the worst headache."

"Who taught you that?"

"Helos."

My brother smiles in a vaguely distracted manner, scratching the back of his head.

"Try one," I suggest, choosing an untouched flower and sucking the nectar from its depths. The little pearl dissolves with a sweet floral aftertaste.

Weslyn's eyebrows arch as he runs his tongue along his teeth. "My mouth feels numb."

"That will only last a moment."

Nodding again, he studies the shrub, the corners of his mouth sinking lower. "Do they travel well? If I pick a few."

It takes a little while for me to understand. "For Finley?"

He looks at me, a bit of sadness in his gaze.

"You can store them in this," Helos says, producing a small vial like the one that holds the cat's tongue. "I brought a few from the shop. It's worth a try."

He shows Weslyn where to break the stems, and we gather a small collection.

By the time evening falls, we've long passed the southernmost point of the lake. Once again, few animals and no people have crossed our path, and again, their absence sparks a warning in me. I wrap my cloak around my shoulders in the cool mountain night air and attempt to dismiss it as luck.

Weslyn asks to take first watch, which Helos overrules on the basis of experience. He does build the fire, though, under our supervision, and my brother even offers him a compliment on fast learning. Amazing the difference a couple of weeks living out-doors can make.

Since the stars tonight are impossible to see through the canopy and clouds, I roll onto my side, away from the fire and watchful eyes. Sleep seems a difficult feat out here, but my awareness drifts into nonsense before I can revisit all the usual haunts, and soon enough I'm flying over mountains and far out at sea.

I wake with a start.

I'm not sure how long I've been asleep. The firelight glows softer than before, but the flames still snap like thunder cracks, punctur-ing the screams lingering in my head. My heart is pounding force-fully enough to wake the forest. Dimly, I realize my face is wet.

Prior to this journey, it had been a long time since I'd woken up with tears on my cheeks. This is the fourth time it's happened in two weeks.

Every night, I watch my home burn over and over, the flames coming close enough to lick my skin. I don't know how much of what I imagine is even real; my brain forges the details I can't remember. I scream as faceless shadows fling Helos from one of the tree bridges. I feel their hands on my shoulder, ready to cast me in after him.

Tonight's dream is already fading, but I know the river loomed large, its black waves closing resolutely over Helos's head.

Moving ever so slowly, I wipe the tears from my eyes, dreading the thought of Weslyn catching me in this state. I have no desire to fall back into nightmares, but still sleep finds me quickly. As I'm drifting in and out of consciousness, I almost think I hear notes that don't belong—a melody low and soothing. I'm gone before I can capture it.

"Hold on," Helos warns, stepping up beside me.

After another uneventful morning, we have reached the edge of a meadow studded with alpine flowers and windblown grass. The mist that sheathes the giants' realm shouldn't be too far beyond the other side; if we're lucky, we might reach it today.

Using a hand to shade my forehead, I strain my senses to scan the meadow's periphery. Beneath an unbroken blue sky, a mass of wheat-colored stalks converges near the grassy center, crowned with swaying violet globes and nearly waist-high from the look of it. Shorter ones are studded throughout the rest of the field, their blossoms more lilac than violet.

"Is something wrong?" Weslyn asks, stepping closer and fisting the straps of his pack.

Helos squats to smell the flowers lining the outskirts. "I don't recognize these."

I twist to Weslyn. "This meadow wasn't here before."

"Is that a problem?" he asks, running a hand through his curls. "It looks empty enough from here."

"Empty of large animals, maybe," I reply. "Not empty of life."

"Let's go around," Helos suggests, rising to his feet and rolling his shoulders back. "It's probably not worth the risk."

I'm inclined to agree. With a small cough, I lead us around to the left, keeping my footsteps well clear of the meadow. The others fall in behind me.

The ground begins to shake.

Not this again. I throw my arms out, both for balance and to stop the others from advancing. There's an uneven rhythm to the trembling, as if heavy weights are striking the earth. The ground rumbles upward before and below our feet, elevating us on a downward slope.

"Back up," I order, spotting the movement through the trees. A series of boulders, all different sizes. The stones are barreling toward us, fanned out in a half moon stretching left, right, and center—crashing through the underbrush, cracking a spruce fir straight in two. A blur of red fur streaks past me, scrambling for safety. "Go!" I shove them toward the meadow, where the land lies beautifully flat.

We pound across the border and onto the open ground, trampling the lilac-crowned stems beneath our boots. We're halfway to the center when the boulders cascade past the tree line and into the meadow, then immediately shatter into rivulets of pale pink blossoms.

All of us pause to watch the threat dissipate. A few rogue strands of wind carry the flowers across the meadow and up toward the sky. I pull a feather-soft petal from my shirt and frown. "Cherry blossoms."

Helos huffs a nervous laugh. "Better than granite, I suppose."

As quiet settles over the land once more, we shift our attention to the stalks around us. They're taller here than on the outskirts; several of them reach past my waist.

"Well," I say, peering around us. "I guess we've made it this far."

Helos brushes drops of water from his arms. "Wet, isn't it?"

I nod. Dew still clings to most of the purple globes.

Weslyn starts for the southern end, leaving us to follow. Soon I have to lift my elbows in order to clear all the stems.

"Are they growing taller?" he asks, brushing a few stalks from his path.

I blink. When did they get so high? Suddenly, the tops crest far above our heads, as if we're walking a cornfield in Telyan's sprawling farmland. My pants are damp with moisture.

A few steps later, Weslyn halts. Lifts a heel, then grinds it into the earth.

"What is it?" I push my way through the towering stalks. I can hear Helos swearing beside me.

"Listen," Weslyn says, gaze still fixed on the ground. "The leaves are all crunching." He swivels toward us. "But it's not autumn."

Bending abruptly, I sweep my hands along the earth, which is mostly bare dirt. A finger of fear strokes the length of my spine.

"Weslyn," I say, rising slowly. "There are no leaves."

He blinks at me. "What?"

"There are no leaves on the ground."

"Yes, there are." Helos crouches low and grabs at the earth. "But they're wet and soggy as anything in here. Look."

He extends an open palm. Nothing's on it. Only empty air.

"We should leave," I tell them, heart hammering in my chest.

"What?"

"There's nothing on your hand, Helos!"

"What are you talking about, I've got a—"

He breaks off. Drops his hand.

"What do you see?" he asks. "Around you, right now. What are you seeing?"

"Stalks," I answer cautiously. "Higher than our heads. They're golden brown, like wheat."

The color drains from his face.

"That's not what—"

Weslyn inhales sharply, balling his hands into fists.

"What?"

"The water. It's burning."

I stomp closer and study his forearms, bare beneath the rolled gray sleeves.

"Do you not feel it?" he asks, clenching one of his dry wrists. "How is it not hurting you?"

"There's nothing to feel!"

Helos swears and slaps his ankle, then lifts a pant leg. "Fire ants." He stomps around, but I can't see a single insect.

"What's going on? Why are we seeing different things?" Weslyn demands.

"It's not just seeing," I reply. Scrunching my nose, I circle in place. "Do either of you smell smoke?"

They stare at me blankly.

"Let's go," Helos says, grinding his shoes into the invisible insects.

"Which way is out?" I retort.

Each of us points in different directions.

"I know this is south." Lips pressed thin, Weslyn lowers his hand. "I was walking in the same direction the whole time."

"That's like trying to cut a straight course through the woods," Helos says. "You may think that it's easy, but eventually, all trees start to look the same."

"I could see where I was going until a few moments ago."

"We've pretty well established that you can't trust what you're seeing!"

"Fire," I breathe, gesturing behind Helos. "We have to move."

"There *is no fire!*" Helos shouts.

The flames are coming closer, licking the stems with greedy limbs, the acrid scent singeing my nostrils. They can't be more than ten paces from us.

"What if there is?" I shout back. "Who's to say which is real? What you're seeing or what I am?"

Weslyn exhales slowly. "We need to—"

"Move," I say, tugging Helos out of the fire's path. Feathers are needling the inside of my skin, offering, insistent. "I'll fly above and—"

The world goes dark.

I freeze.

Shake my head. Rub my eyes with the heels of my hands.

"What is it?" Helos asks close to my ear. "What's wrong?"

"I can't see," I mutter. The snapping of the flames has died away, along with the smell.

"Anything?"

"Nothing." Panic is throwing itself against my rib cage, rattling my chest. I can feel the feathers poking through my skin.

"I don't think shifting will help," Helos says gently, touching my arm and sounding suddenly composed, more controlled. "Whatever this is, it's affecting our senses. That won't change in another form."

"So how do we do this?" Weslyn asks, the voice farther off than I remember him being. With an effort, I urge the feathers to recede. "What do we trust if we can't trust our senses?"

I mash my eyelids together, then open again, to no avail.

"We trust each other." My brother's tone is decisive. "If anyone hears anything odd, or spots an obstacle, we avoid it. No matter if the others cannot."

I nod, but Weslyn doesn't reply.

"Agreed?" Helos presses.

"Yes." Weslyn's voice is rather breathy. "And in that case, we should move."

"Why, what are you seeing?"

"Rattling." He pauses. "I hear rattling."

"Like a snake?"

"Like *many*," he says.

"Then let's go." I take a step to the side.

"Not that way!"

My heart leaps into my throat. His voice rarely raises beyond its usual pitch. "You lead us, then," I say at last.

At the sound of boots crunching something like hay, Helos places gentle pressure against my shoulder blades. Maybe thirty paces later, color and shapes flood my vision.

"It's back," I say, resisting the urge to cry out. "I can see again."

Weslyn glances back from up ahead.

The landscape around us has changed. No longer do towering stalks mask the horizon. Instead, sunflowers blanket the grass, their damp yellow tops playing host to dozens of bees. Yew hedges clump around the perimeter, evergreen and unnaturally shaped, nothing that would normally grow in these parts.

We follow Weslyn for a time, swerving around barriers we cannot see, ducking low to the ground when he drops. I steer them clear of a giant ravine in the earth and make them cover their ears when the piercing cries grow so loud, I'm afraid they might shatter our eardrums. At one point, Helos yells for us to follow him before they grab us.

Somehow, we never seem to close the distance between our current position and the meadow's edge. All we do is track nearer to the border, and in the span of a blink, it recedes.

After our escape from opponents we could not see, Weslyn and I trail Helos with dispirited steps. When the better part of an hour has passed, Weslyn halts without warning.

Wide-eyed, hands fisted, he stares rigidly into the distance.

"What are you seeing?" I ask, noting the veins that appear ready to jump out of his skin.

Weslyn only stares.

"Tell us," I urge, as Helos retraces his steps.

Weslyn shakes his head. "It's not an obstacle."

"Then what is it?"

"It does not matter." His tone sharpens. "It isn't real."

"How do you know?"

"I know, all right?" He waves a hand vaguely in my direction. "Keep walking. I will follow."

The manner in which he speaks wards off further questioning, and in response, my stomach clenches in irritation. I don't know why he insists on shutting down any time I get close. Twisting away, I catch Helos frowning before he leads us onward.

"Does anyone else see storm clouds?" he asks after a while.

"Everything keeps changing," I groan, struggling to tamp down my frustration. The meadow has recently become a bog, tepid water and wan, wilting reeds. Along the border, puffs of steam arc skyward in fractured spirals. "The sky looks dark now, but it wasn't before. First I saw the stalks, then a garden, then a streambed. Now it's more of a swamp, and the outskirts are always—"

I grind to a halt, my response trailing off. And that's when I realize.

"What do our surroundings look like to you?" I ask. "Whatever you're seeing, is it wet?"

"Now it's a grove of hickory trees," Helos replies. "Surrounded by pockets of mud."

"It's open for me." Weslyn shrugs. "Like a barley field at harvest time, but after rain. It's damp."

"I bet it's the dew," I say firmly. "Or whatever the water is. I think that's what's affecting our senses." Moisture has beaded along my arms and seeped into my shirt and pant legs. The boys perform matching examinations of themselves.

"If you're right," Helos says, "then we should try to dry off. But even if we do, as soon as we try to leave the meadow, we'll just get wet again. The only way out is through the damp."

"Maybe that's just an illusion to keep us here. If we're dry, we might see a path."

"Or there could be levels to it," Weslyn puts in, sounding tired. "Maybe the wetter we are, the worse it gets."

We fall silent, considering.

"Let's change," I say at last. "There's no harm in trying. Dry off and put on new clothes."

After a beat, Weslyn sheds his pack and turns around. Helos and I follow his lead. Grabbing the worn towel from my pack, I strip off my damp pants and shirt and rub my skin until it's dry. Then I throw on a fresh set, green and gray, noting gratefully that the moisture on my boots hasn't seeped inside. When everyone is ready, we straighten and face the tree line.

It's much closer than it looked before, maybe twenty or thirty paces away. Around us, the lilac-topped stalks are back, but there are small gaps between the bunches, and none reach higher than our calves.

I confirm with the others that we are all seeing the same.

"Okay then," I mutter, studying the ground before us. "Step carefully."

Moving at a turtle's speed, we advance toward the perimeter with delicate, tentative steps. The motions feel faintly absurd, but I'd rather have my wits about me, and I don't break from the course.

"The river take me," Helos mutters, throwing his arms behind his head.

"Just follow us," I say, "even if you touch it. We're almost out."

Someone inhales sharply, and my ankle brushes against the stalks. I grit my teeth against the moisture. The view ahead hasn't changed.

When we're only a handful of steps away, Helos exclaims loudly from behind.

"What's wrong?" I pivot quickly, seeing Weslyn turn in my peripheries. "Helos?"

My brother is stamping the dirt, the movements rapid, frantic.

Then he drops into the ground, and the earth swallows him whole.

FOURTEEN

"Helos!"

I launch myself at the spot where he vanished and tear at the earth with reckless abandon, my fingers soon stretching into claws. The lilac stalks bend around me, brushing my arms, my ankles. I don't care. My claws churn desperate tracks in the dirt, but my brother's head does not emerge.

Suddenly Weslyn is yanking me upright, away from the place where Helos disappeared. I scream and spit like a wildcat, twisting to get free, to resume my search—but he traps me firmly against him, his grip like iron. "Helos!"

"Rora, stop! Look, I'm here!"

Impossibly, Helos materializes in front of me and holds my face in his hands. "I'm here. It's okay, I'm right here."

I stop fighting and blink at him, tears blurring my eyes. "How do I know you're real?" I demand, my voice cracking on the words. "Which one is real?"

"I am, see?" Helos steps outside the meadow, smiling a little.

Weslyn releases his hold now that I'm no longer struggling, and I follow my brother, scraping the dew from my skin. He's still there. When I look back at the place I'd seen him vanish, there's nothing but a yawning crevice just beyond where I was digging. I must have nearly fallen in. "I thought—I saw you—"

"It's all right," Helos says, pulling me into a hug. "We're out of it now."

I clutch the front of his shirt a moment, breathing slowly to try to blot out the panic. The gash in the earth looks deep and dark, probably new, and I twist around to look at Weslyn, who's standing a short distance to the side, hands in his pockets, turned slightly away. He's watching me.

"Thanks," I say quietly.

His expression softens a little as he nods, then looks away.

Helos was right; storm clouds crowded the sky while we were tramping through the meadow.

The rain breaks that afternoon. Leaves and detritus cling to our cloaks while we trudge through the muck, boots squelching in the mud as we leave the cursed meadow far behind. The trees are denser here, and older, their mossy trunks an arms-width wide. Gray-green lichen drapes unevenly along the branches. It gives the area an almost haunted feel.

Thunder crashes far above, and wind continually knocks the hood off my head. For a while I resort to holding it in place with my fingers, then abandon the attempt entirely. Helos keeps looking behind, trying to watch for followers since it's difficult to hear much above the downpour.

I share his apprehension. We've been trekking most of the day, yet we haven't even come across a single elk. In fact, we've seen no animals beyond birds and the occasional ground dwellers ever since crossing the river. It makes no sense. This area is brimming with wildlife.

If anything, given the recent exodus of magical people to the west, and the sudden surge of magic that's drifted east, I expected to find the Vale more crowded. Or, perhaps, some crisis great enough to disrupt the land magic's usual course.

But beyond the swish of the breeze, which has recently turned to rain—there's nothing.

I try to stifle these concerns in light of the more pressing issue at hand. Our current priority is reaching the giants, but advancing in this weather is nearly impossible. I'm about to suggest we seek shelter and wait for the worst to pass when Helos loses his footing and slides a few paces downhill.

For a moment he just lies there on his stomach, not moving. More sinking sand? I'm already lurching forward, but then he shouts something inarticulate and pounds a fist into the earth.

Weslyn gets there first. Wordlessly, he offers a hand and pulls my brother to his feet.

Helos examines his front, which is now entirely covered in mud, and swears.

"Perhaps we should—"

"No," he interrupts, predicting my train of thought. "We've come this far. Let's finish it." The unspoken message is, *Let's go while everything else takes shelter from the storm.*

Wherever "everything else" may be.

I wait for Weslyn to voice his opinion, but he hasn't said a word since the rain began.

"All right," I relent, raising my voice to be heard above the din. "Let me lead for a while, at least."

Helos gestures to the rise behind him, as if to say, *be my guest.* Stepping carefully, I move to the front and take us up the hill, grabbing wispy trees and sticks lodged in the ground whenever I can to help me balance. My boots slip more than once, driving my knees down into the pliant earth, but I manage to avoid any falls worse than that.

We hike for several more hours, into the early evening. To distract myself from the battering wind, from my waterlogged boots and drenched clothes, I order my mind to focus instead on the after—after we save Finley, after Helos and I prove ourselves as harbingers of healing and not death. After I knock some sense into my friend where my brother is concerned, since out here, the distance between royal and commoner doesn't seem so very far. I saw Finley's indecision that morning at Castle Roanin. I can fix this, I know it.

We stop only to choke down a miserable meal or drain our

water supply. During one of these pauses, I uncork my waterskin and hold it skyward, attempting to catch a few stray drops of rainwater. Weslyn mirrors me silently, while Helos massages his ankle.

By the time the ground levels out into a relatively flat expanse, my calves and thighs are screaming, and I have lost all sense of the time of day. But I'm alert enough to call a halt through panting breath when the horizon sharpens into focus. My heart skids in my chest at the sight of the mist before us.

We've reached it.

A thick layer of fog, nearly opaque, drifts like a silvery-blue cloud among the shadowed forest backdrop. It winds through the trees, hugging trunks and hovering waist-high above the grass. The sight is even more unnerving than when seen from the slopes of Niav. I scan the distance, left, right, and straight ahead. The mist stretches as far as I can see.

"What do you think?" Helos asks, stepping up beside me. The rain has slowed to a drizzle, thank fortune, making it much easier to hear.

I shake my head, considering.

"Is it dangerous?" Weslyn asks from my other side.

"Could be," Helos replies, glancing down, then behind. He retreats a few paces and seizes a twig from the ground.

When he's back at my side, he snaps the twig in two and drops one of the pieces into the mist.

It vanishes before it hits the ground.

All three of us suck in a breath. Circumventing this could take hours. And it could ultimately lead to nothing; for all we know, there might be no other way to reach the giants than to trek directly through.

Helos makes a comment too quiet for my ears to pick up, then extends the second half of the twig, dipping one end in the fog while keeping a loose grip on the other.

Nothing happens.

"Strange," he murmurs, waving the stick back and forth a little. Then he drops it into the mist, and it disappears like the other.

No one speaks. We're all exhausted and soaked to the bone, and the thought of trying to navigate a way around this—particularly when we're so close to our destination—is enough to push me over the edge.

I can't fall apart, I remind myself, running my hands over my face. *Finley is depending on me. Don't fall apart. Do* something.

I swivel round and scan our surroundings, hoping for inspiration.

And stop at the sight.

"Uh, Helos," I mutter. Both boys turn, and I point to the stick— both pieces of it, lying one atop the other in the place they were taken from.

"I didn't hear them drop," Weslyn says.

He's right. The sticks haven't made a sound. It's as if they just materialized there out of nothing.

I search the ground at my feet and settle on a small pebble, which I hurl into the mist with all the force I can muster. Then I look down once more.

The stone blinks into existence a few moments later.

Weslyn stoops to examine the sticks. "They don't seem damaged in any way," he says, lifting one, then the other. I try the pebble and discover the same.

"I think we should step into it," my brother declares. "See if it shoots us back to this spot." I gape as if he's grown a second head. "Well, one of us at least. I'll do it."

"Are you crazy?" I exclaim. "A stick looks okay, so you're willing to just plunge right in?"

"We have to try."

"We don't *have* to do anything."

"So you're willing to let Finley die without even trying."

I level a furious glare in his direction. "And if you die?"

He turns away, arms crossed. "One of us should try." And he thinks it should be him.

Selflessness is making him stupid.

"We're not separating," Weslyn says in a gruff voice, chiming in before I can berate Helos further.

"Then we'll all go."

"We can't see what's inside these objects." I throw up my hands, exasperated. "They could look whole on the outside but be damaged within."

"They—"

"Just . . . hold on a moment," I say, "Before you go charging off on a suicide mission." He's convinced the mist won't hurt us, but that kind of imagined kinship with magic can get you killed. And he should know that.

He *does* know that.

Where is this impulsiveness coming from?

Pacing a short distance away, I find a leaf, so fragile it's almost see-through, and pluck it from the forest floor. Then I step up to the mist and release it.

Helos is the first to reach the returned leaf and holds it close to his face, turning it one way, then the other, running his fingertips along its sides. Then he hands it to me to do the same.

"It seems fine," I admit, after a thorough examination. I pass it to Weslyn.

He studies the leaf, then drops his hand. "What's the point of going in if we'll only end up back where we started?"

"Maybe we can push through it," Helos suggests. "Figure out a way forward. Anything's better than doing nothing."

"What about going around?"

"If this doesn't work, we'll try that," I allow, finally willing to accept my brother's plan. "But we have no idea if there's even a break in the fog, and we've been away for so long already." I don't articulate the danger in these two weeks of travel. The implication that every delay brings more people falling ill with the Throes, more deaths.

Six weeks until King Gerar must side with or against King Jol.

Weslyn's rigid as a board, hands clenched tightly at his sides. I realize this must be hard for him, to continually confront a kind of landscape that's long since faded from Telyan. But we really don't have time.

"Finley needs us," I remind him.

The words aren't enough to uncurl his fists, but at least they spur him into motion once more. He strides up beside me, looking straight ahead.

"We'll take one step in. On three," I add, glancing at my brother, who nods and clutches the straps of his pack. "One. Two."

On three, I step forward, just a single step into the mist's cool embrace.

Instantly, power yanks at my body, an invisible force taking hold as icy air washes over me. My hair whips my face, and shock roars in my ears. But before I can say or do anything, the air releases me.

The first thing I do is confirm that both boys are okay. They are—each stands the same distance from me as before, looking equally shaken and bewildered. Then I focus on our surroundings.

Mast-thin lodgepole pines. Sloping green land. The layered shadows of early evening. All eerily quiet.

Unlike it had with the forest debris, the mist hasn't bounced us back to where we started. It's moved us farther north, to the hills near the base of the Decani Mountains. Easily a four-days' hike from the spot we've just left, the place we need to be, and it takes everything in me not to drop to my knees.

I open my mouth to tell them where we are, and that's when the screaming begins.

FIFTEEN

All three of us speak at once.

"What was—"

"Where did it—"

"Was that—"

"A person," I breathe, feeling the air around me constrict. "It sounded like a person."

My claim is met with silence. Muffled shouts sound in the distance, too far away to make out. My legs jerk forward.

"Wait a moment," Weslyn warns, catching my arm and guiding me back to the group. Wind rips through the trees, blowing sodden leaves onto my skin. "We have no idea what's going on, or how they might receive us. We need to figure out where we are. You cannot go charging off blindly."

Another scream rends the air.

But I can.

I'm gone, boots pounding the earth like drums of war. There's nothing to guide me but the cries echoing in my head and the snap judgment of where they had come from. Maneuvering through the forest would be far easier as a goshawk, but I don't want to lose my pack. So I run, the movement pulling at my still-healing stomach. Swerving around the narrow trunks, leaping over arched roots, ducking under low-hanging branches.

It isn't easy. The ground is slick from the rain, and I lose my footing on a descent more than once, slamming into patches of mottled brown-and-green leaves—adder's tail. A short slide across the forest floor rips open one of my pant legs at the knee. Flecks of dirt lodge themselves in my hair and on my skin, and some sort of insect stings me sharply in the forearm. I yelp at the pain and smack the bug aside, taking the opportunity to glance behind. There's no sign of Helos or Weslyn.

More shouting up ahead, much louder now than it was before. I slow to a more cautious pace as the signs of a struggle take shape—a low growl, a thumping noise, deep voices arcing high.

"It's getting loose!"

"Cut its—"

Vicious snarling serrates the air, rough and wrinkled, like sandpaper in sound.

The blood rushes from my face.

Horrible sounds. Dying sounds. Strangled, choking, utterly agonized screeching. Pinpricks of pressure jut up against my skin, just beneath the surface, fighting to break through. Whiskers in my cheeks, then feathers all over. As if my body can't decide which need is more urgent: to hide or to flee.

I will not hide, I resolve, rebelling against the first stings of numbness, the coolness spreading through my limbs. *I will not flee.*

I step forward.

The forest opens up into a grassy clearing peppered with wildflowers. I hover at the perimeter, several paces behind the tree line, melting into the shadows as the scene before me sharpens into focus.

There are three men—one of them only steps away from me—in uniforms of navy blue, with red detailing on the cuffs and collars. *Eradain colors.*

One of them is on the ground.

It's hardest to look at him, at the narrow face contorted in anguish, the deep crimson patches staining his front. The maimed stomach that's been ripped to shreds, flesh and intestines spilling onto the grass and coating the knife at his side. Bile collects in my throat.

A caegar stands over him, the elusive mountain wildcat with hypnotic powers, a massive swath of wired netting tangled around its back paw. It's bleeding heavily from a cut on its flank.

"Grab the net," shouts the man across the clearing, tall and younger looking, with torn up arms, white skin, and a beard a lighter shade of gold than his hair. His comrade in front of me angles forward with obvious reluctance, leaping backward when the caegar fixes him with its furious gaze.

The wildcat prowls toward him, as I knew it would. You can't run from mountain cats. You can never run.

But in numbers, you have a chance of beating one.

"HEY!" I shriek, leaping into the clearing and turning my face away a moment before that massive feline head swings in my direction. The man beside me nearly jumps out of his bones. I ignore him and focus on the caegar's small, rounded ears, on its shoulder, on the muscles rippling beneath its tawny fur as it takes a step forward. I know its game.

"What the—"

"Don't look it in the eye," I warn, cutting him off. "Do not meet its gaze." The men must have struck the caegar first; these cats are solitary creatures who only attack when their prey is alone. I glance at the net that has snared this one's paw.

"Get out of—"

"If its eyes find yours, you're lost," I say, voice rising so the one with golden hair can hear. The mangled man has fallen silent. "If you run, it will give chase, and then you're dead. Raise your arms and your swords. Make yourselves appear as big as possible."

"Listen, girl—"

"*DO AS I SAY!*" I bellow, not to force my point, but to startle the caegar. It flinches at the outburst, then growls as I step closer to the man on my left. Our shoulders are almost touching.

He spreads his arms wide, as do I, shouting all the while. The caegar steps toward us, and I yell even louder. *Where's Weslyn? Where is my brother?*

Every nerve in my body is on fire. Arteries, veins—the tingling has returned, blossoming from my core to my extremities. No. I won't. I can't. These are Eradain men.

The one with golden hair has started mirroring us, and the caegar takes a step back, fangs bared. Deciding.

I struggle to remain focused on the scene in front of me as my fingers stretch and sharpen. The decision to fight, the need to stand my ground—my body is demanding lynx, though this wildcat would be twice my size, and it's taking every trace of strength I possess to beat the claws back and resist the shift.

I lift my leg to step toward the caegar—and collapse.

The tingling in my legs is no longer the soft patter of raindrops. It's needle-sharp, pulsing the length of my calves, insisting on a shift. I look up at my quarry, and in my distraction, I stupidly catch its gaze.

The prickling sensation recedes, quickly replaced by a spreading paralysis that prevents me from moving—or feeling—my legs at all. The man at my side grabs me under the shoulder, struggling to hoist me up onto feet that no longer hold my weight. I yank my arm from his grasp and stare at the cat. The cat stares at me.

I lean toward it.

The few remaining whispers of reason thrash against my thoughts, demanding that I stop. That I stand. That I scream. The man beside me is yelling the same, tugging me to my feet each time my legs buckle, but the sound of his voice is growing as muddy as those of the forest around us. The caegar prowls toward me, and despite the haze in my mind, I find that I want it to.

The man releases my arm and steps away.

Someone blocks the view in front of me.

"What—" I try to ask, but my tongue lays heavy in my mouth. No sound comes out.

He says something, the person standing there. My brain can't make sense of the syllables. I blink hard, shake my head, blink again. *Focus.*

The pants blocking my view—black. The hair crowning the back of the skull—brown. This means something to me. It should mean something.

Focus.

I jostle my legs—and find that I can move them.

Dizziness skews my senses as I surge to my feet, but the fog lifts at last. Weslyn. Somehow he's here, standing before me, sword drawn. A broad stretch of steel the only thing separating us from the caegar.

"Hasn't anyone ever warned you about their eyes?" he murmurs, keeping his attention on the scene before us.

"Shut up," I tell him earnestly, royal or no.

And I swear by the river, he smiles.

Making every effort not to let the caegar catch me off guard again, I peer around his shoulder. Helos is still nowhere in sight.

As if the thought has summoned him, my brother races past the tree line and into the clearing, stopping directly beside us.

Now there are four of us together. Not to mention the one across the clearing, who looks utterly bewildered by the presence of so many newcomers. The wildcat looks at all of us, blood still dripping from its flank, and curls a lip in warning. It takes a couple of steps backward, then turns to flee—and stumbles over the wire netting.

People explode from the trees, four by my startled count and all wearing the colors of Eradain, firing a device that ejects a dark net from its mouth like a web. It barrels into the caegar with the force of a mountain gale, sending the wildcat tumbling to the ground and enveloping it in a barbed blanket.

"Grab it!" shouts one of the newcomers. She and her comrades rush to the fallen caegar, twisting the ends of the net into a knot of sorts and dragging their catch toward them. The wildcat writhes and scores the earth with its claws, screaming as the wire netting digs deeper into its fur.

"What are you doing?" I yell, ignoring the stuttered protest from the uniformed man beside me and lurching forward. "It was backing away. It was leaving!"

Helos utters a hurried warning.

"Bloody ends, stay *back*!" answers one of the men. The cat's flank is heaving to an irregular rhythm, lungs striving to draw breath despite the cords burrowing into its skin. Its pupils are dilated to twice their normal size. It's frightened.

The sight triggers a blaze of fury in me—pure, unadulterated wrath as forceful as a thousand suns, coursing through my veins.

FORESTBORN   183

Surrounded, hunted, forced from its home. In the Vale, neutral territory. A haven. There can't be more than a couple dozen caegars
in all of Alemara. Their magic is dangerous, yes, but that doesn't
justify attacking them out of nowhere, and this one doesn't appear
to have done more than defend itself.

"Why are you—"

The man with golden hair rushes forward and runs his knife
through the cat's shoulder.

"No!" I cry, watching in horror as he dislodges the red blade and
staggers backward, triumph smeared across his features. The caegar's
body slackens.

"The river take you, Kallen," growls one of the people clutching the net. "You know the rules."

"Do you want to get the son of a bitch back in one piece?" the
man with golden hair—Kallen—replies, northern accent cutting
the words short. "Least now it can't put up such a fight."

"What is wrong with you?" I demand, tearing free of Helos's
grasp and marching right up to Kallen. "Take off this net!" I turn to
the others even as they continue dragging the feeble wildcat away.

"We're finishing the job. Who the bloody ends are you?"

"Let it go!" I say, and Kallen knocks my collarbone so hard it
jostles my balance. A hand finds mine again, tugging me backward
for only an instant before pulling away. I swivel round to Weslyn,
who's clutching his hand and swearing softly. Then I look back at
Kallen, whose gaze has dropped to my fingers. Where claws have
materialized, unsheathed and dagger-sharp. Deadly.

Wide eyes meet mine, the connection lasting only a moment
before he raises his bow, points it at my chest, and shoots.

SIXTEEN

The arrow misses by a hairsbreadth.

"Move!" Helos cries, still clutching my arm where he pulled me to the side a moment before. I tug free and we separate, creating a more difficult target. Weslyn shouts to get the man's attention—a diversion, I realize instantaneously, as does Helos. We rush toward the attacker from either side, me with claws still drawn, ready to try to disarm him.

Another arrow whizzes past my face, snatching a few strands of hair. My heart fires through my chest as the four people clutching the net release their quarry and raise their own bows.

We're outnumbered.

"Run!" I command, just as Kallen shouts, "Grab her!"

At the order, the quiet one who endeavored to get me on my feet when the caegar's paralysis took hold lurches forward from where he's stood, spellbound, ever since the wave of reinforcements rushed in. He intercepts me as I reach the edge of the clearing, grabbing my arm in a halfhearted sort of way.

I don't hesitate. I raise my other hand, twist toward him, and slash my claws over his forearm.

The young man cries out, releasing me at once. The feeling of torn flesh lingers beneath my nails as I escape the clearing, Weslyn and Helos a few paces to either side.

Shadows lay heavy across the earth, casting the forest into a murky, underwater sort of darkness. I tear through the trees, fighting to divert my panic into something more productive. *Run, run,* urges the lynx, and this time I agree.

Thorns snag my ankles, and I go down, severing the stems with my claws and tearing my hands in my effort to untangle myself. Not far behind, our pursuers are crashing through the underbrush, shouting commands at one another. I wrest free and surge to my feet, hurtling after the boys.

Something's moving to the right, keeping pace with our group. Helos senses it, too, but he doesn't pause to examine it any more than I do. Every trace of concentration is channeled into remaining upright and avoiding the branches that almost seem to be reaching toward us. Wings start poking through my back, but again I resist the shift. I will not abandon them.

Weslyn drops a minute later, his shout fracturing upon the ground's impact. Breath catching, I slam to a halt, sheathe the claws, and double back, grabbing his hands and hauling him to his feet. Then we're off again, darting right when an arrow lodges itself into the tree beside him.

The hunt, the chase, the desperate flight through wilderness— the years dissolve in a rush of memory, and it's like I never even left. The only difference is the boy at my side, and the way the land lies motionless, strangely quiet.

Before, it might have trembled beneath my feet. Plants might have sprung up out of thin air, altering the path on a whim. Then a pine's wintry breath, roaring through our ears, temporarily deafening us to our surroundings.

Now there's nothing. Only silence, shadows, and mist.

Mist?

Helos shouts my name, but too late—I've barreled straight into the silver-blue veil.

It seizes hold of my body at once. Cold air slaps at my face, so hard I have to close my eyes. Determined not to leave the others, I attempt to free my legs, circle my arms, *something*. Each effort is a waste; my limbs are cemented in place.

And then it's over.

Eyelids shutter open, and my heart stammers in relief at the sight of Helos and Weslyn to either side. Both entered the mist. Both made it through.

I spin around to check for signs of pursuit. The armed men and women aren't there. Nor is anything else familiar.

We're not in the same part of the forest.

Adrenaline blazing, the three of us lock eyes, then turn back to see where the mist has delivered us this time.

A vast, circular meadow stretches before us, several times larger than the clearing from which we fled. Dozens of orbs of white light hover a few paces in the air, illuminating vibrant green grass that reaches past my ankles and clusters of violet, bell-shaped polemonium flowers. Smooth, silver-trunked aspens skirt the edges— enormous, reality-defying trees easily twice as wide as I am tall, broader and loftier than their ordinary counterparts in every respect. We're standing at the edge of this open expanse, sheltered amongst plants with low-hanging leaves as long as my arm.

Three figures are seated in the clearing. Their backs stretch toward the sky—cream-colored cloth upon skin the colors of sand: tan and charcoal and slate all at once. They're perched on boulders the size of young trees—huge stones by most standards, yet no larger than ordinary chairs for the legs that graze their sides.

Weslyn exhales in disbelief, and the sound must be loud as an eagle's cry to their enormous ears, because all three heads turn toward us.

We've found the giants.

None of them rise from the rocks.

Nobody speaks.

Then, "You come with blood on your hands."

It's the one set farthest back that speaks, her voice low but clear. A round, smooth sound.

My gaze drops to my hands, which are smudged with dirt and blood where the thorns pierced the skin.

"You will leave. Now."

"I didn't—"

"*Go.*"

The ground trembles at the word, and half of the lights blink out. A swath of blackness and swirling grit takes shape in the darkness, rising like a scene out of a nightmare.

Weslyn steps back.

"I only cut my hands on some thorns!" I exclaim, holding my palms out in a placating gesture. "I didn't kill anything."

The giant who stood, now discernible for what she is, looms far above us, a thundercloud ready to strike.

"Please. My name is Rora. This is Helos and Weslyn. We need your help."

Silence, so complete that for a moment I fear I've gone deaf. Then one of the seated giants rises, too, and closes the distance between us in three strides.

The ground trembles so severely at the movement that Helos grabs my shoulder to remain upright. Directly above, the giant's shoulders stand higher than an elm, his arms the length of an entire story, his trunk-wide calves stretching taller than our bodies. We have to tilt our heads back all the way to glimpse his face.

I barely have time to process the turn of events before he bends and seizes one of my hands, pinching it between a thumb and pointer finger as long as my forearms. It would take him half a thought to reduce the bones to dust.

"There is death on you," he proclaims, studying the skin. "But it is still to come."

Light flickers in the dimmed orbs once more, and the surrounding aspens begin to creak despite the absence of wind. The giant releases my hand, seeming appeased, but his declaration has had the opposite effect on me.

"What do you mean?" I say.

He blinks slowly, his emotions difficult to read due to the absence of eyebrows. In fact, there's no hair on any of their heads. It's as if they have been carved from stone, beings of the earth itself.

"Do you mean animals I hunt for food?" I persist.

"No."

A chill worms its way down my spine. I have never killed anything—or anyone—other than prey.

Three hastily scribbled words bob to the surface, mocking.

"You speak our language," Helos observes.

The giant appraises him for several heartbeats. "We speak many languages."

And with that, he returns to his perch atop the boulder, all three of them seated once more. The restored distance does little to soothe my apprehension.

Helos continues when the ground has stilled. "We seek an audience with you."

Are the aspens growing louder?

"We know," says the one who ordered us to leave, who insisted I have blood on my hands. She's watching us with open curiosity.

"What do you mean, you know?" I ask.

"The only way to get here now is through the mist, and the mist puts things where they belong."

I allow myself only a few moments to wonder at this information. "Did you create the mist, then?"

"Is that what you came to ask us?"

Well. "No," I reply, uncertain.

More trembling in the earth, then, a beat that pulses up through my legs. Two more giants step into the clearing, equally lithe and towering, appearing decidedly less calm than the three seated on the rocks.

"What's this?" one of the newcomers demands. "Hutta?" There's a low reverberation beneath the words, like he's speaking and humming at the same time. The hair rises on the back of my neck.

"They seek an audience," our communicator—Hutta—replies.

"Send them away."

"But there are soldiers out there," I say, trying to ignore the way the grass beneath the angry one's feet is turning brown. The way that line of brown is creeping across the meadow and toward our feet. I glance at Weslyn, who's supposed to be the negotiator on this trek. He hasn't uttered a single word. I add: "We only just escaped."

Admittedly, I expected this bit of news to elicit some sort of outcry or alarm. *Any* sign of concern, at least. Instead, it's met with silence.

"Did you hear me?" I say, temper flaring slightly. "There are humans in the Vale, uniformed humans from Eradain. Does that mean nothing to you? Nonmagical people don't belong here."

The brown grass leaps forward in a sudden rush, the stain spreading beneath our boots. We struggle in vain; the blades lengthen and wind their way up and around our feet and calves, no doubt a mark of the giants' influence, until we're encased up to the knees. The grass's grip is rigid as stone.

"No, they don't," the angry one says, his pronouncement humming with the unspoken threat. His companions only watch curiously, making no move to interfere. I swear the trees are moaning now.

"We're not human!" I exclaim, tugging against the bindings. To my left, Weslyn peers at me like I've offended him, the color drained from his face.

"*He* is," comes the reply. "There's magic on the two of you. But you are still—"

"My sister and I are shifters," Helos says, adopting a stranger's form momentarily to prove it.

"Why did you bring him here, then?" the second latecomer demands, slightly breathless. The sound is like wind brushing water. "You should know better. Which realm are you from?"

"We live in Telyan," I reply, smarting at the condescension. "But we're from here, originally."

"Where exactly is 'here'?"

I swallow. "Caela Ridge."

At once, the scene before us changes: the grass releases Helos and me so suddenly we stumble forward, off-balance. The seated giants rise, the two latecomers step toward us, and all five of them begin to speak.

Without thinking, I grab Weslyn's and Helos's arms to steady us.

Hutta, who I see is slightly smaller than the rest now that she's standing, stares at my hand on Weslyn's arm. I drop it. "That isn't possible," she says, and though her voice is quiet, the rest fall silent. "Everyone in that village was slaughtered."

I bristle at the word. Like livestock.

"I've offended you," she observes.

My eyes narrow. "Our parents were among the ones murdered."

Weslyn glances my way, but I continue staring at Hutta, not yet ready to see his face. I've never told him that our parents didn't die of natural causes.

"Do not mistake my vernacular with callousness," she replies. "It was a grievous tragedy." She fixes Weslyn with a stormy look.

"We are not all interested in making war," Weslyn says, finding his voice at last. To his credit, I suppose, it doesn't shake a bit. "Telyan is eager to repair the relationship between our nations."

Now it's my turn to stare at him. He's never shared *that* bit of information before.

His words are met with more silence. The bindings on his legs hold.

"This one's royalty," the giant who examined my hands observes at last. His tone carries an unpleasant note.

"What makes you say that?" Weslyn asks.

"All human kings have an air about them."

"I'm not a king."

"Are you not?"

Weslyn takes a deep breath, then releases it. "My intention is genuine."

"Indeed," agrees the angry one, nodding once. "And you would be the one to repair things?"

"Will you join me?" Weslyn counters.

"That is not an answer."

"It is," Weslyn insists. "A relationship requires two parties. Surely you are familiar with the vernacular."

A pause.

"Why have you come?" Hutta says at last. Not to Weslyn—to me.

I'm glad for the chance to intervene before Weslyn starts a brawl with beings four times his size. "We'd like to make a trade."

Her forehead wrinkles, like ripples on the shore. "Of what?"

Well, this is it.

I stand tall, hands at my sides. "Magic has begun cropping up in humans. Only nonmagical people, and most of them are gravely ill or already dead."

"Most of them?"

"A few have appeared unaffected by the magic."

Her eyes crinkle at the corners. "Unaffected. Do you think so?"

I wait for her to clarify. She doesn't.

"One of the afflicted is our friend," Helos cuts in.

She holds up a hand. "Enough. You have come for stardust, I presume." I nod. "You are not the first."

"We don't claim to be," I say.

Hutta tilts her head back. "Tell me. How is the land in the human realm? How is the magic there?"

"The land is dormant," I reply, a little hesitant. "Though I assume the stardust would change that."

"Not unless you allow it to sink into the earth. Are you planning to do so?"

"No," I admit, taken aback by this piece of information. "Only to heal the afflicted."

"As I thought," she says. "Humans do better on sleeping terrain. Magic only makes them angrier, and so more dangerous." She cricks her neck to the side and watches Weslyn. "That is why we left."

"So the presence of stardust alone is not enough to revive the land?" he asks, undeterred by her pointed comment.

"Of course not. It must be ingested by living beings to have any healing effect, and the same goes for the land." Her voice ticks up at the end, like he's stupid. "It must seep into the ground to cause any restoration, and even then it would take time. Rain may cure a drought, but not overnight."

I was wrong, then. The land east of the river will remain immobile, after all. Weslyn slumps a little in relief.

"You see? You want the magic only when it benefits you. Why should we allow you to take any?"

"My people will die," he says roughly.

"And that should concern us? Humans are always the ones creating problems. Your *people* are petty, guided by greed and fear. It was true in Fendolyn's lifetime, and it is still true today. Oh yes," she adds, when his expression darkens, "we hear whispers of what's happening in the east, the growing unrest among the three realms.

Why should we intervene? We tried that once. *We* gifted you the loropins, urged you to rule on truth and logic rather than baseless emotion, and still you choose to ignore us and destroy yourselves over ugly squabbles. If humans are the only ones falling ill, perhaps that would solve the problem, would it not? At least we would still have our refuge across the river." Her attention slides to me, as if to gauge my reaction to this narrow-minded stance.

"You wouldn't for long," I say, frustrated by her coldness. "Eradain is preparing to strike the Vale, not just the other realms."

A wave of shock ripples through the giants.

"Explain," demands the angry one.

"Gladly. If you allow us to make our trade," says Weslyn. "We have brought a gift."

"Which is?"

"Seeds from the trees in the Old Forest. An emblem of Telyan."

Reluctant interest flickers through the group.

"The forest around us grows thick and strong," Hutta says, her voice guarded. "We have many trees already. Why offer us more? What value is there in such a trade?"

My heart sinks. If the giants reject our offering, we have nothing more to give. A refusal would condemn Finley to death.

Weslyn rises to the challenge before I can muster a response. "The Old Forest outside of Roanin is just as ancient as any west of the river, and more so than any other woods east of it—the trees there don't grow anywhere else in Alemara. It's a remnant of the wilderness here, a bridge between Telyan and the Vale. Those seeds tie our lands together, just as a gift of stardust would. Does such a symbol mean nothing to you?"

A trained negotiator, indeed.

"Show us," says the one who examined my hands.

Weslyn produces the box from his pack, for the first time since that day in Geonen's shop, and the grass releases his legs at last. In fact, the entire stain of brown recedes, until the meadow is a vivid shade of green once more. By the boulders, the giant who examined my palm crouches and holds out his own. Weslyn hesitates.

The giant seems to guess his thoughts. "Do not dishonor me," he warns. "I am no thief."

At that, Weslyn strides forward and places the box in his hand, the prize no bigger than a thimble would be in ours.

The giants converge around the box, rattling the earth in their movements; Weslyn stumbles a bit on his return to my side. They examine it with great interest, conversing in a language I've never heard before. Several minutes pass in which Helos, Weslyn, and I dare not speak to one another. This is the moment we either succeed, or things go terribly, terribly wrong.

"This friend of yours," the one holding the box says, addressing Helos and me. "He is human?"

We nod.

"And he has earned your trust," he continues.

I glance at Helos, who only looks up at the giant with undisguised desperation on his face. "He's earned our love," I say simply.

The five of them look up at the words, study us, then straighten.

"Clouds cover the sky tonight," the one with the box says. "You must wait until tomorrow to retrieve your stardust. In the meantime, you will tell us all you know of this strike."

Joy courses through me, powerful as the river. Finley, saved. The Fallow Throes, *over,* brought to heel before the scales tip into catastrophe. I imagine the looks on King Gerar's and Violet's faces when they see us, then grin broadly. Beside me, Weslyn sags in relief, his face lit with emotion I've never seen on him before, while Helos just covers his face with his hands, silent.

"Thank you," I say, since I'm the only one who seems capable of speech at the moment. "We'll return tomorrow."

"No need," he says, and this time he smiles. Not a cruel smile. Genuine warmth. "Come with us."

SEVENTEEN

The giants' home is a picture out of a dream. The grass that blankets the forest floor is so vibrant a green, it must never have experienced a dry spell in its life. And it's feather-soft; as we follow the five giants through the silver aspens, the blades caress my legs, gentle as whispers. No signs of those vise-like brown stalks. Flowers I've never seen before paint the ground sapphire blue, purple, and white, their colonies thickest around the base of tree trunks, while the trickle of running water streams in from somewhere nearby.

Unlike in Caela Ridge, nothing here is constructed in the trees. In place of layered ropes, dark green vines cascade down from several branches. Others have wrapped around the trunks. Their stems are thick, about the size of a fist in diameter, and strewn with leaves a hands-width long. Farther back amongst the widely spaced trees, there are large nests of moss dotting the ground.

Giants walk the earth before us, the ground humming in their wake. There must be a dozen at least, all clothed in crinkled, cream-colored fabric—tunics with sleeves that fall just past the shoulder and wide-legged trousers that barely pass the knee. Their lean arms appear almost too long for their bodies, spindly echoes of the spires atop Castle Roanin. All wander near at our approach.

They explain our presence to one another in our language, as a courtesy I'm sure. Unlike the dynamic back in Telyan, the giants don't seem to be governed by hierarchy. Instead, they all speak as equals. Each of them gets an opportunity to examine the box of seeds, and though their language switches to one I can't understand every time a new giant looks, they seem pleased with what they see.

They give their names then, sounds that are unfamiliar to my ears, and Helos, Weslyn, and I respond in turn quite cheerfully. Everything seems easier now that we're here, safe at last. Our way is lit by those small orbs of light, floating immobile amongst the trees. They're not of flame—the light is frosted and white, like oversized crystals on a chandelier. Helos pauses to exchange his muddy shirt for a clean one, then we follow them to a crackling fire pit.

"Another gift," says Guthreh—or was it Guthteh?—gesturing to the pit. Birds are roasting on metal spits suspended above the fire.

"Which part?" Helos asks amicably. "The birds or the spits?"

"The spits." Guthreh holds up her hands. "We caught the birds."

He glances back at me, and I can't help but return his grin.

My levity fades when I glance at my own hands, looking for the death on them that giant claimed to see.

"Rora?"

I nod, shrugging off the worry. "I'm fine."

The meal is the best we've had since Niav—roasted grouse, huge leafy greens, oversized wild onions and tomatoes. We have to carve the food into edible bites, though, since the giants down the vegetables like handfuls of seeds and eat the cooked birds whole. We all take seconds when offered, using items from our packs as plates since theirs are longer than our arms, then attack the mound of half-crushed raspberries piled near the center. The giants join us on the ground, jarring our bones each time one sits despite their apparent effort to do so gently.

As we eat, we tell them of our journey, of Finley and the people of Telyan, and how Helos and I came to live there. They seem especially curious about our childhood, but we recount only the outskirts of those years; this feels too pretty a place to delve into an ugly past.

Things grow tense when they ask after the Prediction readings. I notice Weslyn avoids our gaze when he explains the last seven years, and the giants offer no comment, just consider his words in silence.

As for myself, I'd like to cover my ears and block out the reminder. Instead, I study the ground before me, jaw clenched tight. Over the last week, I've been so preoccupied with getting us here that I had nearly forgotten about the Prediction, and being its rumored subject, entirely.

After we've eaten our fill, one of the giants—Corloch, he reminds us—yields his nest, inviting us to sleep there for the night. The halo of moss is the size of a small house and fits all three of us easily.

Right away, Helos and I fall into quiet conversation. Weslyn, however, remains fairly removed; he stretches out on the opposite side, using his pack for a pillow. Hardly any time has passed before his breathing slows and deepens.

Helos rolls his eyes and points with his thumb.

"I think we may have broken him," I whisper in amusement.

"Or fixed him," Helos says.

Crickets chatter and click around the peripheries, piercing the night with their song. After a time, I risk another glance at the sleeping Weslyn, whose features are drawn, almost troubled. As if he, too, suffers in sleep. I wonder what kind of memories might haunt him.

"Did you miss it at all?" Helos asks, running a hand through his hair. "Being here."

My eyebrows arch in disbelief, only for me to realize the corner of his mouth is twitching. The question is so knowing, so absurd, that suddenly we're bent double from laughing. A hopeless, heady charade of trying and failing to stifle the sound, a long-needed release after days of tightly coiled tension. And it feels earned, everything safer in this protected corner of the Vale, because we're *here*. We actually made it. We won.

"The giants have it pretty good, though," I say, regaining my breath. "Peace and quiet, and plenty of birds to catch."

"No, it's too easy to hear yourself think here." Helos waves a hand. "I'd probably go mad if I had to stay."

I study him a bit, sobering, trying to gauge how serious he is.

"Speaking of which—" He opens his mouth, then shuts it again. "I'm sorry."

"What? Why?"

He rubs an arm, like he's bracing himself for a confession. "I forgot what it was like. Being here, back in survival mode. And I let that distract me since crossing. I haven't been there for you like I should have been." He says it all in a rush, as if he's nervous. *Back in survival mode*—because for him, Roanin is the soft place to land, the apothecary shop his calling, whereas I don't think I've ever stopped running. "In any case, that's over now. I promise."

His tone is a bit desperate despite the smile, pleading for me to forgive him when there's nothing to forgive. I search his face in confusion. "You're allowed to be affected by the past, you know. Remembering doesn't make you weak."

Perhaps a bit of a joke coming from me, since the pain of the past has always been my main source of vulnerability, the mold that shaped the person I've become. Habits born from what we suffered and all the times I chose wrong, designed to maintain control and make me a person someone would stay for. Could love.

My brother only shrugs.

"Helos," I say, firmer now. "You can't just shut every bad thought into a box and throw away the key. Sooner or later, you're going to collapse under the weight."

His face transforms from remorseful to indignant, the descent into defensiveness rapid and unfamiliar. Eyebrows knit together, lips pressed tight. "Better than letting them consume you."

Blood rushes to my cheeks. "You're an expert then, are you?"

"Never mind. Forget I said anything." He rolls onto his side, keeping his back to me. Then, as if returning to himself, he quietly adds, "Get some sleep."

The food has soured in my stomach, and I watch his hunched form for a while before switching to the gathering darkness, uneasy. My brother and I have always been a team. We don't fight, not really.

Despite the peaceful surroundings, rest is slow to come.

Dawn has long since stretched its wings by the time I awaken the next morning. The only murmurs in the breeze drift in from songbirds and the stream, but I know further sleep isn't possible. Behind closed lids, I watched the soldiers' faces and heard the caegar's labored breathing and the thrum of arrows flying from angry bows. *Finishing the job,* Kallen growled, over and over in my head. *Finishing the job. Who the bloody ends are you?*

When the ground begins to shake, I jolt upright to wake the others in case of an earthquake—but it's only the trembling footsteps of a giant. Exhaling in relief, I grab my pack and set out in search of a place to bathe, noting that while Helos is still fast asleep, Weslyn is nowhere to be found.

I follow the stream barefoot, deep into the woods, wending around clusters of overgrown firs until the water branches off in two directions. For once, I feel no pressure to hurry or scan my surroundings for threats. Today feels like freedom—from danger, from worry—and the sensation is as unfamiliar as it is welcome. The tributary I choose leads to a small, blue-gray pool rippling out from the base of a waterfall. I shed my clothes and lower myself in, using a cloth to scrub the grime from my skin.

Despite my newfound ease, I can't help but try to figure out how those soldiers could have gotten here. The only crossing is in Niav, but they can't have used it; Minister Mereth would not have been interested in our offer to spy if she knew they were here already.

Jol must have already begun surveying the Vale.

My attention sharpens at the scrabbling to my right—not a man, but a small creature perched on one of the branches, wings outstretched as he collects his balance. He's like a fox in miniature, but raven black, with furry wings nearly twice the size of his body. Nightwing.

There's a brief period in which the two of us lock eyes—he on his branch, and me sitting knees-to-chest on a shelf near the edge of the pool, water lapping gently against my collarbone. Then he launches from the branch and, in a few rapid wingbeats, settles close to the waterfall, apparently deciding I'm not worth his fear.

Slowly, methodically, my hands tease out the knots in my hair while I watch the little nightwing from the corner of my eye. He's crouched low to the rim, his tiny pink tongue swiping the water in rapid strokes. The sight catches me off guard, brushes the dust from a truth long-buried beneath the sediment of trauma and time. I have spent so many years fearing the danger in this stretch of land, I had forgotten there's beauty in it, too. Beauty, and life.

When I have banished every trace of dirt from my skin, I climb out and throw on the cleanest item of clothing I possess: the lavender dress. Then I empty my pack of its contents and dunk the clothes and worn towel into the water one by one, beating and rinsing them as thoroughly as possible before laying them out to dry.

To my surprise, when I locate Weslyn, he's already seated amid a group of six giants, beard shaved to shadow once more, gesturing with his hands in the midst of some passionate recounting. The sight is oddly uplifting, an unexpected feeling considering I spent the first half of this journey wishing simply to be rid of him. But lately, the apathy between us back in Roanin feels as distant as the city itself.

Across the way, Guthreh sits cross-legged with one palm resting on an enormous knee, the other cupping her chin. She's looking down at Weslyn without blinking.

"—thinks killing all magical beings is the key to destroying magic."

"Then he's correct, in a way," says Guthreh. "But he does not understand why."

Several heads twist in my direction as I approach, Weslyn's last of all. He starts to smile when he sees me, then works his mouth into a straighter line, as if confused by his own reaction.

"You're talking about King Jol?" I ask, chest tightening as I take a seat beside him.

"Humans have never understood the connection between magic in the land and the beings it inhabits," Guthreh says by way of reply. She points a bony finger in my direction. "They're the same. Of the same magic, only divided among different hosts."

Weslyn leans forward, resting his elbows on crossed legs. "Scholars have speculated as much."

Guthreh appears unimpressed. "But do they understand the implication? The magic east of the river has begun to fade, you say?"

Weslyn nods. "The land there rarely stirs anymore. Outside of the Fallow Throes, it's almost as if the magic is dead."

Dead.

Before, the idea might have brought relief, to have a permanent respite from the terrain of our youth. Sitting alongside these ancient people, though, the word feels far too heavy and final.

"It is not dead, not yet. Magic will always fight to survive." Guthreh shakes her head. "But it will not last forever. Every day now, segments leak into the sea and vanish like mist."

I straighten in shock.

"It's true. Though imperceptible day by day, the magic *is* slipping away. But like calls to like, and so long as magical beings walk the earth, drawing their counterpart to the surface, the land's magic will continue to flourish. It will grow stronger, or at least stave off the gradual weakening."

"Like magnets," Weslyn says.

Guthreh appraises him for several moments. "Like seeds. They are born with magic in their veins, and they awaken magic where they go. When they die, their magic returns to the soil."

Like water, I add silently. Rising from the ocean. Gathering, falling, returning. "But I feel no different in the east than I do in the Vale."

"Your survival is not dependent on the land's magic, and one shifter alone is not enough to call it forth." Guthreh pauses thoughtfully. "But if it vanishes entirely, your kind—all magical people, and animals—*will* weaken over time. And you will die." Guthreh's attention flicks back to Weslyn. "If not sooner, whether by natural causes or targeted attacks."

I let the idea float together, blurred around the edges as if viewed through water. Wilderness razed, and meadows paved with roads. Human settlements stretching across the entire continent. Perhaps, once they felt more secure at home, they'd even open their borders once again to those across the sea. Magic might become myth, and folk like me, no more than a dream.

Guthreh sighs as if in finality. "You would have us go to war. Perpetuate these attacks. But we only want peace. We moved to the Vale to avoid human conflict, not participate in it."

"I'm trying to *stop* further attacks," Weslyn counters. "Against your people and mine. But I fear the only way to secure peace will be to fight back against those who seek to undermine it." He frowns. "I would have you help us, yes."

The pieces shift into place. "You think your father will say no to Eradain."

His silence is answer enough.

"Remaining here does not mean we condone what might happen," Guthreh says.

"Doesn't inaction amount to the same?" Weslyn challenges.

I stare at him, recalling our conversation in Willahelm Palace when I posited roughly the same thing. I hadn't expected my words to have any real effect on his attitude.

"What you must understand," says Hutta, one of the giants who greeted us the night before, "is that it does no good for us to stand against the people of the north. We already tried interfering, long ago. If you really wish to fix the problem now, opposition must come from within."

"It will," Weslyn insists. "I ask only that you stand with us when the time comes, not that you stand alone. You once urged my people to act on logic rather than emotion. I thought you'd want to hold us accountable."

"And we will," Guthreh replies, a hint of threat in her voice. A warning to back off. "When the time is right."

"The time is *now*," I say. "There are soldiers in the Vale, practically on your doorstep. They tried to carry off a caegar and called it some kind of job. King Jol has made his intentions perfectly clear."

She eyes me wearily. "The prince told us this already."

"Well?" I demand. "Don't you want to know what they're doing here?" My words are met with more silence, then two of the spectators mutter in a different language. "I don't understand. What's the problem? Why do you hesitate?"

"There is a way to these things," Hutta replies at last, studying me with an expression I can't interpret. "You mustn't rush forward before knowing the whole story. There is danger in acting reactively."

"Better than doing nothing at all."

Weslyn murmurs a word of caution, but I shake it off.

Hutta only stares at me. "Ah, shifter. You have been among humans too long."

The word lights the match.

Shifter. Monster. Girl.

Who the bloody ends are you?

No more.

"My name is not *shifter*," I spit, surging to my feet. "It's Rora."

Hutta starts to reply, but I'm already gone, thundering off without a destination in mind.

Weslyn catches up quickly.

"I think that went well," he observes in a dry voice.

I just continue marching.

"You have to remain calm in a negotiation."

"How very diplomatic of you," I retort. Feeling out Minister Mereth, establishing ties with the giants, rescuing Finley—how many reasons for coming on this journey did he have, exactly? Have and not tell me? My eyes cut over to him in the emptiness that follows.

He's grinning.

I nearly stumble over my own feet. It's the first time he's smiled, really smiled, at me. It's not his brother's smile; not as open, not as easily given. But I decide the subtlety of it makes it even better.

It dissipates some of my anger.

"What you said back there about doing nothing." I stop to face him. "You didn't used to feel that way."

He holds my gaze. "I do listen when you speak, you know."

A twinge of anxiety courses through me, but he's walking again before I can make sense of it.

"Come on, I'll show you."

I follow him to his pack, which he pulls onto his lap after sinking into the grass. I sit opposite him, surprised to find it feels natural now, replaying the moment he stepped between me and the caegar. *Hasn't anyone ever warned you about their eyes?*

"Here," he says, pulling me from my thoughts. I take the proffered book from his hands—not the one he reads, but the one he writes in, the one he's never let me or Helos see.

The light brown leather binding is travel-worn. I run my hands over its crinkled surface, amazed he has managed to keep it dry and whole, before opening to the first page. Then I look up at him.

"It's okay," he says. "You can read it."

So I do—the first page, then the next, then the next. It's an account of our journey, but the contents aren't sentimental; they're notes. Things Helos and I said and did—tips for traversing the wild. For surviving. I flip through the pages, spotting illustrations and diagrams interspersed throughout the text. Sketches of plants I said were poisonous, Helos's fire pits, honeysuckle blossoms folded back to reveal the tiny pearls. The holly hare's razored teeth, and even the widow bats. It's wonderful.

He smiles again, and I realize I said the last part out loud.

"It is, though," I insist, flipping to an illustration at random. "These are really good, Weslyn."

He opens his mouth to speak, hesitates, then settles on running a hand along his cheek. He makes no move to take the book back, only watches my face, as if waiting for me to say more.

Wind teases the ends of my hair, smelling of blossoms and pine.

A few drops of water patter across the open page, shattering the moment. I flinch backward, slamming the book shut on instinct. It's a mantis butterfly, with wings so dazzlingly blue they're almost glowing—water droplets sprinkle down from the tips with every flap. This one flits away at the fuss, but another few come to take its place, hovering mischievously over my head, then Weslyn's. His own personal, miniature rain cloud.

He ducks away, swearing softly and throwing his arms over his head.

And I just laugh. For the second time in days, weeks maybe, I laugh before I can remember my masks or the usual stony set of his mouth. Before the memories of this place and the weight of our mission settle over my bones once more.

His attention flicks back to me, at the way my shoulders are shaking with mirth. After a beat of deliberation, he drops his hands grandly as if conceding defeat, scrunching his nose a little when the butterflies' barrage meets its mark. It's all so absurd I can't help but laugh again, louder this time, and he maintains his false composure for another moment or two, three, before dropping his head to his chest and laughing, too. Like he's trying to hold it in, but can't. Like he needs the respite as much as I do. And I realize with a pang that I haven't heard him laugh since that day in King Gerar's throne room, before the messenger came rushing in.

"Stop it," I say at last, not to him, but the butterflies, swiping a gentle hand to scatter them.

Weslyn laughs again and shakes his head, brushing the water from his loose curls, his gray button-down dotted with moisture. The gesture makes him look younger, somehow. Less weighed down.

Warmth brushes my face and whispers to life in my chest. An unexpected impulse I've only acted on in a borrowed form, one that makes the voice inside my head whisper, *Danger.*

He watches me a moment, unblinking. "Listen—"

"Thank you for showing me this," I say abruptly, handing him back his book and berating my accelerating heartbeat. "I should see how Helos is getting on. There's a stream that way, if you want to wash your clothes." I stand before I can interpret the look on his face.

Realizing I have to make good on my word, I leave in search of my brother, wringing my hands roughly as I walk. It makes no sense, the flicker of feelings all wrong. Weslyn is the difficult one. Hardheaded. I hardly even know him—yet there was his book between my hands, freely given. The farther I walk, the more the adrenaline subsides, but I have trouble dismissing his expression from my thoughts. I think I'm disappointed, too.

There isn't a cloud in the sky, and the sunset that evening is one of the prettiest I've seen; brilliant shades of orange, lavender, and pink are streaked across it, the canvas a dramatic backdrop for the canopy above. Almost time.

We dine on similar fare as the night before, joined once more by several of the giants. I'm still aggravated from our earlier spat, but no one alludes to it. Instead, the meal is a pleasant affair, and even Weslyn laughs now and again. I'm still not used to the sound.

When the first crystal stars appear in the sky, we process past the moss nests and the rippling pool to another clearing toward the edge of the woods, near the place where the earth meets the sea. Helos trails in the giants' wake around the meadow's perimeter, keeping up whatever conversation they've begun, but I take a seat in the grass. Weslyn joins me.

The nights are growing cooler, and a shiver passes through me as I cross my legs and lay my arms across them. Neither of us says anything for a while. I catch my brother's eye at one point, but he glances away quickly, chatting animatedly with the smallest giant. Odd.

"I still don't understand," Weslyn mutters, the first to break the silence. "Why didn't the mist bring us here the first time?"

"You heard the giants—it puts things where they belong. Maybe helping those people was more important." My thoughts recoil, conjuring the caegar's bloody flank and terrified eyes. "Even if they didn't deserve it."

"More important to whom? The mist?" He huffs quietly in disbelief. "Would have been easier if it had just deigned to admit us on the first try."

Legs crossed, he tears at scattered blades of grass, then chucks them into the distance and leans back on his hands. A few strands of hair have fallen over his face.

"You're afraid for your brother," I respond at last. He turns his head away. "That makes it easy to deal out blame. But you can't fault the mist for doing what it will. It doesn't have a consciousness like you or I do, doesn't feel empathy or take sides. It just is." I track the giants' progress around the clearing as they free oversized vines from the branches, smiling when Helos tugs on one several times, only to have it fall on his face. "You can't assign intention to magic. I told you, it's neither good nor bad. It doesn't fit human labels, can't be put into a box any more than you or I can."

Weslyn doesn't respond for a while. I'm learning, though, that his silences are not always for shutting down, but for thinking. So while I wait, I tilt my head back to the sky and breathe it in. The darkness is familiar and unfamiliar all at once.

"And you feel you've been put into a box?" he says at last.

It's not the part of my little speech I expected him to pick up on, but I nod anyway. "Of course."

"The Prediction."

I hug my knees against my chest, studying the sky again. "Not just that."

The silence that follows feels slightly expectant, which elicits a strand of nerves. Though I've faulted him before for shutting down on me, I still find myself pleading that he won't push on this. Not right now, when I feel I can finally relax, and when that day by the riverbank seems so far away.

"You love the stars," he says instead, and I feel a twinge of gratitude.

"I like the dark," I tell him, smoothing the hem of my dress. And really, I'm not looking at the stars. I'm gazing at the velvet-soft night between them, its warmth an infinite void of colors and complexity and depth. It's not as bright, but to me it's beautiful.

"I used to fear it," he confesses, smiling ever so slightly when I raise my eyebrows. "Probably not something a potential future king should admit."

I wish he hadn't mentioned the king thing. It broadens the distance between us.

"Though I doubt I'll ever see the throne," he muses, as if reading my thoughts. "Not with Violet next in line."

He doesn't sound sorry about it.

"Does that bother you?" I ask.

He shrugs. "I don't need to be king to make a difference. Besides," he raises an eyebrow, "it would be difficult to murder my sister. She's too clever."

My eyes narrow suspiciously. Did he actually make a joke? "Maybe you can go to university once she's queen."

He seems surprised by the suggestion. "I'm meant to train as an officer. That won't change even if the sovereign does."

"And that has to be forever? What about what you want?"

Weslyn studies me calmly, almost with sympathy. "I *want* to do my duty. I don't begrudge my title or the responsibility it brings, Rora. I'm not my brother." He shakes his head a little, marking the giants' movement around the perimeter. "I just would have chosen a different role, that's all."

I'm trying to act normal, as if hopeful energy isn't suddenly coursing through my veins, but it's hard. This is the first time he's said my name in four years.

You have everything, I would have replied even two weeks ago. *A life without baseless judgment and a family who loves you. I'd hardly say you're stuck.* But I remember what he said about serving to spare Finley, assessing the future and reshaping his life for the sake of someone else's, and I think a box might still be a box, however velvet its walls. "Well," I say, feeling encouraged by his use of my name, "What would you study if you could go?"

He straightens a little, warming to the subject. "History," he answers, like the word has been building inside him. "The sciences. And—" He breaks off, looking almost shy. "You'll laugh."

"Why would I laugh?"

Weslyn doesn't answer for a while, just tosses blades of grass into the distance. Suddenly far more the boy on the horse than the somber soldier prince. "Architecture," he mutters. "I think there's a lot we could do to improve the cities' infrastructure. The farming towns, too. If we could just—you said you wouldn't laugh!" he protests, but now he's smiling too, happiness contagious in this peaceful place.

"I'm not," I tell him earnestly, though I'm unable to staunch the ridiculous grin that's taken over my face. "I think that's smart. It suits you."

And it does. Overseeing planning grids and building projects, refining the kingdom's smaller intricacies while the crown handles the larger picture—all those people in Grovewood he knew by name. I can see it.

Weslyn nods his thanks and looks away, the ghost of a smile still playing at his lips.

I hate that I'm looking at his lips.

A rush of wind slivers through the clearing, and I hug my legs tighter against the chill. In contrast, Helos appears to lean into it, spreading his fingers and letting the air twirl around them. Anything to ground him in the present, I'm sure. I'm relieved to see his bearing is lighter here than out in the woods, more relaxed, and he glances over to check on me before sidling away with a smirk.

And then I understand why he's absented himself.

"Now that you've interrogated me," Weslyn says, "can I ask you a question?"

Yes, Helos is definitely keeping his back turned now. I'd like to chuck a rock at him, but there are no stones lying around.

"Does anything good ever follow those words?" I reply, uneasy with the way his tone has sobered.

He seems to take that for permission. "Why do you cry in your sleep?"

Now it's my turn to feel taken aback. "You noticed, then?" I remark, stabbing at humor. He remains serious as ever, though, so I relent. "I have a lot of nightmares. From the past."

He nods once. "Back in Roanin, when we devised this plan—I didn't consider what it would be like for you, to have to return."

There it is again. An invitation to share more. A door left open, if only I choose to step through. I know little about friendship, but I've been raised on instinct, and mine is thrumming a warning.

If he knew the truth of what I am, I would lose him.

"You never asked," I agree at last, but I soften it with a smile.

He doesn't return it. "I should have."

"Sorry to interrupt," Helos says, making far noisier an entrance than is strictly necessary. He plops down on my other side, setting the small box we had used for the Old Forest seeds on the ground beside him. "I'm supposed to leave it open. The giants said that not enough stardust drifted down in the daylight to provide the supply we need, so they're going to tap into their 'vault.' They told me it's time."

"Time?" Weslyn repeats, still looking at me.

As if in answer, the giants grab hold of the vines they've collected, wrapping the ends around their palms like bandages. Fireflies dart around them in frenzied anticipation, as if they know what's coming. The white orbs blink out one by one, until the only remaining source of light is the star-strewn night sky.

To my astonishment, the giants begin swinging the vines, higher and higher above their heads until the ends sweep across the treetops. The resultant breeze lifts the hair from my shoulders. I hear the stems connect with leaves, like bear grass in the wind. Weslyn straightens beside me.

Specks of light cascade down from the treetops, winding and twirling like autumn leaves. There are hundreds—no, thousands—millions of lights shimmering down, silver and pearly white and iridescent gold, glittering in the blackness.

Stardust.

Steady as rain, gentle as mist, the particles glide to the forest floor. Some settle on my hair, others over my outstretched legs. They're surprisingly cold to the touch, but I make no effort to brush them off. Though the giants said it would have to be ingested to do its work, I still find myself searching within me for a sign, some change wrought by making contact with this concentration of consummate magic. *Like calls to like.*

There's no singing in my bones. No metamorphosed blood in my veins. And it doesn't repair the cuts on my hands or my stomach.

Tenderly, I pinch a few bits of dust between my fingers. The beads are ice-cold and tiny like sand. Before I can change my mind, I pop them into my mouth and swallow.

At first, the chill moves like a blade, traveling down my throat and beyond. Then it softens to a glow, almost how it feels when shifting. I can feel the cuts on my hands and stomach stitching back together.

Helos extends a hand of his own but makes no move to swallow any.

The giants continue to swing their vines, and the fireflies swirl higher, dancing with the dust, the meadow their ballroom, as it spirals to the ground. It's the most beautiful sight I have ever seen.

The boys to either side of me say nothing. We just breathe, content to witness in silence, and suddenly I feel it.

A twinge of release. A chink in the armor. A slackening on the tether encasing my heart. As if pools of water have been drained from my lungs, and finally I can breathe easy again.

Happy.

For the first time, in a long time, unbroken, untainted, peace.

EIGHTEEN

The following morning dawns clear and bright. I awaken only when Helos shakes me gently, having slept fitfully through the night; my restless thoughts kept turning over the events of the evening, and one particular exchange that taunted me loudest of all.

You never asked.

I should have.

"I thought an early start would be best," Helos says, as I pull on clean clothes and shove the dress to the bottom of the pack.

I just nod. Truthfully, I'd like nothing more than to fly—there are few better ways to clear a cluttered mind than by soaring far above the ground. But I can see the way he keeps running his hands through his hair, feet shuffling. And really, I'm as anxious as he is to get back on the move. There's no telling what state Finley's in back in Telyan, and besides, I'm growing tired of living on the road again. I'm ready for this journey to be over.

Once everything is in order, I hoist my pack over my shoulders and trail Helos to the stone circle where four giants are seated, Hutta and Guthreh among them. Weslyn is there, too.

Adrenaline brushes through me, unexpected and difficult to ignore. I settle next to Helos, not daring to check until my traitorous eyes shift of their own accord. He's watching.

Yes, the sooner we leave the confusion of this place, the better.

I accept the proffered breakfast eagerly, grateful to have a use for my hands.

Corloch says sometime in the coming week, they'll be sending a message to Weslyn by black-tipped caw. Once we return to Telyan, Weslyn is to send one back with updates on the situation with Eradain, as well as King Gerar's plan of action. No mention of trying to track down the people who tried to kill us.

Not enough. It's not good enough, and I long to tell them so. Instead I keep quiet, wrestling with my own conscience. King Gerar ordered us to find what might be causing the resurgence of magic, and the anomaly of those Eradain soldiers practically fell into our lap. The logical next step is to investigate, but whenever I try to work out a plan, the only image that manages to stick is that of the loaded bow aimed at my chest.

We depart the stone circle shortly after, bidding farewell to all but the two giants who come to see us off. Weslyn has the box of stardust tucked safely into his bag. I had examined it first, only to find it surprisingly heavy in my hands, easily the weight of two rabbits. Too heavy to enable my unvoiced idea of carrying it back to Roanin on wings. No matter—we cannot lessen the load, or there won't be enough to go around.

We're halfway through the clearing in which we arrived when the giants halt, lodging themselves on the boulders. Even with the massive stones there to intercept their weight, the ground still quivers at the impact.

"You will find the mist where you left it," Hutta says, nodding toward the other end. "Remember, you must ingest the stardust in order for it to heal. And make sure it remains dry—outside of a living body, water is not compatible with magic." She examines each of us in turn. "Good luck with your people."

"My brother would have liked to meet you himself," says Weslyn. "Thank you again."

She only nods. The other says nothing, so we utter one final goodbye and resume our crossing.

"Rora."

I swivel round, facing Hutta in surprise. We've scarcely gone more than ten steps.

"A word," she says, gesturing for the two boys to stay where they are.

With minor trepidation, I return to her side, wondering what she could possibly have to say that she doesn't wish Helos or Weslyn to hear. Perhaps the reprimand for insulting her the day before is finally coming. She stares at me. I stare back.

"You've held on long enough," she says, her voice soft as wind-swept reeds. "It's time to let go."

Let go? I blink at her a couple of times. "Let go of what?"

Hutta's mouth stretches wide in a smile. "Good luck, Rora."

Unease hits the pit of my stomach. I don't know how to respond, so I say nothing, just pick my way back over to the boys. Their faces are more apprehensive than curious, and I know their attention is focused elsewhere. The border. The mist. We have no choice but to depart that way, and the last time we were outside of the giants' domain, we had been on the verge of capture. There's no way of controlling where it spits us out this time—or whether or not the soldiers will be there, waiting.

I lead them onward.

"Just . . . focus on Finley," Helos says, attempting to reassure us. Being strong, like he said he would. It doesn't comfort me as it once did. "That's where we're needed. Maybe concentrating all our energy on him will send the mist a message."

I don't respond. Weslyn keeps his eyes trained forward, but he nods all the same.

The eerie silver-blue veil materializes as soon as we reach the other end of the meadow; it can't be more than a stone's throw past the tree line. I step into the woods and tug a thorny, leafy stem away from our path, holding it in place until Helos and Weslyn have both reached my side.

"And if those soldiers are there?" Weslyn asks, gripping the hilt of his sword.

I study that grip, then follow the line up his arms, past his chest, to the expression on his face. Quiet, but edged. Solemn, but composed. Clear. I often forget that he's been trained for situations like these, but looking at him now, it's hard not to think of it.

I release the stem. "How many could you take?"

"At once?" He pauses to consider, fist still wrapped around the hilt. A warrior's stance. "Three. Possibly four."

Four? Merciful fortune. "If you're exaggerating—"

"I'm not." No boasting, no defensiveness.

He's not.

It feels odd, now that I'm starting to get the fuller measure of him. Not a military man, but a cerebral boy forced into a soldier's body, softness scrubbed into a harder, impenetrable shell. As if the frown he so often wields is not a weapon, but armor. My thoughts return to the scene with the caegar. There were six of them then. Would Weslyn have tried to fight if I had not ordered him to run?

"The thing is," I voice hesitantly. "I've been thinking. Shouldn't we try to learn what those people are doing here?"

Weslyn's brow furrows. "That might be difficult to do if they're intent on killing us."

"But if they're not there when we return, we may not have to fight them. We could track them down in secret, so they wouldn't know we're following. They captured a caegar—why? They could have killed it straight away, but they didn't. Where were they taking it?"

He runs a hand along his face. "My father would want us to find out if we can."

I glance at my brother, who has been silent throughout this exchange. "Helos?"

He grips the straps of his pack. "Our priority is reaching Telyan. All of us, all in one piece."

"What about the rest of our mission? You would leave without figuring out what's going on?"

He drops his shoulders and bites his lip. "I'm not saying I like it. But securing the stardust has always been the most important part, and we've done that. We have the cure. We should bring it to those who need it."

Old habit whispers that I ought to side with him. Helos has always been the one to help others, after all, to judge what's best for them, no matter the cost to himself. But—

"The humans might not be the only ones in danger. Think of that caegar. Haven't you noticed how quiet it's been since we crossed the river? What if Eradain really isn't waiting for assistance from Telyan and Glenweil before striking the Vale? Other animals could be captured or dying. The magic could be dying."

"*Finley* is dying." My brother almost never cries, but all of a sudden he looks close to it. "Back in Telyan, right now. And we can save him."

Weslyn's mouth pinches tighter, and guilt hits the pit of my stomach. I agreed to this quest to save Finley. I still want to save Finley.

But it feels wrong to leave the Vale without at least trying.

"My father's orders were clear," Weslyn says, with a hint of defeat. "Rora's right, we should track them down if they're not already waiting to ambush us. But I agree with you," he adds, when Helos crosses his arms. "We cannot delay too long. We'll give it four days to find out what we can, five at most. Then we return to Niav."

"How can you—"

"I know what you would say," Weslyn cuts in. "But it's the right thing to do. I'm sorry, my hands are tied."

For a long moment, they just stare at each other. Weslyn scarcely more than a statue, Helos fidgeting with his golden shirt, ready to step right out of his skin. Back with that strange, wild-eyed intensity he wore when pinning Weslyn to the tree, as if he has a mind to do it again. I don't understand whatever's passing between them, but before I can think of a way to ask, Helos relents.

"Come on, then," he says, sorrow warring with frustration in his voice. He leads us right to the edge of the mist, then nods to me, making sure I'm ready. When Weslyn mirrors the gesture, we step into the veil as one.

I don't struggle against the invisible bindings as they yank me forward yet again. Instead, muscles clenched, I survey our surroundings the moment the air around us settles once more—a deer that flees at our sudden appearance, a break in the pines just ahead.

No Eradain soldiers in sight.

I crane to catch a glimpse of the white tail disappearing into the brush. Light brown coat and cream-colored breast. Not a deer. A caribran.

Finally, a larger magical creature spotted. But the dirt beneath my boots remains silent and still, no razored pine needles or sentient peppervine strangling its prey, no ground shifting quicker than a falling star. The feeling of wrongness lingers.

Since the absence of people does little to reassure us, we move as one to the break in the trees, each of us still on our guard. We're back at the lake, only farther north than when we'd first encountered it. It's a lucky break. Judging by the mountains' proximity, we should be able to reach the area where we lost the soldiers in little more than a day, if we move quickly.

And we do. An unspoken sense of urgency has taken hold; the sooner we can gather this information, the sooner we can leave, and all of us are eager for journey's end.

We pick our way along the shore in silence, making unprecedented time. Helos charges ahead, with Weslyn following close behind. I bring up the rear, keeping an eye on the sun's position in the sky. By the time my brother turns us farther east, long beyond sight of the lake, we're all in need of a rest.

None of us stop. Instead, we push on through the dense, quiet woods until it's practically a contest over whose stomach growls the loudest.

"Helos," I call.

He swerves to a halt, hovering a moment before swinging the pack from his back. "Ten minutes," is all he grants.

Weslyn pulls some nuts from his pack. While the two of them are occupied with food, I take the opportunity to relieve myself, walking a good distance away until I'm sure neither can see. Though I strain my ears for any sound of approach, there's nothing beyond the usual rustling and creaking trees.

The surrounding stillness has begun to unnerve me. Like it isn't simply quiet west of the river. . . . It's *empty*.

Voiceless and rigid, halfway asleep. It's made the trekking easier, true, and I suppose I ought to be grateful for that. But the lingering dregs of relief are mixed with increasing despondency.

Where are the people like me, the forest walkers and whisperers? The elusive moose whose melodic calls ring out like a symphony of bells, or timber bear cubs play-fighting outside of moss-covered dens? Gemstone beavers who lure mates with iridescent tails, and teal-striped hummingbirds that collect acorn tops like crowns? More and more, I'm finding in my heart a sorrow I never expected to feel.

Weslyn is missing when I return.

"Where is he?" I demand at once, finding Helos simply sitting among the twisted roots of an old oak, toying with a piece of crinkled parchment. He shoves it into his pack as soon as I appear.

"He offered to fill our waterskins. He said he would stay close."

"You let him go by himself?"

Helos peers out to his left, then back at me. "He's getting better. I think he can manage a short time on his own." His eyebrows arch in amusement. "You're welcome to go and check on him, though, if you're concerned."

"Of course I'm *concerned*," I reply. "There could be more of those soldiers around!"

He nods his head to the side again. "The stream is just out of sight—we passed it on the way here. If anything threatens him, we can be there in an instant. Sit," he says, gesturing to the grainy ground before him.

After ensuring that I can hear the faint trickle of running water myself, I do as he suggests. I'll have to refill my own waterskin before we move on. "What were you looking at, anyway?" I ask, straightening for a better view of his pack.

He holds his empty hands up and shrugs. "Just a leaflet I brought from Niav."

I do another scan for danger before broaching the topic on my mind. "Listen. I have an idea."

"I know what you're going to say," Helos murmurs, carving tiny slits into the dirt. "And I do want to know what's going on here, okay? But I have to save him. Whatever that fading magic means for us, for others like us—" He drops his head a fraction lower. "I can't lose him, Rora. And I can't be in two places at once."

"You don't have to be," I say, forcing him to meet my gaze. "You and Weslyn can bring the stardust to Finley and the others. I can stay."

He recoils at once. "You're not staying here alone. It's too dangerous."

It's true, the notion of separating would have felt inconceivable to me before. It still nearly is, but suddenly the issues at stake feel far greater than a question of what I want. "Clearly, the Vale is not like it was before. I can shift—"

"You're not staying here alone."

"But think about it, Helos! If we split up, you can get a jump on delivering the medicine, while I finish the job King Gerar gave us."

"By the river, Rora!" Helos punches the ground with his fist. "Just . . . stay here with me. Finish the job like we planned. Then we'll figure out our next step."

Another fight, and not even two days have passed since the last one. Something's unraveling between us, and I've lost the thread as to why.

"You don't have to spend every hour protecting me," I remind him. "I'm just as capable as you."

"I know you are. I just—" He breaks off, brushing the hair away from his forehead. Already, exhaustion appears to be sweeping away the sudden burst of adrenaline. Sweet Helos, his earnest face the very portrait of a torn heart. "Stay with me. Please."

Though my throat pinches at the sight, I let the moments drift past before responding.

"I'm going to fetch Weslyn. He's been gone long enough."

My brother's brow furrows. I haven't promised anything, and he knows it. But he doesn't speak again, so I grab my waterskin and leave the camp.

The narrow stream is indeed just a short distance downhill;

Helos has hardly left my sight when the first stretch comes into view. The babbling water wends between silver aspens and over slick, flat stones jutting out from its center, gleaming in patches of sunlight. A little farther along, Weslyn is crouched on the opposite bank, wrists submerged in the fast-flowing stream. His eyes are closed.

"Sleeping on the job?" I ask when I'm close enough, watching his hands fly to his sword in the moment before he spots me. His shoulders sag, and his mouth relaxes into a subtle smile.

Something's unraveling between us, too.

"You startled me," Weslyn observes with a touch of humor. "This is becoming a pattern."

"You're lucky it's only me," I reply. "You shouldn't let your guard down."

He runs a hand along the back of his neck, still grinning. "Always one for reassurance. You sound like Brock."

"Brock?"

"The arms-master."

Ah. Yet another person who showed little pleasure in my existence. "Well, he's right."

"You took your pack with you," Weslyn continues, pushing to his feet and hefting his and Helos's waterskins. "I couldn't refill yours."

"It's all right." I move opposite him and dip mine under the surface. "You chose a good spot, at least."

"Moving water only. I remember." The confidence in his voice hedges on boredom.

"Yes, well, it could still be contaminated," I mutter.

"No doubt you'd poison it to teach me a lesson."

Insulted, I open my mouth to object, then shut it again when I see his expression. He's teasing me.

Off-kilter, I swallow my response and take a couple of swigs from my waterskin.

Weslyn leans lazily against a tree, watching me. "I have managed to survive twenty years on my own, you know."

Not on his own. Not like my brother and me. "Please. You grew up in a castle. They practically spoon-fed you."

"Not true," he says. "Growing up in a castle has its challenges."
"Oh?"

He nods very seriously. "People were always there trying to *do* things for me. Anywhere I'd go. Very annoying."

I bite my lip. "I'm sure."

"And Astra," he says mournfully, as if the name holds the weight of the world. "I said one day I wanted a dog, assuming my parents would either say no or wait awhile to let the excitement build. But they just . . . gave me the dog." He speaks as if it's a true puzzle.

"You are insufferable," I murmur, but I can no longer hold back the smile.

Without warning, a flock of crows erupts from the treetops nearby, a sudden, feathered mass of flapping and shrieking. I start so violently I nearly lose my footing on the bank.

Weslyn's arm shoots out to steady me, but I regain my balance on my own, forcing a deep breath and crouching again by the water's edge. "Sorry."

"Are you okay?"

No. I dip my waterskin back beneath the surface and focus on the stream's bracing chill, cradling my wrist like silk. Count the stones, smell the fresh air, anything to lock out the hammering in my chest, the flush of embarrassment heating my face. "It's nothing."

Rather slowly, Weslyn crouches to my level on the opposite bank.

I have a mind to tell him I'm fine again. But when my gaze flits to his I see concern there rather than judgment, and I think that maybe—maybe I can admit this.

"Sometimes it's like I never left." I speak as if to the ground. "A noise will make me jump, or I'll feel an ache where I injured myself years ago, and suddenly I'm a child again, stuck in a scene I thought I'd buried for good. Which is stupid, I know, because so much time has passed, but I can't help it, the thought of returning to—" I break off, suddenly aware I'm rambling. Feeling utterly exposed.

"Yes?" Weslyn says, the word gentle.

I hesitate, not knowing how to continue. But since he never seems to need to fill a long silence, I suppose there's no need to feel bad about it. "It sticks with you," I say at last, then shake my head.

"It can be difficult to remember I'm in the present, that's all." I pull the waterskin from the stream and fasten the cork back into place in one swift motion.

"That sounds difficult," he says after a time, still crouched there.

I shrug, my throat somewhat tight.

"I'd like to help."

"You do," I assure him, before I can think better of it.

There's a moment of silence. Then another. "I do?" he asks, watching me carefully.

I swallow. "Yes."

A shout rends the air.

I'm on my feet in an instant, water tumbling down my wrists and over my boots. Was it—? Another garbled shout, and this time I'm sure of the voice.

Helos.

I surge up the hill as fast as I can manage, stumbling once or twice on an unstable bit of footing—whether from roots, rocks, or a surge of magic, I neither know nor care. Weslyn must have jumped the stream, because his footsteps are pounding the earth just behind me. Branches scratch my skin and yank my hair, but the stings barely even register. I have only one thought, and that's to get to my brother.

The sounds of a struggle grow louder as we reach the campsite. Heart writhing in its cage, I hasten to make sense of the scene emerging before me.

There's Helos, in elk form, surrounded by blue-clad men. How many? There must be six at least, maybe seven. One by one, they're smothering him in ropes.

Without thinking, I scream his name.

The men's eyes are on me straightaway. Seconds later, two of them break apart and tear in our direction.

Pulling his sword, Weslyn shoves me aside, half a second before his blade connects with another's. Three more uniforms have sprung out from our left, a second wave that neither of us spotted in our panic. I barely have time to fear for him before cool air rushes through my body and my clothing rips apart. Claws out, hackles raised, I shift to lynx just in time to deflect one of the two men charging me, rolling onto my back and kicking out with my hind legs.

His body is powerful; I can feel the strength in his muscles as I send him crashing onto his back. By the time I've leapt to my paws, he's already twisting to the left, gasping, heaving, desperate to restore the breath I've knocked from his lungs. I don't stop to think. I don't consider my options. Before he has time to swing his sword back into position, I clamp my jaws around his throat and rip.

Warm blood showers my snout and floods my mouth, over my gums and beneath my tongue. But I don't loosen my hold. Instead, the taste sends me into a sort of frenzy, and I tug harder, tearing and maiming until the jerking beneath me ceases abruptly.

The second man is backing away, staring in horror at the sticky liquid dribbling from my jaws down the front of my coat. I have half a mind to spare him, but the predator instincts are thundering through my senses, and he's clearly making for his comrades again. No doubt to help subdue Helos, who's thrashing about like a wildcat himself. Ears pinned close to my head, I close the distance between us in four strides and pounce, digging my claws into his back and finding the soft spot beneath his jawbone. He stops twitching long before his friend.

When I raise my head once more, the scene has already shifted. A man's sword-tip catches Weslyn just above the knee, but Weslyn doesn't falter. He intercepts the blade with his own and slams against it several times before dislodging it from his opponent's hands and slicing his sword through the man's midsection. To my left, one of the men around Helos is on the ground, emitting strangled cries of agony as his shaking hands clutch blindly at the long, bloody gash severing him from neck to navel. Another man bears similar wounds on his legs and drops a moment later.

Amazingly, I think we might actually be winning, but then out of nowhere, reinforcements appear. Again. Now there are five men around Helos once more, two of them fresh, holding fast to the ropes that bind him. I charge toward my brother as he shifts to fox and attempts to wiggle out of the cords now hanging loosely off his smaller form. He manages to rid himself of a few, but one of those ruthless men delivers a vicious blow against the back of his skull, and he falls to the ground.

Falls, and doesn't get up.

I snarl in rage, paws flying toward the group.

One of them spots my approach and shouts a warning as he raises his bow. I manage to clear the arrow speeding toward me—barely—but a sickening cry from behind sends me sliding to a halt.

Weslyn, who I've only just realized was steps behind me, has dropped to his knees. His fingers are turning scarlet where they clutch at a black-fletched shaft imbedded in his sword arm, midway between the shoulder and elbow. My blood freezes in my veins. The arrow pierced him.

A man from the newest wave of reinforcements is limping toward him from behind, the only one out of—I look beyond him, merciful fortune, there are *five* bodies on the ground—that he hasn't killed. Weslyn hears him coming and releases his arm, grabbing his blade with his left hand and stumbling to his feet. Sticky blood drips down from the arrow wound as he steadies himself—then staggers to the side.

I look toward the group carrying Helos, which has begun a hasty retreat through the trees, then back at Weslyn, who's already falling.

This will only take an instant. I race toward the man and duck around his feeble swordwork with ease, bringing him down swiftly now that I know how it's done. Weslyn tries to stand again—and fails. I just whip back around, ready to return to my brother and finish off the rest of the men who dared to touch him.

The forest before me is empty, save for the dead.

Helos is gone.

NINETEEN

They took my brother.

I have no idea how they tracked us, or how far they've gotten. I don't even know if Helos is still alive.

But he's gone, and they've taken him, and it's taking every drop of effort for me not to fall apart on the spot.

I turn to Weslyn, who's on the ground with the black-fletched arrow in his arm, clutching at his knee, his face contorted in pain. I can't tell how grave his injuries are or how much blood he's lost, and he's my responsibility. *Please,* Violet said, and I promised Finley he'd be fine. I'm charged with protecting him.

His eyes connect with mine, and he whispers a single word: "Go."

The command may condemn him, but it isn't a choice for me, not really.

I run.

My paws fly across the forest floor as easily as my wings claim the sky. The ashen, earthy scent of magic hangs faintly in the air, still far weaker than it used to in these parts. I cling to the sight-and-sound trail of scuffed dirt and quivering vegetation, uniformed pant legs rubbing together and the thumping footsteps of rubber-soled boots. Every stride pierces my heart with a thousand knives. Patches of blood are smattered across the ground, and on the leaves, Helos's scent.

And then, without any warning whatsoever, the trail ends abruptly.

I crash to a halt and pause an instant before retracing my steps. Impossible. It was clear enough only moments before. My ears strain to relocate the party, but the only remnants they detect sound underground, which makes no sense. I search the area thoroughly, scrabble at the forest floor, even lurch a few paces farther ahead in the hopes of picking the trail back up. But my eyes and ears aren't wrong.

It's simply vanished.

Panic rips through me then, so forceful that my bobbed tail brushes out. Do they have magic? But no, that would be impossible; humans cannot wield magic. They're simply gone. My brother is gone. And I've killed people.

The reality of that begins to sink in. I didn't just fight them off. I ripped their throats out and can still taste blood between my teeth. I don't even want to know what my coat looks like.

And I don't regret it.

I think that should be impossible, but it's the truth. They were after my brother—and my friend. It was us or them, and I chose us. I chose us, and I don't regret it.

I'm not sure what that says about me.

I try to imagine what Helos would have done, were our situations reversed. Throughout our childhood, our survival strategy was always to run away. Evade, outsmart, hide. Wait for the danger to pass or flee so far away that we lost it.

What would Helos have done?

This is the question that plagues me as I perform another thorough examination of the area. But the trail is truly gone, sight, sound, and scent, and I'm forced to admit defeat.

Overwhelmed with despair, I tilt my head to the sky. A mournful yowl erupts from my throat, high-pitched and piercing. I send the sound into the forest around me, hoping that somehow, wherever he is, Helos can hear it and know that I'm coming for him. Hoping that he's even alive to hear it.

But first, there's someone else who needs saving, and at least I know where he is.

I pick my way back to Weslyn, limping after a thorn catches in my paw. Fortunately, beyond that, I seem to be unscathed.

He's right where I left him: slumped onto the forest floor, white shirt stained scarlet, alone except for the slain men around him. The fur rises along my spine. He's breathing heavily and dangerously pale, clearly exerting a great deal of effort to keep silent.

Even to my weaker nose, the putrid scent of death hangs heavy in the air. I count nine bodies in total—the one whose belly Helos slit with his antlers has since expired. Apprehensive, I glance up through the cracks in the canopy, where vultures have already begun circling overhead. Cursed fortune.

When Weslyn finally catches sight of me, his eyes widen significantly. He looks afraid, and I honestly don't blame him.

I need to pull the arrow free and assess the seriousness of his wounds. To do that, I need to shift back to human. Normally I would do it without a second thought—it's just another form. But for some reason, being naked in front of him suddenly feels different, and I find that I don't want to.

Don't be ridiculous, snaps the voice inside my head. *He needs you.*

Steeling my nerves, I pad over to my pack and sit beside it, looking at him expectantly. He closes his eyes.

Though I hate the thought of traveling in a dress, the pants I ripped today were one of only two other pairs. For all I know, there could be more of those men nearby, and I can't risk ruining a second set. Checking once more to ensure his eyes are really closed, I shift to human, remove the thorn from my hand, and quickly pull underthings and the lavender dress from my bag. Heartbeats later, I'm kneeling at Weslyn's side.

"Let me look," I instruct, trying to ignore the wariness in his expression. When he doesn't offer the wounded arm, I reach for it myself and gently remove his other, soaked hand from beneath the arrow shaft. Fortunately, the hole is close to the edge; it seems to have cut through more fat than muscle. The pain must be horrendous, but still—he's lucky.

A quick inspection of the remaining tears in his clothing reveals the other cut a little above the knee, but that one seems shallow enough, thank fortune. I have to disinfect them, and I have to stop the bleeding, but I'm not a healer.

"My bag," Weslyn says through gritted teeth.

I snatch it from the ground and drop it at my feet. Though I'm hesitant to rifle through his things, he's in no state to do it himself, so I flip the covering open and peer inside.

It takes some time to find what I need. I end up laying out some of his belongings on the ground—clothing, food, the book, and the journal. I leave the box of stardust where it is; his injuries don't look severe enough to merit using any of that precious supply, and I won't risk it going anywhere other than the inside of a pack. At last, I produce the roll of bandages and the vial of disinfectant that he used on me. There's no needle or thread, so after I free the arrow, we'll just have to hope that a tight enough binding will stop the flow of blood. I don't want to think about what will happen if it doesn't.

"I'm going to take this out," I tell him, indicating the arrow and attempting to sound confident.

Weslyn opens his mouth to speak, but before he can protest or dwell too long on the anticipation of pain, I fist the shaft and break it in two. Weslyn swears fiercely and drops his head, gasping as I slide the pieces free.

"Sorry," I breathe. As tenderly as I can, I roll back the sleeve until it's up to his shoulder. My fingers are covered in his blood, as I'm sure my face is still covered with the blood of the men I killed. I can feel it starting to dry.

I reach for the shirt I tore when shifting to lynx and use it to wipe the area as clean as I can, a process not made easy by the flowing cut. When I soak an untouched stretch of fabric in the disinfectant, Weslyn stiffens visibly.

"Don't be a baby," I say lightly, hoping to take the edge off of his nerves. Then I press the cloth against his skin. This time he can't stifle his groan.

"Almost done," I lie, being careful to clean all of it. Then I wrap it tightly with the bandages.

By now, Weslyn looks close to fainting. I slap his face a little, trying not to dwell on the feeling of stubble scraping my palm, desperate for him not to leave me alone in this clearing. Not yet. "Don't fall asleep," I say, though I don't know if that's actually necessary.

"Just . . . painful," he breathes, blinking slowly.

Overhead, the meddlesome vultures are loitering. I scan the trees for movement before applying the same treatment to Weslyn's leg, then wipe my hands and sit back, exhausted. Nothing to do now but wait. The bandage around his arm has soaked through a little, but the blood hasn't reached all the way around, so I'm hoping that means it's tapering off.

Weslyn catches my eye. "Helos," he rasps.

The word is a blade to my stomach. I shake my head, wishing I had another wound to treat. Anything to distract me from my failure to rescue my brother.

"I lost him," I say. It comes out little more than a whisper.

"Is he—?"

"I don't know!" I exclaim, tears welling in my eyes. I cross my legs and bury my face in my red hands. "I don't know. I lost the trail." An avian cry pierces the air, and I allow myself another handful of heartbeats before lifting my gaze to the sky once more.

"You're worried . . . about them?" Weslyn asks, gesturing vaguely to the birds.

"Not them." I watch him wince as he clutches his leg and realize we're going nowhere just yet. "About whatever else might have seen them."

We sit in silence for a time. Ever so slowly, the sounds of the forest start to surface again. Creatures coming out of hiding after the disturbance has cleared.

Never in my life have I felt so utterly alone.

"Rora."

I lift my tear-streaked face.

Weslyn is struggling to keep his eyes open. "Sorry, but . . . I think . . . I'm going to faint."

I release a huff of air and almost smile in spite of myself, torn between a desire to shake the life out of him or kiss him.

"It's okay. Lie down and shut your eyes."

He does as I say, leaving me to scan our surroundings for any signs of movement. Scout, and rack my brain for a clue as to where those men might have taken my brother. My fingers tighten around the skirt of my dress—and my head snaps up. Helos and hands.

With a glance at Weslyn to make sure he's not watching, I step carefully over to Helos's pack and sink down beside it. My eyes well up as I sort through his clothing, shirts he may never wear again for all I know. *Stop it.* He's still alive. Surely he must be.

My fingers brush against loose parchment. Delicately as I can, I extract the folded paper that Helos clung to throughout the river crossing and restore it to its original shape.

It's Finley.

Finley in strokes of black ink, a drawing cut from a leaflet. Messy hair across his forehead, cheekbones carved through an oval face. Standing—back when he could without pain—yet slouching slightly despite the formal attire. I run a fingertip across the tailored suit and vest beneath. Finley would have hated these, but I'm smiling all the same. He was healthier when this portrait was created. Untouched by death's proximity.

The thought of Helos clinging to this cutout makes me want to bury my face in my hands once more. I cannot lose him. I will not lose him.

But for now, he isn't here, and Finley's just a picture, and Weslyn's breathing has deepened into sleep. I'm alone in these evil woods, with only my thoughts and the dead for company.

The marrow sheep arrive more quickly than I anticipated. Pale brown coats, white rumps, massive horns curling to either side of a head that could crush a person's skull with a single blow. Carrion pickers of the Vale, hunting for bones to strengthen their horns. The bodies of the Eradain men are still strewn about where they fell.

Fortunately for us, or perhaps a sign of the Vale's weakening state, there are only two sheep. I manage to frighten them off in lynx form before Weslyn comes to.

"We have to move," I tell him, rousing him from his stupor once they're gone. I hold out a navy button-down from his bag. "Put this on."

Weslyn doesn't argue or demand an explanation for my rummaging through his belongings again. Instead, he accepts the offering and attempts a one-handed change while I take sudden interest in cataloging my food supply. I'm onto the fruits when he holds out the ruined shirt.

"Leave it," I say, indicating the ground. "Can you stand?"

He drops the shirt and pushes himself to his feet, keeping most of his weight on his uninjured leg.

"That one doesn't hurt so bad," he explains when he sees where I'm looking. "I just don't want to push it, in case it starts bleeding again."

I appraise him critically, unable to determine whether or not he's lying. His voice sounds stronger, at least. "All right then. Let's go."

I place his things back in his bag and hoist it over my shoulder, ignoring his protests. I grab Helos's bag, too, since he'll definitely need that when we find him. The weight of three packs is almost more than I can manage, but I lead us in the direction I ran in earlier without complaint, the track the men took when they stole my brother. We barely make it a hundred paces before Weslyn staggers against a tree.

"Sorry," he mutters, panting heavily. "Just need to rest for a moment."

I glance between the way forward and Weslyn, torn. After a brief deliberation, I make up my mind. "We'll stop here for the night."

"No, let's keep going."

"It's okay," I assure him. "We've moved far enough from the bodies. We should be safe." Another lie, but what am I supposed to do? He can't even walk.

He glares at me like he knows I'm lying but doesn't press it further, just sinks to the ground right where he is. I place the packs down next to him and survey the area for any signs of animal tracks or snake dens. When I'm satisfied nothing is about to leap out at us, I set about building a small fire, then pull some dried meat and way-bread from my pack.

Weslyn drops off for a while, and by the time he comes to, the sky has grown dark.

"Drink some water. And eat," I command. He grumbles a little but does what I say. I wish I still had that cat's tongue to lessen the pain, but our supply ran out long ago, and I don't remember the look of it enough to go searching.

"That sound," he says, taking a bite of dried meat and nodding in the direction of the faint pops, like sticks snapping into pieces.

"Probably just some squirrels rummaging for food." I repress the urge to cover my ears. Powerful molars grinding bones into dust. Fortunately for us, marrow sheep have little interest in heartbeats.

He pulls his waterskin from his pack. "You said you lost the trail. How?"

My shoulders sag. "I don't know. It was just—there one moment, gone the next. As if they'd vanished into thin air, or the ground had swallowed them whole."

"Could it have?"

I imagine Helos imprisoned beneath the forest floor. Buried under layers of sediment and rock, my hallucination from the meadow come to life. I shake my head helplessly. "It's possible." In which case, how could I ever hope to follow? "For a moment, I thought the trail led underground."

He pauses. "We have to go after him."

"I'm going to." And I will. Even if it means leaving Weslyn on his own for a time. I can do that, if I have to. If it means giving Helos a chance at survival.

Can't I?

"We're going to," he amends.

I give him a once-over. "You can barely walk, Weslyn."

After a while, he says, "Wes."

"What?"

He smiles a little. "You saved my life. You may as well call me Wes. Anyway, I'm better now." As if to prove it, he starts to stand.

"Stop!" I exclaim at once, having no desire to watch him faint. "You need to rest."

"I'm fine."

"You're an idiot. Sit down."

He obeys, grinning. "What if I told you I could have you beheaded for calling me an idiot?"

"I'd call you a liar, too," I reply. "And I'd laugh, because you'd have to make it all the way back to Telyan to issue that order, and you're in no state to do that at the moment."

He doesn't reply, and my thoughts grow serious in the silence that follows.

"I killed those men," I say quietly. Their faces have plagued my thoughts alongside the image of Helos being hit in the head.

Weslyn's expression is grim, but determined. "You did what you had to do."

"I know. And I thought that was enough, earlier. I didn't regret it." I watch him for a few moments, waiting for him to judge. "But their deaths achieved nothing. Helos was still taken. I killed them for nothing." My voice chokes a little on the words.

"It wasn't for nothing," he says. "You saved me. And you stayed free. If you hadn't, you would not be able to rescue your brother."

I laugh without humor. "I don't know how to save him. I don't even know where he is."

"But you're going to try."

I nod. "I have to."

"We'll go at first light," he says. "You can start by taking me to the place the trail disappeared. Maybe we'll find a clue you didn't notice before."

I eye him dubiously but don't object.

"Those men," he continues, when he realizes I'm not going to contradict him. "They were wearing Eradain colors."

I tug at my hair. "I know."

A pause. Then: "I killed many of them, too."

If Brock were here, I imagine he'd be proud. I only feel sick. Calm, lethal precision; I examined the bodies earlier while Weslyn was recovering.

Wes, I correct myself.

"Had you ever done that before?"

He holds my gaze. "No. And I hated it."

My heart twists. "Despite your training?"

"They train us to do the job when there is no other choice. Not to take pleasure in it." He rubs at his bandaged arm, wincing slightly. "I don't think anyone should."

Silence falls again. Around us, conifer trees huddle close in the light of the flickering flames. I switch my attention to the crackling fire and the crickets' lament in the air, the soothing scent of burning cedar. Anything to distract me from the fear for Helos threatening to eat me alive.

"It's my fault he was taken," I say, pressing my hands into my forehead. "I'm the one who insisted we stay. I may as well have led him straight to them."

"I argued for it, too," Wes reminds me. "If anyone is to blame, I'm as responsible as you are. But Helos agreed. He knew what he was doing."

I shake my head, unconvinced. "All he wanted was to bring Finley the stardust. He—they're close, you know. Or," I stumble, confused. "They were."

Wes leans back on his good hand, nodding once. "They were."

Hearing the past tense from somebody else only adds to my sorrow. Does he know, or has he had to piece it together alone, as I have? And if Finley has confided in him, does he know why his brother would keep Helos away when the misery of that decision is written so plainly across his face?

I realize, right then, that I'm angry with Finley. To have found that kind of love and choose to keep it at bay with nothing more than a word, no sensible reason I can see—it's wasteful. Insulting, even, to people like me, who have never been so lucky as to have the choice at all.

I peer closely at Weslyn's face and realize it doesn't matter. He doesn't seem ready to spill his brother's secrets, any more than I am mine.

"Do you miss Finley?" I ask instead, swallowing my frustration. I've never really asked him about his relationship with his brother. Not directly. But personal questions always seem more acceptable at night, and I did just save his life, as he pointed out.

He runs a hand through his hair, appearing to weigh his response. "He told me to trust you, you know."

"He did?"

"Mm. The night before we left."

I try and fail to imagine that conversation playing out. "Well, we both know you're too stubborn to actually listen."

Wes smiles a little. "After my mother died, it was—difficult. My father became a shell of himself. I tried to help, but it frightened me, the change in him." He falls quiet, his gaze a bit distant.

For a moment, I try to picture him as a scared, grieving boy, not as the stoic, steady appraiser he's always been in my presence. It's difficult to envision.

"Violet is the one who pulled him out of it. I don't think he could have done it without her." He draws one of his knees up and loops his arm around it. "But I couldn't have done it without Finley." Eyebrows arched in amusement, he nods at the surprise on my face and glances away. "He's my little brother. I'm supposed to look out for him. But somehow he's gotten it into that thick skull of his that it's his job to look after me."

Now it's my turn to smile. "I think it works both ways."

"To answer your question, I miss him, yes. More than I can say."

He looks at me then, expression turning serious once more. "We're going to get Helos out."

"And the rest of your family?" I persist, looking down at my palms and brushing past the reassurance. "You must miss your mother, too." Something is building inside me. Burning. Demanding release.

Wes grazes a hand along his beard. A long time passes before he speaks again. "I saw her in the meadow, the other day. I knew it wasn't real. But still, it was—" He takes a breath. "Difficult to look away."

Sympathy lances through me as I remember how she managed to make me feel hopeful in so short a time. "What was she like?"

"Clever, like Violet. Kind, like Fin."

And you, I almost say, but I bite back the words. For so long, I have mistaken his reservedness for severity. But it's not. He's just quieter. Serious. Slow to trust.

Like me.

"You loved her," I say simply.

He studies the ground. "It just didn't make sense. She was the one who taught us to ride, she was an expert. To fall like that, on the day you both arrived . . ."

My back tenses reflexively.

"I'm not blaming you," he continues, sensing the change in me. "It was my own problem, and I'm sorry if it hurts you. But for a long time, I couldn't look at you without thinking of her death. I resented you for coming, for being there that day, because maybe if I had not had to—" He pauses the sudden torrent of words, tugging at the grass. "I was wrong," he admits, and I don't contradict him. "But I can't stop thinking that if I had been there, if I hadn't volunteered to take you and Helos to the castle, I might have been able to stop it."

"You couldn't have changed it," I tell him.

Wes looks at me sadly. "You don't know that."

"I know that you can't keep torturing yourself about it," I say, more gently now. "And I don't think she would want you to. The odds you could have done anything to prevent that accident are very small."

He falls silent for a long while. Around our meager fire, the night presses closer, as if offering a hand to hide us from the world. Clouds cover the moon tonight, but a few stubborn stars are glimmering through the wisps.

"Sometimes I think it's just easier not to feel at all," Wes mutters.

There's a rawness to the words, a soft honesty in his voice that makes me wonder if he's ever said that aloud.

"Does that make you happy?" I ask after a moment.

His jaw tightens, just a little. "It's not—it wasn't—about being happy."

"Is that why you came on this journey, then?"

He blinks at me.

"That's why you're trying to help your father and save your brother? I saw you with those people in Grovewood, Wes. You make a good show of it, but you don't seem to me like someone determined not to feel." I find I'm actually grinning. "In fact, I think you might be very bad at it."

He laughs at last, surprised and heartfelt, and it feels like a victory.

"Have I just risked execution again, for telling you you're bad at something?"

"If you have, you'll have to join a queue," he says, shaking his head. "Naethan tells me that every other day."

He looks down again, calmer now.

In light of his openness, the thing building inside me has sharpened into claws, needling my insides, insistent. The painful awareness that I'm lying to him, even now. I don't know if it's the fact that we're alone in these woods, or just the baffling, endless patience in his bearing, but I can't shake the conviction that if he's going to put his trust in me—this person I now understand is damaged but so inherently good, just like Finley said, who feels so deeply and listens and owns his mistakes without prompting—he needs to know.

I drop my gaze, fiddling with my hands.

"I don't miss my mother," I confess into the dark. Already, it's the tip of madness, putting the worst of me on display. But it's out now, can't take it back. "She abandoned us when we were only a few years old. Humans attacked our village, I don't know why, and she fled without taking us with her. She left us there to die." I pause to gather breath, old grief tightening its fist around my heart. "They must have killed her after she left, because we never saw her again. And I'm almost glad, because sometimes I think I hate her, Wes. I try not to, but I do."

Speaking the words aloud brings a strange mixture of mortification and relief. I'm terrified to see his reaction, but when I steal a glance at last, he's only watching me intently.

"At the giants, you said both of your parents were murdered. Your father?"

How long has he been waiting to ask that? "He was shot in the back after our house caught fire." I press my lips together. "In front of me. He was helping me escape."

Wes opens his mouth, closes it again. "Rora," he whispers, sadly.

I shake my head. "Helos and I ran for our lives. He told us to. But when we returned the next morning, no one was left."

"No one? Why did those people attack your village?"

"I don't know. The wondering still keeps me up at night."

Wes doesn't speak for a while, and my nerves twist into knots. I have never spoken this much about my past, even with Finley, despite all his pressing. Not with anyone other than Helos, who lived it, too. After a time, I start to worry I've made a mistake in telling him these things. My fingers dig at the ground.

"I figured you were—orphans," he acknowledges at last, stumbling over the last word. "But I thought your parents must have died just before you came to Telyan. I had no idea—" He breaks off. "I'm sorry."

I shrug a little, like it isn't a big deal, like it's not the biggest deal in the world. "Helos has always been enough. He's always been . . . better than me. It should have been me who was taken."

"Don't say that."

"No, it's true. It should have been. But it wasn't, because it never is. Did you know I left him to drown once?"

The confession clearly startles him. And it should. My heart is screaming at me to shut my mouth before I ruin his impression of me forever, but now that I've started, I can't seem to stop. It's the worst truth of all, the shame a brand upon my soul.

"I did. When we crossed the river to enter Glenweil. He insisted I wait on the bank while he went in first, to make sure it was safe. Of course it wasn't. He only swam a short way into the water before the current swept him under. It was slamming into him, he couldn't keep his head above the surface, he was drowning, and I was watching him there from the bank. And I—" I break off. "Did you know that shifters can take three animal forms in the course of their lives? We can't choose which. They just appear at a moment of greatest need." I swallow bitterly. "My brother was drowning, and I wanted to save him. I *tried* to save him, I ran to the water, and do you know what my body did?"

Weslyn only stares.

"It shifted to a stupid bird! So I could fly across instead of swimming and maybe drowning, too. I stood there watching my brother dying, and my core, my deepest self, thought the right response was to flee and save myself." My voice is wobbling precariously now. "Do you know what my third form is, besides the hawk and the lynx? It's a mouse. So I can hide. A lynx, so I can defend myself. Helos's two forms appeared when he needed to save *me,* not himself." A small sob. "I bet my mother saw it, whatever in me that's gone wrong, and that's why she left. I guess I hate her, but I also can't blame her. At least if you had been there the day your mother died, you would have done the right thing. I *was* there the day Helos almost died. And I didn't. I'm not a good person, Wes."

And just like that, the dam within me breaks, and the tears that have been threatening to fall all day flow freely. I hate crying in front of him, in front of anyone, really, but it's all just too much, and I can't imprison myself any longer. I press my palms into my sodden eyes until it hurts. I know he's going to leave now that he knows, and he'll be right to, but even so I can't keep holding on to this suffocating guilt. The self-loathing. The conviction that I'll never be enough. I am just too tired.

Impossibly, an arm wraps around my shoulders. It only makes me cry harder.

"What was it you said about torturing yourself?" he says quietly.

"That was different," I insist, sniffing a bit.

"Mm." He rests his head on top of mine.

"It was."

"There's nothing wrong with you, Rora. You said yourself you couldn't control what form you took. But you could control whether or not you went after him, and you did. Your mother's choice does not reflect on you."

I don't know whether I should fight him or thank him, but either way, I can't seem to gather enough breath to say anything at all.

"You're the bravest person I know," he murmurs. "I'm sorry I was too stupid to see it sooner."

He doesn't speak after that, just lets me cry, lets me alert the entire forest to our presence. Sturdy. Steady.

The oak.

Because as it turns out, his heart is not hard at all.

We wake at first light to an altered campsite. Where the fire had burned for most of the previous evening, patches of wildflowers have sprouted in clumps: star-shaped violet columbines and stalks of magenta fireweed as tall as my calves. It's hard to appreciate the sight.

Somewhere in the Vale, Helos spent the night alone. He could be frightened, and hurting, and doing fortune knows what with those soldiers in charge. And the more time that passes, the less likely we are to ever find the trail.

As Wes and I start to collect our things, the sounds of scuffling pinch the air to my left. It takes me several moments to spot the peeku crouched among the rocks; with his round body and dusty-brown fur, he appears practically an extension of stone.

My muscles lock up the instant our eyes connect, and his tiny nose quivers as it sniffs the air. He's smaller than a holly hare and infinitely more dangerous. "Wes," I whisper. "Don't make a sound."

Slowly, Weslyn lowers the waterskin from his lips.

I nod to the rocks where the peeku is squatting and raise my hands to cover my ears, in an exaggerated fashion so Wes knows to copy. Behind me, his confusion is a near-tangible thing, but to my relief he's keeping quiet. Move toward the creature, or move away—I'm trying to figure out the best course of action when fangs puncture the peeku's neck and snatch him to the ground.

The changeling wolf's fur returns to gray, his body rippling into existence out of seemingly nothing. The river take me. Peeku may be adept at camouflage, but the wolves here are practically invisible when they choose to be. Before I can decide how to re-act, this one makes a quick appraisal of me and Wes, then vanishes into the undergrowth with his prey clamped between his jaws, tail streaming through the brush.

It's over so quickly, my thundering heart is still catching up when I turn to Wes and rise. "Can you stand?"

He shoots to his feet, wincing at the jolt to his wounds. "What was that?"

"Changeling wolf," I reply. "And he did us a favor; the peeku's cry can be deadly." Wes looks at me like I'm speaking a different language. "Let's go."

"What if there are more?"

I turn back to the trees, peering into the morning haze. "If there are, we won't see them. The only thing to do is carry on. That peeku was small prey, though; I imagine he was hunting alone."

Take heart, the world is at balance—that's what Father would say. But I don't see how that could possibly be true in a world where Helos is gone.

I insist on carrying Wes's pack again despite his protests; he's assuredly in an enormous amount of pain right now, and I wonder how much effort it's costing him to not complain. At least he's able to keep a fairly steady pace, though he still limps a little.

It doesn't take long to reach the spot where the trail dropped off. I recognize it by sight, even without the aid of my lynx eyes. This is the place I lost all trace of my brother. Its features are branded into my brain.

We pace around the clearing for a while, then beyond, then back again. Looking for any echo of disturbance. A speck of dried blood, maybe, since that man with the torn legs disappeared with the rest of them. There's nothing.

Any hope the morning dug up is severed at once. I have no idea what to do.

Right when I'm about to suggest I shift back to lynx to see if there's anything those heightened senses can pick up, Weslyn suddenly stops, standing straight as a rod.

"What is it?" I demand.

He doesn't reply right away, just backs up a few paces, then walks forward again. Halts at the same spot. Jumps a little on his good leg.

"What are you doing?"

He steps to the side and bends down, tugging at the grass and roots covering the place he just vacated. I'm at the point of questioning his sanity when his hand yanks on a particularly knobby root, and the ground opens up.

Adrenaline courses through me. There's a hole about as far across as my arm, right there in the forest floor.

The entrance to a tunnel.

"You did it," I breathe, hardly able to believe my own eyes.

Wes appears just as stunned as I am. "This explains why the trail went underground."

For a few moments more, we linger there, staring into the pit. A wooden ladder descends into its belly, though it's too dark to make out the bottom. I ready myself to shift at the slightest sign of movement within, but there's no sound, no light, not a single human head surfacing to investigate.

Cold trail.

"Are you sure you want to go down there?" Wes asks, without any real conviction to the question. "We don't know how far it goes, or what might be waiting on the other side."

I take in the tight mouth. The curling hair. The dark honeyed eyes creased in concern. "He's my brother," I reply. Then I plunge into the darkness.

TWENTY

Some darkness is familiar. Gentle and warm. Safe. And I am not afraid of it.

This darkness is the thieving sort. It robs me of my vision and my courage. Of rational thought. It's the kind of darkness that blinds me, that makes the sky and the world feel infinite, and me, very small.

I can't navigate the tunnel like this.

"I'm going to have to shift," I whisper to Wes, who's right behind me. I made it only three or four steps past the bottom of the stairs before stopping.

My words have a slightly muffled quality to them, which makes me suspect that the cavern doesn't stretch too far above our heads, and that it isn't lined with stone.

Wes mutters his agreement. "I can carry the bags with my left arm." When I say nothing, he senses my hesitation. "It's okay. Really."

I'm sure his injured leg would disagree, but since there's no other option, I remove my shoes and clothing—he certainly can't see me here—and stuff them into my bag. I hand him his first, then Helos's and mine. As soon as I can feel he's gripping them tightly, one slung over his back, I let go and pull from the air around me, body shrinking and stretching out as the tunnel comes into focus.

The scents of those men and, yes, my brother, break upon me like a wave against the crags. The track is long and narrow, probably no broader than an arms-width apart. As I suspected, the walls and ground are made of packed earth.

There's no telling how far ahead it stretches, but this is the way my brother came and the only way is forward. I pad on, my lynx paws silent against the dirt.

It quickly becomes apparent that Wes is not moving at a good pace, even accounting for his injuries. I double back and touch my nose to his free hand, and he flinches so forcefully that he swears, no doubt having jostled the arrow wound.

"Sorry," he whispers. "I can't see a thing."

I position myself close enough to his side that he can rest a hand in my fur. When he gets the message, I lead us through the tunnel.

It's impossible to tell how long we're there for. Hours, maybe, or so it feels. Between the gaping emptiness ahead, the total silence other than our halting movements, and the hand burning into my back, my nerves stand fully on edge. I push past the uneasiness, driven by the knowledge that each step brings us closer to Helos, and each minute wasted might well lessen our chances of saving him. His captors must have had lanterns or torches of some kind to guide their way, because the tunnel smells faintly of smoke.

When at long last we reach the opposite set of stairs, hunger is raking the walls of my stomach. I halt and shift back to human, grabbing my pack from an unsuspecting Wes and dressing as quickly as I can in the black.

"The stairs are just ahead," I tell him when I'm ready to go. "I don't know where they let out, or whether anyone will be there. It will probably be dangerous." I hesitate before making the offer I think I must. "You don't have to come. You're not bound to Helos like I am. And if we don't make it out of this, there will be no one to bring the stardust to your people."

"I wouldn't make it back to Telyan without you, anyway," Weslyn replies. "And if you think I'm staying behind, you really don't know me at all."

With that, he brushes past me and leads the way up the stairs, feeling each step with his foot, judging by the sound. I am desperately afraid for him, but I can't deny that I'm relieved I don't have to face this alone. I bump into his back at the top.

"I'm going to push and hope that it opens," he explains, so quietly the words are almost lost. "As soon as we're out, make for cover."

I sort of want to point out that I'm the last person who needs instruction on avoiding detection and seeking shelter, but I simply murmur my assent. We wait for a few moments, straining to hear any movement above, but nothing reaches us.

"On three," he says at last. "One, two—"

The flap above the stairs flies open, and Weslyn and I explode from the tunnel. The sunlight is blinding after our time underground, and it's a battle to keep my eyelids open long enough to find refuge. We're still surrounded by trees, thank fortune. As soon as he shuts the entrance, I grab his hand and pull him behind the nearest trunk.

We stand there in silence for an indeterminate amount of time, listening hard for any signs of an approach. As the seconds tick by and it becomes clear that no one is coming after us, I realize how closely we're pressed together—and that he hasn't let go. A blush rises to my cheeks.

"I think we're safe," he whispers. His breath seems to be coming a little quicker, but I suppose that's from our mad dash out of the tunnel.

I nod and drop my hand. "I'm going to scout around."

Leaving him to hold Helos's pack, I peer around our tree, listening hard for more people. The firs here are spread farther apart, and many of them are too thin to hide behind. I spot a good one a short distance away and brace myself, then dart around it to try to catch my bearings.

We're close to the edge of the woods; the tree line is just ahead. Beyond and underfoot, the grassy land slopes upward, cresting into the rolling hills that blanket the base of the Decani Mountains. We've shifted north, farther so than the scene of the caegar attack. I locate my next tree at the top of the knoll ahead and sprint up the rise, breath hitching in my throat as I lodge myself against the bark. Then I look out.

A vast stretch of open land sprawls before me, undulating in gentle curves that ought to be occupied by herds of caribran, their velvety summer antlers arcing high. Instead, the hills are empty, sparsely vegetated, and overwhelmingly brown. The hue is out of place in a wilderness as lush and overgrown as the Vale, and it definitely wasn't here when Helos and I were. In fact, judging by the position of the mountains straight ahead to the north and west, and the slice of the river just barely visible far, far to the east, I'd estimate we're close to where . . . where . . .

My muscles lock up as the truth seeps in.

This is where Caela Ridge used to be.

The ancient trees and overgrown greenery. The ghost town of wooden houses and bridges that haunt my dreams in half-baked form. All of it is gone.

This tree line I'm hiding among isn't natural. The woods should reach a little farther out. My gaze comes to rest on a dark rectangular structure crowning a low plateau in the distance, seated closer to the base of the mountains. It's tiny from here, but the fact that it's visible at all suggests that it must be quite large in actuality. Creeping along the forest's edge, I scan the dirt for boot prints until my suspicions are confirmed.

There are tracks, so subtle I would have missed them if I hadn't spent my life learning to recognize disturbances like these. The men went this way, which means that whatever that structure is, is most likely where we'll find Helos.

I pop up to tell Wes—and find myself facing a bow with the bowstring pulled taut, an arrow two handsbreadths from my nose.

Fur pokes through the skin along my back as I stare at the wooden tip, mouse instincts yanking on my core. The figure wielding the weapon has a freckled, ivory face framed by blond ringlets streaked with silver and gold. She studies me through silver eyes, the irises shiny as stardust.

She's a whisperer, which means I can't shift to animal—she'll be able to persuade me to do what she likes.

"What do you want?" I choke out, and her lips squeeze together in warning.

The ground pulses through the soles of my boots as weighty footsteps thud to a halt somewhere behind. I risk a glance over my shoulder, and my fists tighten further at the sight of the massive timber bear hunched a short distance away. It must be her companion. Its paws are as big as my head, the claws as long as my little finger. The whisperer quirks her chin toward it.

I shake my head. In a heartbeat, she fires the arrow just past my ear and pulls another one into place. Her chin jerks toward the bear once more.

My boots feel heavy as lead as I force one in front of the other, the bear tracking my funeral march through hooded eyes. It circles around and leads us away from the tree line, no doubt receiving instruction from the whisperer through whatever channel she has tapped into in its mind.

Seven more whisperers are standing where I left Wes, each with silver- and gold-streaked hair, each human in appearance except for the silver eyes. Their forest-colored tops are cut with no sleeves, revealing the glimmering, golden rings that surface on their left arms like a second skin for every new species they learn to compel. Some have only two or three encircling the wrist, about the width of a fingertip; others have rings extending all the way up to the shoulder.

Those are the ones to fear the most.

"I found another one," calls my captor as I stumble into their midst. Her voice has a brusque quality to it, not unlike the clipped speech of Eradain. An older-looking man with a partially shaved head shoves Weslyn in front of the group and signals to my captor, whose face falls as the bear lumbers away. Wes clutches his injured leg and scans the length of me as if checking for damage.

"That's far enough," says the man, raising a palm. I stop.

At first, nothing happens. Then a rope slides over my boots, and I look down to find it's a snake.

In fact, there are several snakes, a dozen at least, all milling about the ground where Wes and I have gathered. Their stone-patterned bodies are capped with two heads; the blue-striped one has the ability to spit fire, the red one venom. The one on my shoe curls itself around my calf, and bile rises in my throat.

"Let me explain how this will work," says a short, large-waisted woman, her warm beige face marked by thin brows, a broad nose, and a small, wary mouth. She steps toward Wes and me as her comrades form an outer circle. "You will tell us everything you know about the building beneath the mountains. What it is, why your people have come, and what you aim to do." Pausing for obvious effect, the whisperer curls her long, streaked raven hair behind her ear. "If you don't, the snakes will scorch your legs until they char. If you do, and I think you are lying, I'll sink an arrow into one of your limbs." She strokes her bow rather lovingly. "I warn you, I'm a terribly good shot."

"We don't know what it is," I begin.

She raises the bow.

"We don't! We came to find out."

Wes stares at me pointedly. *What building?*

"And why would humans take sudden interest in the Vale?"

"I'm a shifter," I say. "I used to live here, at Caela Ridge."

Her eyes narrow. "Those shifters were massacred."

My stomach curdles at the pronouncement. Pulling from the earth beneath her boots, I lengthen my hands and feet, stain my hair yellow with streaks of silver and gold, extend my torso, reshape my nose—on and on, until I know I'm a perfect replica of the whisperer who brought me here.

"You are a ghost," the short woman murmurs, her pupils dilating as she stands a little lower in the hole I've created. To the side, my captor swears loudly at her stolen image as several others raise their bows once more.

"I am just as real as you are," I insist, returning to my natural form. "And you're slowing us down. We're looking for someone who was taken from us."

"Typically it's best *not* to provoke armed captors," Wes cautions under his breath.

"And this one?" the man asks, kicking a smattering of forest

FORESTBORN 249

debris in Wes's direction. The snakes hiss at the disturbance and undulate closer to us. "Are you a shifter, too?"

"Human."

The bows pivot in his direction, and someone spits at his feet.

"Stop that!" I demand.

"Why?" The man with the shaved head closes the distance between us in slow, deliberate strides. The serpents part before his feet. "Is this the kind of friend you're searching for? Another human?"

I swallow the lump crawling up my throat. "My brother. I think he might be in that building you spoke of."

Wes peers toward the top of the knoll I climbed.

After a long pause, the short woman mutters a few words, and the rest of them lower their weapons, some visibly reluctant. "We have lost people, too," she says. "Ones who have gone out alone. Normally, you can hear the humans' stomping from far away. Somehow, they have figured out a way to move in silence."

"We found a tunnel," says Wes. "That may be how they're getting around."

"Show us."

The snakes disperse, slithering into the trees with a few indignant outbursts of flame and venom. Limping a little, Wes leads our group back to where he and I burst through, and the whisperers exclaim openly when they see the trapdoor.

"How long has that building been there?" I ask.

The short one fingers her bow, the movement etched with tension. "A few months, perhaps."

"A few *months*?"

"You did not know?"

I steal a glance at Weslyn, who's surveying our surroundings with appraising eyes. "I live east of the river now."

"You stay with them?" spits my captor, her lip curled in disgust. "Even now?"

Wes rubs his bandaged arm but says nothing.

"What of it?" I say.

"Forestborn do not belong with humans. Not anymore."

"Forestborn?"

She narrows her eyes. "People like you and us. You were born with magic in your blood, were you not?"

The word tugs on the deep recesses of my memory. A term from childhood, maybe, or perhaps the flicker of recognition I feel now is only imagined.

"You still have a home here, a community—family and friends you can turn to," I counter at last. "We had nothing."

"We?"

I bite my lip. "My brother. The one I'm trying to rescue, and yet I'm wasting time here talking to you!"

"It is folly to try to enter that building," says one that looks younger than the rest. His arms are all corded muscle, his dark brown hair tied into a knot at the nape of his neck. A black-tipped caw is perched on his shoulder, its blade-sharp feathers precariously close to the boy's rich brown skin. "None of our scouts have ever returned. My cousin, for one."

"What about the animals you control? Why don't you send one of them?"

His eyebrows raise. "We've sent birds," he admits. "They are the only ones that returned. But they do not have sufficiently complex language to describe what they see. They can only report simple words: humans, shelter, hunters, danger, death."

Weslyn appears bewildered by all this talk of bird words, but I've latched on to only one.

"My brother is not going to die," I say. "Not while I'm still breathing. One of my animal forms is a goshawk. Let us go now, and I'll scout out the building and tell you what I find."

The man with the shaved hair quirks his head, considering. "If you go, you will not return."

I grasp the straps of my pack tighter. "I will."

"I can help as well," Wes offers at once.

"No," says my original captor, shoving Wes's injured arm hard. I lurch toward her, but she has an arrow nocked and pointed in an instant. "We do not treat with humans. Not since their kind forced us from our home."

"Peace, Yena," the youngest one says, earning a few scowls from his companions before turning to me. "Your friend can stay with us while we wait for you."

Reluctantly, I urge my clawed hands to return to fingers. Wes folds his arms, but I nod.

"Will you walk with me back to the tree line?"

I agree after a brief hesitation, catching Wes's frown out of the corner of my eye. The bird on the boy's shoulder squawks at my approach, its ruffling feathers clicking together like metal, but it falls silent when the boy tilts his head. He gestures for me to lead the way, his streaked hair glimmering in the sun.

"My name is Peridon," he says quietly, falling into step beside me. "And yours?"

I eye him warily. "Rora."

He nods. "My cousin is small, with brown skin and long, curly hair." He worries his bottom lip. "Her name is Andie. Will you look for her?"

This boy really doesn't look any older than I am. Than Finley.

"I will," I say, and the set of his mouth relaxes.

The tree line comes into view before long. When we reach it, the whisperers murmur a few parting words of luck, then retreat a bit into the woods. They seem to be intentionally giving Wes and me space.

To say goodbye, I realize. They clearly don't expect us to see each other again. The knot in my chest tightens.

Wes steps closer when we're more or less alone. "You know, I think you might be getting better at negotiating." I knock his good arm lightly. "What did that one with the bird say?"

"He wants me to look for his cousin."

Wes gazes at the sky a short while, then back at me. "What if they're right, and you don't come back?"

"I will."

"And if you don't?"

I bite the inside of my cheek. "Do you have any better ideas?"

He tugs his hair with both hands, then sighs loudly. "No," he admits, sounding defeated.

"All right then. Watch my stuff."

"You're going now?"

"My brother could be dying for all I know!" I exclaim, not willing to admit the other, even more terrible possibility. "Of course I'm going now!" In truth, my sleepless night is beginning to drag me under; my head aches, my limbs hang like rocks, and mild nausea coats my throat.

"Okay, you're right, I'm sorry," he says quickly, as I stow my pack behind a tree. I look again toward the low-lying hills, trying to gauge the distance.

"It would take me forever to cross that as a mouse," I muse, half to myself. "I'll fly over, then find a place to shift again."

He appears as if he's going to caution me with another warning, so I cut him off before he can shape the words.

"Wes."

"Rora."

A small light dances in my chest at the sound of my name, but I can't let that distract me. "I spent nearly a decade learning to survive. This is what I do. And I'm good at it." I realize it's true, now that I've said it aloud—the past may have weakened me, but it also made me strong. "If you're going to keep objecting, I'll just tie you to a tree and be done with it."

He smirks. "Using what rope?"

I take a step toward him. "Then I'll knock you out instead."

"Fine. Don't let me stop you. This is the part where you strip, I take it?"

I can't help it. I'm still not used to this side of Weslyn, the one that calls me by my name and makes wry jokes. I smile wickedly. "Feel free to look away if it embarrasses you."

He folds his arms and leans against a tree. "Not at all."

Well. I actually do need to strip, and he's not looking away. Rather than ask him to turn around, I try determinedly to remember the ambivalence with which I regarded nudity for my entire life up until the past few days. *Just another form,* I tell myself over and over as I shed my boots.

Doesn't work.

I fix him with a look, and he raises his palms and turns around. I wrap my underthings in my dress and shift to hawk within a handful of heartbeats. Then I'm rising into the air, the wind buffeting my outstretched wings, racing toward the mountains and, with any luck, Helos.

TWENTY-ONE

I gain a decent amount of altitude before sweeping over the low hills, trying to ensure that my presence goes unnoticed. Far below, I can make out a few remaining tree trunks cut close to the ground, stragglers that their killers couldn't be bothered to remove entirely. I don't understand the purpose of such destruction, but the lack of coverage will make liberating Helos even more difficult, if he really is there. After spotting a couple pairs of soldiers patrolling the open expanse, I can only hope Wes and those whisperers have enough sense to remain hidden.

I soon realize the site is more extensive than I first believed. Up close, the building I saw before is a forbidding, rectangular block that stands a couple of stories high, with dark gray walls that match the mountains behind them and no windows save for a handful set in a row just below the roofline, narrowed to hardly more than slits. Looming behind that is a tall, circular, wooden tower, and an ugly, squatter building with a chimney poking out of the roof. Three long, walled-in rows stretch to the right of these monstrosities, gleaming unnaturally in the sunlight.

I maintain my height as I fly closer, knowing I've only got one chance to pass over. At most, two. Any more than that, and onlookers might find my behavior suspicious. Well, more suspicious than a goshawk that has left the refuge of the forest to explore this barren domain. But there's no help for that now.

I keep my flight speed slow to the point of casualness. Only a bird searching the sky. It works to my advantage that I have a lot of experience with committing quick observations to memory; one pass over the silver rows is enough to tell me what's down there, and the realization makes me so ill I nearly lose control and abandon my avian form.

Instead, I fly straight ahead, beyond the compound and toward the nearest mountain. There's a deep fissure carved into the rock face, where a flood of mismatched stones has caved in and settled like an empty riverbed, widening in its descent and spilling all the way down to the ground. I alight near the top of an enormous fir tree shadowed at the base of the range—and nearly lose my purchase on the bark.

My blood, my beak, my veins, my very bones feel strange. Mismatched. At once chafed and soothed, kindled and doused. As if something is rubbing them raw one instant and healing them the next. The cool air sits unnaturally heavy in my lungs, and I take a few moments to steady myself and ensure that I'm still breathing. There is something wrong about this place.

I force my attention back to the walled rows below.

They're cages. Rows of cages, all out in the open to the side of the rectangular building. And they're occupied.

From the safety of my lofty perch a short distance away, I examine the enclosures in greater detail. Many of the magical people and creatures I kept expecting to see in the Vale are here. There are more caegars, some pacing their cages with taut whiskers and tails brushed out, others merely lying there. One keeps pawing at its eyes; I wish I knew why. There are birds, beautiful birds with red breasts and multicolored wings. Loropins. The bird whose feathers have cast a pall over my existence at the hands of the humans who wield them. In all my time living in the Vale, I only ever saw two. Here there are five.

What exactly is this place? A cruel menagerie? The conditions are terrible: slick stone floors enclosed in double-layered walls, the interior one made from crosshatched wire, the outer lined with thick, vertical black bars. Farther down the rows, there are more captives: marrow sheep and widow bats; nightwings splayed out on the floor as if sedated; an indeterminate number of two-headed snakes, curled up in an impossible knot of bodies with neither beginning nor end; caribran whose hooves normally draw grass from the ground, regrowing the blades they eat, except that beneath their feet here, there's only concrete. There are changeling wolves and gemstone beavers, even a couple of timber bears whose limbs have been bound so tightly, they must be in total agony.

My pulsing dread deepens when I take in the people. In the row nearest to me, there are six whisperers with silver-and gold-streaked hair, and four people who might be shifters given their entirely human appearance. Across the aisle from them, three forest walkers in adjacent cages rub at their bark-like, birch-patterned skin, ghostly in the sunlight. The farther they get from their home trees, the more their bodies fade, and one of these is nearly transparent. And at the end—

My heart speeds into overtime. A short-statured whisperer with brown skin and dark curls tumbling down to her waist. Andie, I'm guessing. And in a cage near hers—

Helos.

He's alive! At least, I think he is. I'm fairly certain. He must be. He looks terrible, though, even from here. He's wearing some sort of rags, his eyes are closed, and he's slumped in a corner of his prison at the end of the row nearest to me. Not moving.

I need to get a closer look.

I drop to the ground, hop a few steps toward the plateau, and shift to deer mouse. At once, my vision weakens dramatically, blurry enough that it's far easier to detect movement than any real details around me. But this is the stealthiest form I've got, so I really don't have a choice. As quickly as my tiny legs will carry me, I scurry up the rest of the slope, using my whiskers to navigate through blades of grass more than twice my height. Soon enough, the land levels out, and then I'm hurrying toward the metal cages as if my life depends on it. It probably does.

Helos doesn't stir when I crawl between the bars and the

crosshatched wires forming the cage's outer walls, the gaps so tiny
that escape would be impossible for any of the creatures I have seen
imprisoned here. I walk directly over to him, hesitate, then brush
my whiskers against one of his bare feet.

Nothing happens.

A wisp of anger spirals through my limbs, settling over my
bones. *You're not leaving me,* I think. *Not you, too. Never you.* I abandon all pretense of gentleness and slam my body into his foot with
all my might.

Helos flinches awake and withdraws his outstretched leg at once.
There are a few moments of sleepiness and confusion, and then he
reaches a hand down. I crawl onto it and let him lift me toward his
face, which is filthy with smears of grime and dried blood.

Rora?

He doesn't speak the word aloud, just mouths the syllables. I
squeak a little in response.

How did you find me?

I have no way of answering in this form, and there's no chance I
can risk shifting to human, so I simply tap his fingers with my tail.

He rotates his head in either direction, checking for threats,
then brings his face even closer.

"Look, Rora," he whispers, so quietly it's amazing any sound
comes out at all. "This is a bad place. I don't know what exactly
they're up to, but I can tell it doesn't end well for the prisoners. The
caegars—they blinded them. And they—"

He hesitates, teeth skimming his bottom lip.

A chill fingers the length of my spine. Eyes with the power to
hypnotize prey—gone. A magical species robbed of its greatest
asset.

"Listen," he says at last. "I know you wanted to investigate this
further, but please. Don't risk your life to save me. Go with Weslyn.
You have to save Finley."

I bite his hand.

"Finley," he repeats. "You already have what he needs. Please.
It's . . . important to me."

And what about what's important to me? I want to ask. *What about your own life?* His selflessness is going to get him killed. If he were any other shifter, no doubt his imprisonment would trigger his third and final animal form. But it's my brother, whose instinct is always to protect others. His moments of greatest need will never be to save himself.

I think of his fingers smoothing the wrinkles in Finley's portrait. Of Finley himself telling me "the answer is no" to a question I never heard, when his expression suggested anything but. That Helos might never see that face again, that he might die here, alone, so far away from everyone he loves, is completely unacceptable.

I bite harder, causing him to nearly drop me. He doesn't, of course.

We stare at each other for the span of several heartbeats. I can tell he's trying to convince me that he's not worth it, and I'm trying to convey to him that he's always worth it, that we're a pair, that we don't separate. We just don't. We go together, always.

"We have an understanding, then," he whispers. We certainly do not, but there's nothing I can do about that now. I signal that I want to be let down.

He lowers his hand, then wavers a little. I know he's about to attempt some sort of goodbye, and I won't have that, so I dash out of the cage before he can speak to me again.

Now to make a plan.

Sticking as close to the bars as possible, I make my way down the evil line of cages. With my limited vision, it's difficult to tell if any of the imprisoned notice my passing. The air reeks of sweat, filth, and a horrid odor I can't quite place. Even more disturbing is the quiet constricting them all. None of them are trying to communicate or force the doors to their cages. It's as if they've already given up hope.

I wonder how long they held on to it.

And just like that, I realize the implications of rescuing Helos but leaving the rest of them caged. The notion makes my stomach turn.

One thing at a time.

I'm almost at the end of the row when the screeching of metal doors fractures the silence. Desperately, I press my body into the dirt as footsteps thunder across the earth. Two people, soldiers maybe, approach the place where I'm hidden.

They halt, by my estimate, two cages away. Relief quickly fades to dismay as the sounds of a struggle reach my ears. That's a forest walker's prison.

From what I can hear, she's putting up a good resistance. Then there's the scratch of a match being lit, and the smell of smoke wafts toward me. I can't see what's happening, but there's an anguished cry, then another, then nothing as the party—now three instead of two—leaves the relative safety of the cage.

Fighting to control the panic creeping in, I flit toward them, keeping as close to their heels as I dare. The scent of sweeter smoke lingers in the air; one of the soldiers might be carrying a cigar. We reach the end of the aisle and turn left, walking past the two other rows until we come to the side of the building. The ashen wall towers high above me, an impassive giant shadowing my tiny features. Before I can pause to consider what may be inside, a set of double-doors swings open.

I don't waste time deliberating. The soldiers pull the forest walker inside, and I take my chance, squeezing through just as the doors slam shut behind me. The impact is so loud it's nearly deafening.

A long, wide corridor stretches into the distance, little more than a harshly lit blur to my mouse eyes. The soldiers move right, so I make straight for the opposite wall and hope my brown fur blends in well enough with the cold floor. There's movement behind me, to the left of the double doors.

My whiskers pick up the vibrations in the air; one of the soldiers has opened an object mounted on the wall next to the doors. I can't see what she's doing, but a distinctive rattle rings through the air.

Keys! Rows of them, judging by the chimes. With any luck, they're the keys to the cages.

Straining my ears, I hear a small latch click shut and metal grating against a lock. So one needs a key to access the box of keys.

I keep still as stone as the soldiers stomp past, their prisoner positioned between them. Since it's the only lead I have, I trail behind as best I can until we stop before an open doorway—the second room on the right.

"Mohr!" barks one of the soldiers.

In a matter of moments, someone emerges from the room.

"Take this downstairs while I lock up."

This, I soon learn, is the forest walker. Mohr joins the soldier with the cigar, and the two of them shunt their prisoner down the hall while the remaining soldier enters the room. I dart in behind her, and my heart fires through my chest.

There are several figures here, some sprawled around a circular table, some on a couch, some pacing the room. A hornets' nest. The stench of pipe smoke taints the air, along with the thuds of darts hitting their mark. My nose and whiskers assemble the rough picture, moving frantically even as the rest of me remains desperately still. Though I listen hard for the sound of keys, it's difficult to hear over the raucous voices. *Where did that soldier go?*

Moving as quickly as I dare, I skirt the edges of the crowded room, sticking to as many shadows as I can find. A table leg here, a crack in the floorboard there. As it had when I met Ambassador Kelner, the Eradain accent prods the corners of my mind, like there's a familiarity to it whose origins I've forgotten. My nose sifts through the cloud of smells, suddenly latching on to one that curls my spine. Earth and ash, concentrated in a figure nearby.

Magic in the midst of Eradain soldiers.

The realization is nearly enough to send me off-course. The Fallow Throes, or are they keeping one of the prisoners in here for some reason? *Focus,* I remind myself, peeling my thoughts away from the distraction, searching for . . .

There! I creep toward the soldier who opened the key box. She's standing in front of another mounted object, scratching notes in something on the counter before her. So where's the—

"RAT!"

I'm gone before the broom hits home, flying through the door, then out into the hall. The linoleum floor trembles beneath the footsteps pounding behind me. Fighting panic, I tear down the corridor with no sense of direction or destination other than *away*. The broom slams down beside me once more, so near and so forcefully that it would have snapped my spine had it been a mere finger's length closer.

I swerve abruptly to the left, then right again, then left and straight through an open door. My infinitesimal lead enables me to skid against the wall directly beside the entrance, just around the corner. My heartbeat radiates through every crevice of my body.

The pursuer flails into the room, mercifully overshooting my hiding spot by several paces, and I use the opportunity to race back out. There's a closed door across the corridor, and though I have no idea what new danger may lurk behind, I scramble for the crack underneath it. My body is just small enough to squeeze through.

The room is lit by a single source of light. Judging by the smell, it is also empty.

Not knowing whether my pursuer will think to check this room, I make haste for the safety of a large wooden desk. Several long moments crawl past as I crouch beneath it, shaking and trying to calm my fraying nerves. My thoughts drift to the whisperers doubting my return, then Weslyn expecting it, and the latter steadies me.

After a while, as the room remains quiet and no one makes any attempts to enter, the space around me begins to take shape. My whiskers detect a number of objects scattered throughout it, and my nose picks up the distinct scent of parchment.

Maybe there's information here that will tell me about this place.

The door I crawled under was shut, which suggests that this room has limited access. The oil lamp is lit, though, which means whoever works or lives here can't have intended to be gone for very long.

I'll have to be quick.

It's an enormous relief to return to my human form, but there's no time to dwell on that. I cross the room in three strides and bolt the door; the sound of a key rattling the lock should give me enough warning to shift back to mouse. Then I locate the oil lamp and examine the walls. No windows. Good.

A large map of Alemara has been mounted on the wall opposite the desk. Bright pins are stuck throughout the Western Vale. I don't know what they signify, but it's clear these soldiers have been working here for a while. A red one pierces the place where Caela Ridge used to be, and I feel a stab of rage before turning away.

The desk itself is strewn with folders and papers, the former all bearing the vile stamp of Eradain's standard: a gold crown encased in a scarlet sun with five rays, all centered over a navy blue backdrop traced with black. More are in the drawers, which prove unlocked except for one. I rifle through them all, trying to make sense of the charts, illustrations, and blocks of text without messing up the order or placement. Never have I been so grateful that everyone on this continent speaks the same language.

In one folder, there are a number of logs, some sort of records for experimentation findings. Trials on prisoners involving medicines and weapons. Horrible illustrations accompany the notes, dozens of roughly hewn sketches, many immaculately detailed and stomach-churning. Too many. I slap the folder shut.

The next one holds accounts of all the earthquakes that have shaken Alemara in the last seven years, growing in frequency but not much in magnitude. Another contains lists of dates and numbers stretching back several months ago, all of which are meaningless to me.

I try the locked drawer again, and footsteps sound in the hall.

Instantly, I shift back to mouse and dart over to the wall, positioning myself right beside the door. The steps come closer and closer—then they pass.

Though my nerves are just about spent, I'm still contemplating trying for more information when the lock rattles ominously, and the door swings open.

Bootsteps, so close to my face I can smell the pitch and blood splattered across them. While I was careful to leave everything the way I found it, I have no intention of sticking around to discover whether I slipped up. I run from the room, fasten my side against the corridor wall, and scurry to an untried set of double doors at the end.

This time, it takes much longer for someone to come and open them, and there's no crack underneath that I can crawl through. Instead, I'm forced to wait there, silent and still. I don't dare backtrack all the way to the set of doors I came through. There's no guarantee those would open any sooner, anyway.

I wait.

The key. I need a key to free Helos. The key to the cage is in that mounted box, and the key to that box is . . . Where? My best guess is in that room with the soldiers and smoke, but it's still only a theory. For all I know, the woman I followed keeps the key on her at all times.

I wait.

The first question, of course, is how Wes and I are going to make it in here undetected. The one idea I have is risky, but then again, I suppose there are no safe options when planning a prison break.

One thing is clear: we have to move right away. Today. After my restless night and the prolonged state of adrenaline from being here, the idea alone makes me weak in the knees. I have no choice but to push through the exhaustion, though. I have to get Helos out before they try one of those . . . *experiments* on him; I don't know what exactly they're searching for, but it was clear enough that not every subject makes it out alive.

At last, the doors swing open and I rush through, relieved beyond words to be outside once more. I run and run, hardly even aware of where I'm going—and almost slam headlong into a wagon parked outside.

Hollow bones, decaying flesh—the stench of death is so overwhelming I nearly gag. It's what I smelled before, smelled but couldn't place from afar. Corpses are piled atop the wooden slats, and now I know why the Vale seemed so empty, why many of the cages weren't filled.

They're not just holding people and animals prisoner here. They're killing them.

TWENTY-TWO

When I rejoin the group, back in human form, pack in hand and very much alive, the whisperers size me up like I really am a ghost.

"Are you okay?" Wes demands, taking two steps toward me before stopping just as quickly. "Is Helos alive?"

I nod, and he releases a long breath.

"What of my cousin?" Peridon adds, straightening the bow across his back. "Did you see her there?"

"I think so."

His face erupts into a smile, and his people start conversing in low, urgent voices.

Wes peers closely at my face, brow furrowing. "What is it?"

At that, Peridon leaves the group and paces over to my side, his watchful gaze now holding all the intensity of a mountain cat's. The black-tipped caw on his shoulder flaps its wings indignantly. Aside from a few brave birds chattering nearby, the air around us falls unusually silent and still. Almost like that day in the Old Forest with Finley, as if the firs themselves are holding their breath to hear what I have to say.

Maybe they are.

I tell them everything I encountered, from the compound layout and cages to the map and papers. Weslyn's eyebrows knit together, but that's the only change I can see as he absorbs the information. I suppose he has experience receiving news with a more or less neutral face. The whisperers mutter occasionally in indecipherable undertones, until I end with the wagon.

Nobody speaks for a time. I spend most of it staring at the ground and running my feet continually through the grass. Those men I killed. I can't stop thinking about their bodies lying alone, whether carnivores that have eluded capture will follow the scent and eat them. Or perhaps they'll yield instead to the slow decay of time, until all that remains is a collection of bones—that is, if the marrow sheep left any.

We didn't even bury them.

"What were the people there wearing?" asks Wes. "The same uniforms as the ones we met in the woods?"

I shake my head. "I couldn't tell. Mice don't have good eyesight. But Eradain's standard was on the papers."

"*Eradain,*" hisses Yena. "The human filth. I might have known."

Peridon's caw croaks, and he strokes its feathers while making soft, soothing sounds. "Yena used to live there," he explains.

"It sounds like King Jol grew tired of waiting," says Wes, running a hand over his mouth. "He must have begun his mission to take the Vale."

I ball my hands into fists, fury warring with anguish deep in my gut. The idea of a second Rupturing frightens me as much as it would anyone, but murdering magical beings as a preventative measure is not the answer. It should not even be a question. "We have to save them."

For a long time, Weslyn just returns my stare. I know what he's thinking, because it's what I'm thinking, too. If we stay and attempt to liberate the compound, there's no telling how long that might take, or if we could even manage it ourselves. We might even die in the attempt. Either way, if the Fallow Throes continues to spread, his people—his *brother*—would be lost.

Finley. My friend, his kin. Helos's . . . what?

It's . . . important to me.

Helos's love.

If we choose to save Finley, how many more here will die before we can return?

How many more will die in Telyan if we stay?

"How do you plan to do that?" asks a girl with a prominent nose who looks to be around Violet's age, though she has none of the crown princess's force of presence.

I work the knots in my shoulders with weary fingers. "I don't know yet. Do you have an idea?"

Her deep-set eyes flicker nervously to her companions, and she raises her own shoulders practically to her ears.

"I think—" Wes breaks off, considering some more. "I think any attempt we make on our own would be too risky. We need help." Another pause. "Our greatest chance of success lies in telling Minister Mereth and my father. If we try to free them ourselves and are taken in the attempt, or killed, this secret will hold for longer. People back home would only assume the wilderness killed us."

"That's your solution? To bring more humans into our land?" Yena grinds a heel into the ground. "The Vale is now the one place we can live without harassment. We want to rid it of your kind, not make room for more."

"Not all humans are bad," I protest. "Weslyn, for one, along with his family." Wes's eyebrows lift a little. "I know things are tense, but King Gerar of Telyan is a good man. At least, he tries to be. He could help."

"How? By sending enough troops to outnumber Eradain's? They could destroy half the Vale in their skirmishes for dominance. It's ironic, is it not? So often, these people look for danger in magic when they should be looking to each other." She raises her chin. "Humans always seek to control one another. To conquer." She spits the last word. "*That* is their nature. And just as they will never break it, so we can never allow that poison to overtake the one refuge we have left. You believe the southern king might help. But even if he wins, who is to say he won't simply stay and claim the land for himself?"

"Would you rather do nothing?" I challenge. "The poison you speak of is here already, yet I just went into that compound alone!"

She purses her lips.

What would Helos do? I wonder in the silence that follows. Then I stop myself. It's not Helos's choice to make. It's mine.

And that makes the consequences of what I'm about to do so much harder to bear.

"I agree with Weslyn," I say at last. "We'll rescue Helos and your friends who were captured and return to Telyan. And then we will have to return for the rest with greater forces." I don't mention bringing the stardust to the afflicted—for all I know, Yena could try to steal it from Wes to prevent us from rescuing more humans.

The whisperers shuffle their feet.

"What is it?"

The short one who seems to be in charge lowers her chin a fraction. "We cannot help you in this quest."

My mouth drops open. "What about your friends? I saw several people in there. In *cages*. What about Andie?"

Peridon glances at his leader. "Feren—"

"No. You would have us launch an attack without a plan, and without enough fighters to pose a threat. We cannot disguise ourselves as you can."

I step forward. "I didn't say—"

"You did not think. If we fail, and in these numbers we *will* fail, what will stop them from destroying the rest of our home like they did yours? Perhaps you have no one to account for but yourself, but I do, and I will not risk a massacre."

My nails stretch into claws, and I make no effort to beat them back. "They're already seizing your people one by one. Whether you choose to risk it or not, they are coming for you. For all the forestborn."

The word sits strange on my tongue, but I can tell it holds a significance among them, so I say it anyway. *People like you and us.* A collective. The idea of it stretches and settles deep between my ribs, rousing a glimmer of warmth despite the circumstances.

For several long moments, we glare at each other, Feren examining my claws and I sizing up the weapon on her back. At last, she jerks her head for the others to gather around her. "I thank you for the information and wish you luck with your brother," she says, dipping her chin once. "We will tell our clan what you've learned. Come."

The group retreats into the woods, one or two of them glancing behind as they go. Peridon lingers a few beats longer, clearly torn between staying and obeying.

"I'm sorry," he says quietly. "I wish I could help you." With a final, tortured glance, eventually he, too, vanishes from sight.

We're alone.

It's familiar, of course, the dreaded place in which I'm used to being. But it still stings. Flexing my fingers, I'm considering going after them to make another appeal when Weslyn steps before me, leaning heavily on his good leg.

He nods once. "So what's the plan?"

Gratitude pulses in, easing the usual tangle of loneliness and frustration. Rolling my shoulders a little, I take in the gravity of his expression, the lack of concern for the help we might have had, and lost. Even injured, he's still here. And so am I.

I clasp my hands before me. "You're not going to like it."

My flight back across the hills holds none of the usual joy. I glide high above the stretch of yellow brown, a shadow of vengeance tracing the ground below. As I predicted, Wes was vehemently against the plan. He wanted to stake out the compound longer, account for as many variables as possible. Ordinarily I would agree, but he didn't see the cages like I did. He didn't feel the way death and despair hang over the place like a veil. There's no time for further planning.

I come in from above, training my eyes on the watchtower and scanning the roof for a place to land. Overlapping tiles lay smooth and flat across it, but there are perches in the small ridges running the length. I drop quickly, the hunter's approach, descending only when I'm above the tower. My talons grasp for purchase, hopefully no more than a pebble loosed from the mountains.

I have rarely seen Wes as angry as he was when I told him he had to stay behind. His reaction didn't surprise me; by now I realize how much he hates feeling useless. I feel no guilt, though. It was out of the question for him to come. His wounds would prevent him from fighting well, if it came to combat, and he has no way of disguising himself. Not like I do.

Forcing that distraction out of my mind, I focus on an adjoining staircase in back of the tower—it must lead to an entrance. After scouring my surroundings for an enemy's approach, I alight on the rail.

Windows make up most of the tower walls, which means I'm now in plain view of anyone inside.

Immediately I drop to the platform, shifting to mouse just before I land. *Stupid. You'll have to do better than that.* The impact rattles my teeth, but at least it was quiet. I wait for several heartbeats, listening hard for alarmed voices or panicked feet.

There's nothing.

The door is just across the landing at the top. From here it's simple, really, as there's a good-sized gap beneath it, plenty of room for me to crawl through. Yet my feet feel rooted to the floor.

I force large gulps of air into my tiny mouse lungs. Nothing to count up here, no surroundings I can pinpoint with enough detail to blot out my nerves. I have only the facts before me and the spiraling anger clutched close to my chest. I don't know how many soldiers are in the tower. I don't know how well my plan will work, or if it will succeed at all. But I know what I can do, particularly if someone needs me.

And Helos needs me.

I crawl under the door, right in the corner, and hold myself still against the wall.

There are only three people in here, likely as good a set of odds as I could have hoped for, all sitting at shallow desks set against the far windows. I can't pick up the scent of metal blades; with any luck, that means they're unarmed. The majority of the room feels fairly empty.

I'll have to move fast.

Using vibrations in the air, I locate the biggest one, seated on the left by the windows overlooking the cages. The element of surprise

FORESTBORN   271

will buy me only a moment—best to take him out first. Sticking close to the wall, I patter around the edges of the room until I'm under his desk, uncomfortably close to his greasy boots. My body is quivering.

I allow myself another minute to steady my breathing. Then I step out from under the desk and shift.

My fist slams into the side of his face before he has time to react. His body staggers off the chair and onto the floor, just as the other two watchtower guards leap to their feet. Gawking openly, they reach for weapons that aren't there as I sprint toward them, feeling the power of the muscles I've gained by switching to the form of the man I just knocked out.

The first one is quite small and demanding that I freeze—a kick to his chest catapults him to the ground. I prepare to deliver another blow when I catch sight of the object hurtling toward me.

Without thought, my body shrinks into goshawk and contorts backward, my wings flapping frantically, out of reach of the wooden chair now broken upon the floor. Though the small man I just knocked down is struggling to push to his feet, clearly winded, the woman who aimed the chair demands immediate attention. She's headed toward some sort of contraption mounted on the wall.

I fly forward before she can sound the alarm, shifting back to human and toppling both of us to the floor. Instantly she rolls to the side, dislodging me, and scrambles back to her feet. I grab her ankles and yank, bringing her down once more, then punch her in the throat before she can right herself. It's a risky move; I can only hope it didn't kill her.

By now, the smaller man has successfully gotten to his feet, but his suffering lungs and the sight of his comrade now duplicated, naked, before him is enough of a distraction. An instant later he joins the other two in the bitter surrender of unconsciousness. I smile smugly at his inanimate form. With humans, nudity can be just as much a weapon as feet and fists.

Panting heavily, I return to my natural form and consider him more closely, my moment of levity already slipping away. He's young, now that I really look at him. Probably not much older than I am. I wonder what his family might be like, and whether they know he's here. I wonder what his name is. Then I'm glad I don't know.

I shake my head, scattering the fragments like leaves in the breeze. I can't let thoughts like this distract me. He's old enough to know what he's doing. I make quick study of the three options in front of me before settling on him.

Moving quickly but methodically, I shift my features until I'm a replica of the boy—shorter stature, stubby fingers, eyes the color of the sea, thick black hair cut close on the sides. I make my vocal cords thicker as well; all I have to go on are a couple of sentences, but I think I get the voice close enough to pass. Then I strip him of his uniform, making a few final adjustments—thicker arm hair, wider biceps, squatter torso—before slipping on the clothes.

The uniform is dark blue, the color of the sky between twilight and midnight. The wide, short-cut sleeves are starched and hang rather stiffly around my arms. I tuck the shirt into the pants, add the belt, and finish with the black socks and shoes. Then I check my work against the two still-clothed guards to make sure I've got it right.

My gaze falls again upon the motionless form of the boy whose identity I've stolen. I know I should ensure that none of the guards can sound the alarm before I've freed Helos. But he didn't wake this morning thinking it would be his last, and surely there's at least one person waiting for him back home, someone who loves him.

I don't want to be a killer.

I remember Weslyn saying, *I don't think anyone should.*

Logic wins. Ordering myself not to hesitate, I smother them all with shaking hands until their hearts stop beating. Then I wipe my palms on a uniform and vomit against the wall.

There is death on you.

"I'm sorry," I whisper to the corpses, biting back a fractured sob.

Please, fortune, don't ever make this easy on me.

After a glance through the window to confirm that Helos is still in his holding cell, I slip from the tower room—don't think about them, *focus*—and descend the creaky wooden stairs, willing there not to be a guard shift anytime soon.

Unfortunately, I didn't really get a chance to observe how this boy moves. Judging by the age gap between him and the other two, I'm guessing he's of a more junior rank. Still, his role is the captor, not captured, so he can't be too insecure. As I make my way from the base of the stairs to the double doors opposite the first line of cages, I settle on my walk and attitude: confident, but not seeking to draw attention to myself.

Nobody intercepts me as I pass through the doors. There are a few people in the corridor, all dressed in the same navy uniforms as the ones in the tower. I stride with purpose toward the second room on the right. That's where the soldier I trailed my first time in this hall went after messing with the box of keys on the wall, and though I'm not positive the key to that box is inside, it's a place to start, at least. Before I reach it, I pass another room—more of an oversized closet, really—with the door swung wide on its hinges, revealing a collection of tools: rods, ropes, torches, netting. My lips press together until they ache.

I can guess what those are for. Magic may give most of the prisoners unique abilities, but it doesn't give them heightened strength against brute force or the power to escape a tangled mass of ropes.

The second room, which looks to be some sort of recreation room now that I can see it clearly, is brimming with men and women as it was before. None of them acknowledge my presence when I enter, but I imagine that luck won't hold for long. I also don't see a single magical person, despite the scent I picked up on before.

Keeping my head down, I walk the outskirts of the room, tracing the path the previous soldier had taken before I lost her. I examine each person through downcast eyes, searching for any signs of illness.

There are no covered ears or pained expressions. None of the people are on the floor, grasping at sanity through fracturing wills. That makes no sense. If the magic I scented had come from a human, someone in here ought to be dying.

Unless the source is a shifter.

A particularly raucous band of laughter snares my attention, and I follow the turned heads and slapping hands to the apparent source of the joke: a familiar face in the opposite corner of the room. Short, dark hair, broad shoulders—it's one of the men I saved from the caegar, the one who tried to haul me to my feet when I'd been paralyzed. The one I slashed with my claws to get away.

He's just . . . sitting there. Not talking with anyone, seemingly indifferent to being the butt of mockery. Only sitting, eyes unfocused. He might be the one, yet he appears just as healthy as the rest.

I have no time to reflect on it further. I reach the end of the second wall and spot a small board mounted above a counter. The board is lined with rows of hooks—and keys. Hardly able to believe my luck, I take one step, then another, then another—until I'm facing the board.

"Olin, are you deaf?"

I jump in my skin as the voice sounds directly to my right. I had heard someone call for Olin but had no idea it was meant for me.

I know that voice.

The man at my side looks exactly as I remember him. A little older than Olin. Long, muscular arms. Severe jawline. Golden hair and beard that contrast sharply with his eyes, which are dark as flecks of coal.

I can still see his hands driving a knife through the caegar's shoulder.

I can still see mine pressing against Olin's nose and mouth.

"What are you doing?" Kallen demands in an undertone, his northern accent gruff.

My heart is beating wildly out of control.

Captor.

Butcher.

How many innocents in that wagon fell at his hands? Does he see their faces behind closed eyelids or feel the life gasping from their bodies, as I still can of the people I've killed?

There's no way he could recognize me now, not disguised as I am. And yet—what if?

"Mute now, too, are you?"

The accusation snaps me back into character.

I take quick stock of his posture and tone, trying to assess whether he and I are friends. He's angry, but he's speaking quietly rather than making a scene of it, so I think maybe we are.

I don't like to think about what that says of the boy I'm impersonating.

"What does it look like I'm doing?" I reply in a low voice, matching my "friend's" tone and accent as best I can. "I want to check on one of the shifters. He was acting kind of funny."

"What do you mean, funny?"

I don't comment on the way the blood rushes from his face, only shrug noncommittally.

"That isn't your job," he persists. "Let someone else handle it and get back in the tower before someone notices."

I fix him with a pointed look. "It's my job to keep watch, and that is what I'm doing. If you're scared, you don't have to come."

The color returns to his cheeks. "Idiot, you can't go alone. The commander would have your head."

So much concern. Where was it when I was in the forest saving his life?

He snatches a key off the board. We really must be friends, then, if he's willing to accompany me to keep me out of trouble.

"Thanks," I mutter, and he rolls his eyes in a way that promises Olin will pay for this act of loyalty later. I turn to follow him out of the room—and freeze.

"Changed your mind, have you?" Kallen asks dryly.

I don't reply. I don't move.

On my first visit to this room, I heard the sound of darts hitting their mark and thought little of it. Now I see what I couldn't as a mouse: the target mounted on the opposite wall. It's a painting of a woman. A woman with olive skin, brown waves cascading down her back, Helos's nose, my cheekbones—the same, narrow face shape as my own. Nearly the same *face* as my own, just a few years older. And eyes I'll never forget, because they were the last part of her I saw before she ran.

It's my mother.

It cannot be. But it is. Her resemblance to Helos and me is so striking, it's irrefutable.

What in the world is she doing *here*?

"Traitorous bitch," says Kallen, following my gaze.

I want to ask who she is to these people, why a wrinkled painting of her is mounted on the wall to be used as nothing more than target practice. I want to ask this man if he knew her. But I bite back the slew of questions on my tongue; I have no idea how long he and Olin have known each other, what they've talked about, or what's common knowledge to everyone here. The wrong question could give me away.

I attempt to school my features into a mask of contempt and grumble a few words that hopefully pass for assent. My throat chokes on them.

A thought bobs to the surface then, so sudden and sharp it outshines all others in this moment: I have to get Helos out before somebody notices the resemblance. Whatever the reason she's here, she is clearly reviled. No connection to her could be good.

Without a word, I brush past Olin's friend and lead the way out of the room.

I feel like I am burning and drowning all at once. Fire singes my skin, incinerates my veins, a writhing mess of confusion and sorrow and rage and fear so overwhelming it's difficult to walk, to breathe. Kallen catches up to me and reaches the key box first, which he swiftly unlocks. The rows of keys are arranged to match the cages outside, so it's easy to find the one I need. I snatch it hastily so he can't see how my hand is shaking.

Then we're out the doors and into the late afternoon sunlight, blinding and branding and burning, burning, burning. My mother. My *mother*. I can't make sense of it. I wasn't prepared to have to face her ghost. Wasn't—

"What are we looking for, exactly?" he asks roughly. By now, I realize anger is his mask for fear.

"He was pacing his cell," I reply, inventing the answer as it falls from my mouth. The forest walker who was taken inside on my previous visit is still missing from her cage when we pass it. "He looked agitated. Like he was waiting for something."

Helos comes into view, isolated at his end of the row save for Andie two cages away. He isn't pacing. He's sitting motionless in the corner.

My companion slows his gait. "He looks fine to me," he says, which is absurd because my brother doesn't look fine at all.

"Let's just be sure," I insist, and to my relief he follows, albeit reluctantly.

Helos lifts his head when we reach his door. His expression is defiant, haunted, but he makes no move to stand. He recognizes the man at my side, too.

Kallen appraises him critically. "Well, I don't—"

The rest of his sentence is cut off as he crumples to the ground. My knuckles, which were already sore, now ache so painfully I have to clench my teeth. They'll certainly bruise, but by the river, it was worth it.

Helos leaps to his feet, swaying a little on the spot as I unlock the barred gate, then the fenced one. "Who are you?" he demands.

"Rora," I say, quietly so Andie won't overhear. I have no wish to leave a trail. "It's Rora."

My brother blinks in astonishment. "What? How did you . . . ?"

"There's no time," I rush on. "Let's go. I took care of the guards in the watchtower, so the way should be clear enough. Weslyn is—"

A horrible, blaring horn rends the air, so loud I cover my ears involuntarily. There's movement at the watchtower. I turn back to Helos, whose panicked expression mirrors my own.

"They found the guards," I say. "We have to go *now*."

"You can't."

I spin around so fast I almost knock Helos over in the process. The voice belonged to Andie. "What?"

She watches me mournfully from where she sits in a tattered, long-sleeved tunic and pants, silver-eyed, her streaked hair curled in ringlets. Her legs are crossed tight beneath her curvy body. What she makes of the fact that a soldier is helping a captive escape, or whether she's guessed the truth, I have no idea. "He can't leave. They're all on high alert now, and I heard one say the king is eager to see him. This *particular* shifter." She raises her eyebrows. The truth, then. "As soon as they find his cage empty, they'll loose their dogs and scour the hills and the woods across the way. You wouldn't make it a mile."

"You really think they could find us in all that land?"

"Not them. The dogs."

No. No, no, no. I didn't make it this far to fail. There has to be a way. There must be. *Focus!* Maybe in my disguise, I can distract them while Helos runs. Maybe I can . . . Maybe . . .

Disguise. Distract.

Shift.

"Helos," I say urgently. "You have to switch with me."

"What?"

"Switch with me!" I repeat. "Do it! I'll stay here and pretend to be you, so they don't think to search the woods. You'll have time to get ahead—grab Weslyn and make for the river. I can shift to mouse when things return to normal and crawl out of the cage, then fly to catch up. I can escape, but you can't. Quickly, Helos!"

He sees the logic in it, or maybe exhaustion has weakened his ability to argue, because he's already morphing into the borrowed form of Olin. Once he has the features right, I assume the face I know best in the world, and we switch clothing in a mad dash. He's moving rather gingerly, but there's no time to ask about it now.

"When you're far enough away, stash the clothes and run for your life," I instruct, pushing him outside the cage. "Carry the shoes if you can. I don't know what they've done with yours."

Now that he's out and I'm inside, the reality of what he's about to do seems to sink in. He plants his heels.

"Rora, I can't let you do this," he says. "I can't—"

"Weslyn is in the woods, across the hills and to the left of the compound. Find him and keep moving toward the river, okay? The dogs can't track us once we're across."

"Rora!"

I don't give him another chance to object. Instead, I shove him backward, turn the key in both of the locks, and throw the key to his cage—*my* cage—as far into the trees at the base of the mountains as I can.

And I slam the gates shut.

TWENTY-THREE

As soon as Helos has gone, I throw myself down in the corner of the cage, rumpling his hair—my hair—into a state of disarray. I don't have the bruises, and only half the grime, but there's no help for that now. Hopefully my captors will assume that shifters are fast healers.

I try not to think of Helos's stricken face and instead picture him far from here, escaping across the open land when no one is looking.

Several people are hurrying down the line of cages toward me.

I exchange a quick look with Andie, who has been staring openly, before turning back to the concrete beneath my feet. How long has she been a prisoner here? My gut tells me she won't give me away, but better to secure her loyalty just in case. "I know your cousin Peridon," I tell her in a low voice, risking one last glance out of the corner of my downturned eyes—shock is written plainly across her face, but fortunately she has had the sense to look away.

The uniforms have arrived; there must be half a dozen at least. One of them hastily checks Kallen's pulse before calling back, "He's still alive, Commander." Gone are the easy grins, lounging limbs, and bawdy humor of the recreation room. The soldiers, or whatever they are before me, stand stiff at attention, mouths drawn tight, eyes trained on someone moving quickly to the front of the group.

Everything about him speaks of authority: the stripes and

badges on his red-accented uniform, the way the others part to let him through, the manner in which he carries himself, the force with which his frigid gaze now knifes through mine.

"You are responsible for this?" he says, gesturing to the body in the grass. It's a statement, not a question.

I frown in confusion and say nothing.

"What happened here?" he demands again. "Speak, or I'll cut out your tongue and be done with it."

I look again at the fallen man, who will likely revive at any moment. "He had some sort of fit. I don't know more than that. I'm not a healer."

A storm brews on the commander's sun-darkened face. "Yet your own injuries have healed quite well."

I don't reply.

"He can't have come alone. Who was with him?" he asks, turning to his reports.

There's a brief moment of silence. Then one says, "It looked like Olin."

"*Olin,*" the commander repeats, marching to shove his face a finger-length in front of the person who answered him. "*Olin* is currently lying naked and dead in the blood-forsaken tower!"

The soldier blanches slightly.

"So," the commander continues, pacing back to my cage. "One Olin is in the tower. Another is seen walking the grounds." The soldiers seem to hold their breath in the quiet that follows. *"Who let another shifter infiltrate the camp?"*

No one answers. Their fear is palpable as they start eyeing one another, as if unsure which of them might be an imposter.

"This base is on lockdown," the commander announces, shaving my bones to dust. "Everyone will report to my office for questioning. If anyone is seen trying to escape, you grab a bow and shoot on sight."

He calls six men and women forth immediately, barking questions that are meaningless to me. I suppose their answers are satisfactory, because he sends them off to secure the compound a moment later. Three now remain, along with the unconscious one.

Leave. Please leave. Please.

"Failed to break you out, though, didn't it?" the commander muses aloud with a wicked sort of pleasure, eyes resting on me. "Or maybe it didn't come for you at all."

It. *It.*

I hide my hands behind my back.

He's looking for a reaction, but I won't give him one. I'm well versed in masks.

"Tell me, shifter, where is the other one? Why is it here?"

Again, I give him nothing.

"Get him out."

The commander holds up a key, which someone uses to unlock my doors. My heart is hammering loud enough to wake the dead. I didn't realize there'd be a master key. I need them to leave me alone, so I can vanish. I need—

But the doors are open, and the three remaining soldiers grab on to my arms and haul me roughly to my feet. They appear nauseated to be touching me, but their holds remain firm as they twist my arms painfully and shove my body forward. I attempt to dig my heels in, but there's only smooth stone underfoot, no grip my feet can catch. All too quickly, we're out of the cage and standing in front of the commander.

He holds my gaze for several heartbeats. Then he sinks a fist into my stomach, completely without warning.

My torso attempts to fold over of its own accord, but the soldiers maintain their grip on my arms. All I can do is stand there, wheezing and blinking back tears. The pain is stunning. The commander watches me with cold appraisal, studying the effect of his actions. Then he hits me again.

This time I do drop to the ground; my captors have loosened their hold slightly, perhaps interpreting my silence as an inability to fight back.

The commander tilts his head. "I thought, by now, you would have learned the futility of resisting."

Pressure mounts behind my shoulder blades, clawing, insistent.

But I can't shift and escape, not with this many eyes on me. The commander only just gave the order, and already soldiers are swarming the grounds, crossbows at the ready. Odds are I wouldn't last long. Not at this range. Not when there are no roots to trip them or trees to hide behind. No, I have to wait—but it's taking every bit of willpower I have to beat the wings back.

"Now then," he says, squatting in front of me and talking over my ragged breathing. "I'm going to ask you again. What do you know about the other one?"

The welling numbness and blinding ache in my gut are blocking out most other thoughts. I need to catch my breath, but my lungs can't seem to draw in enough air, and I'm certain I'm going to vomit from the strain of resisting the shift. In answer, I spit at the commander's boots.

He stands abruptly. "Bring him."

The men try strong-arming me to my feet, but my legs will no longer support my weight. I'm still holding on to human by my fingertips, but the instant one of the guards puts a knife to my back, the battle is lost. My body shrinks, wings burst forth, and I catapult into the air with all the force I can muster.

Hands clamp around my legs and yank me back down, despite each powerful thrust of my wings. I twist and shriek, aiming to puncture their skin with my talons, and then a cloth drops over my head. My vision teeters, and the world goes dark.

I blink once. Twice.

Harshly lit white walls scald my irises, and I duck my head toward my chest, attempting the small feat of twitching my fingers. I find the bones stretch into wings instead, and dimly, it occurs to me that I'm still in hawk form.

I adjust my hold on the borrowed matter and shift back to human, thankfully having the wherewithal to assume Helos's form instead of my own. My limbs feel battered where they lay curled up on the floor, and pain is knifing a merciless rhythm through my skull. None of that changes the fact that I need to assess where I am, though, so I shove my palms against the chilled tile and push myself upright.

The room that holds me is small, smooth-walled, and not as bright as it seemed upon waking. Confusion mingles with dismay when I realize there are no windows through which to check the sun's position. Nor is there any furniture beyond the oil lamps, a chamber pot, a thin, woolen rug, and two curve-backed, uphol-stered chairs scraped across it. Everything else is cold stone and closed in, no escape except the door through which we must have entered. Someone has stacked clothing against one of the walls.

Since panicking won't help, I cross the room and pull on the purple top and loose black pants. The fabric rests surprisingly soft against my skin. I don't expect the door to give at my touch but try the handle anyway, pressing my lips together when the lock rattles in its hold.

Stretching the kinks from my muscles, I trail the perimeter of the room, scanning for any crevice I might slip through as a mouse. Back in the corners, against the floor. There's nothing, and I have no idea how long I've been here.

I slam a palm into the wall, and the door flies open.

Incurring a wave of dizziness, I throw my back against the stone, cradling my aching hand. It takes a couple of moments for my vision to focus.

A short man holding a tray of food steps over the threshold, two bulky guards quickly filling the gap in the doorway behind him. Both hold loaded crossbows aimed in my direction. Black arrows poke out of quivers belted at their waists, the same ones that cut a vicious hole in Weslyn's arm.

The tails are feathered.

And suddenly I'm seeing what I couldn't before. A childhood memory snatched from the fold, its edges gaining clarity with every new encounter. The room around me dims into irrelevance as Father's face takes shape in my mind, the familiar, earnest blue eyes and light brown curls crowning an aging face. Fragmented images from the last night I saw him alive.

"You have to be brave now, Rora," he said, crouching before me at the tree line and cradling my tiny face in his warm palms. Flames devoured the buildings around us with roaring apathy, their heat scalding. Everywhere, people were screaming, fighting to get out. "That's it. Be brave, just a little longer. Go with Helos. Your mother and I will follow."

"Don't leave me!" I cried, just as Helos appeared beside me, wild-eyed.

"Make for the trees—the forest will protect you. Don't separate, do you hear me?" Father grabbed Helos's shoulder. "You stay together."

Our neighbor, an older woman who had always baked us sweet breads, dropped to the ground beside us, an arrow protruding from her neck. I shrieked and bit my tongue hard enough to draw blood.

"Quickly!" Father exclaimed, placing a hand on my back and urging me forward.

"But you—"

He loosed a strangled noise as a black-fletched arrow sank into his back with a horrid thud. He landed facedown in the dirt. He didn't move.

"Father!" I screamed, collapsing beside him. "Fath—"

The word choked in my throat as thin arms wrapped around my waist and yanked me backward.

"Come on!" Helos cried, nearly lifting me off my feet.

I writhed in his grasp, screaming, fighting to free myself and crawl back to our father's side while he bled onto the forest floor.

"We have to—"

"Here."

Without quite meeting my gaze, the short man sets the tray on the ground with shaking hands.

I hardly even see him. The food, the soldiers, all of them mean nothing to me. I stare only at their arrows as the group retreats through the door, and the bolt slides back into place.

I don't know how long I linger there, stationed against the wall, my consciousness tethered to the past. Old embers buried between my ribs are rekindling to a blazing roar. The weapon that killed my father, my mother's portrait mounted and studded with darts—the pieces circle for prominence in my brain, linked by a single word.

Eradain.

I wipe the exhaustion from my face and struggle to cast the

thoughts aside. Now is not the time to solve that puzzle. Memories won't help me escape.

Since I really am hungry, I assess the tray's contents—red grapes, a block of cheese, and a cut of crusty bread. All fuel that might combat my fatigue, and my throat nearly cries at the sight of the water glass beside them.

I don't touch any of it.

Instead, I remain like that, staring at the door for an indeterminate amount of time. I try to picture Helos in the woods, Helos running free—at last, his safety guaranteed because of my help. I came for him without a second thought, and this time, it worked.

I smile a little, despite the violent pulsing in my head.

When at last the door opens once more, a handful of soldiers sweep into the room and snap to attention, making way for the man cutting a path between them. It's not the commander from yesterday. This one is tall, lithe, and . . . well, *young*. Younger than most of them.

My stomach crawls to the floor.

Looking at this man is like looking in a mirror. His skin has the same olive tones, though his eyes are green. His hair the same thick waves, though it's cut a little shorter and gleams darker—a striking shade of black. His nose sits more prominently on his face, his eyebrows a little wider. These differences do little to disguise the similarities, though. He's a slightly distorted version of Helos.

His expression, which was neutral at first, curdles a bit at the sight of me. Nobody speaks for a few moments.

"Do you mock me, shifter?"

He sees it, too, then. The resemblance. I shake my head, not bothering to hide my surprise; it could only help me in this situation.

He peers at me awhile longer, then smooths the anger from his face in one quick sweep and assumes a sort of half smile. His chin nods toward the untouched food. "It's not poisoned, you know."

As if to prove the point, he bends to pick a grape from its stem and plunks it in his mouth. Then he sinks into one of the chairs, knees splayed wide. "Sit," he says, extending a palm to the seat across from his.

I remain where I stand, and one of the soldiers fingers the crossbow at her side.

The seated man follows my gaze. "Leave us," he commands to the crew assembled.

A woman steps forward. "Your Majesty, it isn't safe."

Your Majesty? Could this be Jol? This boy-king who looks little older than my brother?

He turns back to face me, his features quite relaxed aside from the calculating eyes. "Do as I say."

The soldiers shuffle out, closing the door behind them.

Most people in King Gerar's court were afraid to meet my gaze for more than a few moments. Not this man. His eyes lock on to mine, and though they are the same shape as Helos's, they contain none of his usual, gentle warmth. "Sit," he says again.

I don't see any weapons on him, and I'm not exactly keen to have those soldiers called back in. So I sit.

The king leans back, setting an elbow on the arm of the chair. His collared shirt is dyed a dark color reminiscent of dried blood, an image that reminds me vaguely of Helos's disguise at Willahelm Palace. "I must apologize for my commander's behavior," he begins. "I would have intervened sooner, had I arrived before you were drugged."

My gut still prickles. I say nothing.

"What is your name?"

As if I would ever entrust him with it. His tone may sound civil enough, but he speaks with the measured, tightly controlled countenance of a man who has not gotten to where he is by asking the wrong questions.

"The hawk is an interesting form to take," he continues, passing over my silence. "Let me see. Hawk, fox, elk, is that right?" He counts them off on his fingers one by one, before lowering his voice a little. "Already three forms at such a young age. You haven't exactly lived in comfort over the years, have you?"

There's a bitterness in his tone I don't understand any more than the apology, the dismissal of guards, the food, and the relocation.

"In that, we are alike," he says, as easy as if we're already friends. "Some would say it makes us stronger. Would you agree?"

I truly don't know what game he's playing at. But beneath the shrewd expression, I detect a hint of genuine curiosity, and maybe that's why I reply, "Perhaps, but not enough to warrant the trade-off."

A glint akin to approval gleams in his eyes. "How is it you came to be here?"

"I was attacked," I say, since surely he would have received the report by now. "By your horrible men."

"Horrible." He shakes his head. "You judge me. That much is plain. But a good leader does what's best for his people, as I'm sure you can understand."

"All of his people, or only some?" I retort.

He studies me with a guarded expression, his reaction as indecipherable as Violet's ever are. "Who else knows you're here?"

"No one."

"No one," he echoes, sounding faintly amused now. "That doesn't explain what happened in the guard tower."

I blink and hope it passes for confusion.

"With whom do you live?"

"I live alone."

"Where?"

"The wilderness."

His eyes narrow a fraction. "Careful, now. Vague answers will not work with me. Tell me: Where is your home?"

Mentioning Telyan is certainly not an option, but the reminder of it brings unwanted images to mind. I imagine King Gerar erecting a prison compound like this one within his borders, his people's fear and hunger and anger taken to such extremes that they follow Eradain's lead and build cages, order executions. Whatever apprehension I felt at the idea of Telyan's land running wild with magic, I see now that a future without magic, one filled with more prisons like this, would be far worse.

"My home was destroyed," I say, settling on the truth.

"And where was that?" he asks. A trace of steel has entered his voice.

I raise my chin, a fraction of a challenge. "Nothing remains but the dirt on your doorstep."

A shadow crosses his face, along with the slightest hint of triumph. "You lived in Caela Ridge," he guesses. When I grant him nothing, he reaches into a pocket and withdraws a small square of wrinkled parchment. He unfolds it, then leans forward and holds it to my face. "Do you know this woman?"

Never in my life have I been so grateful for the years spent in Castle Roanin, honing my standard expression into one devoid of emotion. I take in the tiny painting of my mother now as if it means nothing to me, even when I notice a detail that drives a spike straight through my heart: she's wearing a crown.

"Is she royalty?" I ask, the weight of truth closing in. My limbs feel close to boiling. I curl my fingers reflexively, seeking that familiar jab of nails digging into palms, just enough pressure that the pain distracts and centers me. But I unfurl them just as quickly. Fists signal emotion.

"Answer the question," he commands, the friendly manner dropped away. "And she *isn't* anything, not anymore. She's dead."

It's obvious he dropped that fact in the hope of gaining a reaction. It doesn't work; at least, not in a way that he can see. "It was many years ago," I say truthfully. "I don't remember her." The room is quiet for a short time. "Did you kill her?" I can't help but add, in as neutral a tone as I can manage.

It must not have been as convincing as I had hoped, because a slight smile pulls at the corner of his mouth. He sits back, lifting his chin. "Her head decorated my father's gate for many weeks. Does that bother you?"

He speaks as if describing the weather.

Claws. Blazing. Biting. Threatening to break through the surface. I bend the entirety of my attention and my will to those hands, forcing them back, beating them back, *back*. He doesn't know about the lynx or the mouse, and I'm going to keep it that way. I must, if I am to have any hope of escaping. It's the only leverage I possess.

"Who was she to you?" The king has not broken eye contact. He's scouring for recognition, pressing me to reveal the connection that he's clearly already guessed. Torturing me even worse than fists or weapons ever could.

And it's working. I can feel the bindings threatening to snap, my entire body straining against the dam. Snippets of conversation with Wes slide into place with this new information—Daymon's murdered wife, the paintings of my mother, the crown. The echo of her appearance etched into this king's features, this man who is certainly Jol.

My mother had another child before us. My mother was a queen. My mother was murdered.

And this man is my half brother. The beloved ruler of Eradain, a kingdom founded upon the very principle that no one with magic in their blood should ever hold the throne.

A torrent of emotions overwhelms me, astonishment and anguish and unadulterated wrath. "Is that why your father murdered her?" I ask before I can stop myself. "To keep your secret safe?"

I've leapt through several points in the conversation in asking that, enough that I expect him to take time to process. In an instant, however, Jol has yanked me to my feet and slammed me against the wall so hard the back of my head rebounds. The forearm pinned across my collarbone is frighteningly strong, and I glance down at the sharp point biting between my ribs to find it's a knife.

"What has that fool Gerar promised you?" he asks, his breath singeing my face. "Because whatever it is, your plot will fail. Do not make the mistake of thinking me weak."

In the charged silence that follows, I scour my memory frantically for the bits of information Wes told me about Jol, anything that could help me out of this. Something about a difficult childhood. Problems with his father, a hero to his people. And then I realize.

"Gerar?" I whisper, my headache searing as lightning bolts.

Jol's mouth pinches a fraction. "Do not play stupid with me. I know who you are; I can see it in your face. And I know your home is in Telyan. You have been traveling with Gerar's eldest son, have you not?" He frowns. "Unfriendly sort of man."

"That's because he sees right through you," I spit.

"Good," he says with a twist of a smile. "We're finally getting somewhere."

I writhe in his grasp, but the knife point only presses harder. "You know nothing."

"I know plenty." A few strands of hair have fallen across his face in the struggle. "I received word two weeks ago that the prince was traveling with two shifters. My ambassador encountered a Royal Guard with quite a lot to say. And then, of course, there was the girl who looked so remarkably like Mariella. Who is she, I wonder, another bastard child from mother dearest?" His voice breaks a little on the words, undercutting the viciousness. I can recognize the subtle sorrow threatening to break through as easily as my own. "A lot can happen in two weeks, you know."

I flip through the pages of my memory with unbridled desperation, feeling the mouse fur now cushioning my back. Two weeks ago, we were in Grovewood. The ambassador. The inn.

One of the Royal Guards?

"That Gerar is consorting with magical people, even after the terms I laid out for him, is no great surprise to me." A small smile mars his face. "Though I did warn him of the consequences."

Say something, my mind is begging me. But I'm truly at a loss for how to escape this. In the wake of Jol's ultimatum, King Gerar's actions are as good as a slap to the face. We were ordered to keep Jol from finding out, but instead, we have forced his hand. And back in Telyan, King Gerar and his advisers all believe we still have time.

I have to warn them.

"But consorting with my blood and withholding their identity from me, despite the centuries-long peace treaties between our kingdoms?" Jol clicks his tongue as if disappointed. "Why, one might even call that treason. Tell me, which one of you has he been grooming for my throne?"

I shove him hard in the chest, and whether it's because he allowed it or anger has given me heightened strength, he stumbles back a pace or two and lowers the knife.

"No one is plotting against you," I say urgently, my mind reeling. "If King Gerar ever guessed at my lineage, he didn't tell me." And then, from whatever part of me snagged on the hitch in his voice: "You don't have to choose this path. Let me help you."

He studies me a long while and laughs once, a low and humorless sound. "Consider your options, brother," he murmurs, eliciting cold shivers down my spine. "I am not so heartless as to leave you without a choice. You can renounce your ties to Telyan and join me back at court, where you may, in time, prove yourself worthy of my trust. Your sister, too, if she likes." He chews on the words as if debating adding more. "Or, the two of you can side with your southern patron, and I will send him his usurpers' heads in a parcel." He pauses, considering. "Then again, perhaps Gerar will be dead before you make up your mind. After all, there is a Prediction to consider."

I launch toward him in fury, but he must have seen it coming, because he's already shouting for reinforcements. The door slams open and soldiers file in, forming a barrier between me and my half brother.

"Choose wisely," Jol says, backing away until he's nearly at the door. "And if you breathe a word of what we discussed to anyone on this base, then their deaths and those of your travel companions will be on your conscience. All it will take is one word from me." He smiles. "You have three days."

I run for the exit, but someone throws his arms around my torso and forces me back from the door. "Jol!" I shout, but he's already gone.

My captor shoves me so hard my back collides with the wall. Again. "The next time you address His Majesty so informally, I'll cut out your tongue, beast."

With that, the soldiers disperse, and I am left alone in the room.

TWENTY-FOUR

I ram my body into the door. I down the glass of water and shatter it, attempting to use the shards as lock picks. All my efforts yield are bloody fingers, and I sink to the floor, pressing my stinging hands into my shirt. When the shirt stains through and the bleeding doesn't stop, I forego my prior caution and shift to lynx, where I'm able to lick the wounds until the blood clots. I have no choice.

A lot can happen in two weeks.

He's going to launch an attack. Now, when Telyan isn't prepared. He thinks King Gerar is, what, plotting with me or Helos to take his throne? And he knows that the three of us have been traveling together; even now, soldiers may be scouring the woods for Weslyn and me. I reassume my brother's form and crouch against the wall, racking my brain for a way to escape.

I can't stop thinking about the betrayal. Jol must have been mobilizing ever since one of the Royal Guards . . . I rifle through the potential traitors. Naethan, Ansley, Carolette, and Dom. The latter two seem more likely, but then again, maybe the most skillful turncoat is the one I'd least expect. Though aren't the first two Wes's childhood friends?

I clench my jaws together, hard. Yena was right. These humans always search for danger in me when they should be looking at one another.

Throughout the next several hours, soldiers burst through the door at regular intervals; I can't figure out the reason for these surprise entries beyond preventing me from sleeping. When the first group enters, I consider shifting to lynx and throwing myself at them, but I cannot imagine I would get very far. I could try to escape once more as a mouse, but they'd scour the corridor the moment they saw the room was empty, and it probably wouldn't be difficult to spot my fleeing figure. I need a smarter plan than that. So I keep still while they clear away the glass without comment, and the rest of the water arrives in wooden bowls.

The same man with the shaking hands brings me every tray of food. His face bears only the suggestion of wrinkles—he looks about the age Father was before men like these murdered him. I wonder if sustaining a high priority prisoner is considered an honor or a punishment at this compound, but either way, the sight of his nerves and his uniform begins to rile me. I'm the imprisoned one here, not him.

"Care to switch places?" I taunt on his third visit, aching from the effort of maintaining Helos's borrowed form. He nearly drops the meal in front of me. "The service is pretty good, I hear."

"Silence," barks one of the soldiers by the door.

It would be easy, so easy, to tell them my suspicions about Jol's magical parentage. But I can't yet bring myself to have their deaths on my conscience, not if there's another way.

"Won't even look at me," I say instead, addressing only the tray bearer. "Too scared? Ashamed of what you do here, maybe?" His step falters midway across the room. "Look at me," I dare him.

He does, and in that moment, I'm not sure which of us manages to act more alarmed. His irises *change,* brown to blue, before settling back into their original color.

I saw it. I don't know how it's possible, or how long he hopes to hide it, but I show him I know his secret the best way I can.

I shift to assume his form, but with blue eyes instead of brown.

"Filth!" he screeches, stumbling backward. One of the others draws his sword. "I'll cut out your eyes! I'll break your neck, I'll—"

"What is the meaning of this?" Jol demands, soaring into the room as gracefully as a falcon.

The man snaps to attention so quickly, it's a marvel he does not break. "Your Majesty," he exhales, wringing his hands like a sodden dishcloth. "I—"

"Have no business hurling threats at my guest. Remove yourself from my sight."

His *guest*. I nearly gag. The man collapses into a hasty bow before walking backward to the door. When he meets my gaze a final time, I smile at him.

The remaining soldiers yank his gaping form into the corridor and shut the door behind them.

"Have you decided on my offer?" Jol asks, helping himself to his chair.

I nearly laugh in his face. An Eradain soldier with magic in his blood, right at the heart of their prison. A king with magic in his blood, at the seat of their government. The layers of deception and hypocrisy at play are astounding.

"What kind of life would await me in Eradain?" I reply, deeming it wise to pretend I'm actually considering it. "Why should I believe you wouldn't just kill me there?"

He appraises me thoughtfully. "I see no reason to waste talent unnecessarily, should you prove to have any of value."

"It's a business transaction, then."

He smiles. "If you are searching for sentimentality, I'm afraid I will have to disappoint you. In my experience, it does not get you very far."

"King Gerar would disagree," I can't help but add.

"Oh, I don't doubt that," he says, seriously. "And look at where working with him has gotten you."

I glare at him through narrowed eyes.

"I will get you a new attendant," Jol says, rising abruptly and heading for the door. "You have two days left."

True to his word, the tray bearer doesn't return. Every so often, however, Jol reenters the room, asking if I will accept his offer. Each time I deflect, and he departs seemingly unbothered. No sign of knives or more brutal tactics ever since that first meeting, and I still can't figure out why.

The only thing I have to mark the passing time is the mounting strain in my body. The ache in my head is blossoming into body-wide discomfort. First as knots in my back, then pinches along the lining of my stomach. Cords tightening inside my calves, and pinpricks jabbing the soles of my feet. It's becoming increasingly difficult to maintain Helos's form; pretty soon, my two days of borrowed matter will be up. At least by then, the boys will hopefully have had the sense to obey my orders and run far away from here.

By Jol's fourth visit, I'm close to fainting. Lack of proper sleep and holding borrowed matter has rendered me nearly incapacitated, but the thought of Wes and Helos going free has me desperate to buy them as much of a lead as possible. I remain in Helos's form.

By Jol's fifth visit, my body has betrayed me at last.

He makes it only a couple of steps into the room before halting. "What is this?"

Breathing rather heavily, there's little explanation I can offer him beyond the obvious. My hair falls in waves just past my shoulders, and my hands rest limply in my lap. In my natural form once more.

The sight arrests Jol where he stands. He seems to undergo a kind of transformation; his eyes are splayed wide, his fists are balled, and despite the distance between us, I could swear he's started to shake.

"You," he whispers, and I don't know whether he means I'm his half sister, not brother, or whether he's simply seeing the ghost of his mother.

"She left me, too, you know," I say. "Before your father murdered her."

For the first time since meeting him, Jol appears incapable of responding.

"I know what that feels like," I continue. "But you have nothing to prove."

This, at last, stirs him into anger. "You know nothing of me or my life," he hisses, and there's a hint of emotion in the words. Defiance. Or loneliness.

"Then tell me."

He exhales slowly. "Does this mean you accept my offer?"

In the silence that follows, whatever sliver of him may have begun warming to me slams shut. His expression returns to one of cool indifference. Detached.

"You still believe there is value in sentimentality," he observes. "I see now I will have to break you of that notion, if you choose to live and wish to survive at my court."

My pulse accelerates. "Jol—"

"Commander!"

The vile man enters the room a heartbeat later, along with three other soldiers. His lips curl into a sneer when he sees me. "Your Majesty?"

Jol straightens and places his hands behind his back, his eyes never leaving mine. "Put her in the shed." The commander becomes near gleeful, until Jol specifies, "Alive."

Someone's jaw drops a little, but no one objects. Instead, I'm hauled roughly to my feet and dragged back through the corridors and out into the open air, trying to make sense of my surroundings. I tilt my head to the sky and could swear I catch a glimpse of black circling overhead.

I force my attention back to eye level. The shed. I saw the logs and diagrams, the experiments they perform here. *Please don't let the shed be that.* I'm still appealing to fortune when we reach the squat, concrete building near the watchtower.

A soldier throws open the door and covers her mouth with a fist.

The stench hits me before the sight.

Horror-struck, I yank against my captors' hold. Attempt to kick them in the groin. Scratch, bite, break. None of it works, but it does earn me another punch to the gut. I clench my teeth at the impact.

"Don't forget, shifter, I have plenty of techniques at my disposal," the commander murmurs close to my ear, when we're standing at the precipice. "A finger broken, perhaps, or a toenail removed. Don't worry," he adds, noting the look on my face. "None of it would kill you."

A moment later I'm tossed through the opening and into a nightmare. Into the "shed," whose floor is covered wall to wall with corpses.

The impact of landing might be the worst sensation I have ever felt.

"Don't bother trying to beat down the door," the commander cautions in a carrying voice, across the exit's threshold. "If you do, we'll have crossbows at the ready."

He slams the door shut, casting me into near-total darkness, save for the murky light from a few slitted windows scattered throughout.

Corpses. Corpses everywhere, from all different people and animals. Empty eyes and stacked limbs and decaying flesh. The stench of rot scalds the back of my throat, crawling into my lungs, so thick I can practically sink my teeth into it. Resting only an arm's length away is the missing forest walker, her body clear as glass, save for the smudged edges. Hastily, I stumble barefoot toward the door, tripping, shrieking, choking on sobs as the bodies roll beneath me.

I'm desperate not to vomit, not to tarnish these lost souls any more than they already have been, but there's no help for it. I retch and retch.

"Let me out!" I scream when I've emptied my guts, any pretense of composure completely impossible. No one answers, and my body is too drained to offer escape in the form of an animal. I tip my head to the ceiling and look for an opening of any kind, one I can fly through once I have recovered enough strength. There's nothing.

I'm shaking so violently it's a miracle I haven't stripped the skin from my bones. There's nowhere to stand, nowhere to sit, nowhere to *exist* that isn't on top of someone; the bodies cover the ground completely. I press my fists against the metal door and struggle to calm my hiccuping breaths. I need to think. I need to breathe. But I can't. I can't think of anything other than the victims beneath my feet, the ones who can no longer breathe, the ones whose lives were stolen from them.

And for what? Because they were born with magic in their blood? Because they failed whatever tests were forced upon them? Because they weren't human?

It's all wrong. The executions. The biases. This campaign to empty the land and destroy the magic within, as if that could possibly justify preventing another Rupturing.

At last, something pushes past my horror and disgust. The sob in my throat breaks through, and then I'm crying. Proper, hysterical crying, a mess of tears and snot and swelling, whether from sorrow or fury I don't know. It occurs to me that this could have been Helos, how close that was to becoming reality, and I cry even harder. Cry and scream and scream some more.

I think of Simeon, ramming his elbow between my ribs at Castle Roanin. I think of Dom, declaring me a monster, and Seraline's sister making the symbol to ward off bad fortune.

And suddenly, I'm not angry at my mother for abandoning Helos and me, for choosing to flee and save herself. I'm angry at those men with their black-fletched arrows who forced her to choose in the first place.

The knowledge is a revelation, along with everything else. My mother had a life before she had us. She had a husband and a son and a home of palace walls. Weslyn told us once that Jol's mother—*my* mother—left Oraes before she was killed, but he never said how long she managed to live in hiding. She must have fled to Caela Ridge and given birth to Helos and me a few years later.

And before that, she was a queen. A *queen.*

What does that make Helos and me?

A threat, it seems, in Jol's mind.

There's so much I need to ask her, so many gaps in the story that only she can fill. And she's gone. Murdered like the rest of the forestborn in this room, with no ability to think or speak or act or *know* anything, ever again.

But I'm still breathing.

This is the thought that grants me clarity as the day drags on. The door is the only way out, and that way is being watched. So I'll have to find another one.

I take a breath and face the room once more.

There's an opening built into the wall opposite mine, an arch made of brick that recedes into shadow. It may lead to nothing, but it's a start. After steeling myself another moment, I walk slowly, agonizingly, across the room, shifting the bodies out of my path to the extent that I'm able.

When I reach the arch, I find it stretches back far enough for me to take several steps in, if I can work up the courage to cross the soot-covered floor without shoes. I hesitate, then bend a little and take a step forward. A sharp point jabs the sole of my foot, and I bite back a cry, lifting my leg to brush away the debris. They're shards of bone.

Bile rises in my throat. Using the sides of my feet to brush away what I can, I carve a path to the back and press my hands against the wall. No openings that I can make out, but if a fire has been lit here, as I'm starting to suspect, fire needs air to stay alive. Which means there must be an opening somewhere. I look up.

There's a thick slab of metal grating, so crusted and black with soot that it's difficult to make out in the dark. The opening to a chimney. I slide my fingers through the gaps around the greasy, gnarled rods and pull. A bit of debris rains down on my head and shoulders, and the fresh cuts from the glass shards scream in protest, but the grating doesn't budge. I try again, lifting my knees so my whole weight is hanging on the bars. Nothing.

By now I've regained enough strength to hold a shift, for a little while at least. So I shed my clothes and shift to lynx, then fasten my jaws around the grating. A foul taste enters my mouth, but I don't allow myself to stop and consider what it might be. I pull, and this time the metal groans a little in protest.

I don't know how long I remain there, working to loosen the grating. My jaws are aching like thunder by the time I release it and sink back onto the floor. The metal won't yield.

This can't be the end. Not when I've actually found an escape I can fly out of. Fighting not to give in to despair, I shift back to human and shove my shirt in my mouth, trying to scrape the taste from my tongue. Then I stumble back into the room, chest heaving. Think, Rora. *Think.*

Air feeds fire. Fire breeds smoke. Smoke needs a means of escape, if the soldiers here are meant to enter this room after a fire without breathing it in. I scan the walls and find what I was looking for: small metal vents, like the chimney's grating in miniature, set into the walls a good distance apart. There are four in total, and I work my way over to the first with a surge of hope.

It doesn't give. I huff in disbelief and move to the second, brushing my fingers against my shirt; they're rubbing raw in the effort, and a couple of the wounds have reopened. The second holds as fast as the first, and this time I don't muffle my scream of frustration.

Only two left. I choose the one that's farthest away and move until I'm directly in front of it. A couple of the bars here are missing from the set, so I shift to lynx and examine the opening. My heart nearly bursts at the sight.

The metal has begun to rust. When I've secured a firm grasp with my teeth, I yank, and the grating screeches free.

The opening in the wall is just wide enough to work. I whisper one final apology—and a promise—to the bodies around me. Then I take my chance and fly into the gap, shifting from goshawk to mouse when my talons start to slide on the metal. Exhaustion is eating at my body; the strength I've regained is almost spent. I have no choice but to carry on as long as I can, though, so I scrabble through the metal tunnel, whiskers twitching.

At last, the passage ends in an opening the size of a brick. Night proper blankets the world outside, and the fresh air cleanses my lungs like a stream. I take a minute to listen for the sounds of restless guards standing watch, but it seems they've left this side of the building unmonitored. I muster the final dregs of strength and shift to goshawk, letting my wings carry me quickly, quietly, away.

TWENTY-FIVE

I find the boys only a short distance from where I'd left Wes. They didn't obey my order to move on after all.

Helos pushes to his feet the moment I explode into the clearing. Weslyn, who was pacing, jerks to a halt, hand on his sword. I drop to the ground and shift to human, regaining my natural form with a gasp. They're at my side in an instant, a jumble of limbs supporting me under the arms and offering me my pack. I recoil from their touch as if it burns.

"Take it easy," Helos murmurs, retreating as I pull on underthings, dark brown pants, green shirt, socks, boots—the movements mechanical, made by quivering fingers. "You're okay."

"I told you to head for the river!" I choke out.

"You think I could leave you?"

Wes turns his back while I change. I think I should be grateful, or at least feel *something,* but I'm having trouble focusing. A shield of fog thicker than mist has somehow permeated my brain, obscuring most threads of rational thought.

"You're okay," Helos repeats. "You're—what happened to your hands?"

They're bleeding again. Wes swivels round, and I lower my arms, looking up at him and Helos. Both visible in the moonlight, whole and breathing and mercifully alive.

But not safe. Not yet.

"We have to move," I rasp, as Helos withdraws bandages from his pack. "Jol kno—"

"Look at me, Rora," he says, very seriously, dropping the bandages and taking my face in his hands. "Did they hurt you?"

"*No.* Not me, they—wait, did they hurt you?" I ask, instinct thrumming a warning.

But Helos shakes his head.

"Then listen to me. Jol knows the three of us are traveling together, and he knows King Gerar is working with shifters—"

"What? How?" Wes says.

"—And he implied that's as good as a refusal of his terms. He's going to attack."

"He was there?" Wes asks, at the same time Helos exclaims, "Now?"

"How should I know?" I snap. "If he doesn't give the order now, I'm sure he will soon!"

Despite Helos's alarm, his hands are steady as they tend to my own. "Rora—"

"I'm *fine*," I insist, but this time when I look at my brother, I don't see the dark brown eyes creased in concern, the skin bruised but flushed with life. I see bodies, some whole, some severed, crawling in insects. The scent of decay lingers in my nostrils like tendrils of smoke.

I dry heave into the grass.

"What's wrong with her? What happened?" Wes demands. His voice sounds like his hands feel, holding my hair back while I gag. That ridiculous thought propels an even more ridiculous impulse to laugh. Instead, I start trembling harder—chest, arms, hands, everywhere. I can't seem to stop, and the wall of fog thickens.

A hand to the back of my neck. "She doesn't feel feverish."

"She's in shock."

"From what?"

"I don't know."

Something soft brushed across my mouth, wiping away any stray saliva.

"She's right. We should move."

"She's shaking. Take this."

Something draped around my neck, bulky and warming. I glance down. A cloak.

"Rora."

I shake my head.

"Rora," Helos repeats, more insistent this time. "I need you to stand."

I snatch my arm away from the hand that grabs it.

"*Stand,*" he commands, regaining his grip.

Dimly, it occurs to me that he's not being cruel. He's being me, were our situations reversed.

I let him help me to my feet, only to have my knees buckle on the first step.

"Hold her while I shift," Helos says, releasing me. Suddenly there's a new pair of arms supporting me, one wrapped around my waist, the other resting gently under my arm. Awareness of the touch to my waist pricks through the fog, kindling a flicker of feeling, something strange and stupid. I will it to retreat, even as his hold remains steady.

Helos appears beside me shortly after, bobbing his antlered head. An elk. Understanding dawns, and the part of my brain that's working properly abhors the idea of having to be carried. The rest, however, is finding it difficult to stand, let alone resist. My brother kneels to the ground, and I clamber onto his back. Then without another word, he stands, and we flee.

Whether by fortune or the Vale's design, no one catches up to us in the days to come. Which is a miracle, because we're not moving fast. Wes is still limping from the leg wound that he claimed didn't hurt much. Helos is weak all over, not yet healed from our skirmish in the woods—he walks evenly, but slowly, appearing uncomfortable under the weight of his pack. And I—well, there's no point in pretending I'm fine.

There is death on you.

I don't know whether he meant the people I would kill or the victims I would join. I'm not sure I even care anymore. I'm having trouble caring about a lot of things.

There's a heaviness between my ribs that hasn't lifted since my escape. It's a strange sensation, almost like burning. As if the memories from that day are searing a hole through my heart. Every once in a while, the ground beneath my feet seems to shift, and in those moments I shriek and stagger a few paces to the side. Once I stumble right into Wes, who winces at the impact to his injured arm. Another time I swing onto a low-hanging branch, just to avoid touching the forest floor. Because in these moments, twigs, acorns, and grass turn to arms, eyes, and fur. I can feel them on my neck, my shoulders, my back—I'm lying there again, cast into the chamber, fighting to keep my head up before I'm buried alive. Buried in flesh and rot and bones.

I can still smell it.

The boys try to soothe my wasted nerves by assuring me it's all in my head. A memory, only a memory. But it isn't just a memory—those corpses and those prisoners are still there, even if we can no longer see them.

This is the fact that shapes my thoughts in the coming days. As we travel, I pass the time by imagining the Vale as a conscious being and the prison as a parasite, leeching its lifeblood acre by acre. In my fantasies, the woods and the mountains come to life. Trees seize the soldiers with gnarled roots and crush them, snapping their bones and squeezing their lungs until they no longer draw breath. The mountains bellow in fury, thunderous roars that shake the earth and rip chunks of rock from the cliff faces. Under such duress, the buildings and the cages collapse in broken heaps, but the prisoners remain untouched. Rain falls then, a healing mist that seeps through their fur and into their skin. And pockets of wind carry them to safety.

These thoughts of destruction give me comfort, and in turn that comfort disturbs me. Sometimes I fear I might be turning into the monster Dom claimed me to be.

Then I remind myself that whatever danger may be taking root in my mind, I have seen its mirror image enacted tenfold by humankind. Violence gets its wings by choice, not by nature, and I am no more monster than they.

Regardless, as I lie awake at night, reliving the horrors of the compound after triple-checking to make sure that the boys are still breathing, only sleeping, nothing more—I can feel it there, sprouting in my core. The seed of vengeance planted deep in my heart.

Wes and Helos seem to be getting along with each other better than they had before. I wonder if my absence had anything to do with it, whether concern over my safety somehow brought them together. Then I dismiss the idea that Wes would have been so concerned. Then I wonder if he might have been.

Stupid. Strange and stupid.

In time, I tell them about Jol's interrogation and the shed. Peridon's cousin I never managed to speak to more—I should have freed her when I had the chance. Helos alternates between swearing loudly, asking questions, and coming close to tears. Weslyn says little, but I can read his dismay in his face.

Both are rattled when I tell them about the traitorous guard.

"One of them must have told Ambassador Kelner we were traveling together." Speaking the words aloud is like drawing poison from a wound. "They're the reason he's known about us for weeks. The timeline fits."

After hours of hiking, the three of us are sitting cross-legged in a circle, Weslyn's knee grazing my own. He's not moving away, and I'm grateful for the tether to the present.

"One of the Guard, a traitor." He tests the syllables like foreign words. "I don't understand it. None of them would—"

"Clearly they would. It's simply a question of who."

Anger twists in my belly as I recall Dom shoving me into an alley, Carolette making the sign to ward off bad fortune. Even the quiet acceptance from Ansley and Naethan might have been a lie. Their king swore them all to silence, but one of them talked anyway, and now Telyan will go to war because of that.

Well, not just that.

"Dom was clearly against us," Helos says. "Carolette, too." He runs a hand over his shoulder. "Ansley was quiet, maybe too much so. Naethan—"

"Impossible," Wes interrupts. "Naethan and I have been friends ever since we were boys. The notion is laughable. And Ansley would never. She and I trained together, we were—" He stops and looks down, cutting that thought abruptly at the roots.

"Rora?" Helos says, looking pointedly at my claws.

It's an effort to sheathe them, but I do. "There's something else."

I tell them about our mother. That she was Jol's mother, too, and how Kelner spotted the resemblance between us in Grovewood. I reiterate Jol's suspicions that King Gerar knows our parentage and has been planning some kind of secret coup. Saying it all aloud, it sounds impossible to the point of absurdity.

"That's impossible," Helos whispers, because we're of one mind, always.

I shake my head. "I saw the portrait. Two of them, actually. It's her."

He just stares as if he's never seen me before.

"And you're absolutely certain it's your mother?" Wes asks. "You did say you were very young when you last saw her."

I glare at him. "I'm sure. She looked like us. So does Jol; all he had to do was see Helos to guess the truth. You've met him before, haven't you?"

Wes holds my gaze awhile longer, then looks at Helos. Well, more than looks. Studies.

While he studies my brother, I study him. His beard has grown longer over the last few days, his skin darkened a shade by the sun. The pack set beside him bears a small rip near the top, and the clothes on his back are rumpled and smudged with dirt. Not to mention the bandages underneath.

How far he's come from his castle life.

In time, he nods, slightly wide-eyed. "You do look alike," he admits, speaking to Helos. "Very much so. I don't know why I didn't see it before."

"Were you ever really looking?" I ask quietly.

He doesn't answer.

"Think," I urge Helos. "What do we know about her life before us? Nothing. And Jol is, what, seven years older than you?" Well, more or less. "Weslyn said she left Oraes before she was killed. The timeline's entirely possible; she must have taken refuge at Caela Ridge. And those people who led the raid—I bet you Daymon sent them. The soldiers in that compound had the same arrows as the one that killed Father."

Helos blanches as heat rushes through my body. To hunt your own wife.

"But that means—" Weslyn runs a hand over his beard. "Are you saying that Jol's mother was a shifter?"

I nod. "He could be one, too. Who knows how much magic she passed to him."

"Magic in the Holworth line," Wes echoes, mystified. "If the people there knew, they would turn on him."

"We should tell them," Helos says gruffly.

"How would you prove it?" I counter. "Our mother is dead. Unless Jol himself shifts in public—which we don't even know he has enough magic to do, if no emotions have triggered this already—the only way to be certain would be to get a shifter in there. One who could smell the magic on him in an animal form and speak out about it. Assuming anyone would even believe them." I shake my head. "In any case, I don't think he's stupid enough to allow that to happen, not while—" My voice drops away, more pieces settling into place. "He's eliminating magical people from the continent. He's burying the truth."

Helos frowns. "Then why didn't he kill you or me when he had the chance?"

I don't have an answer to that. But playing through my conversations with Jol once again, another connection clicks at last— the reason his accent sounded familiar. In my limited memory, my mother's accent wasn't as strong as his, but it was there.

Northern brusque.

"He's right about one thing," Wes says, looking thoughtful.

"My father must have guessed the truth, or at least suspected it. If you resemble your mother as closely as you say, he will have spotted the similarity. He met her—and Jol, for that matter—several times."

I contemplate King Gerar's refusal to send me north, despite Violet's entreaties. "I'd like to ask him."

"And on that note." Helos fixes me with a piercing look. "If our mother was a queen, what does that make us?"

Even with the blackness clouding my head, that invisible barrier severing me from reality, a small shiver runs down my spine at the words. "Wes?" I ask, since this is more his territory than ours.

Wearily, he massages his forehead. "Daymon is the one who carried the Holworth blood. You're not part of his line, but the current king is your half brother." He shakes his head, shrugging a little. "It's conceivable you could have some claim to the throne."

I imagine it then. For one horrible, fascinating moment: me, a shifter. A girl who doesn't even know how old she is. A princess of Eradain.

I find it doesn't fit at all.

"I wouldn't want it," I say.

"Wouldn't you?" Helos says in a quiet voice.

I stare at him, astonished.

"Think about what Jol is doing. The prejudice he perpetuates. The atrocities he's committing." He takes my hands in his, gaze locked on to mine. "If you had the chance to stop him, remove him from power altogether—wouldn't you?"

It takes a moment for me to register it—the exact thing Jol suspected Helos or I have been plotting, straight from my brother's mouth in less than an hour since learning his lineage. Yet the future he suggests is so removed from anything I ever imagined for myself that it's nearly impossible to picture. I want to stop Jol, yes, to fix this broken world, and for the first time in my life, I'm starting to feel I have the capacity to. Scars and selfish thoughts at times, but also—courage. A good heart. But to become responsible for an entire kingdom? To rule?

I yank my hands from his, afraid of what he's suggesting—and ashamed of my fear.

"You would not have an easy time of it," Wes points out. "Rulers are not often deposed."

Helos frowns, the lines of his face no longer echoes of laughter and light. They are hard lines now, serious and severe. Weighted.

Sharp as antlers.

"Surely genocide would be reason enough," he says.

Wes doesn't contradict him.

Magical beings dying west of the river. Humans dying to the east. When will it be enough?

"Let's keep moving," I say. "I want to finish this." The sooner we get the stardust to Telyan and warn the court, the better.

At the allusion to Finley, Helos's face transforms into something softer and sadder. Without a word, he leads the way onward.

And doubles the pace.

We reach the riverbank three days after fleeing the compound.

The water is as imposing as I remember, the riotous current churning violently as always. The roaring grates loud enough to block out my fantasies, at least. To Helos's and my surprise, it's Wes who identifies the place we landed first. Even from a distance, he recognizes the curve of the shoreline and the thicket of reeds near the water's edge. Though he tries to shrug it off, it's obvious he's proud of himself, and somehow the sight draws me further from my despair. Like a small ray of sunlight peeking through the blackness. I laugh for the first time in days.

We slow our pace now that we're getting so close, not wanting to overshoot the stretch where we're supposed to attract the Niav watchmen with smoke signals. We keep our eyes trained on the opposite shore as we walk, waiting for the city to come into view.

When the first buildings appear on the horizon, it's immediately apparent that something is wrong.

An enormous cloud of smoke funnels up from the earth, swathing what we can see of the city in an unearthly shadow. River breeze carries the stench of flames right to us.

Niav is burning.

TWENTY-SIX

"Fortune save us," I breathe.

"What's happening?" Helos demands. "Did a fire break out?"

I think of the people we passed in the street. Minister Mereth in her palace atop the hill. Did anyone make it out in time?

Mangled limbs. Bloodless lips. Death, death, dea—

"No," Wes replies, both hands behind his neck, staring as if he can't believe what he's seeing. Unaware of the nausea stroking my throat. "Look there."

I can't make out what he's pointing to, but Helos can.

"A flag."

Wes swears softly and starts to pace. "Eradain."

"What?" I exclaim, close to retching. "You're sure?"

He nods, and the smoke stuns us into silence. Niav, attacked. Glenweil's capital, burning. That realm is still neutral, at least officially. Has Jol's patience with opposition simply expired?

I face the others, stomach plummeting. "Do you think he's already attacked Telyan, too?"

Helos pales, but Weslyn only looks at me, like he's thought of this already. "We have to find some way to cross," he says firmly. Though his voice sounds calm enough, I see the fists bunched at his sides. "We cannot go this way now. We don't know if anyone will be awaiting a signal anymore, and we don't want to risk encountering someone from Eradain."

I see his point, and I think I agree, but—"There's nowhere else to cross," I say miserably.

He stares at me beseechingly. "Is there *truly* nowhere else? Nowhere opposite Telyan?"

I open my mouth, then close it again. "I mean, the river is narrower there. But it runs through a gorge, and the current's just as strong." He remains silent, and I realize he's waiting for me to make the decision. Helos is still staring at the opposite shore. "I suppose we could at least look," I relent. My brother appears as hopeless as I feel, but he nods anyway.

With a final glance at the burning city, I lead the way back along the shore, retracing our steps from only moments before. The quiet stretched between us has turned ominous. *His family is in Telyan,* I think wretchedly. Not just his people, but his family. The ones he loves most in the world and would do anything for.

Let them all be safe. Please, let them be safe.

At one point, Wes loses his footing in his haste, but otherwise there are no mishaps on the despondent trek south. We travel a few steps into the tree line, just in case someone is keeping watch on the other side. After a while, the Purple Mountains decorate the opposite shore, the forested peaks standing sentinel in the sunlight. From this distance, they do indeed look purple-tinted, and it's a beautiful sight, so at odds with the danger only a short way to the north.

But despite our strenuous pace, we're losing the race against the sun. By the time we're nearly parallel with the peaks, it's sunk below the horizon.

"We're going to have to stop for the night," I say, bringing the group to a halt. Wes takes another couple of steps forward, but I grab his sleeve. "We stand little enough chance of making it across as it is. Attempting it in the dark would be suicidal."

He wants to object. I know he does, but he can't. Not this time.

"We'll start again at first light," I promise.

He opens his mouth.

"First light," I repeat, firmly this time.

He holds my gaze a long while. The fear he's trying so hard to disguise is breaking my heart, but I can't back down. I won't. I wait until I see his shoulders drop, feel the muscles relax beneath my grip. When the rest of the fight has finally left him, I release his arm.

We reach the gorge by midmorning.

It's a foreboding sight. The land on our side of the river is still dotted with sun-stricken pines, but the other side is barren, a few scraggly bushes comprising the only vegetation beneath the mountains. Far below, the river rages southward with its usual fury. The drop on both sides is dangerously steep, too steep to climb down or up. Helos and I exchange a look.

"Let's keep going," I suggest, attempting to convey greater confidence than I feel. By some perverse turn of events, it seems it's become my job to keep their spirits up. That used to be my brother's role.

Neither of them responds. Instead, we follow the curve of the cliff face in a gloomy silence, keeping an eye out for any descents that look promising.

As we walk, the walls of the gorge do begin to shrink, albeit gradually. The river narrows as well, more so than I remember. It won't be much farther now until we reach the edge of the Vale, and the Elrin Sea beyond.

As time passes, it becomes clear that this is not going to work. A shallow bank has emerged far below on the opposite shore, but even with that and the rather drastic narrowing, the current still races as wild as ever. Perhaps it's possible we could make it across, but it would be a huge risk.

A few paces directly ahead, the earth melts away in another severe drop. Beyond, brilliantly blue water stretches as far as the eye can see, glistening in the sunlight. We've reached the sea.

On the opposite shore, Telyan continues on farther south, the land curving slightly to the east. Eventually, it will sharpen to a point. This is the edge of the Vale, though, and the end of the road for us.

Wes chucks a stone in frustration, anger slipping through a crack in his usually controlled veneer. Helos says nothing, just sinks to the ground with his pack against a tree. We have only two choices now: risk flagging down Jol's soldiers, or risk the raging current.

I'm tempted to join Helos on the ground. Instead, my gaze sweeps the gorge once more, searching for a solution that is not there.

I won't fall apart, I tell myself, images of Finley hurting, Geonen's daughter hiding, Andie sitting cross-legged in a cage—all of them—flashing across my mind. I have seen death, and given it, and I won't condemn my friend to that fate. I've kept to the outskirts of the world, but I won't leave others to do the same, won't perpetuate the cycle any longer. That kernel of conviction, new and delicate and flickering, sparks to life once more, warming me like a shield against the misery and the injustice of how we could survive imprisonment and actually retrieve the medicine we set out to find, only to be thwarted so close to home.

Home.

The thought is a shock. My entire life, I have thought of Helos and myself as little more than wanderers, orphans with few friends or any place to call home. We lived in uncertainty for so long that part of me always feared Telyan wouldn't be more than a short stint.

The city hasn't been kind to us. Helos lives in secrecy every day, hiding his true nature, while I'm criticized for mine more often than not. But it's been four years. Helos and I both have jobs we love and a place to live. We have a royal family who will be indebted to us upon our return. More than that—they may even *want* us around. King Gerar defended me when everyone implored him to send me away. Finley befriended me when no one else would. Violet understood me well enough to know exactly what to do to strengthen my loyalty and resolve: she hugged me. And Wes—he's not the person he was nearly a month ago. He's my friend.

And I'm not the same girl. I'm done with sticking to shadows, done with accepting abuse without retaliation. Maybe I can make Telyan a kinder place for us after all. Maybe I can make it a proper home.

This hope, more than anything, is enough to make me desperate.

"Please," I whisper. Scarcely more than a breath.

For a few heartbeats, there's nothing save the sound of a few lonesome birds and the river below. And then I hear it: creaking, breaking, crashing.

Helos leaps to his feet, and the three of us charge forward, heading north once more to locate the source of the crack now echoing through the gorge. It doesn't take long.

A tree has fallen across the ravine.

For several long moments, we just stare at it, blinking stupidly.

"What are the chances of it falling right where we needed?" Weslyn asks, clearly wary.

"Coincidence," Helos says.

Wes appears unconvinced.

"Remember," I tell him. "You can't anthropomorphize the magic. It doesn't take sides or grant favors. The only driving force it has is to survive." I pause, considering. "And given the number of magical beings they're slaughtering at that prison, I wouldn't blame the Vale for feeling threatened. The land itself felt wrong in that place. Even the mountain was cracked."

Helos pivots toward me. "What did you say?"

"The mountain was cracked. You must have seen it."

He stares at the gorge for an endless moment. Then he tilts his head toward the ground, marching a few steps away, then back.

"Helos?"

"A crack in the land," he says, in an agitated manner. "Magical people and creatures being murdered. Magic feeling threatened, appearing east of the river. You," he switches abruptly, smacking Wes's arm with the back of his hand. "You must have had plenty of tutors growing up in a castle. What did they teach you about the origin of magic? Why did the Rupturing occur?"

Weslyn's eyes narrow, and I feel rather tempted to shove Helos myself. "The energy beneath the surface became too great," he responds in a low voice, like he's annoyed he has the decency to answer. "The magic broke through and fractured."

FORESTBORN 317

"It *fractured*! Magic couldn't survive where it was, so it erupted and cracked the land."

"So?"

"Magic will always fight to survive," I murmur, starting to catch where Helos is headed.

"This is it," Helos says. "The disturbance the king told us to search for. The source of the magic east of the river."

"I don't understand," says Wes.

"Rora had the measure of it. Eradain begins taking steps to eradicate magic from the Vale, and a mountain fissures at the site where magic's hosts are being killed. Those two facts aren't coincidence. They're *linked*." He turns to me. "You're right, I did see the crack. I just didn't think anything of it."

"What are you saying?" Weslyn asks. "Another energy event split the land without anyone noticing?"

"Not the land. The mountain." Helos scrapes his boot across the ground. "Think about it," he presses. "Magic fights to survive. If it felt truly threatened, it would try to preserve itself. And what better method to try than one that has worked already? Jol thinks he's preventing another Rupturing by eliminating magic from the continent, but he's only making the problem worse. The land is already cracking again, only less dramatically than last time. Except the fracturing magic still needs a place to go." He folds his arms tightly before him. "And this time, it seems the hosts are no longer compatible."

"Oh," I exhale. Wes twists toward me. "The Fallow Throes."

A gust of wind sweeps through the gorge, and I bow my head against the worst of it. The thinner branches and leaves on the fallen tree flutter like insects in the gale. Helos is right—this must be why magic surged across the river.

"Those papers I found in the compound dated back to several months ago," I say. "That's when people started getting sick, around the time Jol's compound started functioning."

"But Fin only became sick a few weeks ago," Wes points out, massaging a kink in his shoulder. "If the mountain cracked months ago, how could its magic still be affecting people?"

"It would take a long time for the pieces of an event like that to settle," Helos reasons.

"Months?"

My brother shrugs. "Illnesses affect people differently. Maybe it takes longer to surface in some than others."

"Or maybe the mountain wasn't the only crack in the land," I say. "Maybe there have been smaller ones we haven't noticed." My gaze falls on the fallen pine spanning the gorge. "Like this tree."

An uneasy silence hangs in the air.

"Look, debating this is not going to help the afflicted right now. We have the remedy they need, and we're lingering too long. We need to cross."

Wes examines the tree bridge and the yawning emptiness below, his expression heavy with apprehension. "Are we going to try that?"

I roll my shoulders back, already determined. "Yes, we are."

Before anyone can object, I step up to the edge. The trunk is wide, about the length of my arm across. But it's round and flecked with branches, and the drop is a long way down. I don't fear heights—spending part of life as a goshawk will have that effect—but even I feel a little dizzy at the sight.

"Rora," says Weslyn, just as Helos says, "Hang on."

"Listen." I cut them off, swiveling to face them. "It's either this, or we swim across. The latter has a larger chance of ending in drowning."

"This could still end that way," Helos snaps.

"But it's the less likely of the two."

He doesn't appear impressed by this reasoning.

"Why don't you shift?" Wes suggests. "You can fly across."

The words spark the old guilt, along with anger. A picture of Helos dropping below the surface flashes through my mind. Never again.

"We're not separating," I say, insistent. *And we're all making it across,* I add silently, unable to bear the thought of any alternative. "Besides, I still have to get my pack over there."

Before they protest again, I step around the towering roots and out onto the trunk.

The first couple of steps are not so bad. It's when the ground beneath the tree falls away that moving forward becomes a lot more difficult.

Walking ever so slowly, arms spread wide and occasionally gripping a branch for balance, I tell myself this is the same as crossing a log on land. My feet wouldn't slip then, and I would be moving much faster besides. No reason they should fail me now. A gust of wind buffets my hair, abruptly dousing my imagined words of comfort. It wasn't strong enough to interfere with my balance, but who's to say the next one won't be?

What about the boys?

"Do you think I should crawl instead?" I call without looking back, determined to keep my voice as relaxed as possible. I'm desperately afraid for both of them, neither of whom have a winged fail-safe should they fall.

"I was about to ask the same thing."

It's Wes's voice, much closer than I expected it to be. I pause and glance behind. He's joined me on the log, arms stretched out and bare where he's rolled his gray sleeves above the forearm.

I thought I was nervous before; it's nothing compared to how I feel now.

"Are you okay?" he asks, searching my face briefly before his eyes are drawn back to his feet. The river rages far below, a roaring beast of churning waves and blue-white spray.

For so long, masking my emotions from him was simple. Routine, even. Now it's an effort to school my features into a calmer palette. "I was just thinking about the wind," I say, turning forward again, as casual as if discussing the chance of rain later in the week. Anything that might temper his terror, though my own heart is ripping a hole through my chest. "It would be harder to knock us off balance on all fours."

He doesn't reply immediately. Then, "I'm afraid to lower myself down."

"Okay. Let's keep going like this for a while. Helos?" I raise my voice at the end.

"I'm here," he calls back from farther away. "I don't know if it's strong enough to hold all three of us. I'll go last."

Good, I think. My nerves can't handle both of them on this tree bridge at once.

Our pace is agonizingly slow, but eventually we reach the midway point. The second stretch looks harder; there are several more branches around the top half of the tree, and the trunk narrows visibly. "Halfway there," is all I say. From behind, Helos shouts encouragement.

We're only a quarter of the way from the other side when it happens. Another gust of wind kicks through, this one much stronger than any that have come before.

I wobble.

An arm strikes out, quick as a viper, steadying me. But the movement throws off Wes's balance, and he cries out. I whip my head around and reach for him, just as he goes down.

His body hits the trunk, half hanging perilously over the side, hands scrabbling desperately for a hold on the bark.

"Hang on!" I shout, dropping onto all fours, Helos yelling in the background. Wes lifts an arm and reaches farther, trying to wrap it more securely around the trunk. I stretch out my hands, but his pack is already pulling him back toward the water.

He slips over the side.

"WESLYN!" I scream, as he plummets toward the river. "WES!"

I'm scouring the waves frantically, hardly giving thought to my own security on the tree, desperate for his head to break through. I wait another instant before rising, shedding my pack, and hurling it with all my might onto the land ahead. It hits, and I go down.

The descent through nothingness lasts no more than a handful of heartbeats. I slam into the water with the force of a bear, engulfed at once by the waves.

Cold water surrounds me from every angle, yanking and twisting me this way and that. Eyes clamped shut, cheeks puffed out to preserve the air in my lungs, I flail wildly in the darkness. I have no idea how far down I've sunk, or which direction the surface is in, and panic begins to consume me.

Up. The one thought that cuts through the rest. Swim up.

But which way is up?

I force my eyes open just enough to make out the haze of light, then kick and claw toward it with all the strength I possess. My lungs are going to burst, they're going to burst—but I break through the surface, gasping and choking.

The churning water bellows in my ears, enraged and ringing with ire. Wes is ahead; I can see his head above the surface now, arms fighting desperately to stay afloat. The weight of the pack keeps pulling him under for long stretches.

I throw myself forward, riding the current, swimming toward him as fast as I can manage. Spray clogs my nose and mouth, and I'm forced to stop and cough every few strokes. I consider shifting to lynx, but I don't know that that would make me any stronger.

I swim. I spit. I swim more.

In the chaos, a flurry of driftwood surges past my spiraling arms. Before I can try to warn him, one of the pieces collides with Wes's head, and I inhale another mouthful of water when I shout for him.

My arms close under Wes's just as he's about to sink too far to reach. His body is a deadweight in my hands, and for a few terrifying moments I'm pulled beneath the surface. The sounds of the world above grow muffled.

Then we're out again, and our shot at salvation appears up ahead: the banks of Telyan curving out to meet us. Using all of the strength that remains in my body, I fight toward it, one arm around Wes's chest, the other churning the water. The current slows the closer to shore we get, and in time my feet strike rocks and sand. I keep swimming over until it's shallow enough for me to stand, then drag the unconscious Wes toward me, over the rocks and onto the bank. Then I collapse.

For several moments, all I can do is lie there on the muddy river-bank, coughing water that burns like fire, my breath coming in horrible, sticking gasps. A sharp pain razors through my chest and upper back with every inhale, and my limbs feel heavy, so heavy. Waterlogged. Completely exhausted. It takes everything in me to dig my hands into the soft earth and drag myself forward, then upright.

I crawl to him.

The sight of Wes lying broken on the ground is enough to drown me anew. His arms have been cut up even more than mine, some wounds still bleeding, others covered by the debris that caused them in the first place. His chest—is it moving? Frantically, I place my hands on his stomach and lower my ear to his mouth. My hands rise, then fall. Barely.

"Wake up," I sputter, my hoarse voice choking on the words. "Weslyn. Wes!" I cradle his face in my hands, smearing dirt in his beard. "Why did you try to save me?" I murmur furiously, lowering my forehead to his. "I have wings."

He doesn't answer. Eyes closed, hair plastered to his skin, he looks deathly pale and utterly vulnerable. One of my nightmares from the last few days come to life.

It's wrong. So wrong. Like Helos honing his horns into weapons and Finley keeping him away. Like patients dying of a relentless illness, away from the people they love. Like cages and corpses, and a mother leaving her children to die. This cold, expiring thing is not my friend. It's not Wes.

Panic thrums through every crevice of my body.

I don't know what to do. I don't know what to do. I need my brother, but he's still on the other side of the river; I can just hear him shouting from the top of the gorge. Once again, I've crossed without him.

The next ragged breath I draw sends me into another fit of hacking. And an idea hits.

As soon as I've stopped coughing, I press my hands into his chest. Nothing happens. I push again, harder this time. And again. And again. When I think my arms are about to break, I push still more, until I cannot push any longer. Desperately, I check his face.

Nothing happens.

"Wake up," I whisper.

If he can hear me, he shows no sign of it. Hot tears scourge my cheeks as I cup his face once more with my left hand. With my right, I brush the hair back from his forehead. I want him to look at me. To pierce me with those warm honeyed eyes that people say give strength in the darkest of times. But his eyes remain closed. Slowly, I lower my face and press my lips against his. They're cold.

Then I turn my head toward the river. Where his pack is still somehow, miraculously, lying. The pack with our treasure.

Make sure it remains dry. The giants' only instruction. *Outside of a living body, water is not compatible with magic.*

Finley. Nelle. All the people who have fallen ill, and all those still to come. To fall. The Fallow Throes that will spread and spread, consume the kingdom, because we failed. We traveled all this way—and failed.

It's torture to leave Weslyn's side, but I have to know.

I open the pack, treated to repel moisture from the rain—but nothing so strong as a river. Water has seeped into the bag and through his belongings. I extract the leather-bound journal and set it on dry land, cracking at the sight of its damp exterior. Then I find the box and hold it in front of me.

The seal is airtight. At least, it's meant to be. But when I open the latch and lift the lid, the stardust is no longer iridescent and glowing. The minuscule, pearly white beads the size of sand have darkened to charcoal. My head shakes of its own accord as I run a pair of trembling fingers through the lot. It's coarse against my wrinkled skin. Dull and lifeless. Grainy—

A gasp escapes my lips.

There at the bottom, deep in the corner, the faintest silver glow. Like embers of a dying flame, scrambling for a lifeline, a foothold, anything in the wood, the air.

I'm scooping it out and carrying it to Wes before my mind can catch up to my legs. A tiny chance, an impossible chance, a sliver of hope.

Then logic snatches the reins.

Even if this pinch survived the river, I can't use it. It's meant for
Finley. If no one else, at least save Finley. It was my devotion to
him that made me agree to this quest in the first place. A journey
that almost killed my brother.

Coolness is kissing the inside of my fist, where the precious dust
is sheltered within. I can't use it.

I think of Wes's voice, quiet but measured, reassuring, and
imagine never hearing it again. Never feeling his arm around my
shoulders and his head resting on mine, his touch both a ground-
ing presence and a promise. *What was it you said about torturing
yourself?*

I imagine losing that future, that splinter of a future that's
taken root in my mind, with this stubborn, difficult, wonderful
person, who learned the very worst of me and, somehow, still
wanted to stay.

A sob breaks my throat.

A collection of images that will no longer come true.

I can't use it.

But then, what am I supposed to do? Deliver one dead son to
King Gerar in exchange for the key to saving another? Impossible.
And what if I did? What if I save it for Finley and, fortune forbid
it, he's already gone?

Finley. Weslyn. I'm ripping at the seams, torn in two.

Please, Violet said.

I kneel by Wes's shoulder.

Across the river, high above, Helos is waving his arms frantically, screaming at me. But his words are swallowed by the roar
of the current and my desire not to hear them. I'm sure he can just
make out my closed fist and has guessed what I'm planning to do.

And that's another problem. If I save Weslyn, I doom more than
my friend. I doom the boy my brother loves.

Can I do this to Helos? Betray his trust in a way that might be beyond reconciliation? Helos, who has sacrificed everything for me.
Helos, the noble. Helos the good.

I look at Wes's face, and know the answer. I have always known it, because it's who I am. Clever and compassionate and courageous and strong.

But not that selfless.

I part Weslyn's lips and let the stardust fall between them.

TWENTY-SEVEN

For several torturous moments, nothing happens. Wes remains immobile as ever, and in his silence I'm left to contemplate the magnitude of what I've done—and the fact that it may have been for nothing. What if I was too late, for the stardust or for Wes? What will Helos say?

Tentatively, I raise my eyes to the gorge. He isn't there.

Feathers prick my skin. But before I can continue the search, Weslyn jerks awake.

Violent coughs rack his lungs, so pronounced that his entire body shakes. It's the most beautiful sound I have ever heard. Heart thundering through my chest, I help him roll onto his side when I see the effort he's making. His hands dig into the muddy earth, scrabbling for stability as he purges river water from his system.

When his haggard breathing finally relaxes into quiet wheezes, he pushes himself upright.

For a while, he says nothing. Just sits and breathes. And in this silence I look at him. Really look, see the skin mud-caked and dripping, the broad chest rising and falling, the taut arms supporting his weight. The thick brows, the eyes wide with the relief of the almost-dead, the mouth I grazed with my own. All of the things that were almost taken from me. I look and look.

At some point I realize he's thinking these things, too, because he's looking at me and my tear-streaked face, and then he's pulling me toward him, and then he's kissing me.

Kissing Wes is nothing like kissing the person I pulled from the river. It's bracing and warm and wonderfully alive, mouth against mine, fingers in my soaked hair, hands on the back of his neck. Closer, closer. Greed for this thing the river tried to take. His grip falls to my waist, where drenched clothing still clings to my skin, and I pause in my tracing of his shoulders, down his chest, to rest a palm briefly over his heart. Reassuring myself of the pounding heartbeat, the spark still within. The life I almost lost. Perhaps sensing my distraction, he soon reclaims my attention with a trail of kisses along my jaw, down my neck, and my own rather strangled heartbeat tells me the move is entirely unfair.

Eventually I have to pull away to catch my breath, and when I do, he wraps his arms around my torso, steady and strong, not yet willing to let go. Which is good, because neither am I. I rest my forehead against his, savoring the feeling of his skin beneath my fingertips and his breath against mine. Not human and shifter. Not a leader of his people and the rumored subject of a prophecy.

Us.

For a few precious moments, just us.

I laugh a little, feeling lighter than I have in weeks, months probably. Weslyn smiles and brushes my tears away with his thumb, murmuring something that lights a thousand fires in each nerve, every trace of my skin.

And then he snaps back, alarm painted plainly across his face.

"The box! Fin!"

He pushes to his feet and locates his pack after a brief but frantic search, and all too soon, here is the moment I've been dreading, when I might lose what I've only just gained.

He tears through it, comes up short, then spots the box lying open nearby. The ashy dust within.

His entire body sags. Limp. Defeated. "Ruined," he says, like he's already standing in the future, exhausted from digging graves. "It's all ruined." His voice breaks a little on the word, and suddenly I'm longing to hide the truth from him. Aching to let him believe his survival is only by chance.

But something grew between us that night by the fire, when we shared the painful truths we keep hidden from the rest of the world. Perhaps the hardest thing for either of us to give another, but we gave it, anyway.

Trust.

And I refuse to betray that gift, however painful.

I gather myself, then say, "There was a little left."

Slowly, fractionally, his gaze lifts from the box to me.

The silence is terrible.

"Wes—"

But I break off at the sight of my brother charging up the shoreline toward us. He made it! He crossed!

"RORA!" he howls, in a voice so vicious I instinctively leap to my feet. I will my heart to beat normally, attempt to stem the adrenaline leaking through my veins. This is not an enemy. He's my brother.

Only, I've rarely ever seen him this angry, and never at me. Face red and limbs flailing.

He looks dangerous.

"You didn't," he begs, crashing to a halt before me. "Tell me you didn't."

"Helos—"

"How much was left? After the river, was there any left?"

I swallow. "Enough for one."

"That was his chance!" he cries, arms swinging madly. "His *one* chance, the whole reason we left Telyan."

"Finley is not the only one—"

"—the one who mattered to us."

The cold words fracture the silence like shards of glass. All Wes does is turn back to the river, the only sign that the blow landed. I lock on to my brother, staring at him like I've never seen him before. "There are others we set out to save," I say again, anger mounting. "And barely any stardust remained. I had no choice."

"Of course you had a choice!"

"He was dying!" I yell, looking at Wes, who's looking away.

"*Finley* is dying," Helos pushes out through gritted teeth. "Remember Finley? Your friend? Or maybe you've forgotten, blinded by a pretty face."

"Don't you *dare* say something like that," I tell him, still unsure of how to navigate this attack. I've been blamed, I've been shouted at, yes—but never by him. "Don't you dare tell me I don't care."

"Your actions speak for themselves."

"Helos," Wes mutters, taking a step forward. "That's enough. It's done."

"No, *you* don't get to speak!" my brother retorts, shoving Wes away.

"You think you care more than I do about what happens to my own brother?" Wes challenges in a rising voice, still a bit hoarse from the river.

"Yeah, maybe I do," Helos says, pushing him again.

"Stop it!" I cry, stepping between them. "This isn't you. Everyone here loves Finley. You know that."

He scoffs loudly.

"Maybe we can return to the giants," I suggest. "We made a good impression. I'm sure they'd give us more."

"We have nothing else to trade," Wes replies, eyes still avoiding mine. "And I need to return to Roanin. I must warn my father about the attack on Glenweil; I'm sure they will come for Telyan next."

Helos swears. "Back to the start with nothing gained. The whole journey, a waste."

"A waste?" I echo in disbelief. "Have you overlooked the compound? What have *you* forgotten for a pretty face?"

"You know what I mean," he says impatiently.

"No, I don't. If you would set aside your own grief for an instant, you'd remember there's more at stake now than our own problems. You think I don't feel awful? Or that I don't wish there had been another way?" I'm shouting at this point. "What would you have done, Helos? Can you decide one life is more valuable than another? What gives you the right?"

He shakes his head. "By the river, you're so selfish, Rora. I don't believe you."

The words are as callous as a slap to the face. I recoil, stunned.

It's the way he said it, like I'm dirt beneath his boot. The fact that he specifically chose the fear that tormented me for so many years.

"You can't mean that," I whisper. And he can't, because he knows me better than anyone in the world, and if he means to wound me as badly as his words suggest, I really am lost.

His expression relents a fraction, as if he's coming to his senses at last. He runs his hands through his hair, and for a moment his mouth tightens in shame. But he does not take it back. Unable now to separate himself from the truths he would rather not face. Unable to pretend ugliness does not exist in his world. The wall has come crumbling down. Our journey through the Vale began it. My actions on the riverbank have seen to the rest.

"Is there a way out of this gorge?" Wes asks quietly. He wishes I hadn't used the stardust on him. He's still not looking at me, and it hurts, it hurts, it hurts.

Helos glares daggers at him, then jerks his head back in the direction from which he came.

I watch my brother a moment longer, needing him to recognize his own mistake, the hurt he has inflicted. Maybe I should have expected this, even without my betrayal. Maybe he was bound to snap sooner or later under the weight of too much caring.

Or maybe I've been wrong all along, and there's no such thing as Helos the good and Rora the bad. Maybe we're just . . . us.

I was the one who wanted to investigate the soldiers further. I argued we should stay. Helos is the one who refused, his need to protect everyone he loves blinding him to the greater issue at stake. I have always thought of that protectiveness as a mark of his selflessness, an inherent goodness. But now I see the danger to it, how others may be left by the wayside, eclipsed by his singular focus. I never saw it before, because it has always been just him and me. Growing up, there was no one else for him to worry about, nothing else at stake beyond keeping us alive.

It's true I'm not willing to yield everything like he so often is. But I'm beginning to understand there's power in the balance. To live, not in the black and white, but the gray space in between. Selfish and selfless, present and past, old sorrow and newfound joy—I can alternate between them, there is room inside for both, and that duality freed my brother from imprisonment and death. It saved my friend and brought me home.

I was wrong that day in the woods. Nothing's unraveling between Helos and me. I've just come to see my brother for who he really is—a person with flaws, same as me.

The thought should be comforting, but right now it's only disappointing.

I storm past him, reflecting miserably on how my brother could be the one to hurt me more than anyone.

We stick to the base of the mountains, making our way east without speaking. The morning sun shines directly in our eyes, untempered by a single tree. The land here is more brown than green, uncomfortably open, and there's no birdsong or tiny mammals scurrying underfoot. Even the grass grows in dwindling clumps.

It's empty. Little better than the stretch of land separating the compound from the forest's edge. I press my fingernails into my palms, the half-moon marks tethering me firmly to Telyan. To the present.

The soil's depressing infertility certainly mirrors our mood. I remain in the lead for the rest of the day, marching determinedly under the weight of my pack. It was waiting for me at the lip of the gorge where it landed, and I find its presence comforting. Almost like a shell to shield me from the brooding boys behind.

Helos has fallen far to the rear. Resentment and distance yawn between us, biting and unfamiliar. He won't take back what he said, any more than I can take back what I've done, and I'm only too content to let him linger.

Wes is keeping just a few strides away, walking steadily now that the stardust healed his wounds, but he says nothing. Looks

332

at . . . nothing. All I get is a muttered thanks when I hand him some of my food—most of his was ruined in the river—and even that's only a single word.

It's torment. I long to recapture the closeness between us. I want him to assure me that this changes nothing. But even in my day-dreams, I know the wish is folly. I've used his brother's only salvation to save him instead, and even if a part of him is grateful to be alive, I've still condemned his brother to die. We both have, and he without having made the choice himself.

I would do anything for Fin.

Not only by venturing forth into a wilderness that might kill him as soon as shelter him. Not just by giving up the path he wanted and pursuing a career as an officer, so his brother could continue to learn and dream.

He would have accepted death when it came for him and saved the stardust for Finley. He doesn't have to tell me that's what he would have done. I know. I don't regret the choice I made, but I know.

The truth of that—and Helos's bitter accusations—have tainted what we've become.

Reaching the Old Forest the next day is like stepping into a dream, one that's a perverse mirror of our first journey through. Our silence is just as strained as it was then. But this time, I can't look at Wes without feeling the ghost of his hands around my waist, the pressure of his lips on mine. Helos hurls no chestnuts at me, only anger and quiet judgment. My only comfort lies in the woods around us, the dense undergrowth and ancient oaks embracing me like old friends. It's difficult to find consolation in it like I did before. The trees and the security they provide still matter, but the two boys behind me matter more.

The sky is beginning to darken by the time the first spires of Castle Roanin appear through the branches. The sight is like a tonic to Wes, who lurches forward the moment he spots them. As I follow, memories of our last day at the castle drift to the surface— King Gerar standing in the courtyard, hands gripping his eldest son's shoulders. Back straight, dignified in sorrow. *Go safely, Son.*

The guards standing sentinel while Violet took me aside, confiding in me. Briefly, I recall what Wes said about his sister wanting me to spy for them. I wonder if King Gerar will be more amenable to the prospect once we deliver our news.

I have no idea how to face Finley and tell him I chose to save another. My friend who called me by my name long before anyone else in the castle. The one who never, not once, bowed to superstition like the rest of his court. Worse, there's a chance I'm too late to tell him anything at all.

Despite my resolution to change things for the better here, old trepidation pricks my skin at the thought of walking those halls, so it's with some relief that I learn we'll be using the secret door hidden in the complex's outer wall. The one Finley led me through nearly a month ago, when we escaped the castle's prying eyes the morning of the Prediction. Wes doesn't want to cause a scene.

"I don't mean with you and Helos," he clarifies when he sees my face. They're the most words he's spoken since the river. "I mean me. I've been away awhile."

Of course. Because he's a prince, and his reappearance will cause quite the stir throughout the castle. The reminder is yet another blow to everything we have built. Out in the wilderness with nothing but sky and starlight to shield you, it's easy to blur the lines between royal and shifter. Easy to forget.

Wes and I reach the edge of the Old Forest, and the ivy-covered door comes into view at last. The castle's northern façade towers beyond. Thankfully, there are no smoking turrets or crumbling patches; it seems that Jol hasn't yet reached Roanin. When Helos catches up a minute or two later, he looks white as a sheet despite his air of bravado. I'm sure I catch a tremor in his hands before he shoves them into his pockets.

Regardless of the ire between us, I'm determined we should walk the castle together. Prediction or no. I step toward Helos, meaning to loop my arm through his; whatever's inside the castle, we'll face it together. As we always do.

But at my approach, he straightens his shoulders and pushes forward. Without a single word.

I feel the force of his anger like a physical wound.

Wes knocks twice on the door in quick succession, as King Gerar apparently told him to do. I hover beside my brother, knowing my presence is of little comfort to him right now, and hoping Simeon isn't on duty this evening.

Several heartbeats pass.

Then another few. And another.

The door remains shut.

Wes lifts his fist and knocks again, harder this time. Another pause.

Still there's no answer.

"Maybe they're off duty?" I suggest. None of us brought the key with us.

Wes steps away from the wall, head tilted back to examine the top. "Give me a boost," he says.

Helos approaches, forming a step with linked fingers. Wes goes up and over, dropping quickly onto the other side. A few moments later, the door swings outward.

My brother and I slip inside, making a quick appraisal of the estate as Wes fastens the door behind us. The grounds are empty.

"Follow me," Wes instructs, leading the way across the complex and into the castle. At my side, Helos is painfully tense. Apprehension flows off him in waves, and it's starting to rouse my own sense of unease. Wordlessly, we walk the unlit hall, the mounted oil lamps cold and dark.

The grim feeling intensifies as we pass from the corridor into the western wing, then through its high-ceilinged entrance hall with the crystal chandeliers and portraits of horses and hounds. All empty.

"Wes—"

"Come on."

Picking up the pace, we cross the red antechamber and reach the central atrium, its vaulted ceiling stretching three stories high. Weak evening light filters in through long windows, casting the room in the pale blue of twilight. Shadows collect on the massive marble staircase, and it, too, is empty.

Something is wrong.

Helos and I exchange a glance as Wes crosses to the center of the room. He turns about, halts, and calls out. His voice bounces off the walls, echoing in the silence.

For several long moments, there's nothing.

Then a blur of gray streaks through the foyer, nails scratching against the marble floor.

Astra!

The hound barrels straight into her master. She's grown thin; her wiry coat is dull and disheveled. But her tail wags furiously as Wes drops to the ground and throws his arms around her.

I have never been happier to see that dog. The sight of her is almost enough to give me hope.

Then I see the fresh marks on the floor.

"What is that?" Helos asks as I crouch over the track that stretches all the way to a far side of the room. Astra left a trail in her wake.

I run two fingers through the lines. "It looks like . . . frost."

We all turn to Astra, who licks the back of Wes's hands and wags her tail, still delighted by the return of her boy.

The next moment, she vanishes into thin air.

I cry out in alarm, pointing to the empty space where she had been. Wes shoots to his feet. But no, she's there, over by the windows, dropping into a playful lunge while another streak of frost paints the marble floor between us.

"Astra?" Wes chokes out, as if she might have the explanation.

"She disappeared," Helos says somewhat breathily, his voice infused with less venom than before.

Wes whistles an arcing string of notes, and Astra appears at his side a heartbeat later, her transition from there to here little more than a wisp of color. He crouches low, holding the sides of her face and breathing heavily. "No. She ran."

She licks his nose.

"But she's just a dog," I protest weakly. "There's no magic in her. If there were, she would be dying or dead."

"You've reported a few people with magic in them who seemed in perfect health," Wes reminds me.

"This is more than perfect health," Helos says. "This is an ordinary animal with a magical ability. That hasn't occurred since—"

"The continent first fractured," finishes Wes.

The implications creep toward us like shadows.

"But I thought they were all incompatible now."

"In the prison compound," I say, the detail surfacing for the first time since my horrid escape. "One of the guards who was assigned to me. His eyes changed color."

"He what?" Helos gawks.

"His eyes. It was a shift." I pause. "A tiny one."

Astra sits facing us with her ears perked, clearly unfazed by our alarm.

"And in Niav!" I exclaim, my voice rising with the revelations. "The guard who led us from the gate to the palace looked blurry around the edges. I don't know how else to describe it. I thought it was a trick of the light, but maybe it wasn't. Maybe she was turning translucent."

"Translucent."

Silence falls.

"Like a forest walker," Helos adds dryly.

"What are you saying?" Wes asks. "That there are shifters and forest walkers being created all over again?"

Helos shakes his head. "This is unbelievable."

"And no one has noticed?" Weslyn continues, sounding skeptical now.

I shrug. "Last time it took years for the transformation to evolve. Maybe they're only at the very beginning stages."

"Plus, do you really think someone who finds himself with a magical ability is going to parade it around town?" Helos says. "You know how your people are these days."

Weslyn holds my gaze so long, it's almost like it was before. "Have you noticed that no one has appeared in this room while we've been speaking?"

Hair rises along the back of my neck. People dying of magic's touch. Others granted the beginnings of magical abilities.

Where is the court?

Where is the king?

Weslyn takes a step back and glances wildly around the room. Then he bolts for the stairs.

He climbs them two at a time, Astra streaking ahead and trailing frost, Helos and I scrambling to keep pace. We search the northern wing first, Wes forcing entry into Finley's chamber at the end of the hall.

The doors open with a bang, revealing nothing but an empty sitting room—the hearth cold, the windows fastened shut. Helos crosses the room in a few quick strides and thrusts open the double doors leading to Finley's bedroom. There's nothing.

"He's gone," Helos says, voice cracking on the words. Wes throws his hands behind his head, clearly making an effort not to panic.

I just stare at my brother. Helos, who crossed the room with zero hesitation. Helos, who knew exactly where to go, even though he's always let me believe he never went inside the castle after our audience with King Gerar.

By now, I'm not surprised.

I'm hurt that he kept it from me.

Helos's gaze connects with mine, and he seems to wilt ever so slightly under my stare.

Wes is the first to leave, sweeping down the hall and around the corner. Helos and I follow, but I quickly break away from my brother's side to keep pace with Wes. The web of resentment spins in both directions now.

Together, we search the rest of the castle. A section of rooms I learn are Violet's quarters. King Gerar's. Wes becomes frantic, darting into chambers and down corridors with feverish haste. Astra leaps beside him into each of the wings, the kitchens, the armory, the library. Wes calls out. He throws open doors. He pounds the walls with his fists.

There's nothing but silence.

With a shout of defeat, he slams his back against a wall and sinks to the floor, throwing his hands over his face. The sight is as out of place as the empty rooms around us. Wes is the steady one. Wes is the ship that charts a course through rocky waters. I've never seen him so undone.

I want to say something that will make it better, but I've been here before and know there are no words that will. Village or castle. Forest canopy or stone walls. The details make no difference. He's returned to an empty home.

Helos calls my name just as I'm about to sink onto the floor beside Wes. I pace over to the window, following my brother's outstretched finger south, out onto the grounds below. The city is visible in the near distance.

There's no fire. No charred ruins of a once prosperous city. Instead, the buildings appear just as they always have—gray and russet stones, the clock tower, swirls of close-quartered, gabled roofs. But the roads are as empty as the castle itself.

Usually at this hour, there'd still be plenty of people out and about. Now, not a single person can be seen walking the streets.

Roanin is completely deserted.

TWENTY-EIGHT

"I don't understand," Helos murmurs, the first to break the silence. Wes has joined us at the window, still as a statue as he takes in the quiet.

"There are no signs of a struggle," I point out. "Perhaps they evacuated the city."

"But why?"

I shake my head.

Quiet descends once more, so absolute it reminds me of that morning Finley collapsed, the smothering dread as we stared down the circle of outstretched branches. I peer into the hollow city, scouring for a clue, any at all, poking out from those narrow, winding lanes.

At my left, Weslyn straightens abruptly and steps back from the window.

Then he takes off down the corridor without explanation or warning, Astra tearing ahead.

Helos and I exchange startled looks and hurry after him.

Wes is running so quickly that we don't catch up until he's already back in Finley's quarters. They are ringing with the crashing sounds of furniture striking the floor. I slam to a halt just past the double doors leading into the bedroom, clutching at a stitch in my side and appraising the space in alarm.

Weslyn is dismantling it. Lifting the mattress from the large, four-poster bed, tossing the blue silk duvet onto the woven area rug. He opens a wooden cabinet and rifles through the drawers, then dumps a series of shirts out the side, heedless of our arrival.

"Wes—" I begin.

He doesn't reply. Breathing hard, he pivots to the crowded bookshelves built into the wall and begins scanning the spines with a finger. Astra is pacing circles around him, clearly unsettled by his mood.

"Do you—"

"Give me a moment," he says, pulling a couple of volumes from the shelf. After leafing through their contents, he drops the books and crouches beside the lower levels.

The next time he pulls a book from the shelf, a wooden disk clangs against the exposed floorboards.

Helos and I rush over, just as Weslyn releases a long breath.

"He's alive," he says, examining the wooden disk a heartbeat longer before handing it to me. The dull, sanded sphere is small enough to fit inside my palm, notched with an array of numbers and lines. I don't understand.

"It's a calendar," Wes explains, seeing my confusion. "I made it for him, long ago. He found the design in a book."

"How does that prove he's alive?" Helos demands, grabbing the disk and holding it close to his face.

Wes smiles a bit. "It's dated five days ago. And he left it for me to find."

I take the winning book from him and read the cover. *Waterfowl of the Low Country Lakes*.

"It's a book about birds," Helos says, exasperated.

"Waterfowl," Weslyn corrects him. "The *w* is for Wes."

My attention shifts to the books strewn across the floor. They all begin with the same letter. "Why choose this particular book, then?" I ask. "The low country. Did he go south? Some place near water, maybe?"

"A valley?" Helos suggests.

We each fall silent for a time.

"Come on," Weslyn says, looking slightly more heartened. "My father would have left instructions."

Seizing this thread of hope, he leads us deep into the castle once more, this time at a slower pace. There's a renewed sense of purpose in his stride; the mission, and Finley's message, have given him something to latch on to. He takes us down the grand staircase to the ground floor, boots striking the marble with ringing footsteps. I don't realize our destination until we're almost upon it: the throne room.

Unlike most of the other entryways we've come upon, the doors to the hall are swung wide open. It's this fact, more than anything, that triggers the warning bells in my head.

Astra whimpers and jerks to a halt.

"Wes . . ."

"The council room is just beyond this hall," he interrupts confidently. "There's a door at the back."

But that's not my concern. These doors are rarely kept open. I quicken my pace until I'm several strides ahead of him and reach the entrance first.

The sight bowls me over like a stone to the gut. I don't know what I was expecting, but this is worse. Far worse. Nausea coats my throat as I swing around, desperate to prevent my friend from seeing.

"Wes, stop." I lend as much authority to my voice as I can.

"What?"

"Please. Don't look. Please."

The second "please" catches him, and he hesitates, trying to read what's beyond in my expression.

"What's going on?" Helos asks, not heeding my warning as Weslyn has. He passes straight into the throne room. And stops.

Now Wes can no longer restrain himself. Clearly apprehensive, he steps up to my side and confronts what I so fiercely wish I could shield him from.

The hall is empty, save for the pair of silvered thrones set upon the dais at the far end.

King Gerar's head is mounted on a post between them.

Wes stares. He stares and stares, so long I'm tempted to turn his face away by force. But I'm afraid to touch him. And because he stares, I feel an obligation to face it, too. The brown-and-silver waves crowning King Gerar's head. The tan cheeks once flush with life now dull and graying. The crystal eyes gazing at nothing. The lips slightly parted as if breath might pass between them still.

Astra slips inside the hall and presses against Weslyn's leg.

I do not understand. I don't see the point of it, don't see how fortune could be so cruel just as my wasted heart had begun to heal. King Gerar was always kind to me. He offered Helos and me protection, even in the wake of his wife's death, and treated me as a person of value rather than a harbinger of doom. More than that, he had every opportunity to exploit the power granted to him by royal blood, none of which he took. He had been a good king.

Go safely, Son. The words echo in my mind, over and over, a scythe cutting through the field of grief. The final blessing of a father fated to die.

I can't help but wonder if this is what my mother looked like when her first husband speared her head on his castle wall. In a way, I'm grateful I don't know. There's no memory to call upon, no sight to haunt the rest of my days alongside that of Father's death. The same will never be true for Wes.

I step in front of him, a near-perfect match for height, blocking out the view of his father. He doesn't appear to see me.

"You can stop now," I say gently. Helos is walking the length of the hall, down toward the end. I know he's going to examine the two notices that have been nailed there, one against the back of each throne, but I don't watch his progress.

Wes's jaw is clenched tight with such force I'm afraid he'll break it. He doesn't acknowledge my presence, but tears are pooling at the base of his eyes.

I suspect he'd want me to look away, but I'm loath to turn my back on him. I don't want him to feel, even for an instant, that he's alone. So instead, I watch the quivering skin, the rapidly blinking eyes, the enormous effort he's expending to keep from falling apart.

"Here."

It's Helos. Wes's eyes cut to him, so I allow mine to as well.

He's holding out one of the posters, where a few rows of text are scrawled across the parchment in big, bold letters:

> *King Gerar Danofer, Sovereign of Telyan, has been found guilty of consorting with two shifters and plotting treason against an allied king.*
>
> *As an insult to his people and a direct violation of the terms of his alliance with King Jol Holworth, Sovereign of Eradain, these acts are found punishable by death.*
>
> *Let this execution serve as warning to all who would debase themselves and their kingdom in such a manner.*

"I don't believe it," I whisper, after we've all read the message. My brother watches Wes carefully, then turns to me. "There's also this." He raises the second piece of parchment.

It's a note addressed to us.

> *To Mariella's children,*
>
> *Yes, I know that's what you are. We did not meet or part on friendly terms, but I would like to rectify that. If you should return to Roanin and see this, I ask that you come to Oraes, so that we might better understand one another. There is much I'd have you tell me, and much that you should know.*
>
> *-J. Holworth*

I squeeze the bridge of my nose between my thumb and forefinger, exhaustion suddenly threatening to overwhelm me. "He cannot be serious."

"What does he mean, 'much that you should know'?" Helos says.

I shake my head. It's difficult to think of anything other than King Gerar's head mounted on the post behind me.

I did warn him of the consequences. Jol's jeering slithers through my ears. Mocking. Triumphant. I didn't just condemn Wes's brother to die. I condemned his father, too.

I could swear the head at the end of the hall is screaming, drowning my mind with the sound.

I glance at Helos, nails serrating my palms. Two shifters journeying together with a member of the royal family. Both of us standing here in this hall.

Maybe the two of us really do mean death. Maybe we've cursed the Danofers after all.

"Leave me," Wes says abruptly, in a voice so firm that for a moment, I see only the prince he was before, cold and unyielding. "Please," he adds, shattering the veneer with a single cracked plea. "I would like to be alone with my father."

Neither of us argues or attempts to offer words of comfort, much as it tears me apart to do so. Instead we leave Wes to his grief, turning to shut the doors behind us just as he falls to his knees. A single sob is audible before the clasps latch firmly in place.

We don't see Wes for the rest of the night. Helos and I barely even speak to each other, though the shock of death has healed some of the divide between us. Instead, I tell my brother I need to lie down and split off, wandering the corridors with a pilfered oil lamp until I come to an unlocked door that yields a red canopied bed. I'm not sure whose room this is. No doubt they'd consider my presence an invasion of privacy.

I don't care. I set the lamp on top of the wardrobe and cross the thick rug in a few sullen strides, dragging the curtains closed and shutting out the night beyond them. Then I collapse onto the bed, arms and legs still sore from the river rescue, not bothering to shed any of my clothes. My pack is somewhere else in the castle, and its absence is almost a relief; I'm not even sure where I left it.

An indefinite amount of time passes as I stare at the cloth crowning the bedposts. The flickering light from the lamp casts odd shadows across the red fabric, and I watch the dance with muted detachment. This time, I don't hide from my fears or my sorrow. I don't bully myself for feeling them in the first place. In the gathering darkness of the stolen bedroom, my limbs sinking into the feather-soft comforter beneath me, I confront my emotions head-on. I grieve for the deaths I have witnessed and for Wes's loss. I lament the way things have changed so quickly between Helos and me. I mourn the friendship I fear I've lost, and I even let the hatred and resentment I have harbored toward my mother dull to a slate without shine. Whether her reasoning had been selfish or selfless, I cannot change the choices she made any more than I will ever know the truth. I know, however, that I will not let other people's mistakes dictate the person I become. Not any longer.

Something has changed in me. Pain and grief have long carved a hole through my heart, but what was once hollow and cold now blazes with ferocious fire. Anger and determination. Compassion and hope. The seed of vengeance blossomed into an overwhelming sense of purpose, its roots stretching through my body and encasing my bones with the strength of any in the Old Forest.

As the light from the lamp dims to black and the thoughts swarming my brain subside to a distant hum, what amazes me most of all is that in the midst of so much sorrow, I could feel freer than I ever have.

By the time I find Wes the following day, I know what I have to do. The thought frightened me at first, but by now I've made my peace with it. All that's left to do is tell the others.

He's in the study with Astra at his feet, staring out of the windows. The same place I used to meet with King Gerar on occasion. Something I will never do again.

They both look up at my approach. The skin around Wes's eyes is red and raw, and his hair falls in a state of gentle chaos. It's clear he hasn't slept any better than I have. More than anything, I long to reach a hand up and run my fingers through the dark brown curls, smoothing them into submission. I imagine his eyes closing at my touch.

But his gaze remains wary, and betrayal still hangs heavy between us.

My hands stay at my sides.

"I have something to say to you," I murmur.

He takes a deep breath. "Don't apologize," he says. "You did only what you believed was right. I don't blame you."

The words have a practiced air to them, like he's thought long and hard about the situation, analyzed it from every angle like a good prince should. Like a king.

A king to his subject. Not a boy to the girl he held in his arms and kissed until she was breathless.

My throat constricts. "I'm leaving."

He uncrosses his arms, eyes widening. "What do you mean, leaving?"

"You need to find the missing court. Find your people, and your family." I pause, bracing myself. "But every day you spend looking, every day spent rebuilding, is another day that prison endures."

He closes the distance between us in a few small strides, putting a hand out to still Astra when she tries to follow. "What are you saying?"

"Maybe stardust is not the only way to cure the afflicted. If magic is only holding on to these people because it's searching for a way to survive, maybe we need to give it another option besides incompatible hosts." I look him straight in the eye. "The giants told us that magical beings awaken magic where they go. That as long as they walk the earth, magic will continue to survive."

He waits.

"I am going to destroy the compound and free those prisoners, bring some of them east if I can. If we can remove the threat and reawaken the earth, perhaps the magic will stop fracturing the land and looking for new hosts." I swallow. "Maybe it will let go."

"You don't know that will work."

"No. But I'm going to try."

"Rora—"

"I can't leave them there, Wes. I have to do this, whether or not it impacts the Fallow Throes." I take a breath. "And then I will do what Violet wanted. I'll go north. To Eradain."

He starts visibly. "Are you mad? You cannot believe Jol's message; he would sooner kill you than make peace."

"Probably," I say, feeling the tiniest seed of doubt in spite of everything. He had that chance already—and didn't take it. "But his people need to know what he's doing in the Vale."

"And if they know already? Know and condone it?"

I hesitate, but only for a moment. "Then I'll have to change their minds, after I find a way to free those prisoners. Or change his."

Free them and awaken the land in the east, properly, the way it ought to be. I have seen the cost of relative safety, of dormant magic, and it isn't worth it. Will never be worth it.

Let the centuries-old divide between east and west crumble. Let magical beings cross the river and finish what the mountain started. If our journey to the Vale was the coming of the tide, my return will be the strike that unleashes the storm.

My wilderness kin. Forestborn.

Community.

Wes looks at me searchingly. Opens his mouth, then shuts it again. Nods once. "Helos will help."

Now comes the hardest part. "Helos isn't coming. He's going with you."

"What?"

Breathe in. Breathe out.

"I haven't told him yet. But you need his help, and he needs to do this. He needs to see Finley while . . ." I don't allow myself to finish the thought. Nor do I mention the concern I'm now struggling to dismiss entirely, no matter how badly I want to believe it has nothing to do with us. The one that hisses two shifters and death. That it really might have been a warning after all.

"I think I know where they are," Wes says softly, watching my expression change. "Fin and the rest. Fendolyn's Keep."

"The garrison?" I wrack my brain for a visual of the military base where Wes was meant to train. In all my years of gathering intel for King Gerar, he never sent me to that elusive place. All I know is that it's farther south, and intentionally difficult to find.

"It fits," Weslyn assures me, running a hand through his hair. "The base is hidden in a valley. There are lakes there. It's where—" He breaks off, the words slightly strangled, as if he does not want to continue. "Violet would take our people there if she felt Roanin were under threat. I know it."

I nod, unable to do more than hope that he's right. "Then you'll be able to help her soon. I'll meet you there when I'm done."

His gaze searching, Weslyn shifts closer, just a little. "Rora—"

I smile slightly, not sure I'll ever be tired of the way my name sounds on his lips. "I'll be okay. I'm good at disguising myself, remember?"

Wes doesn't try to talk me out of it. He doesn't tell me it's too dangerous, or beg me to stay when he knows others would suffer. He just raises a hand to the side of my face, hesitating a moment before gently sweeping a few strands of hair aside.

It's the first time he's touched me since the river. Hope rushes in, flooding my charged nerves like the tide and sweeping away some of the fear as footprints from the sand. Maybe he really did mean the words he murmured on the riverbank.

"Come back," he says quietly, holding my gaze for a few precious moments.

My eyes chart a course across his features one last time, composing a map to carry with me in the weeks to come. "Look to the skies," I whisper.

Then I'm gone.

It's a strange feeling, walking the city with Helos without the fear of being seen. The morning has dawned clear and cool, better traveling weather than we had on our prior departure. A day has passed since I told the boys of my plan. As much as I have dreaded our parting of the ways, I cannot bring myself to delay any longer.

Wes is back in the castle, preparing for his own journey. We haven't spoken since that conversation in the study. I've stayed away; he needs time to grieve, and much as I want to help, I think my presence only makes things worse right now. Each time he sees me is another reminder of the choice I made. The same kind of reminder he experienced following Queen Raenen's death.

Besides, any steps we might make toward reconciliation would make it only more difficult to leave.

Now it's only my brother and me, me with a pack and him without, matching each other stride for stride. He hasn't spoken in several minutes.

My plan for the prison and Eradain didn't shock him as much as it had Wes. The fact that I expected him to go with Wes and not me, however, had raised his eyebrows to the sky.

"I promised I wouldn't leave you, and I meant it," he'd protested, folding his arms tightly in front of him. "We go together. Always."

I shook my head. "This time you have to. Finley needs your strength, Helos. And you need him. Hey," I said, grabbing his arm as he turned away. "Look at me." It took a few moments, but he finally did. Tears were collecting in the corners of his eyes. "This can work, reawakening the land. We can still save him."

Helos squeezes the bridge of his nose between thumb and forefinger. "Since when have you ever been an optimist?"

"Since yesterday."

He blinks at me.

"Two days ago, this plan didn't exist." I smile. "Today it does."

Helos huffs a laugh, running a weary hand over his face.

"I've seen the way he acts around you," I continue.

"Like he can't bear to look at me again?"

"Like he never wants to look anywhere else."

His jaw clenches.

"It's okay to be selfish sometimes. Save him like you saved me." *The answer is no.* A question I've guessed the sense of by now, even if I'll never know the wording. "Change his mind."

He'd broken a little, then. But in the end, he agreed. For the first time, choosing someone other than me.

Now, as we reach the western edge of the city, we slow to a stop.

"You're going to know the Old Forest by heart at this rate," he jokes softly. I'm going back the way we came, across the tree bridge and up through the Vale. I don't want to risk encountering people on the mainland, and I feel sure there's another river crossing into Eradain. Jol and his soldiers have moved between them somehow. If that fails, I can always fly, but I would rather not be left without a pack and supplies.

I study the trees before me—ancient, towering, welcoming. "I already do."

"Good weather for traveling," he adds, examining the sky and echoing my thoughts from moments before. One mind. Even when he hasn't forgiven me. I can read it in his face.

"Helos."

He peels his gaze from the sky.

"I love you. And I'll—"

"Stop it," he says, cutting me off and hugging me tightly. "Don't say goodbye. Don't you do that."

For a few moments, we simply stand there, holding on to the one thing that has always been constant in our lives. My brother and me. Two shifters in a land that's changing. Remnants of the magic that's building once more.

Then he releases me, and I curl my hair behind my ear, smiling. "I was going to say I'll see you soon."

With one final look, I grab the straps of my pack and head for the woods.

I make it only a few steps before something hits me between the shoulder blades. My head snaps back, then I grab the object from the ground and pocket it. It's a pebble from the riverbed, but it's also love.

"Easy as always," I say, returning his grin. "Try harder next time."

Then I let the shadows of the forest embrace me once more, turning my thoughts to the journey ahead. Jol may want me to come to him, but I'll do so on my terms, and with a plan of my own. His pretty words don't fool me; I know little kindness awaits me in a kingdom that would rather see me exiled or dead. Still, someone has to hold him accountable for his actions, and that person may as well be his kin.

Perhaps King Gerar's advisers were right, and my brother and

I really will bring about the end of a royal line. But it won't be because of three hastily scribbled words on parchment.

It will be because this misplaced tension and punishing fear must end. I'm not the subject of anyone's prophecy, there to assign meaning to however they like, but my own person, a *good* person, my actions determined by my will alone. I'm one in a pair of shifters, both of us bent on mending the cracks in this broken world. Survivors.

And to people like Jol, that's infinitely more dangerous.

ACKNOWLEDGMENTS

Writing is famous for being a solitary pursuit, hours and hours spent penning a story that exists only in your own mind. But I've learned the path to publication is not one you wander alone, and I'm lucky enough to have had so many wonderful people supporting me on this journey.

Thank you to Hillary Jacobson, agent extraordinaire, who saw something in my writing and—with boundless insight and encouragement—helped me see it, too. I am so glad to walk this path with you.

To my editor, Lindsey Hall, who breathed new life into this story when I needed it most, and who continually amazes me with her wisdom, enthusiasm, and infectious energy. I'm so grateful to be on your team.

To Melissa Frain, aka Coach, who made my dream come true.

Endless thanks to the team at Tor Teen—my colleagues and friends. You inspire me with your unrelenting passion for all things magical and twisted. Special thanks go to Devi Pillai, Lucille Rettino, Eileen Lawrence, Sarah Reidy, Giselle Gonzalez, Rachel Bass, Anthony Parisi, Isa Caban, Andrew King, Sarah Pannenberg, and Jeff LaSala. And of course, thank you to Rhys Davies for drawing such a stunning map of Alemara, as well as to Lesley Worrell and Katie Ponder for creating the beautiful cover!

To AJ Stuhrenberg, my forever best friend, who has brainstormed revision strategies and talked me off the literary ledge more times than I can count. My God, I owe you so much cake.

To Bess McAllister, the Éowyn to my Merry, writing sister and honorary twin. It's your turn next.

Thank you to early readers Ali Fisher, Dave Rosenkranz, Amy Schettino, Edwin Rivera, Alex Cameron, and Hilary Mauro for your insight and support in the book's initial stages. I am particularly grateful to Clara-Ann Joyce, my nature-loving friend with the heart of an Ent who helps me bring Alemara's topography to life, and to Ryan Meese, Rora's #1 supporter, who always insists I Do the Thing and close all the plot holes. I'm sure I missed a few and look forward to hearing of them in due course.

Thank you to Curtis Dozier, my former college professor and mentor, who once told me to stop apologizing for what I write. I haven't forgotten, and I'm trying.

To every reader, bookseller, blogger, and librarian who decides to give this book a chance.

And finally, to the family Rora always wanted, the family I am immeasurably lucky to have: to my dad, who instills in me his love of literature, adventure, and the outdoors; to my brother, best friend, endless advocate, and fellow cat enthusiast; and to my tireless mom, who teaches me strength in femininity and the value of hard work, and who saved every one of my childhood stories in a folder she's kept all these years. Mom, I'm afraid this one's too big for the folder, but I think you'll find it fits perfectly on a bookshelf.